Virtuoso

KATRINA VINCENZI

First published in 1994 by
Black Lace
332 Ladbroke Grove
London
W10 5AH

Copyright © Katrina Vincenzi 1994

Typeset by CentraCet Limited, Cambridge
Printed and bound by Cox & Wyman Ltd, Reading,
Berks

ISBN 0 352 32907 6

Black Lace novels are sexual fantasies.
In real life, make sure you practise safe sex.

Prelude

ROME, 1989

The lights dimmed. He stood alone on the stage, a tall, slender figure dressed all in black, a violin clasped loosely in one hand, bow in the other.

He could feel the heat of them, sense the press of bodies confined in orderly rows, hear the rustle of programmes, the soft murmur of intimate voices, the whisper of silk-clad legs crossing and re-crossing. Scented skin, heady and musky, perfumed the air.

Closing his eyes, with a finger he caressed the satiny contours of the violin from head to neck, shoulders to waist, belly, back and bottom. The smooth varnish of the Guarnerius was the silken texture of a woman's skin, cool and flawless, waiting to be warmed. Raising the instrument to nestle the chin-rest against his neck, he felt the familiar stirring deep in his groin. She was passive now, this smooth, silken creature, awaiting his touch. She would scream in ecstasy, moan and whimper and beg . . . but first he'd coax the soft murmurs, the little gasps of delighted surprise as he explored her leisurely, intimately.

The woman. Dark, with brown, silky hair, wrapped in garnet-coloured velvet. A fine old Burgundy. A conceit, he knew, but a pretty one. They'd drunk a glass as he traced the curves of her body through the plush warmth of the velvet.

Lifting the bow, he began slowly, just floating across the strings, a feather-light caress misting the skin. The rustle of programmes stilled. The notes traced the nerve endings, slipping into secret hidden places, discovering the intimate hollows.

The sound kissed their ears softly, like a small tongue. Delicately it licked the outlines, licked the curves and contours. He was flirting now, teasing the strings, warming them.

Naked beneath the velvet. Nipples hardening to his eyes, to his touch. Dark red wine flowing over her skin, pooling in her navel, rushing to the plume between her thighs.

They could feel the sound on their skin, subtle and stirring, potent with promise, rousing and arousing. They were open and eager now, waiting and ready. He sensed it as surely he heard her moan, ripe and inviting, thighs and lips parted, reaching for him. The violence curled in his groin, simmered under his skin.

The deliberate kindling. The slow burn. The tension was palpable now. Bodies strained forward in their seats, eyes narrowed and muscles clenched.

He felt the sweat beading his brow, felt them simmering, felt the air grow warmer and closer, felt the lust. He was hard now. With deliberate, agonising slowness he traced the note, then paused, longer than the score allowed. Felt them wait, suspended, in thrall to the next sound, the next sensation.

He could feel her aching for him, becoming the red-raw wild thing that shivered at his touch, moaning and mewing. He knew the fury then, the blood-lust that scourged the strings. With long firm strokes he began to thrust, attacking hungrily, harder and harder, stronger and stronger. Bodies swayed, rocked unconsciously against the brushed velvet seats.

He could feel it building and swelling now, the

waves growing and pulsing. The air was hot, thick and dense as the velvet of her dress, the atmosphere almost stifling. He knew it, could feel the warmth of their bodies, breathless, straining for release. He increased the vibrato, set loose the throbbing, thrilling pulse. It flooded through them, around them, surging and swelling.

The ecstatic, pre-orgasmic thrill of anticipation, rippling on the edge, close, so very close.

The dark frenzy. Time suspended in sensation as he thrust again and again, harder and harder, fighting the waves, fanning the flames. Caught in the adrenalin high, rock-hard, he knew he could play forever, could thrust into her endlessly.

Then, at last, the final explosion, the primitive scream as she came, the spectacular convulsion of sound and fury.

Spent, he lowered his violin with a shaking hand.

As the last thrilling echoes spiralled away, the audience remained dazed and mute, utterly drained. Slowly they roused themselves. The applause, sporadic and disjointed at first, quickly swelled to a thunderous roar. They were greedy now, insatiable for more.

Backstage, hearing the applause, hearing the hunger, she smiled. She'd always been fond of Bach.

Chapter One
Warming Up

GENEVA

'*A*nd it is here,' said the TV reporter in thrilling tones, gesturing to the outlines of a sprawling villa partially obscured by tall trees and an imposing brick wall, 'here at Lake Geneva in Switzerland that Mika, virtuoso violinist who set the world on fire with his passionate, electric interpretations of the classics, has remained in seclusion for over a year in the company of his long-time companion Serena D'Angelo.' The screen cut to a shot of Mika and Serena, Mika dressed in his signature black, and Serena, small and darkly voluptuous in white.

'Companion!' Serena said scornfully to the screen.

'You have a better word?' asked Mika, his voice faintly amused.

She cut her eyes across at him and said nothing.

'The details of the accident which caused Mika's sudden retirement at the height of his career have never been disclosed, but this reporter has learned,' she paused, licked her lips and tried to look knowing, 'that it is unlikely he will ever play again. The secret of his technique that has moved audiences the world over remains locked behind these gates. The magical and mysterious power of his—'

'Bloody vultures,' said Mika, raising one gloved hand to the remote control.

'Leave it darling, just for a moment,' said Serena, sprawled on the black leather sofa and sipping champagne, 'I want to hear the rest of it. Look, they've got a clip of that Vienna recital from two years ago. I never was really sure about that dress,' she added, critically assessing her image on the screen. 'Too many sequins, perhaps.'

'Serena,' he said, 'I'm not interested—'

'And there's Max, right after you signed the contract with him. What a long time ago it seems now. Oh, and look, it's the last recital in London.'

'Serena,' he objected, his voice suddenly harsh. 'I don't want—'

'Listen,' she said, her attention focused entirely on the screen. It showed him alone on stage at the Barbican Hall. The overly refined BBC tones of the TV reporter were suddenly replaced by the strains of the Bach *Sonata in G minor* for solo violin. Even through the imperfect medium of television, the power of the music was palpable.

'Serena,' he began, and turning to her saw the telltale flush mantling her cheeks. She was leaning forward, her breath quickening, utterly transfixed. For a moment he forgot his anger and simply stared. Accustomed to her beauty, the pale flawless skin and glossy black hair, the slanting amber eyes, the lithely voluptuous body, he had almost forgotten how compelling she was when aroused. 'So, it still works for you,' he remarked softly. 'I hadn't realised.'

She looked at him, her eyes hot. 'Don't you remember, Mika? What it was like? I remember the rehearsal in London, I remember—'

'I remember too, Serena,' he interrupted roughly. 'But it's past. Over. Finished,' he concluded, rather desperately, and stared down at his gloved hands. Don't push it, Serena, he warned silently.

'Mika, darling, there must be something we can do, something that—'

Abruptly he switched off the set. 'Leave it, Serena. And leave me alone.'

Frustrated, she looked over at him. The late afternoon sun was warming the sensual planes of his face, highlighting his fair hair. But his blue eyes were cold.

'I'm sorry, Serena. I'm better by myself.'

She hesitated for a moment, wondering whether to pursue it, needle him to some reaction, any reaction. Deciding against it she silently left the room.

Irritated, frustrated, she paused outside the door and looked around the hall with unseeing eyes. The music and the memories had teased awake her nerve endings, roused them from the self-induced torpor of champagne. How she missed the heady excitement of their old life, the roller-coaster highs, the concerts, the parties, the sexual thrills and spills. Since the accident that had so tragically cut short Mika's stellar career, she had remained with him in seclusion, keeping him company when he wanted it, more often being left to her own devices.

He would not, she knew, blame her if she left, returned alone to the life they had shared together. But the ties that bound her to him were too deep to be severed, she thought, absent-mindedly fingering the heavy gold chain around her neck.

Oh, well, she thought wryly, at least I have a hobby. She used to think of it as an art, she realised, suddenly depressed. And it used to mean something, then. The techniques, the props, the various mysterious potions were all part of a fundamental, sensual counterpoint to the intellectual isolation of the music.

She crossed the marble floor, bare feet padding softly on the polished surface, made her way up the large curving staircase, fingers trailing on its carved, cool surface, up to her suite. It was large and extravagantly furnished, a sensualist's paradise with silk tapestries covering the walls, soft inviting mounds of cushions heaped everywhere, plump armchairs and settees, massive Chinese vases filled with flowers. The huge, four-poster bed had been shipped from an exclusive antique dealer in Hong Kong. The windows were latticed, and slats of light played across the black satin bedspread embroidered with snakes and dragons.

Highlighted in various niches were priceless, antique erotic scenes. A wall painting from Pompeii advertising positions available from a certain brothel, acquired surreptitiously from the storerooms of the Naples National Museum. An Arretine, red-glazed cup from the Perrenius workshop, a masterpiece of untrammelled sensuality, men and women, women and women, satyrs and mythological beasts frozen in sensual ecstasy. Temple carvings from Nepal, with a joyous, exuberant sexuality all their own. All periods of history united in celebration of carnal pleasures, distinguished by being the very best, and the most erotic.

Gilt-framed mirrors ran across the length of one wall, mute witnesses to untold of perverse pleasures. She paused, spoke into the intercom that was unobtrusively fixed to the carved headboard of the bed.

'Send Sergei to me.'

He found her seated at her black lacquered dressing-table, shaded in half-light, half-dressed, swathed in silk, puzzling over her collection of erotica. Carved ivory dildoes from Africa, thicker and longer than any male flesh could possibly imitate, with cunningly abraded surfaces. Jade love beads from Japan, designed to be inserted in the rectum and pulled out slowly, one by one, to prolong the sensation at the moment of orgasm. Multi-coloured braided whips in the soft leather of Mexico. Black leather bondage masks. An array of curiously shaped instruments in surgical steel. Perfumes and unguents and oils. Cut-glass bottles filled with strange, aromatic liquids she had concocted herself.

'You sent for me, madam?' he asked casually, his eyes hot on her body.

'Ah, Sergei. Such a delightfully improbable name for a chauffeur,' said Serena, smiling a little. The latest in a string of young male bodies culled from the village, he was young, blond and husky, with a neck like a bull. And equally well-endowed elsewhere, she thought with a shiver of pleasure. Then, too, he was deliciously inexperienced. Or had been. She'd enjoyed seducing him, teaching him to pleasure her, master the sensual refinements she relished. Pain and pleasure. Power and weakness. The conquest had been amusing, and he'd proved an adept pupil. But just recently she'd wondered if he was becoming a little too arrogant, a little cock-sure. And she was . . . well, let's face it, she thought grimly, she was getting bored.

'And what is your pleasure?' he queried, swiftly moving towards her, both hands on the crotch of his uniform, emphasising the bulge in his trousers.

'Yes,' she reminded him gently. 'My pleasure. Just a massage, I think.'

She crossed to the bed, gracefully discarded her white silk dressing-gown and lay face down. Selecting one of the scented creams, he dropped to his knees beside her. Firmly, with long, slow strokes he spread the cream over her back. His hands trailed at the nape of her neck, then moved to her shoulders, down her back, along her sides, just brushing against the swell of her breasts before returning to the column of her spine. Slowly in a hypnotic, circular movement he caressed the cream into her body, moving lower down to the swell of her buttocks. Closing her eyes, she willed herself to remain still, to concentrate on the feel of his hands flickering at the base of her spine, the smooth sensuous feel of the cream against her flesh.

She was already hot, her body roused by the music and the memories, but her mind kept returning to the sombre figure below in the library. Poor Mika! Since the accident he had become remote, almost unreachable. Coldly, resolutely he had turned his back to the world, refused any of the sensual pleasures his music embodied. Knowing he needed time to adjust, she'd accepted their isolation, resigned herself to this lonely existence. But it couldn't last for ever.

Sensing her distraction, Sergei crouched over her and spread his hands along her ankles, forcing her legs further apart. He brushed his hands up to the back of her knees, then down to her ankles, up and down, up and down, each time edging further towards the top of her thighs, the cleft of her buttocks, spreading her legs further and further apart. Tantalising and teasing now, his fingers fluttered gently along the insides of her thighs, brushed the swell of her hips, returned to her back, avoiding the twin globes of her buttocks. She felt herself swelling, growing wet and hot and she squirmed against the satin spread, relishing the friction. Gratefully she abandoned her thoughts, concentrating instead on the waves of sensation flowing through her body.

The telephone beside the bed trilled once, then stopped. He squeezed more cream onto her skin just at the base of her spine, felt her gasp involuntarily as it puddled, then trickled down the cleft of her buttocks, moistening her anus, joining the warm wetness of her hidden lips. Soon his fingers would find the creamy wetness, part the red, wet folds and massage the gnawing ache between her legs.

The phone rang again. Gesturing to Sergei to continue, Serena picked up the receiver.

'Sorry to disturb you, madam,' said the housekeeper, 'but it's Max Schiller from London. He insisted on being put through to you, even though I told him you were—'

'That's all right, Maddie. Put him through,' she said, suddenly eager to hear his voice.

She turned over on her back, propping herself

against the pillows. Sergei poured more cream onto his hands and smoothed it along her throat, her arms, just skimming the top of her breasts, carefully avoiding the jutting brown nipples.

'Yes,' she purred, picturing Max on the other end of the line. Dark, almost swarthy, of medium height, he was strongly built. Only piercing green eyes saved his face from a rather pleasant anonymity.

'Serena? Serena, is that you?' Across the wires his voice sounded faintly distorted.

'Oh yes,' she breathed, as she felt the rough male hands tracing the swell of her breasts, hardly touching them at all, then gently sculpting their curves, kneading the soft mounds. Her nipples were aching and distended now.

'It's very hard to get a hold of you these days,' he grumbled.

'Hard to get a hold of?' she murmured. Encouraged, Sergei quickly discarded his trousers and knelt on the bed between her legs. Languidly she reached out, taking his shaft in her hand, felt it ripple and grow under her touch.

'Well, you have me now, darling,' she murmured, spreading her legs apart. Understanding her instantly, Sergei bent his mouth to the inviting apex of her body. With firm, insistent strokes he tongued the inside of her thighs, stealthily flicking at her mound, retreating almost instantly. She felt the warm trickle of liquid escape, knowing she was growing wetter and wetter. Her skin, freshly shaved, was unbearably soft and sensitive. He pulled at her gently, stretching her swollen lips to his tongue and found her clitoris hard and erect. Firmly he pressed down with his finger, felt the throb of her womb contracting. Lightly he pressed up and down, up and down, felt her grow harder and wetter, felt her outer lips swell as if they too longed for his touch.

'It's been more than a year now, Serena, closer to

two since you've gone into seclusion. You must be finding it unbearably dull.'

'Yes, I suppose it is a little dull like this,' she agreed, fully conscious of her unintended *double entendre*. Hearing her words, Sergei swiftly retrieved the jade beads, raised her hips on a pillow, and parted the lips of her anus with his fingers. Expertly he jammed the first one against the tightness of her back passage, then felt it yield. The rounded coolness of the oiled bead blocking her and filling her was deliciously stimulating.

Almost as stimulating as this teasing conversation with Max.

'Anyway, I've got a proposition for you. A rather novel one.'

'You know how I adore novelty, Max,' she purred, and felt Sergei pushing in the next bead, and the next and the next until only the tasselled pull was left, nestled in the cleft of her buttocks.

'I think we should meet, Serena. Do you see yourself coming to London in the near future?' he asked.

'Coming?' she repeated, pleased with the opening he had given her. 'Not for a long time, I hope,' lifting an eyebrow at Sergei. Carefully he inserted his index and middle fingers inside her, cupping her with his palm. Gently, rhythmically, he pressed against her inner walls, feeling her hot and tight. With his free hand he reached up and captured a nipple between his fingers, flicking the rosy-brown point with his nails.

'I know, you've always disliked London. Well then, I'll come to Geneva. I should be there by dinner-time tomorrow.'

'What's the rush, Max?' she asked, suddenly suspicious. She'd been enjoying her word-play too much to pay attention to what Max was saying. Feeling her tense, her attention diverted, Sergei slowed the rhythm of his fingers inside her.

'Max?' she repeated. But the line had suddenly gone dead. 'Damn,' she muttered, replacing the receiver.

'I wonder what he wants,' she said aloud.

'I know what you want,' said Sergei. 'And what I want. And I'm going to get it.'

Preoccupied, she barely heard him, barely felt his mouth move to her breast. Aware of her distraction, angered by it, he took her nipple between his teeth, bit down sharply. Twisting his fingers inside her, probing deeply, he could just feel the outlines of the jade beads blocking her anus. Using his teeth and fingers in unison, he quickly established a rhythm, biting and jabbing, biting and jabbing.

Distantly she was aware of her skin heating, the blood rising and centring between her legs, the tingling arcs flowing from her nipples.

'Sorry, Sergei,' she said, regretfully ruffling his hair, 'but I really must call Max back. Later, perhaps.'

'Max?' he repeated incredulously. The blood was roaring in his ears, pulsing through his cock. Furiously he threw himself at her, forcing her face down on the pillows, almost knocking the breath from her. Panting, half smothered by the soft pillows, she struggled to breathe. His blood high, he barely heard her curse, and the feel of her writhing beneath him maddened him further. Capturing her wrists in a vice-like grip, he subdued her effortlessly.

'Sergei, not Max,' he growled.

Helpless, she felt his shaft sliding down the cleft of her buttocks, pause at her anus, butt against the tightness of her blocked passage. Trapped by his arms and weight, she could do nothing to fight him. There was none of the teasing, slow build-up, the strength and submission she'd taught him so painstakingly.

'Stupid son-of-a-bitch! You forget yourself, Sergei,' she spat, suddenly angry. 'Slowly and—'

Roughly he forced his hand against her mouth, cutting off her words. Grasping himself with one hand, he positioned the tip of his penis just at the entrance to her back passage, rocked against it and felt her shudder beneath him. The globes of her buttocks were deliciously soft and warm and yielding against his groin. Relishing the contrast of tightness and softness, he thrust his hips harder against her, sliding his pendulous sac along her cleft.

'Feel me here,' he commanded and centred the tip of his shaft at her entrance. Hot and full he felt her muscles contract against him, felt the jade beads, and enraged by this solid resistance rocked harder against her, forcing himself just inside. She gasped and lay still. Impaled by the tip of his member, forcing the beads further into her anus, held immobile by his hands and the weight of his body full-length against hers, she was helpless.

He jerked roughly against her, forcing himself a fraction further inside. With the beads held in her, she was tight and hot, tighter than anything he'd ever felt. He felt her spasm beneath him, felt a curious mixture of pain and pleasure centre on the head of his shaft. His breathing was laboured now and he felt the sweat spring to his brow. He paused, settling his body more firmly against hers.

The ache of his invasion was subsiding a little, becoming familiar and she was conscious of a thready stirring in her blood, as though it was bubbling through her veins. Distantly, she wondered if she was just a little afraid. Or merely excited. *SEX SLAVE REBELS*. It belonged on the front page of some seamy tabloid, she thought. Perhaps she should have seen it coming.

Perversely, deliberately she tightened her muscles, feeling the delicious pressure of the beads, then pushed back, forcing him out. Arching against him slightly she drew him down to her other entrance which was now soft and slick and welcoming.

'Yes,' he grated, remembering the lessons she had taught him. Grasping his member with his free hand, he jammed the head of his rod hard against her and moved himself up and down, up and down, up and down, tracing a path between the two openings to her body, his rhythm fast and furious.

Rocking in response, she felt her hidden lips swell

and warm, throb in anticipation of his hardness, felt herself growing smooth and loose. She was wet and steamy now and he was slick with her wetness. Raising her buttocks just slightly, she drew him into her, felt the hard length of him filling her. For a moment she allowed herself to savour the delicious sensation of being utterly filled with the twin pressures of the jade beads blocking her rectum, his hard rod filling her vagina.

She knew from his laboured breathing, the tensing of the muscles in his arms that he was caught, immersed in the rhythms of his body. And so, mustering all her strength, using the bruising grasp on her wrists as leverage, she suddenly hauled herself up, felt him sliding out of her and twisted beneath him to confront him face to face.

'My way, Sergei. Only my way,' she warned, and tightened her body against him.

Caught by surprise, in the beginning throes of his orgasm, he was mad to find her, grind against her and shoot into her body. But she'd tightened her legs, bucked against him, eluded him, and he found himself coming against the silk sheet that had knotted around her thighs, her nails scoring his wrists.

He shuddered the last of himself into that silken wasteland, and looked up to find her amber eyes smiling at him gently, her warm red lips curved in a delicious smile.

'Since you're so eager, we'll try and get it right,' she cooed. She could call Max later. An hour wouldn't make any difference. She slipped out from under him and padded towards her dressing-table.

LONDON

Max leaned back in his black leather chair, carefully replacing the telephone receiver. Just the sound of Serena's voice, smoky and sultry over the long-distance wires, was enough to make him hard. From the moment he saw her he'd wanted her. Felt an electrical

14

pulse of recognition jangling his nerves the instant his eyes met hers. He remembered how her amber eyes had caught his briefly, then slid away. Serena.

Wild, wanton, untameable Serena. It had been at the first party he had thrown at Maxim's, to celebrate Mika's contract with Disc-O. As founder and managing director of the newly formed recording company, it had been a coup for Max to sign Mika, rising star in classical music and bidding fair to rival Menuhin. Amidst the usual jet-set glitterati she had stood out like some luscious wild flower, mysterious and exotic, dark and enticing.

'The dark woman with the gorgeous legs, over there, who is she?' he'd asked Mika, standing next to him. Seen the slow, reluctant smile.

'Mmm. Devastating, isn't she? Her name is Serena.' Both aware of some hidden undercurrents, they'd sipped champagne, watched the crowd form and re-form, the throng of men surrounding Serena increasing and swelling. It parted for a moment, and she looked over at them, half closing her eyes at Mika and touching the heavy gold chain wrapped around her neck. Max sensed some intimate signal, some curious communication between the two.

'Your, umm . . .' Max fumbled for a word. Mistress seemed old-fashioned, lover too banal.

'Mine?' Mika replied. 'Serena . . . Serena belongs to herself.'

She had come to Max that night in Paris, slipped into his hotel room wearing a white silk negligée and carrying a bottle of champagne. Tight, hot, lush, wet and wild, she'd excited him unbearably with her hands, her mouth, brought him to the brink again and again. She had taken possession of him like some succubus, he remembered, until he finally came in an explosive frenzy he'd never found with another woman. Then left while he slept.

God, how he wanted her. Had pursued her relentlessly after Paris, to be met with casual, friendly indifference. Every stratagem he'd devised had failed. If he was in London, she was in Rome. A hasty flight to Rome, to discover she'd just checked out. A few chance encounters over the years, in Vienna, again in London. Always in the company of others.

And then the accident.

Max sighed and pressed the intercom, summoning his personal assistant.

She appeared instantly. She had been waiting for his summons, expecting it ever since he'd told her to place the call to Geneva.

'Did you tape the TV report on Mika?' asked Max.

'I have it here,' she replied, showing him the black cartridge she carried in her right hand. 'Do you want to see it again?'

At his nod, she crossed the room and slotted the tape into the VCR. Instantly the image of the glossy reporter filled the massive screen.

'The secret of his technique that has moved audiences the world over remains locked behind these gates. The magical and mysterious power of his playing created an unparalleled sensation in the music world for almost a decade. Disc-O, the recording company owned by Max Schiller, has been obliged to honour their negotiated inflation-proof contract worth some estimated £500,000 per year for life. How long will Mika remain in seclusion? How long can Disc-O survive without Mika? How long before Max Schiller issues a public statement? How long—'

'Turn off the sound and freeze it there,' said Max, as Serena appeared on the screen in a glittering white sheath.

'Well?' asked his PA. She was dark and small and vaguely resembled the woman on the screen.

'Well, Sally?' he replied, devouring the sight of Serena. That voluptuous body encased in sequins. That warm, red mouth.

'Well, what did she say? What are you going to do?

We can't afford to ignore the press. This sort of speculation is only going to grow—'

'I'll be going to Geneva tomorrow,' he interrupted her. 'And in the meantime, we'll have come up with some sort of plan. Lock the door.' His eyes were fixed on the screen, his arousal apparent.

'Of course,' she replied and locked the door behind her. She had long been aware of his obsession with Serena D'Angelo. And it was, despite the odds, getting stronger, perhaps even interfering with his judgement. Perhaps it always had.

Max lounged back in the chair, relishing the image of Serena. The white sheath was moulded to her body, emphasising her lush breasts, tiny waist, rounded hips.

'Quickly,' he said.

Sally crossed the room, knelt before him and lowered her head to him. Cunningly she ran a long-tipped fingernail along the zipper of his trousers, testing his arousal through the fabric. Found him hard, bulging, massive. Fluttering her fingers against the cloth she felt him grow. Her mouth moistened with a sudden rush of saliva. Swallowing, she blew against the crisp black linen, wanting him to feel the warmth of her breath. Knowingly she drifted one hand up towards the head of the zipper, her other down to cup his balls, constrained by the twin layers of fabric. Gently, ever so gently, she scratched at his sac, still running her nail up and down along the length of his zipper.

Raising both hands to the waistband of his trousers, she undid the two buttons, slowly and luxuriously the zipper. His penis shot out at her, thick and wild and red like some predatory beast.

Lifting his hips, he felt her slide his trousers down, the rasp of linen and then of silk as she pulled down his shorts, freeing his aching rod from confinement.

Delicately she circled the head of his shaft with her tongue, around and around, creating a circle of numb, aching pleasure. He felt himself growing, engorging, reaching his full length. Tantalising, playing, she took the bulbous tip in her mouth, cupping the soft silky sac of his balls in one hand, while her other hand roved freely along his length in sure, smooth strokes.

Her fingers felt hot and cool, smooth and rough, just as he wanted. Reaching to the nape of her neck, he tightened his fingers, pushed her down just for an instant, indicating his preference.

Smoothly she adjusted her rhythm, clasping his shaft with both hands while her mouth maintained a steady sucking pressure on the head of his cock. His fingers tightened, pressed down on her, forcing her to take more of him in her mouth. Swiftly she responded with a firmer, more rhythmic stroke of both hands on his member. He was too big, far too big. She could only take a small part of him before he was piercing the back of her throat.

She wanted him inside her, filling her with that giant length, wanted to feel her walls clasp him, feel him shoot inside her, empty himself into her. She pressed her thighs together more closely, feeling herself moisten. But the clutch of his hand on the nape of her neck recalled her, and she plied herself to his shaft-head, sucking now in quick eager suction, like a baby at the bottle teat, stopping and grasping, playing and circling with her tongue, all the time keeping a strong forceful lengthy stroke along his shaft.

He felt himself centring, felt the focus of his body gather in the long hard length in her hands and mouth. Opening his eyes, he saw Serena. She was smiling, ever so slightly. What was it the reporter had said? 'The secret lies locked behind these gates . . .'

'Serena,' he said, hardly conscious of his own voice, and gave himself up to the utterly inevitable pleasure of his forthcoming orgasm. As he relaxed to the flow of all his blood, all his energy gathered in his cock.

She felt the muscles of his thighs tremble almost imperceptibly, tensing against her arms spasmodically, knew he was on the verge of losing control as much as he ever could, ever did.

Maliciously she stopped the smooth sucking rhythm of her mouth on his cock and withdrew, flicked her tongue instead along the top of his swollen glans, stilled her hands on the length of him and instead squeezed back and forth, back and forth.

Hovering on the edge, feeling himself grow hotter, he was unaware of anything but an intrusion to the rhythm he wanted. Roughly he clutched at the hair of this woman kneeling in front of him, pulled her head down hard, felt his shaft meet the back of her throat, walls harder than a vagina, more unforgiving, more exciting for all that, and forced himself further down. He came in a flood, shaking and spasming and jerking to the primitive wild calls of his body.

Half-smothering from the length of him in her mouth, struggling not to drown in his bitter-sweet juices, Sally heard him muttering something, but she couldn't quite make out the words. The secret behind the gates?

Slowly the room swam into focus. She was still before him, kneeling, his cock in her mouth. He smiled down at her, as his breathing returned to normal. Freeing himself from her mouth he zipped up his trousers.

She was hot and wet and ready, aroused by the feel of him in her mouth, aching for something inside her, anything of him, fingers, mouth, cock, tongue, something.

'Thank you, Sally,' he said. For a moment, watching her raise herself to her feet, clutching the desk for support, he felt vaguely disquieted, but brushed the feeling aside.

'Lovely. Now let's get to work. We'll have to devise some sort of excuse for, I mean some proposal that I can take to Geneva. Think about it.'

'Of course, sir,' she replied, straightening her clothes, smoothing the hair he'd disarranged in his passion, hating him just a little.

Hastening to the Ladies, she looked at herself in the

long mirror over the washbasins. Her cheeks were flushed, eyes bright and glittering. With shaking hands, she ran cold water over her wrists, splashed her face, all the while knowing it was no use. Defeated by the hot waves still rolling through her, she quickly entered one of the cubicles, closed the door and locked it. Relaxing on the seat she slumped back, breathed deeply. Imagining herself sitting in his black leather chair behind the long glass desk, she parted her thighs just slightly. In her mind's eye she transformed the cool, unyielding surface of the enamel tank against her back into the welcoming caress of soft leather, firmly cushioning her body.

He would be before her, kneeling, pleading, a supplicant to the earthy, juicy delights of her body. And she, preoccupied, would open her thighs a little to his questing hands, feel them trail up the insides of her legs, whisper against her stockings. He would be impassioned and impatient, would try to force her knees apart with greedy hands, desperate to fix his ravenous mouth on her hidden mouth, make her writhe with want.

Eyes closed, she felt herself through the thin covering of her underwear, soaking wet with eager juices. Sighing, she flicked the cloth aside, roughly inserted her index and middle finger, keeping her thumb free for her centre of passion. Expertly she jammed her fingers in, up and down, rubbing, sculpting, stimulating her inside walls, while her thumb flicked her clitoris into hard, red awareness.

And her thumb became his mouth, her fingers his fingers, wanting and willing her into abandoned pleasure at his touch. But she would be coy, aloof, aloof from the pleasure this man could bring, deny him a while, play with him a bit. Closing her thighs, she felt the pressure against her swelling lips, felt the coolness of the unyielding enamel.

She felt the tightness now, the pooling chill of oncoming orgasm, knew it was inevitable. She tensed her muscles, stopped the flurry of her fingers inside and outside, willed herself at peace to savour the torment. Opened her mouth to receive his rough, hungry kiss, the phantom tongue that flicked and drove at hers. Offered her breasts to the impassioned, invisible hands that clutched them a little too roughly. Reckless hands roaming everywhere, wanting her everywhere, legs, breasts, arms. Wreathing her wraith-like, totally enveloping.

She would lie passive as he fed on her flesh, lapping and sucking and darting with his hands and tongue, striving to drive her over the edge. And then he would enter the room, tall and slim and fair, violin clasped loosely in his hand. Mika. Smiling at her, he would bend his bow to the strings, play to her and only to her. She could feel the strings licking at her like the man's tongue, electrifying her flesh, rousing her nerves to fever pitch.

Her hands moved now, taking up the lost rhythm, thumb rubbing her throbbing erectness, fingers pulsing against her echoing walls. She was hot and slick now, and the friction of her fingers created a moist burning trail. She rocked against the enamel seat, felt its coolness as warmth, felt the hands and tongue driving into her, claiming her, heard the pure and elegant staccato vibrating . . . And came in a quick, electric gush, spasming and shaking.

Returning to her desk, she found a note propped against her coffee cup in Max's distinctive scrawl. 1) Compile shortlist of all competitors placed in final rounds of international instrumental competitions in last eighteen months. 2) Book me first class to Geneva on the afternoon flight tomorrow.

Chapter Two

First Audition

LONDON

'You're confirmed first class on the afternoon flight tomorrow, Mr Schiller,' said Sally, looking up as he approached her desk later that afternoon. 'And I've begun compiling a short list, as you asked.'

'Well done,' he approved. It was obvious that she had been working. Her desk was littered with papers, newspaper cuttings and glossy publicity photos.

'But since I have absolutely *no* idea why I'm doing it, or *what* I'm looking for, it's going to take a while,' she said, a distinct edge to her voice.

'Someone special. We'll know when we find her,' he stated confidently.

'Her? I didn't realise you were only interested in female artists. If only you'd told me before—'

'Did I say her?' he asked, surprised. 'I hadn't really thought about it. I'm not sure . . .' his voice trailed off and he knit his brows in concentration.

'Perhaps if you told me exactly what you *are* looking for, it might help! A short list of every instrumentalist in the final rounds of international competitions for the past eighteen months is going to run to at least a hundred names, possibly more! You haven't even said what instrument. Nor how this relates to your trip to Geneva tomorrow. Assuming, of course, you intend on trying to do some business while you're away. Sir,' she concluded bitingly.

'Violin, I expect,' he said, selecting the easiest question. 'We might do with a viola, but I doubt it. We do need Mika. I replayed the video after you left and, well, the press are starting to make waves. We can't afford to keep up these payments indefinitely. Mika can't – or won't – play again. What are my options?' he asked rhetorically. 'Now, I've told Serena I have a novel proposition for her. Which I don't.'

It's just an excuse to see her, you know that, taunted Sally silently. You'd let Disc-O go to hell if it meant you could spend the night with her.

'So,' Max continued, waxing theatrical, 'I can go to Geneva and beg them to rip up the contract. I can taunt Mika with the promise of another player, a violinist, who will outstrip his success almost immediately. I—'

'Unlikely,' she commented dryly. 'Particularly if you want a woman.'

'I can . . . What did you say?' Of course I want a woman, he thought. That woman.

'I said that it's unlikely a woman could equal, or even outstrip, Mika's success,' said Sally calmly.

'And you call yourself a feminist,' he mocked.

'Don't you read the marketing summaries?' she retorted, stung. 'Seventy per cent of Mika's record and ticket sales were made by women. And as far as the researchers could make out, at least fifty per cent of those women previously had no interest in classical music. That's absolutely unparalleled! And the reason is simple. It's because of the way he makes you feel.'

'Yes, yes, we're all fully aware of his electric effect on the audience,' Max began impatiently, but she interrupted him almost at once.

'There's something you're overlooking here. Not one of the critics has come close to describing the way he makes me feel when I listen to him play. Probably because they're all men. They compare his perfect technique to Perlman, his pure interpretative style to Menuhin, but they've never touched on that very special, very personal quality he communicates. It's like being kissed for the first time,' she said, and a small smile curved her mouth. Swallowing, she ran her tongue over her lips.

'How very romantic,' he said, intending it as a snub.

'Yes, utterly romantic at times,' she agreed. 'There's that first soft touch, casual, so artful it seems unplanned. But you can feel the memory of it on your skin, feel it pulse a little.'

'Go on,' he said, suddenly interested, caught by the look in her eyes.

'It's a seduction of the strings, an enticing, beguiling seduction. Soft touches. A kiss, gentle and undemanding, just tracing your lips, relishing the curves, promising more. That's how it starts, anyway,' she said.

'Tell me,' he said intently.

'Well, it all depends on what he's playing, of course. But you know the thrill that you get at the back of your spine, that sort of tingling feeling that makes your hair stand on end when you hear something that's absolutely right?' He nodded. 'There's that and more than that. You can feel his music on your skin. It's like he's playing you. Making love to you. It's like a dream lover, a demon lover. It's like a roller-coaster, like the best sex you ever had. It's physical and mental, because you can actually feel it while you think about the music. It's a seduction. Not something you're familiar with, perhaps,' she concluded, and shrugging she turned back to the pile of papers on her desk.

'What do you mean?' he asked, stung.

I mean you live for a celluloid fantasy, and get your kicks by snapping your fingers for me and still thinking of her, she thought to herself. 'I mean you haven't had to seduce anybody for a very long time,' she snapped.

'Sally,' he began, then paused, totally at a loss. She remained impassive, still seated at her desk.

Her flashes of temper were rare, triggered by the strangest things. He liked her, needed her – she was, after all, one of Disc-O's biggest assets – and what she had just said was undeniably, unpalatably true.

She felt him move behind her, felt the first gentle, apologetic touch of his hands on her hair, sifting through it, parting it at the nape of her neck. Delicately he placed his mouth just at the column of her neck, breathed in the smell of her. Closing her eyes, she willed herself to remain utterly still, concentrating on the feel of his tongue just flicking against her flesh. His hands moved to her shoulders, down her back, then stopped, halted by the back of her chair. She leaned forward just slightly, just enough so that he could run his hands along the full length of her back, down to the swell of her buttocks. Lightly, he traced the swell of her hips, then moved up, brushing against the swell of her breasts. She felt her nipples tighten and tingle against the fabric of her dress, felt the liquid heat between her thighs begin to flow. Crossing her legs, she felt the swell of her inner lips against the thin wedge of fabric.

With one hand on the back of the swivel steno-chair, he turned her to face him. Her eyes were closed, her head flung back. He smoothed his hands along her throat, her arms, then reached down to circle her breasts. Cupping the lush weight in the palm of his hands, he grasped the nipples between his thumb and forefinger, rolling and teasing them against the soft wool of her dress. Then he hardened his touch, pinching the peaks again and again. She felt the electric tingle shoot to her groin, felt herself swell and moisten.

He touched a finger to her lips, pressed down gently, traced the curve of her mouth, then bent towards her and placed his mouth on hers. Questing with his tongue he explored the curve of her lips, tasting and moistening, darting against her teeth and then retreating to the smooth swell of her mouth.

She felt herself growing warmer and looser, rocking

25

to the rhythm of his tongue. Unconsciously she parted her teeth, opened her mouth fully to his tongue, sucked it into the plush warm cavity. Deliberately he hardened his mouth, hardened his tongue, and thrust into her mouth in a hard, jabbing rhythm.

Impatient now and greedy for the feel of her, he hauled her out of the chair, twisted the skirt of her dress around her waist, roughly pulled down her stockings to the top of her thighs, and pressed her firmly against his erection while he fumbled with the zip of his trousers. Annoyed, she opened her eyes, stiffened away from him.

'That's hardly seductive,' she snapped. But her hips rocked towards him, seeking his hardness. She was ready, she knew, slick and hot and waiting to be filled. Still, she reminded herself, there was a point to this exercise. 'Someone really should teach you how to kiss.'

His trousers around his ankles, he felt the fabric of her panties tear away. Pressing her against the desk he entered her in one sharp thrust. Harder and deeper, harder and deeper he thrust into her, revelling in her tightness, her wetness. Feeling her tense and quiver, he felt the impending rush at the base of his spine.

'What did you say?' he asked, barely conscious of his own voice.

'I said,' she replied hoarsely, 'someone should really teach you—' But he drove into her again, and the hard length of him filling her, the delicious friction against her warm slick sex sent her rocketing over the edge before she could finish her sentence. Feeling her convulse around him, throbbing and pulsing, sent him spiralling over the edge scant seconds later.

She slipped out from beneath him, pulling up her stockings and smoothing her dress down over her thighs. She felt drained and elated at the same time. She'd issued her challenge and it had gotten her . . . what?

'Teach me how to kiss, you said?' he asked, his breathing slowly returning to normal.

'That's exactly what I said,' she replied, handing him a towel.

'If you can teach someone how to kiss,' he began, then stopped. Carefully drying himself with the towel, he felt a growing excitement. 'That's the solution, Sally! We get Mika to teach his technique, his method, his secret. We'll find him a pupil. And I was right, as usual!' He felt himself growing hard all over again.

'Right about what?' she asked, unimpressed.

'Right about it having to be a woman, of course! If, as you say, Mika's playing elicited strong emotional arousal in women and captured a previously untapped market – and you're right, I haven't been paying enough attention to the marketing surveys – then a woman should be able to do the same with a male audience.'

'Theoretically, it's plausible enough, I suppose,' she said slowly. At least he was thinking about business for a change. 'But you're assuming that this is a technique that can be taught or transmitted. It may not be. And even if it is, how on earth are you going to convince Mika to teach? Or rather, convince Serena? She keeps him so closely guarded it's impossible to get near him. She'd never tolerate a woman coming between them. In fact, I'm surprised she agreed to your visit at all.'

'She hasn't,' he admitted. 'I fumbled with the phone and then hung up before she could refuse. She'll blame it on a bad connection.'

'That's ridiculous!' she exclaimed. 'What's to stop her from calling you?'

'Nothing. But you'll tell her I've already left, can't be reached, whatever.'

'It's thin, Max, very thin,' she cautioned, unconsciously using his first name.

'And in the meantime,' he continued, ignoring her warning, 'you will find me the most gorgeous, most voluptuous, most talented young violinist currently

27

doing the rounds. Get me a potted biography, too. We'll have to know everything about her.'

'She has to be beautiful?' queried Sally. On the one hand, she found this male preoccupation with beauty mildly offensive. On the other hand, it would certainly make her search easier. For some reason, female string players, like opera singers, tended to be unquestionably, unfortunately, plain.

'Arresting, anyway,' he compromised. 'Get a selection together before I leave tomorrow.'

'That's almost impossible, you know,' she pointed out.

'That's why you get paid so well, darling. Anyway, you have an assistant. Let the divine Eve loose on the problem.'

Typical Max, she thought with a groan. 'The divine Eve is still in New York, as you know.'

'Actually, I'm back,' said an amused voice. They turned to the doorway where a woman with curly platinum blonde hair in a flaming red dress was lounging. She bore a natural resemblance to the early Monroe, which she'd heightened by stencilling a beauty mark on her cheek.

'Eve,' said Max, disconcerted. How long had she been standing there?

'Eve,' said Sally, thinking furiously. How long had she been standing there? 'Thank God you're here. We've missed you.'

'Right. Well. I'll leave you to sort things out,' said Max, sliding towards the door.

'Don't worry, boss,' drawled Eve. 'We'll find your violinist.'

'You heard, then?' asked Sally, as the door closed on Max.

'Most of it,' replied Eve. 'Another crazy notion?'

'Actually, I'm not sure,' said Sally slowly. 'He might actually be on the right track. Even if it is for all the wrong reasons. God, I'm tired,' she said as a yawn split her face. 'Sorry, Eve. How was New York?'

'Never changes,' replied Eve, crossing to the small refrigerator that lurked unhappily in one corner of the room. 'Full of Americans.' And one of them a very special American, whose petro-dollars would fuel the plans she had been harbouring for some time now. Plans that she needed Sally for. But it was still far, far too soon. 'Shall I get you some wine?' Eve said aloud. 'And why don't you stretch out for a while?'

'Good idea.' Slipping off her shoes, Sally relaxed gratefully in the plump depths of the couch. Her office included various amenities suitable for the PA to the director. A couch, smaller than his and in imitation leather, but it was still a couch. A refrigerator rather than a drinks cabinet, but it still kept the wine cold. And her own assistant. Who was rapidly becoming indispensable. In so many ways.

'So what do you think?' asked Sally, sipping wine.

'Well, at least he's thinking about business for a change.' Setting down her glass, Eve placed both hands on Sally's foot and gently began massaging and kneading. 'So . . . you missed me?' she asked, her eyes fixed on Sally's face.

'Oh, Eve, I—' Sally began, tentatively sliding away from her hands, but Eve interrupted her almost at once.

'Come on Sally, you know it'll relax you.' Deftly, giving her no time to resist, she reached up beneath the other woman's dress, felt for the tops of her stockings, pulled them down over her ankles, tugged them off, and resumed her massage.

'But—' Sally began, then stopped herself. How had she ever got herself into this situation? Eve's hands were cool and sure, exploring every muscle, every tendon, slipping her fingers between her toes, pressing her fingers against the soft skin that divided them.

'So we need to find a woman,' said Eve, interrupting the confused train of Sally's thoughts. Delicately she slid out her pink pointed tongue and licked at the instep, then flicked her tongue between the toes.

'Mmm,' agreed Sally, shivering a little as the moist warmth of Eve's tongue attacked the tender skin. Eve did have the most original way of combining business and pleasure, she thought, feeling herself heating.

'An arresting violinist,' Eve continued, slipping her mouth over a toe, then sucking hard. She felt the quiver of response, and gently moved her hand up to the ankle, then to the sensitive flesh at the curve of the knee, all the while maintaining the firm, relentless sucking pressure of her mouth.

Relaxing to the rhythm, Sally settled herself more comfortably on the imitation leather couch, parted her thighs and closed her eyes. The wet sucking feel of a mouth on her toes was infinitely arousing. Then she gasped, feeling the needle-point pressure of tiny teeth nipping at her flesh.

Hearing her, Eve smiled in satisfaction, released one toe from the warm cavity of her mouth, and sought another. She made love to her foot, bathing each toe with warm, moist strokes of her tongue, lapping and licking and sucking. She varied the pressure, the suction, sometimes fierce and hard, then just gently rimming the nail with the point of her tongue.

'It's good, isn't it?' breathed Eve.

'Mmm,' Sally responded, and not wanting to think, not wanting anything to interrupt the delicious warmth spreading through her veins, she stretched her hand to Eve's lips.

Eve, recognising the gesture, deliberately guided the hand to her mouth. Enclosing the length of one slim finger between her lips she sucked at it delicately, pulled it full length into her mouth, pushed it against her palate and then circled it with her tongue. Again and again she lapped and laved, nipped and sucked. Deliberately she held back from touching Sally on her breasts or between her legs, willing to wait until she reached for her. Eve herself was slick and ready, excited by the hardness in her mouth, the tantalising softness of the woman's body next to hers. She crossed her legs, determined to prolong the sensation.

Sally felt her body warming, growing sensitive. How astonishing to feel herself growing so wet simply from this repeated warm sucking of her toes and fingers! Her nipples were hard now, and she wanted to feel that same lapping and lipping and sucking on her breasts, between her legs.

'A woman,' Sally said wonderingly, and reached out to touch the fall of platinum blonde hair that just brushed against her arm.

Feeling her touch, Eve reached below Sally's skirt, slid her hands up her dress, found her breasts and imprisoned them with her palms. Cupping the soft weight, she felt the nipples harden further under her thumbs. Tugging and teasing, she flicked the points with the ball of her thumb in a rhythmic caress. The soft wool of the dress provided another source of friction, and cunningly she rubbed the nipple against it, still kneading it with her thumb.

Sally moaned in response, arching her hips. Her eyes were still closed, her skin flushed. She was ready, Eve judged, expertly assessing the blush rising to her cheeks.

'It is good, isn't it?' she repeated softly.

'Mmm, yes, please, don't stop,' murmured Sally softly, lost in sensation.

Eve's hands stilled. 'Better than with him?'

'Please, Eve, you know—'

'Better than with him?'

'Yes, you know it, please, Eve,' she responded helplessly.

Satisfied, she smoothed the dress up over the curve of Sally's hips, past her breasts, and bent her head to the hard peaking nipple of one while clasping the other firmly between her fingers. She sucked hard, drawing as much of the soft white flesh into her mouth as she could, while kneading and pinching the other with her fingers. Then, using both hands, she pressed both breasts together, so close that the nipples met, and took both of them in her mouth at once. She ran her tongue in circles around this double nipple, sucked hard, then gently caught it between her teeth and bit down.

Sally felt it as an electric jolt running down her spine, rushing to meet the moist burning between her thighs. Wave after wave of sensation rolled through her as Eve continued biting gently at her engorged flesh.

'Flesch,' Sally murmured, 'Of course. The Flesch.'

'Beautiful, soft, lovely white flesh,' breathed Eve around a mouthful of breast. Removing one hand, she trailed it down Sally's belly, lightly feathering through the crisp hair between her legs, plucking at it gently.

'No, I mean the Carl Flesch competition,' said Sally. 'It starts this evening. We can go together, see who's playing.'

'Excellent,' approved Eve. 'But we'll finish this flesh competition first, I think.'

Sally felt the mouth move down her belly, tracing the path the hand had taken, tongue flicking her navel, warm, moist breath on her hair, then lapping delicately at the wet red folds enclosing her centre. Eve circled them with her tongue, moistening the slick flesh even further, then hardening her tongue swept round the hood of her clitoris. Pushing aside the tiny fold with her tongue, she found the little red bud hard and erect, almost pulsing with a rhythm of its own, and took it in her mouth. She sucked and sucked with a steadily increasing pressure until she felt Sally begin to arch, begin to quiver with the first small tremors running through her. She slowed the suction of her mouth, reached up with her hands to capture both taut nipples between her fingers.

Utterly absorbed in this triangle of sensation, Sally felt herself centring, growing and swelling. Her clitoris was hungry, greedy, needy for the next soft pulling pressure, knowing it would be the next, or the next, or the next that would throw her off the edge. She was formless, nerveless, weightless. Nothing mattered now except the feel of this hot little mouth, drinking her in, sucking out all the warm juices of her body. She felt ripe and juicy, like a peach, and Eve's mouth was like a gourmet's knife, savouring the juicy ripeness of her flesh. The pressure of her mouth was relentless, driving her closer and closer to the edge. But still her womb felt empty, aching, needing to be filled.

'God, I can't bear it, fuck me Eve!' she cried.

Expertly, without breaking the rhythm of her mouth, the other woman jammed her fingers together, then thrust them up inside Sally. And feeling the pressure, Sally came at once, an electric gushing convulsion that shot through her again and again.

The phone shrilled once, then fell silent.

'Don't worry,' said Eve. 'I put the Ansaphone on.'

GENEVA

Utterly infuriated, Serena slammed down the receiver.

'Damn it, Maddie, I don't believe it! "I've reached the office of Disc-O,"' she mimicked savagely. '"They're sorry no one is available to take my call." That was Max's private line and I just spoke to him an hour ago!'

'Why didn't you put him off then?' asked the house-keeper, reasonably enough.

'I was busy. And I had no idea what he was leading up to,' she snapped. 'The line went dead right after he announced he was coming here.'

'Does it matter? His visit might do you both some good.'

'I won't have him upsetting Mika, Maddie.'

'Might do him some good to be upset for a change,' she replied ruthlessly. 'It's not right, madam, not right at all.'

Serena's eyes narrowed. When Maddie, who had been with them for years, almost since the beginning, called her 'madam', she meant business. 'What do you mean?'

33

'The pair of you have been moping around here all alone for ages now. Well, almost all alone,' she corrected herself. Better not to mention the string of chauffeurs and gardeners Serena had been toying with. 'All he does is play his old recordings again and again until I hear that damn Bach in my sleep. And all you do—' she hesitated.

'All I do?' prompted Serena silkily, daring her to continue.

'You know very well what you do,' huffed the housekeeper. 'I'm sure I don't and it's none of my business anyway. But it's still not right. And he's not looking well, you know.'

'Mika? He looks beautiful, he's fine, stop trying to make trouble, Maddie.'

'He's too pale and wrapped up in himself. And you know it,' she persisted.

'Well—' Serena began, then stopped. She did know it. Hadn't she been thinking much the same thing earlier?

'Won't do any harm for him to see Max Schiller. They used to be good friends. Be good to have a fresh face, some fresh blood in this place.'

'Fresh blood,' repeated Serena. A small smile curved her lips.

Faintly perturbed by the look in her eyes, the housekeeper turned away. 'I'll have a room prepared for him then?'

'Yes, do that, Maddie. As you say, a fresh face. But I'm not sure how Mika will take it.' A small frown marred her expression.

'Well, I expect a lot of it will depend on how you put it to him,' said Maddie, emphasising the 'you'. But Serena had already left the room.

She found Mika sitting on the terrace, drinking coffee, Midas sprawled on his knees. Pausing in the arched doorway, she smiled at the striking figure he made, dressed all in black, jeans, polo shirt, sunglasses, with a golden heap of fur on his lap. It was,

34

she realised with a shock of surprise, the same pose as they'd used for his last album cover, but without the cat. It had been shot in black and white, she remembered, here on this very spot.

'What is it, Serena?' He spoke without turning to face her, and she felt the familiar thrill of surprise at the acuteness of his hearing.

'Max rang,' she replied, sliding into one of the wrought iron chairs.

'Oh,' he said flatly, evidently disinterested. He was looking pale, she realised, a sort of pallor that had nothing to do with the even, golden tan he'd acquired sitting on the terrace.

'He's coming over to see us, darling,' she said, injecting a note of enthusiasm into her voice. 'He says he has something new and exciting he wants to discuss.'

'Why didn't you put him off, Serena?' he asked, sounding annoyed. His black gloved hands stilled on the cat's fur. 'You know I don't want anyone here.' Sensing the tension, the cat arched, opened large sleepy eyes and hissed.

'Because it sounded interesting,' she lied, stretching out a soothing hand to the cat. 'It's all right, Midas. And I thought it would be good to see him, see what he has to say. Ouch! Damn cat!' she cried, hastily retrieving her hand. A thin line of blood welled up where the cat's claws had scored her hand.

'Ah, Serena, you can lie to me, but you never fool Midas,' said Mika, smiling a little. 'You deal with Max.'

'Aren't you at all curious, Mika?' she asked, troubled.

'Not really. You take care of it.'

'All right,' she agreed, licking the blood from her hand. 'I'll find out what he has in mind. He called it a "novel proposition",' she quoted.

35

LONDON

Eve and Sally sat together in the darkened auditorium. The parade of flesh at the Carl Flesch competition had been undeniably first-rate. But so far all the contestants had been male. Sally's head was aching a little from the effort of concentration, and she felt listless and a little drowsy. Too much sex, not enough coffee, she thought wryly. How had she ever got herself into this tangle, she wondered again. Eve and Max. Max and Eve. Was Eve using her as another rung up the corporate ladder? Was that what she herself was doing with Max? She felt Eve's hand on her thigh and frowned.

'Eve—' she began, but Eve cut her off.

'Look,' she hissed, pointing to the wings. Barely visible behind the plush swells of the curtains a girl was standing, waiting to make her entrance. She was tall and slender, with flame-coloured hair flowing down her back. Her face was in the shadows, indistinct.

'Francesca Tonelli, playing Bach's *Sonata in G minor* for solo violin,' intoned the announcer. The fruity, pompous voice couldn't disguise a note of surprise. The Bach was Mika's signature, a piece he had made uniquely his own. For this girl to attempt it in competition was daring that verged on insolence. What would the judges make of it?

She moved from the wings to the centre of the stage, and in the dazzle of the hot stage lights her hair looked as though it might catch fire. Her skin was flawlessly white, the arms laid bare by her perfectly moulded black dress. Her eyebrows, two dark slashing arcs above pale eyes, were at odds with her pale skin.

'Arresting,' murmured Eve. Watching her raise the violin, nestle the chin-rest against her neck, Eve felt a powerful, visceral response shooting straight from her groin to her nipples. As the girl cradled the violin, clasped the bow, drew it gracefully across the strings,

Eve could almost feel those same cool white hands cradling her, stroking her, gliding across her breasts, her thighs, slipping between her legs to caress the plump lips of her labia. The image was so vivid, so immediate that she could almost feel the fingers slipping inside her, burrowing deep. She shifted in her seat, conscious of the moistness burgeoning between her thighs. An electric tingle thrilled down her spine, raising the hairs on the back of her neck.

Aware that all eyes were on stage, surreptitiously Eve shifted and, spreading the full skirt of her bronze taffeta de la Renta, drew one of her legs up to her seat so that the spiky heel of her bronze sandal rested against her clitoris.

No longer moist, she was wet, rushing towards a torrent. The welcome pressure of the thin stiletto heel against her swollen inner lips was almost too much to bear. If she shifted, moved just slightly, she knew she would come in an instant.

Gritting her teeth, she looked at Sally seated next to her. She was utterly intent on the girl onstage, her breathing coming faster, cheeks flushed. Good. She felt it too. Eve leaned forward, as though to retrieve a fallen programme, and the sudden increased pressure on her clitoris sent her flying over the edge in a quick, incandescent spasm.

The technique was close to flawless, the girl's command of the strings masterful. But her choice of music was her undoing. The Sonata could no longer be played without mental comparison to Mika's passionate, almost brutal interpretation. The applause was guarded.

'Well?' whispered Eve, trembling a little as the aftershocks of her orgasm flitted through her veins.

'Oh, very well,' replied Sally. Their eyes met in perfect understanding. 'But I wonder why she chose the Bach?'

'Shall I find out? Why don't I go backstage, talk to her? She's definitely the one, Sally.'

'Well, I don't know, maybe we should both go.' Sally hesitated, awkward and uncertain. But Eve had already risen, gathered up her bag and programme.

'I think it'll be easier with just one of us. Why don't you mingle? It's intermission, maybe you could get close to the judges, pick up some gossip. I'll be fine on my own.'

Backstage, the atmosphere was stifling, sweaty with nerves and tension. Contestants were gathered together in tight knots, criticising, comparing, gossiping. Eve had no difficulty in finding Francesca Tonelli. She stood alone, fidgeting with an unlit cigarette.

'You played well,' said Eve, going up to her and extending a hand.

'Brilliantly, actually,' said the girl, ignoring Eve's outstretched hand.

So it has claws, thought Eve, amused, drawing back her hand and transforming the gesture by smoothing back her hair. 'I'm Eve Drake. From—'

'Disc-O,' finished the girl. 'Yes, I know.' Close up, Francesca Tonelli was even more striking, tall and slender with high, pointed breasts emphasised by her tight black gown. Her eyes, an indeterminate grey, were fringed with thick black lashes. Her dark, slashing eyebrows gave a faintly sulky, sultry cast to her expression. Eve was entranced. The font of the music-induced passion she'd felt scant moments ago was every bit as enticing as she'd hoped.

She let her hand rest lightly on Francesca's left arm. 'Tell me, is there some place we can talk privately? Without being overheard?' she asked, gesturing to the throngs lining the corridor.

Francesca drew back just slightly, studying the woman next to her. Everyone knew that the two top scouts from Disc-O were in the audience that night. The news had spread like wildfire. Speculation was rife, intensified by the broadcast televised earlier detailing Mika's early career and continued seclusion.

'I've finished for the evening,' Francesca replied, 'And I even managed to get a private dressing-room. They're rare as gold dust around here but I was lucky. For tonight at least.' And maybe, just maybe, about to get luckier, said a small voice inside her head. 'We could talk there, if you like.'

'That'll be fine,' replied Eve, letting her hand move from Francesca's arm up the taut valley of her spine, allowing her fingertips to enjoy the delicate moulding of each vertebra, passing them lightly across the firm blade of her shoulder until they rested on the silken flesh of her right arm.

'That is, if you don't mind if I change while we chat?' said Francesca, deliberately provocative, conscious of the woman's cool fingers resting on her arm. She sensed from the glitter in Eve's eyes that her response had been correct.

'Not at all,' said Eve, feeling the moistness between her still trembling thighs. 'Not at all.' Mutely she followed in the girl's wake as she picked her way past the dwindling groups of friends and competitors along the corridor to her dressing-room.

Once inside, Eve found herself breathing more shallowly, the skin of her cheeks and throat flushing, her engorged nipples jagging deliciously against each fibre of her dress.

'So,' said Francesca, closing the door and turning on the lights, 'What brings you to the Flesch?'

'Well, of course we're always interested in competitors at this level,' said Eve vaguely, watching her lean towards the looking-glass which covered the wall from ceiling to bench top. The glittering bulbs lining its perimeter gave a fairy-tale atmosphere to the small dressing-room. In the glass she could see Francesca's image reflected, the taut high breasts pressing against the tight black gown, while before her the cleft of her buttocks was clearly traced between the straining fabric of her dress.

At that moment Eve was gripped by the same

visceral lust she had felt when she heard Francesca play. Her labia throbbing, she felt her clitoris swelling, growing. Suddenly she wanted, needed, was wild to trace that path so clearly outlined by the dress, thrust with her tongue, with her fingers, between the rounded globes of the girl's buttocks, past the resisting sphincter, deep and deeper still into the unexplored haven of her rectum, wanted to grasp those white breasts with her hands, suck and kiss and bite the flawless skin at the nape of her neck.

Francesca stretched, slowly, luxuriously, and reaching up undid the knot of a band which had, unseen, restrained the riot of her hair. It tumbled in abandoned waves down her back, just brushing the swell of her buttocks. 'And Disc-O needs an infusion of new talent?' she asked, her tone making it more a statement than a question. 'I saw the programme on TV earlier.'

'Disc-O's position is unassailable,' said Eve briskly, professionalism ever intact, while her eyes admired the swell of Francesca's hips. 'Tell me something first. Why the Bach? You must have known what a risk it was?'

'I like taking risks,' said Francesca obliquely. 'Could you help me unzip my dress?'

Eve caught her breath, swallowed a sudden gush of saliva, and walked across to her. She could smell her sweat mingled with the faint trace of perfume. Diorissima. Brushing aside the flame coloured riot of hair tumbling down her back, with one hand she held the two sides of the dress firmly together, and with the other slowly pulled the zip the short distance to just below the base of her spine, then let the fabric fall. Eve could see Francesca's breasts reflected in the mirror, rising in firm peaks, large brown nipples puckering at the sudden rush of cool air. Francesca turned, resting her weight on the bench top, finally facing Eve.

'Thanks, Eve. That zip is in such an awkward spot.' She cupped her breasts in her hands, softly massaging the undersides of the taut mounds. 'And that damn bodice is so tight.'

'Not at all, Francesca,' Eve replied, her mind racing furiously. Was the girl just unselfconscious or deliberately provocative? Whichever it was, she decided, it didn't really matter. The half of her brain permanently devoted to business was calculating, assessing, measuring the force of this delicious creature. The other half was uncomfortably aware of her throbbing attraction.

'Please, do call me Franca.'

'Franca.' Her mouth suddenly dry, Eve could hardly tear her eyes away from the girl's body. Close as they were standing, she wanted to be closer still, close her mouth around those large, jutting nipples, suck them until they were red, until those cold grey eyes warmed . . . yes, her eyes were cold.

Drawing back just slightly, Eve smiled, mentally strapping down the desire coursing through her. Later, perhaps. 'Well, as you've no doubt guessed, we're looking for someone. Someone special.'

'Indeed,' smiled Franca. She smoothed the dress down across her waist, down her thighs until it lay pooled at her feet. Naked now but for a tiny strip of silk encasing her mound, she gave off a powerful aura of sensuality.

'Very special. Indeed, I would go so far as to say you have a great deal of unexplored potential,' Eve replied, her voice cool.

'Potential?' Her voice was even colder.

'For our new project,' interjected Eve smoothly, delighted to have unsettled her.

A knock at the door. 'Hullo? Hullo! Ms Tonelli?' It was Sally's voice, brash but somehow uncertain. 'Eve?'

How delicious, thought Eve. Was Sally jealous, perhaps? Bored? Or had she learned something?

How decidedly inconvenient, thought Franca, confident she had almost had Eve in the palm of her hand. 'Do come in,' she called, stepping away from her dress and reaching for a robe. Slowly she smoothed the short Japanese-style kimono over her hips, looking straight into Eve's eyes. 'Do come in,' she repeated.

As she opened the door, Sally was conscious of the sexual tension in the air, hot, heavy and thick.

'Do join us, darling,' said Eve. 'I think things were just getting interesting.'

'I see,' said Sally briskly, her eyes taking in the scene, the black dress pooled on the floor, the languid pose of the violinist in her scanty kimono, the hot glitter in Eve's eyes. 'Have you given Ms Tonelli any details of our project, the nature of our interest?' she probed, uncertain how to continue. If only Eve hadn't darted away before arranging a cover story.

'I was just getting to that,' replied Eve smoothly. 'But why don't you take over?'

Clever Eve. Straightening her shoulders, Sally walked into the room and, uninvited, sat down on one of the two spindly chairs. Crossing her legs, she gave Eve a swift, probing glance before focusing her attention on Franca. 'Let me get straight to the point. We are looking for—'

'The next virtuoso?' interjected Franca.

Sally cut her eyes at Eve. 'I thought you said—'

'Well, it's obvious, isn't it?' asked Franca. 'Why else would the two top scouts from Disc-O be at the Flesch? Disc-O's been getting a lot of publicity recently . . . not all of it good. You need a new sensation. Like me.' Too bold, she wondered, nerves quivering.

'There's more to it than that,' said Sally slowly. 'A lot more. We are looking for a talent . . . a talent with the potential to capture the same electric, passionate frenzy that Mika brought to the world of classical music. And we are hoping that he will be willing to take this talent . . . shape it, form it.'

'He?' asked Franca, voice trembling slightly.

'Mika,' replied Sally, nodding.

'For that,' said Franca levelly, 'I would do anything. Anything.'

'How delightful,' cooed Eve. 'I thought you might.'

'The circumstances, however,' said Sally, looking daggers at Eve, 'are complicated. Technical mastery apart, the person we select has to have a magnetism, a charisma, a frankly sensual allure. That is, I think, more than anything, what Max Schiller is looking to introduce to Mika.'

'So,' said Franca consideringly, 'let me get this straight. To study with Mika, an opportunity any violinist would kill for, I would have to convince Schiller that I have the . . . sex appeal? Sensual capacity? To interpret the classics . . . or to warrant the introduction?'

'Darling,' said Eve silkily, 'you're going much too fast. We are, after all, compiling a short list. No, first of all, you'll have to convince us.'

'Max is leaving for Geneva tomorrow,' interrupted Sally briskly. 'I think you should come by, meet him, talk to him about the project. Our own recommendations will be made at a later stage. After due consideration.'

'So this is your first choice?' asked Max the next morning, studying the glossy publicity photos.

'She's the first candidate we've short-listed,' corrected Sally. 'Both Eve and I are convinced that more detailed research is needed,' she continued, a bit less confidently. Eve had been so persuasive . . .

'Tell me about her,' said Max, perching on the edge of her desk.

'Her name is Francesca Tonelli. Prefers to be called Franca,' began Sally. 'Began studying at the age of five. First won some acclaim at the Lucerne International Music Festival last year, without the aid of a teacher.'

'Unusual,' commented Max. 'Why don't I remember her?'

'Well, last year, what with Mika's accident—'

'Yes, yes, of course. It was a bad time.'

'And she hasn't done much since. A recording for Deutsche Grammophon, which I've got set up in your office. She's moved from one teacher to another. Has a

43

reputation for being difficult. Eve has compiled a profile for you,' she said gesturing to a sheaf of papers.

'She's certainly stunning,' said Max, intent on the photograph, admiring the curve of her throat, the high, pointed breasts. 'But does she have "it"?' he asked. 'The allure, the presence, the magnetism?'

'Oh, she's got all that,' replied Sally, thinking back to the scene she had interrupted the night before in Franca's dressing-room. 'All that and more. But she won't be easy to handle.'

'Better that way, perhaps. A challenge. A challenge for Mika. If I can convince him to go along with this,' said Max, his eyes intent on the photograph. 'What about the others?'

'It's not Mika you'll have to convince,' said Sally, bitchy for once. 'Anyway, why don't you read through this stuff and listen to the CD? She'll be coming by in an hour or so. As for the others, there are no others. At the moment. Eve and I will continue working on it while you're away in Geneva.' Eve had been so insistent, so determined . . .

An hour later Francesca arrived, swirling into the head office like a torch, her flaming hair in striking contrast to the black cape that swathed her from ankle to neck.

'Sally. Eve. How delightful to see you after last night. And the big boss?'

'In there,' said Sally, gesturing to the door behind her. 'But I think—'

'Ah. Ms Tonelli, I presume?' asked Max, striding through the door.

'Mr Schiller,' she replied, ignoring his outstretched hand.

'Ah. Yes. Well. Won't you step into my office?'

'Thank you,' she said, her voice throaty, as she brushed past him through the doorway.

Without waiting to be invited, she seated herself on the black leather couch and slowly removed her cape. Underneath she was dressed in black, skin-tight trousers and a thin sweater that moulded itself to the curves of her body. She stretched out her legs, crossing them at the ankle. So, Max Schiller, she thought, you're my first hurdle. You want magnetism, charisma, sex appeal? That's right, feast your eyes on me. I have it. Everything you want. Pleased, she watched his eyes drift over her body, pause at her breasts, flick to the juncture of her thighs, linger on the length of her legs.

'So, I understand you're acquainted with the major outlines of what we're putting together here?' asked Max. Her photographs didn't do her justice, he thought. Her eyes, her breasts, high and pointed, the riot of flaming hair. But there was more. She exuded some potent appeal, some blatant female animal quality, as though she were thinking sex, breathing sex, wanting sex.

Yes, that's right, she thought. Look into my eyes, read my thoughts. The ones I want you to read. 'Yes,' she replied softly. Imagine me naked, around you, under you, over you, sucking you, screwing you, driving you to the very edge and beyond.

'And I take it you're interested? If things work out?' he prompted, deliberately vague. She had a remarkably unsettling effect on him. Her eyes were cool, but her body looked hot, and her fingers, long and slim, just brushing away a stray tendril of hair . . . Serena. She reminded him of Serena.

Impulsively, he pressed his intercom. 'Sally? Make that two tickets to Geneva this afternoon.'

Chapter Three

First Intermission

GENEVA

*S*erena looked at her watch again, poured herself a glass of wine, and studied herself in the mirror. She'd spent a long time getting ready, taking a long bath in hot, perfumed water, rubbed oils and creams all over her body, wondering if she was anticipating his hands. Max's plane would have arrived by now. She'd sent Sergei to meet him with the Rolls. She smiled a little, imagining the two men meeting. Sergei, blond, Nordic, bullish; Max, dark, swarthy, muscular – the chauffeur and the tycoon. And the only thing they had in common was her. Or rather, she'd had them.

Walking naked to the wardrobe, she admired herself in the mirror. Her breasts were high and firm, her belly gently curved. Thoughtfully she ran her palms over her breasts, feeling her nipples, instantly rousable, firm to the touch.

The black dress she selected was deliberately provocative, plunging deep at the back and front, barely covering her breasts, barely concealing the swell of her buttocks. She wore no underwear, relishing the silky feel of the fabric against her belly and thighs.

'Fresh blood,' she said aloud to her reflection,

remembering Maddie's phrase. And thought of that long ago night in Paris. Max had been so gentle at first, treating her like some fragile, breakable thing of glass. And how exciting it had been to show him the maenad, the wild, lusty, ferocious creature that lived under the skin, that craved the blood-lust and frenzy.

How exciting to drag him with her into the dark places where the air was hot and stifling, riding and rousing him again and again, driving him to the edges of white fury, utter madness. She had, as always, remained in supreme control, choosing at the last moment to let him come alone, reserving her pleasure for herself. He didn't know, couldn't have known.

But she remembered with faint disquiet the way he'd wrapped his arms around her, soothed and caressed her, gentling her down from the throes of the heights he'd assumed they had reached together. She had felt somehow vulnerable then, as though his tenderness was a cleverly concealed weapon she hadn't noticed. And then he had said those three words that had driven her from him . . . until now.

'Enough,' she said, and heard the muted growl of the Rolls at the door. Inspecting herself one last time in the mirror she found herself beautiful, knew she was irresistible. Still, she reminded herself, better to be careful. Max was a businessman. Keep him off guard, distract him a little, and she'd be able to delicately prise all the details from him, discover whatever hidden agenda he was concealing, without him even knowing. That there was some hidden agenda she had no doubt.

Impulsively she crossed to her dressing-table, felt among the jars and vials and finally selected a sachet of powder in rice paper. A powerful aphrodisiac from a Chinese herbalist, so powerful that it inflamed the senses a thousandfold. Extra protection, she thought.

Hastily she ran down the stairs to meet him, throwing open the wide double doors and opening her arms in a generous embrace.

'Max, darling, I'm so glad you're here at last,' she

said, her voice somewhere between a purr and a growl, and kissed him gently on the lips. He felt the touch of her mouth, soft and inviting, like an electric jolt down his spine.

Imperiously she waved Sergei away with the bags. Her attention fully concentrated on Max, she failed to notice the murderous glare in Sergei's eyes as he left with the luggage. Serena led Max into the spacious lounge, asking about the flight, commenting on the weather. He followed numbly, dazed by the sight of her, the musky smell of her perfume, the whiteness of her skin.

'Yes, I'd love a drink,' he heard himself say, feasting his eyes on her, imagining her naked, pinned beneath him, helpless in passion as he thrust into her again and again. Remembering Paris, he reversed their positions, seeing her loom above him, impaling herself on his shaft, riding and rocking in a furious, driven frenzy. He felt the want curl in his groin, send the blood rushing to his ears.

'Scotch?' she smiled. She could sense his desire across the room, washing towards her in waves and was pleased by it. It made him just that little bit vulnerable, easier to handle, more susceptible to the powder. Still, she was faintly surprised to find herself responding to his presence, feeling that tingle of sensual awareness susurrating over her skin.

With an effort he roused himself, pushed away the tantalising images of Serena nude, open to him, under him, around him. What was it about her that exerted this incredible, erotic pull? She could make even the simple act of pouring a drink unbearably sexy. Watching her lift the bottle, pour out the Scotch, select a few ice-cubes with a silver tong, he was struck by the sinuous grace of her every movement.

'Where's Mika?' he asked, with a slight cough, crossing his legs to hide the bulge of his erection. 'I've been looking forward to seeing him.'

'Mika won't be joining us for dinner. He asked me to

make his apologies,' she lied. What he'd actually said, when she'd broached the subject again, had verged on the unprintable. It had only confirmed her deepening suspicions that Mika was becoming too reclusive, too wrapped up in himself. Perhaps Max's 'novel proposition' would pique his interest.

'How are his hands, Serena? Will he—' he stopped abruptly, shocked by the naked anger in her eyes. Quickly, she lowered her lashes, concealing her expression.

'I've been so looking forward to seeing you,' she said, ignoring his question. She handed him his drink, gently brushing against his arm, before seating herself next to him. 'It's been so lonely here at times. I'm delighted you decided to come.'

He felt the extra husky emphasis on the last word. A small insistent voice in the back of his head repeated . . . Come . . . come in you . . . come. 'I would have come whenever you wanted me, Serena, you know that,' he replied softly.

'Whenever I wanted you, Max?' she mocked gently, seeing the lust in his eyes. There was something else there, something indefinable, something she couldn't quite recognise.

'Whenever,' he nodded, bringing her hand to his lips. He turned it gently, kissed the inside of her wrist, just where the pulse fluttered.

'Finish your drink, Max, and we'll have dinner. Maddie will be furious if it's spoiled,' she said, gracefully withdrawing her hand, rising from the couch and leading him to the dining-room.

'Make yourself comfortable. I'll just fetch the wine. It's a very special vintage,' she promised. Feeling his eyes on her, she glided out of the room and made her way to the kitchen. The wine had already been decanted, as she'd ordered, and two crystal goblets were placed beside it. She felt for the sachet of powder concealed in the folds of her dress and carefully shook

49

the contents into the bottle, then returned to the dining-room.

'Here, Max,' she said, offering him a glass. 'It's quite special. I hope you'll like it.'

Seated across from her at the huge refectory table, the candlelight flickering shadows across the room, he was barely able to keep his eyes off her. The soft light of the candles warmed her pale skin to gold, caught the highlights of her ebony hair. He gulped the wine, hoping to steady his nerves, then caught himself.

'Sorry, Serena,' he said, raising his glass in a toast. 'To us. To Mika. To better times ahead.' God, it was terrible stuff, he thought, barely repressing a shudder. How could such a sophisticated woman have such awful taste in wine? And she'd brought it out especially for him. He'd have to drink it, show his appreciation.

'Better times,' she echoed, pretending to sip from her glass. 'So, Max, why have you come to Geneva?' she asked, spearing an oyster.

'I wanted you, I mean, to see you,' he replied, stumbling a little over the words. He wanted her now, wet and open and aching. The sheer impact of her physical presence was a blow. He could feel the lust snaking through his veins, centring in his groin.

'And how are things at Disc-O?' she asked casually, refilling his glass again. His eyes, she noticed, were fixed on her breasts, as though he were devouring them through the fabric of her dress.

'Disc-O? All right for this year, I think,' he said, meeting her eyes. It was becoming increasingly difficult to concentrate on the conversation, when all he wanted was to touch her, feel her skin, thrust into her again and again. 'Serena, you have the most beautiful breasts, the most beautiful skin. So white, it begs to be bruised.' Had he said the words aloud? He couldn't be sure.

'Disc-O?' she prompted, smiling a little.

'Disc-O. Yes. Well, of course, we can't afford Mika's contract indefinitely without additional revenue. We need a new sensation to replace him,' he said absent-mindedly. 'A new sensation,' he repeated, feeling himself grow harder and harder. 'The sensations I want to—'

'Why are you here then, Max, if you're looking for someone else?' she asked softly.

'Actually, I've already found someone. She flew over with me today. She looks a little like you, Serena. Slender, beautiful hands. Legs that seem to go on for ever. You only have to look at them to imagine them curled around your waist, tightening and shivering—'

'And you brought her here, Max? Why?' she choked, feeling her throat lock on the oyster she'd just swallowed. She sputtered, coughed, and felt him behind her, lightly patting her back, pressing her wineglass to her lips. Involuntarily she gulped. Felt the oyster dislodge. Felt the heat spread through her veins like wildfire.

'Max,' she said clearly, her mind working furiously. 'Max, I . . .'

His senses inflamed by her closeness, he barely heard her. His hand, lightly patting between her naked shoulder blades, stilled. Her skin was smooth as silk, white as snow, an invitation to sex. Leaning forward, he placed her wineglass on the table, put his hands on her shoulders. Gently he touched his mouth to the nape of her neck, his lips hard and hot.

'Serena, I need you now. And I won't let you run away, like you did in Paris.'

His breath was warm on her skin. She could feel the hard column of his body behind the chair, feel her senses stirring.

'Max,' she said, shifting in her chair to face him. 'Why did you bring the girl here?'

But he was beyond listening, beyond caring. Swiftly he caught her by the shoulders, raised her from the chair and pressed her against the length of his body. His hands were restless, impatient, roaming across her throat, her arms, her breasts, dipping between her thighs.

She felt her skin warming to his touch, felt herself becoming loose and pliant. His hands were creating a shivering, tingling sensation on her skin and there was a warm, diffuse glow spreading through her body. Her breasts felt fuller somehow, the nipples more sensitive. The effects of the aphrodisiac, she thought, feeling lightheaded.

His hands were tracing an intricate pattern through the silk of her dress, defining her breasts, just glancing off the nipples, moving slowly down to her belly, her thighs, her crotch, then back again, rousing the blood to the surface. She felt herself swelling, engorging. She could, she realised dimly, be on the verge of losing control. His mouth was warm and moist, tracing the outline of her ear gently with his tongue, then thrusting hard and pointed into her ear in a deliberate parody, mimicking penetration, achieving the first entry to her body.

His hips were thrusting too, hard against the curve of her belly, and she could feel the massive bulk of his erection. Summoning the last vestiges of her self-control, she leaned away, looked directly in his eyes.

Suddenly, forcefully, his mouth was against hers, plundering the soft wet caverns of her mouth with his tongue, bruising her lips with his teeth. Savage now, lips hard, he kissed her again and again, forcing his tongue between her teeth as if he would draw the breath from her body. She felt her blood heating, felt her mouth grow swollen under the pressure of his. Beneath the silk of her dress her breasts were swelling, nipples hardening, aching for the touch of his mouth, his teeth, his hands. She felt the hot liquid ache igniting between her thighs.

She drew away just slightly, gasping for breath. 'Max, I—' she began, but he interrupted her at once.

'Upstairs, Serena,' he said, and cut off her words with his mouth. Deftly he picked her up, cradling her against his body without once removing the pressure of his mouth. Half running, half stumbling, he crossed the hall in an instant, made his way up the staircase, found her rooms with unerring instinct. As he let her fall to the bed, he took in the decor with one swift glance. The pillows, the vases, the flowers . . . the incongruous, faintly menacing collection of erotica displayed on the dressing-table. His eyes lit on the manacles carelessly dangling from the corner of the black lacquered surface.

'Not Paris again, Serena. Not now,' he said roughly, and capturing one slim wrist he chained her to the bedpost.

Hazy, drugged by his kisses, drugged by the aphrodisiac effects of the wine she'd swallowed, she'd hardly been aware of their frenzied passage to her rooms, lost in the hard heat of his body. But the feel of the cool metal imprisoning her wrist jolted her awake. She'd used them countless times, on Sergei, on others, had never felt them herself. It was she who wielded the whip, she who chained the naked flesh to the bedposts, making it passive, helpless.

'No, Max, you don't understand, I never. . .'

'Never?' he asked, his voice almost taunting. 'Then it's another lesson to be learned, Serena.' With her free hand she lashed out at him, but he caught her wrist easily, slipped the heavy steel bracelet around it and fastened it to the bedpost. With a groan of satisfaction, he settled himself next to her.

'Not Paris,' he muttered. His eyes were glittering, unfocused, almost as though he was looking through her, past her. She felt the warmth of her arousal chill a little at the look in his eyes. This wasn't the Max she knew. It was as if some dark stranger, devilish and dangerous, had temporarily taken over. It must be the drug. She'd tasted only a little, while he'd drunk several glasses . . . His hands were rough, impatiently stripping the dress from her body, tugging it aside to free her breasts, and his mouth was hot and hungry.

53

He sucked at her nipples with a terrible ferocity, as if he would draw blood, moving from one to the other with a pressure close to pain.

With her wrists chained she was powerless to slow him, soften the suction. His rhythm was hard, relentless, endless and despite herself she found she was succumbing to his intensity, the pressure of his mouth, the threat of his teeth. Her breasts were swelling, engorging, sucked and pulled into twin globes of pure sensation. She felt the warmth, the tingling awareness flowing through her veins, arcing from her nipples to her fingertips. She arched her back, nudged his hip with her thigh, wordlessly inviting him to explore her further, suck and pull at the core of her, but he ignored her, his attention fiercely concentrated on her breasts.

It seemed as though he would go on forever, leave the rest of her body aching, unfulfilled, when he suddenly rose from the bed and stripped off his clothes. The heat of his skin, the silky pelt of dark hair covering his chest were deliciously exciting, wonderfully welcome after the cool friction of linen and denim. She moved to reach for him, found her wrists chained, found her anticipation mixed with anger.

He found her wet and ready, drove into her at once. His entry was like a blow, filling, numbing her. He was hard and massive, almost too big. It was almost as though he had pierced through the walls of her womb, shot up through her belly, filling her lungs, her throat.

Harder and harder, deeper and deeper he thrust, revelling in her lushness, her tightness, the softness of her breasts crushed beneath his chest. The hard length of him filling her, stretching her and stroking her in long hard thrusts somehow intensified both her anger and her lust. Wildly, convulsively she thrust her hips against his, felt him grinding against the crest of her pubis, teasing the taut bud of her clitoris. It was in anger that she had thrust against him, furiously meeting his deepening strokes, but the delicious friction of his skin against hers, the silky sac of his balls caressing

the taut skin between her vagina and her anus transmuted her fury into simple lust. Her senses heightened
and heightening from the aphrodisiac, excited into a
new awareness, she suddenly lost any desire to be
dominant, for control. Closing her eyes, she willed
herself to be only a physical thing, this wild red pulsing
thing that lay passive beneath him.

It was, after all, only the drug, she reasoned, and
uncharacteristically decided to lose herself in the
vortex. She turned her face away from his, burrowing
into the crisp linen of the pillow, relishing its coolness
against her heated skin.

He stopped then, buried deep inside her. Raising
himself on his elbows, arms shaking with the effort to
remain still, he said roughly, 'Look at me, Serena.'

She rocked her hips against him, willing him to
continue. Knowing that in a moment he would explode
inside her or go mad, he withdrew completely. Hot
and heavy he poised himself just at the entrance to her
body, feeling the slick folds of her curl around him.

'Look at me, Serena,' he said again and slapped her
lightly across the cheek. Startled, her head snapped
back on the pillow and she gazed straight into his eyes.
'It's not Paris, Serena. I'm in control. I want you to
look at me, see me, know that I'm going to drive you
over the edge. No one else.'

'No one else,' she repeated mindlessly, desperate to
feel him back inside her, stroking the fleshy walls of
her womb with his massive rod. She closed her eyes,
pushed against him. Feeling that other mouth search
for him, wet and warm, he drew back and cupped her
mound with his hand.

'Not yet, Serena. Not for a long time. Now say my
name.' With his fingers, he gently plucked at her
swollen lips. Her womb was empty, aching to be filled,
but with the touch of his fingers she felt a new ache, a
moist burning that threatened to engulf her. He found
her core, its budding centre stiff and erect, and
scratched at it lightly with the tip of one finger. Feeling

her gasp as the jolt ran through her, he moved his finger up to the very hood of her clitoris, circled the warm red folds of her labia, careful to avoid the centre of her pleasure. Plucking and teasing, he rolled her sex-lips between his fingers, feeling her grow slicker and softer.

'Max,' she breathed.

'Yes, it's Max,' he growled, his breathing ragged.

'Max,' she repeated, opening her eyes.

He felt her arch, begin to quiver with the first tremors of her orgasm seizing her. Quickly he drew his hand away, lightly stroking the soft flesh of her mound, plucking at it as he had plucked at her nether lips. Furiously she bucked at him, impatient to recapture the rhythm that would send the climax rippling through her, but he drew himself up, straddled her hips and lowered his mouth to her breast. He plucked at the nipple with his tongue and his teeth, using the same rolling rhythm he'd used between her thighs. She felt the liquid ache between her thighs intensify, felt the pressure of a million flickering pin points of light gathering under her skin.

'Max, I want—'

'I know. I know what you want.'

She felt his mouth move down her belly, pause at her navel. He drove his tongue deep into that tiny dimple, jabbing again and again, then moved down to her sex. Grasping her firmly by the hips he raised her to his mouth, lapping and bathing her in firm, sure strokes. His breath was warm and moist, his tongue hard as he sought out the nub of her clitoris. She felt the pulse between her legs like a second heartbeat as he nipped at her gently with his teeth, felt the muscles of her thighs twitching involuntarily, felt herself growing even slicker and hotter. Her body electric, she wanted to clutch his shoulders, drive his mouth even harder against her, but she was restrained by the steel links chaining her to the bedpost.

Intent on pleasing her, tormenting her, mastering

her, he was oblivious to her groans, oblivious to everything except the juicy red folds trembling beneath his tongue and teeth.

She felt herself start to convulse, heard a hoarse cry, not recognising her own voice. Swiftly he was there, poised at the entrance to her body, too big now, too full to slide in easily. Careless of pain, immersed in want, she arched up to him, easing the passage of his member, and with that hot thick length pounding into her she came in a flood, spasming and shaking.

He felt her tight around him, throbbing, her womb shocked again by his hardness. The feel of her tight, wet walls pulsing against him sent him spiralling over the edge in a dark frenzy. Fast and furious he shot into her, spurting out in great jets, before finally collapsing on her body.

'Max? Max, my wrists,' she breathed into his ear. Utterly spent, he used the last of his energy to reach up and unfasten the manacles before falling asleep.

Rubbing her wrists, Selena sighed contentedly. The aftershocks of her orgasm were still rippling through her, gradually decreasing in intensity and she could still feel the hard imprint of him inside her. Even in sleep Max was insatiable, she thought with a smile, as she felt his hands reaching for her. She slipped silently from the bed, wrapping a white silk dressing-gown around her, and bent down to retrieve the garments he'd tossed to the floor in his haste.

As she picked up his jacket, shaking it gently to remove the tell-tale creases, a slender folder dropped to the floor. She leafed through it quickly. Airline tickets, passport, traveller's cheques . . . and several densely typed pages clipped to a glossy photograph of a girl with red hair and dark eyebrows.

Crossing to one of the plump armchairs scattered at cosy intervals throughout the huge room, she settled down to read. A profile of the career of a young female violinist, Francesca Tonelli, prepared by someone with the initials E.D. Typical enough in its way, she realised, skimming through the report '. . . the Lucerne International Music Festival . . . recordings for Deutsche Grammophon . . .' Had she heard them? She couldn't be sure. '. . . Erratic relationships with all her teachers . . .' Again, typical enough. And as she read, fragments of her earlier, disjointed conversation with Max kept running through her mind. Satisfied, she closed the folder, then noticed a slip of paper that had fallen to the floor.

PERSONAL AND CONFIDENTIAL:
SUMMARY BY EVE DRAKE
The personal and professional profile of the subject, F. Tonelli, appears to meet the established criteria, namely, exceptionally talented musically with an underlying sensuous appeal. The main objective, to discover a female artist capable of rousing in a male audience the same emotional response that Mika exerted on female listeners (see Marketing Summary 10/9/91 FFH) depends on exploiting the unknown variable of Mika's method/technique. The secret of his success, his ability to literally 'turn on' the listener, has defied careful analysis. It is quite possible that under Mika's tutelage, Tonelli might learn how to elicit this response. While a difficult personality, she has been heavily influenced by Mika's style and regards him as something of an idol. She is currently under the impression that Mika is considering coming out of retirement to teach a few selected pupils, which accounts for her willingness to enter into negotiations with Disc-O. E.D.

Engrossed in her reading, she didn't hear him stirring, wakening, and was startled to feel his hands, cool and heavy, settle on her shoulders.

'Oh, Max, I thought you were asleep,' she said, hastily twisting to face him. 'I was just picking up the

clothes when these papers slipped out of your jacket.'
It sounded lame, even to her ears.

'What do you think, then?' he asked. 'I meant to tell
you over dinner but—' he stopped and shook his head,
as though trying to clear it. 'Sorry, Serena, it's all a bit
vague, must be the jet lag. I feel a bit – is there any
water?'

'Of course Max, I'll get you some, just a moment.' In
the *en suite* bathroom, letting the taps run until the
water was icy cold, Serena looked at herself in the
mirror. Her face was flushed and her eyes looked a
little furtive. A creature of appetites, not given to
introspection, uncharacteristically she wondered why
she felt . . . guilty? Damn Max! She'd forgotten what
an unsettling effect he'd always had on her. Returning
to the bedroom, she found him sprawled on the bed,
leafing through the papers.

'Here you are, Max,' she said, offering him the glass.

'Thanks, See, my throat's terribly dry for some
reason,' he replied, draining the glass in a gulp. 'It's a
simple enough proposition. The girl really is very
talented and if we can persuade Mika to take her under
his wing for a few weeks, give her a few lessons, it
could be the solution we've been looking for.' His eyes
were clear and limpid as glass. 'Come back to bed,
anyway, while we talk. You're too far away. And
wearing too many clothes.'

Discarding her robe, she slipped between the sheets
next to him and picked up the photograph. The face
seemed somehow familiar, although she was sure
she'd never seen her before.

'And you brought her with you to Geneva?' she
asked, stalling for time.

'Yes, I put her in a *pension* in the village,' Max replied,
taking the photograph from her. He shuffled the
papers into some semblance of order and laid them on
the table beside the bed. 'So what do you think?' he
asked again, drawing her into his arms.

Leaning back against the hard warmth of his chest,

she tried to frame a reply. Her first impulse had been to tell him that it was ludicrous, utterly inconceivable, far-fetched and ridiculous. Mika, of course, could never, would never reveal the secret of his success, why he was able to 'turn-on' his audience . . . What a vulgar phrase! But perhaps there was something in this scheme after all. Perhaps this girl could rouse him from his cold remoteness, rekindle his love of music. Certainly, if Mika were willing, he could teach her a few technical tricks without initiating her into the intricate scenarios they used to construct. Could Max be trusted?

'I'm sleepy,' she murmured, avoiding his question. Turning away from him, she lay on her side, drew the covers up to her chin. Turning off the light, he settled himself close to her, his chest pressed against her back, his groin to her buttocks, his legs tangling with hers. With one arm he reached across, cradling her breasts.

Momentarily she was surprised to feel the warmth and weight of his body next to hers, expecting him to return to his room. Invariably she slept alone, never allowing a man to share her bed for more than a few hours. But tonight it was somehow curiously comforting to hear his steady, regular breathing, feel the heat of his skin next to hers. Cosy and slumbrous now, she felt his erection rising, nudging against her buttocks, slipping between her cheeks. She parted her legs just slightly, just enough to allow him to slide between her thighs, settle between the silky folds of her nether lips. He was big, so big that even from behind, the head of his cock was kissing her clitoris. Curiously he made no move to enter her, but lay still, the hard, hot length of him encased between her thighs. With his arm cradling her breasts, his breath warm on the back of her neck, she drifted off to sleep.

She woke the next morning at dawn, refreshed and with an unfamiliar sense of purpose. Max was huddled beneath the covers, only the tip of his nose visible. Quickly she reviewed the events of the previous night, lingering with some astonishment on the powerful, abandoned performance Max had treated her to under the influence of the aphrodisiac. Her breasts still felt heavy and a little swollen, and there was an unaccustomed ache between her thighs. She slipped from the bed, careful not to wake him, and pulled on her silk dressing-gown. As she padded down the stairs, in search of coffee and Mika, she was surprised to hear herself humming.

She found him on the terrace, already at breakfast.

'You're up early, Serena,' he said, observing her with some misgiving. She looked sleek and satisfied, her eyes and skin glowing with that well-screwed look he hadn't seen in ages. She also looked uncharacteristically determined, he thought, hoping he was mistaken. Once Serena truly set her mind on something, it was almost impossible to resist her.

'I had an early night,' she smiled, pouring coffee for herself and selecting a pastry. 'With Max.'

'Ah, yes. Max. I hope you found out what he wants so we can get rid of him.'

'Well, I found out why he's here, darling. And I think it sounds quite interesting. In fact his scheme has distinct . . . well, possibilities, shall we say?' she said, biting into her pastry with perfectly white, pointed little teeth.

'I told you, Serena, I'm not interested in Max or his schemes,' he replied coldly.

'Read this,' she replied, ignoring the tone of his voice and handing him the folder she'd retrieved from Max's jacket before leaving her suite. 'You'll find it interesting.'

Grudgingly he took the folder and turned the pages slowly, yawning to emphasise his disinterest. But despite himself, his attention was caught by the glossy photograph of Franca Tonelli. With that flaming hair and those dark, slashing brows she was certainly striking. She seemed somehow familiar, though he was sure he had never seen her before. He sifted through his memory for a musical image . . . Vivaldi's *Autumn*

61

of course. All the warmth of summer in her hair, but the chill of winter in her eyes. In the old days he could have used her as Autumn, feasted on her body like a harvest. He could sense just from the photograph that she would be crisp and yielding, ripe and pungent. Firelight for her hair, masses of spicy autumn flowers. Carnations and chrysanthemums in yellow and gold. And she would be the feast, breasts as firm as apples that he'd make red with wanting, use his teeth, his hands, his fingers. Drive into her in long, deep furrows, plough her into the flowers, take her in long, deep ruts.

Watching him intently from across the table, Serena saw that his eyes were slightly unfocused. He had that rapt, absorbed expression she recognised from the old days. 'She's striking, isn't she?' she asked at last. 'And apparently talented as well.'

Or perhaps, he thought, not hearing her voice, with those sulky eyebrows, Ravel would be better. Candlelight. Thick white tapers in heavy silver holders. She'd be wearing silk. The first time he'd take her roughly from behind, no preliminaries, hauling the dress up to her waist. Already he could feel it, pooled at the base of his belly, smooth and cool, contrasting with the heated silk of her buttocks. Holding her by the waist he'd drive in quickly, fill her completely, hurting her perhaps just a little with the force of his entry. Then wait. Let her swell around him like music, soften and stretch, accept and embrace his hard, unyielding bulk. When he had to move, when he could bear it no longer, it would be slowly. To the slow, dark rhythms of Ravel.

'You don't have to commit yourself to anything, darling. Max has her staying in a *pension* in the village. I'll send Sergei down to fetch her. You can meet her, talk to her, test her out. If you felt like it, you might even give her a few lessons, breathing, posture, whatever. You needn't go any further. Unless, of course,' she added, still carefully watching his expression, 'you wanted to.'

'It's impossible, Serena,' he said flatly, finally responding. But his eyes were still fixed on the photograph.

She could feel him weakening. 'Not at all,' she replied firmly. 'Not at all. Besides, we've got nothing to lose. Why not take a chance?'

A chance. It had all begun by chance, by accident really, years ago when he was struggling to be accepted into the first rank. An older woman from the orchestra. Too much vodka after their last rehearsal before the recital. A dark room, heavy with velvet curtains. An array of strange-looking instruments in steel and leather in careful rows. She'd put on a recording of the piece they had rehearsed, poured more vodka, thick and chill, into cut-glass tumblers. Had slipped out of her dress and into the heavy manacles in one sinuous, fluid movement. At her gesture he'd taken the long, leather whip in his hand, feeling foolish, ill at ease. Then, swaying a little from the vodka, he'd felt the music rising in his blood, coursing through his veins, felt his erection swell and grow with the deep throb of the drums.

He'd floated the whip across her belly, her thighs, felt it hiss against her skin like his bow across the strings. Saw her skin redden and warm to its touch. At the final, shattering crescendo he'd come in a blinding rush, furiously spewing himself over her naked breasts. When the final strains had died away, he'd roused himself, seen with horror the welted skin he'd raised with the whip. Falling to his knees, he'd lifted her face to his. And was astounded at the pale, transported ecstasy of her expression.

The night of the concert, as they'd moved slowly through the prelude, he'd felt both strangely disassociated and utterly focused, split between the velvet darkness and the hot, harsh stage lights, felt simultaneously the polished wood of the violin and the soft, naked flesh of the woman. He'd wielded his bow like the whip, scoring her flesh and the notes in an indistinguishable frenzy. When the music ended, he almost expected to see the strings transformed into bruised flesh. The reviews were dazzling. It had been the performance of his life, catapulting him to the forefront of the classical music world.

He'd thought then that he had discovered the secret, how to unlock the passion from the strings, create that soaring, searing, orgasmic frenzy. But of course, he hadn't. It had been Serena who, after his next near disastrous appearance, had . . .

'Mika?'

He looked, found her gazing at him intently, but with the beginning of a smile on her lips.

'You agree? She can stay here for a few days while you make up your mind. No pressure, darling.'

But there was. He could feel the dark insistence in her washing over him. 'Serena, tell me. Why is this important to you?'

'Because . . . because I'm bored. Because you're bored.' She shrugged her shoulders. 'We might be in severe danger of becoming boring.'

He laughed shortly. 'You, Serena? Never.' But he knew her well enough to feel the ring of truth in what she said. It wasn't the whole truth by any means, but then Serena had always had a hit and miss relationship with that quality.

'Well, let's just say it might be fun. We can make up the rules as we go along. Mika?' Idly she fingered the heavy gold chain around her neck.

He remembered the night he had given it to her, the night he had taken Vivaldi's *Four Seasons* to unparalleled heights, found the burgeoning, animal warmth of spring, the heady, hazy heat of summer. And it had been because of her.

'Very well, Serena. She can come to the villa,' said Mika softly.

Another woman might have laughed in triumph,

thrown her arms around him in exuberant delight for having achieved her ends so easily.

'That's fine,' she said just as softly, 'I'll send Sergei now then, and get Maddie to make up a room for her. Max will be pleased. You will see him, won't you?'

'Not yet,' he said abruptly. 'I'm not ready to see him yet. Keep Max amused, keep him out of my way. I'm sure you won't find it difficult.'

'Not at all, my dear,' she smiled. She rose then, and touched him gently on the shoulder before moving away.

Chapter Four

Water Music

'You should pleased, Max, it's what you really wanted, isn't it?' Seated at her dressing-table, idly brushing her hair, Serena looked at him reflected in the mirror before her. 'I must admit I'm rather surprised . . . but very pleased. We may have a . . . coinciding interest in this project. Your "novel proposition".'

'Mmm. Yes. Yes, of course,' he replied distractedly, eyes fixed on her, admiring the curve of her arm as she swept it back and forth. Someone should sculpt her, he thought, freeze the achingly beautiful curve of her elbow, capture it in marble.

'Mika wants to meet her alone. I think strangers are easier for him now, I'm sure you'll understand. We can dine here, in my rooms, or there are a few amusing places not too far away. Sergei will bring her here later this afternoon. So tell me about her.'

Max was looking at Serena with a rapt, absorbed intensity, his eyes moving wonderingly over her body.

'Serena, last night . . . I didn't hurt you, did I?'

She could almost have smiled at the words, but his voice was low, concerned, almost loving. Her mind shied at the word as she saw the direction of his eyes, the pale bruise at the base of her throat just emerging, a relic of Sergei's feeble bid for dominance.

She looked at Max's reflection in the mirror. For some strange reason, she hadn't woken him this morning, hadn't gracefully guided him back to the suite prepared for him. Instead, inexplicably, after talking with Mika on the terrace, she'd gone to the kitchen, asked for a tray and brought it up to her rooms, even pausing to pluck a rose from one of the ornate arrangements in the hall and placed it on his plate.

Suddenly she bitterly regretted the gesture. 'No. No, Max, you didn't hurt me,' she replied, almost shortly. 'Now, tell me about Francesca. What is she really like? Is she—'

'I'm glad.' There was a world of relief in his voice. 'I was afraid, because, I think . . . I think I went a little crazy last night.'

It should have been funny, hysterically funny even, the words he used, the concern in his eyes, his voice. The breakfast tray forgotten on his knees, he was looking at her with intimate eyes, searchingly, enfolding her.

He couldn't be that naïve. She smiled at the mirror, masking her unease. 'Divinely, wonderfully, madly crazy, Max. Now, tell me more about Francesca. Isn't this exciting? And what a coup for you if—'

'Serena. I want to talk about you, about us.'

If the blood froze in her veins, she gave no outward sign of it. With the fluid grace that characterised her every movement, she crossed over to him, deftly removed the tray from his kness, drew the sheet down to his thighs and draped herself over him.

She could feel him swelling beneath her, stiffening under the velvet caress of her lower lips. With one lyrical, lascivious movement she drew him into her, knowing that he was powerless to resist the heated embrace of her inner walls. Half-closing her eyes, she concentrated on the hard length still growing inside her. Deliberately she tightened her inner muscles, clasping him tight, then released him. The rest of her body was perfectly motionless, hands trailing at her sides, and the contrast between the intense stillness of her pose and the measured throb grasping and releasing him, was intensely, deliciously exciting.

He reached out to touch her, smooth away the silk of her robe, but she met his hands with her fingertips, delicately brushing them away while clenching him internally with a sudden powerful spasm that rippled intoxicatingly along the length of his shaft.

Trapped in her body, captive in her silken cage, he felt his shaft grow harder and harder, stroked to utter fullness by the rhythmic pulse she set. Her eyes were amber slits, her face the rapt mask of some ancient priestess absorbed in ritual.

'Serena—'

Gently she touched his lips with her finger, motioning him to silence. Groaning, he gave himself over to her.

Mika had agreed to meet her. A car would be sent for her that evening. She would stay at the villa, for a few days at least. The woman's voice had been soft and smoky, but with a barely concealed edge to it. It was a voice accustomed to immediate acquiescence.

Franca glanced around the tiny room. She hadn't unpacked the night before, so there was little to be done. She dressed quickly, slim black trousers, a thin black silk sleeveless T-shirt and over-sized matching jacket, black leather boots. An indirect compliment to Mika, who always wore black, she knew how well it set off her pale skin and flaming hair. Taming her hair into a twist, she leaned closer to the mirror.

Her eyes seemed huge, her skin too pale. She was nervous, she realised, as she carefully applied some mascara. She hadn't expected things to move this quickly, had been anticipating a few days alone in the village to get her bearings, prepare some version of herself that Mika would find desirable.

Sheer nerve and deliberate bravado had carried her thus far. Eve and Sally, the two scouts from Disc-O, had been easy enough to deal with, and she'd impressed Max Schiller, consciously and deliberately projecting a heated sensuality she was far from feeling. But Mika . . . Mika was a different story. And Serena, the dark-haired, voluptuous siren never far from his side. Everyone knew they were long-time lovers, surely . . . how would she react to Franca's presence? Jealous? Suspicious?

She picked up a book and put it down; prowled over to the window and gazed with unseeing eyes at the picturesque landscape; changed her clothes twice, once into a white cocktail dress which she rapidly discarded, struck by a sudden and irrational dislike for her legs, and then into a long skirt in dull purple. It looked ugly and old-fashioned, and in despair she reverted to her original choice. Eyeshadow might help.

A knock on the door interrupted her. Opening it, she discovered a tall, blond, bullish man in a uniform.

'I'm your driver, Sergei,' he said, entering the room before she could say a word. 'Your bags?' gesturing to the cases on the bed, but never taking his eyes from her body. She had the fleeting impression that the room was suddenly smaller. Under his air of deference, there was something . . . she shook her head.

'Yes, please, no, not that one, I'll take the violin myself,' she managed to reply.

In the plush grey embrace of the limousine's luxurious upholstery, she tried to relax, tried to summon the confident, assured, even arrogant air that she had learned to wear in the competitive, cut-throat arena of the musical world. But she was conscious only of a growing, thrilling anxiety mixed with budding excitement. At last, at long last, she was going to meet him.

Mika.

The superstar of the violin.

The sensual genius of the strings.

The teacher she craved. He would become her master, her maestro, her conductor, would teach her how to summon the passion from the strings that still eluded her.

'If you would care to follow me?' said Sergei. Engrossed in her thoughts, she hadn't noticed that the car had stopped, that he'd opened her door and was waiting for her to get out. She slid out, looked around and received a confused impression of a massive, brick-fronted exterior, soaring turrets, acres of velvety green grass, and then she saw him.

He was standing in the curved archway, leaning negligently against a pillar, a massive yellow blur heaped on his shoulder that, as she ascended the steps, resolved itself into the outlines of a cat.

'Miss Tonelli.' He nodded a formal greeting, did not attempt to take her hand. 'Sergei, thank you. Maddie has put her in the Green Room. You'll take care of things?'

His voice was beautiful, a deep, rich baritone, clear and beautifully modulated, like honey-coated crystal. It was a voice that could tempt saints to sin or lure sinners to virtue. She felt a sudden surge of pleasure at the sound and wondered, irrelevantly, if he knew the power of that voice, knew how it caressed the ears.

His physical presence was somehow shocking, like an unexpected blow. His face, familiar to her from countless album covers, was subtly different in person, the eyes deeper set, the mouth fuller, more sensual. And his eyes were more forceful by far, a blazing electric blue that seemed to pierce beneath one's skin and search through the skull beneath.

'I thought we should listen to you together,' he said, motioning her inside.

'Yes,' she said, swallowing quickly, grimly aware that she must have been staring. Wordlessly, she followed him into the huge entrance hall, heels clicking on the pale marble floor, eyes darting here and there to the carved Corinthian columns embedded in the walls, the huge chandelier, the spindly grace of stray chairs and tiny tables scattered at seemingly random intervals, the massive arrangements of cut flowers.

Opening a pair of huge carved double doors to one side of a spiralling staircase, he stepped aside, allowing her to enter. From the corner of one eye she saw a slim figure dressed in white lingering at the top of the stairs, but when she turned it had vanished.

The room was huge, a shining expanse of marble interrupted by the jewel tones of scattered Persian rugs, antique glass-fronted cabinets containing leather cases, a complicated sound system occupying one entire wall.

He walked over to it and inserted a CD. With a thrill of surprise and disquiet she recognised Mozart, the A major recording she had done for Deutsche Grammophon. She waited uncertainly, awkwardly, watching him as he stood motionless, listening to the music, caressing the cat who was fixing her with an evil, yellow stare.

She let the magic of Mozart calm her, mentally approving the purity of her sound in the first movement, appreciating the skill of the orchestra in developing the sonata-form movement in the second. Nerves tightening, she waited for the third . . . Yes, here it was, *The Seraglio*. She'd never quite captured the exotic colouring demanded by the Turkish Allegro theme, never quite evoked the mysterious flavour of the East.

'You recorded that last year, I believe.'

'Yes,' she agreed, pleased to hear her voice was cool and clear.

He played it again. And again. And again. Hours passed. When he finally spoke, his words surprised her.

'Come, let's have dinner. We'll be dining alone,' he said, stooping to drop the protesting cat to the floor and gesturing to her to follow him.

'Oh? But I thought perhaps Max and—' She stopped,

halted by the force of a withering glance from those magnificent, electric blue eyes.

Wordlessly she stood, then hastened to catch up with him, their footsteps echoing on the marble floor. Glancing at her watch, she was amazed to see that it was eight o'clock. So much seemed to have happened already. He made time somehow irrelevant, stretched it, compressed it, changed it.

Dinner was simple and beautifully prepared. A roast of lamb, delicately seasoned with fresh rosemary, new potatoes glistening with butter, fresh green salad followed by fruit and cheese. He spoke little, said nothing beyond the polite commonplaces of dining together, commenting on the wine, passing the bread and then, after a brief, disparaging remark about the local brandy, had fallen silent.

She was disappointed.

She found her eyes returning again and again to his hands. Encased in soft black leather, the fingers seemed long, shapely and elegant, offering no clue to the disabling injury that had forced his premature retirement.

He used his hands with the unconscious, precise grace of the true musician, idly balancing the heavy silver tableware as though testing the weight of a bow, skimming the faceted bowl of the crystal wineglass as thoughtfully as if it were the varnish of some priceless violin. With his thumb and forefinger he traced the crystal curves in a repeated caress, meeting the ruby level of the wine, then drifting down to the stem, again and again in an hypnotic, almost erotic appreciation of the fine contours of the glass.

He looked at her thoughtfully. Unaccustomed to the company of strangers, he was mildly surprised to find her an almost comfortable companion. Hers was not the sweet, sinuous silence of Serena, which accompanied him effortlessly, but still it seemed she had some appreciation of sound, didn't seek to clutter the air mindlessly.

72

Suddenly full, she toyed with the food on her plate, drank more wine and was conscious of feeling light-headed. A stray breeze stirred the candlelight, casting his face into sharp relief.

He watched her in the warm glow of the candles. Objectively he admired her face, the pale skin, the unusual, slanting eyebrows. She was beautiful, of course, but he had long ago become sated with beauty.

Idly he wondered about her life, the private, inti-mate, intrinsic details that could never have found their way into the potted biography prepared by Max's staff. And he wondered about Max and Serena, now dining alone in another part of the villa, the two arch mani-pulators who had engineered this meeting. On second thoughts, he decided that he might possibly acquit Max.

Suddenly he felt sorry for this flame-haired girl, tool for so many ambitions. 'So they've brought you here to me, Miss Tonelli. You're a pawn, you know that? We both are. But you're the sacrifice to a dying god Serena will never let rest. Doesn't that trouble you?' he said.

For a moment she couldn't believe that she had heard him correctly, but the words refused to disap-pear. A sacrifice? A dying god? What melodrama was this?

'It's not a bad parallel,' he said calmly, as though reading her mind. 'But I forget, you don't know Serena. Have you ever considered the relationship between master and pupil?' he asked, apparently changing tack.

'Frequently,' she said, striving to remain as calm as he appeared. 'But I sometimes wonder if my teachers have. They have all been singularly stupid.' She stared at him challengingly, with a fair assumption of her usual arrogant bravado.

So, she was not a passive tool. Better that way. 'It rests on power,' he explained, ignoring her remark. 'But it rests on power that is not simply imposed. It must be a relationship in which the pupil is willing to trust the teacher's instinct, give him or herself over to

73

the dominance of greater experience. It's a relationship like that between parent and child, but more intimate than that of lovers.' Across the table his eyes were fixed on hers. She felt drawn by them, unable to look away.

'If,' he paused then, drawing out the silence, 'if by some chance you were to interest me sufficiently, I might be willing to teach you.' He heard himself say the words with some surprise. 'But you should understand the nature of the relationship. You would have to be willing to suspend your critical faculties at first, and obey me without question.'

He lounged back in his chair, sipped more wine, wondering whether he was actually contemplating teaching her or merely toying with the idea to please Serena. The Mozart, though, had moved him; gifted as she was, she had failed to etch *The Seraglio* with the sensuous, forbidden incense of the East. He knew how frustrating that could be.

'Read my reviews,' she challenged. 'Technically, I'm flawless. Your natural successor, the critics say. That should interest you, at least a little.'

To her surprise, he laughed. 'The critics say?' he mocked gently.

'Well, one critic,' she admitted. And he hadn't said exactly that.

'You are an innocent. That A major was played by a virginal talent. You're still playing the score, the notes – in an exceptionally brilliant way, I agree – but you are not a channel for the music,' replied Mika.

'Virginal,' she repeated, confused. 'What do you mean?'

'Music starts deep inside you. It's not governed by the mind, by slavish devotion to the score. It is a primitive, primal urge, or even instinct, deep in the bowels of your soul. From there it radiates out, expands to your heart, your breasts, down to your groin, encompasses your most sensual imaginings. You become the violin and it becomes you. It's a consummation.' He stopped then, aware he had come too close to revealing the secret that had fed his genius.

If she had spoken then, even a single word, he would have left the room, had her briskly and unceremoniously removed from the villa, wiped her from his memory.

But she said nothing, sat motionless, head bowed, slanting dark brows drawn together in thought.

When she finally lifted her head, her eyes were bright with unshed tears. 'It was the third movement, wasn't it?' she acknowledged softly.

He nodded, disarmed a little by her perception, disarmed by the tears now coursing unheeded down her cheeks. She hardly seemed aware that she was crying.

Quietly he rose from his chair and stood behind her. 'An audition, perhaps,' he said softly, as though to himself. 'Why not? We'll test your instrument, see if it has any resonance at all. Put your hands on your breasts.'

'What?' she asked, startled, and felt his hands on her shoulders poised and waiting.

'Trust me. Do as I say.' The tone of command was unmistakable, edging the dark honey of his voice.

He demanded a willing submission to his dominance, a blind faith in his genius, obedience without question. She was intensely aware of the warmth of his hands through the supple black leather gloves, intensely aware of the hard column of his body standing behind her, could almost feel the electric waves of energy pulsing from him. To be so near to such musical genius, to find it allied with such a sensual presence was intoxicating, and in that moment she knew this was a man who could do anything with her, that she would submit blindly to his voice, his hands.

'Yes,' she murmured, lifting her hands to her breasts, unsurprised to feel them trembling.

'Good,' he said more softly. 'You must be in tune with your body, in touch with your real instrument.

Focus on the idea that your body is a violin, your fingers a bow. Every instrument has its vibrator and its resonator. The strings are the violin's vibrator. Make your nipples the strings of your body.' And so she brushed her hands against her nipples, feeling them tighten against the black silk.

'Good,' he approved. 'Brush them up and down, feel them.'

She felt the heat rising to her face, felt the tingling sensation that coursed from her fingers to her breasts, felt his hands gently cup the back of her neck, then search through her hair and come to rest at her temples.

'Don't stop until I tell you, you may,' he said. 'Concentrate on your body.'

Closing her eyes she brushed her nipples with her thumb, up and down as he commanded, feeling the softness of the silk like an irritation. Sensitised to touch now, her nipples were erect, quivering with life. There was something profoundly erotic in touching herself, arousing herself as he stood behind her, his long fingers cradling her head.

He must be watching, seeing how her nipples were standing out firmly, confidently, challenging him to warm and suck them.

Standing behind her, he could feel the betraying pulse at her temples, sense her arousal.

'Tell me what you feel.'

'Heat,' she said softly. And she was hot, burning almost. The most delicious, searing heat, soaring through her body, knowing that he was watching her, his eyes fixed on her hands, her breasts.

'Harder,' he said. 'Pluck the string, pizzicato.'

Pizzicato. She tightened her fingers, pinching her nipples as firmly as if plucking the strings and felt the electric jolt ripple through her body, radiating from her breasts to her groin, thrilling her spine.

'Again,' he said, his hands moving gently to her shoulders. 'And again.'

Her nipples felt like twin circles of fire, hot and unbearably sensitive, her breasts heavy and swollen. Closing her eyes, she leaned back in her chair, resting her head gently against his midriff. Through the silk, her nipples were distending, growing, and without his urging she pinched them harder, rolling them between her fingers. She felt the burgeoning moistness between her thighs, the swelling of her lower lips, the first, greedy stirrings of her clitoris. Caught in the sensations coursing through her, she twisted in the chair, would have turned to face him but he tightened his grip on her shoulders, forcing her to stay still.

'Tell me.'

'Still hot,' she murmured. 'But fuller now.'

'And wet?' he suggested, feathering her ear with his breath.

'Yes, wet.' She felt the lips between her legs growing warm and swollen, mimicking her nipples, the hot wet liquid of arousal bathing her groin.

'*Water Music*,' he said softly. 'Think of wet and water and the strings.' She felt his hands slip from her shoulders to cup the curve of her breasts, support the lush fullness that her fingers had plucked to swollen warmth.

'Arco,' he said softly, using the term that directs string players to resume the bow after a passage of pizzicato. 'Arco.'

Almost gratefully she slid her hands over his, relishing the supple coolness of the leather, relishing the sensation of both their hands enfolding her breasts.

'Now find the strings. Touch yourself wherever you feel the strings. Your body is the sound box. Make it vibrate.'

Caught by his voice, hypnotised by the flickering candles, her hands dawdled. And then she gasped as his gloved hands tightened just a fraction on her breasts, causing a frisson of shuddering delight.

'Your hand,' she whispered and then felt it trailing gently down to her belly. Her nerve endings tightened, rippled in an arpeggio of anticipation. She was harp now, as well as violin, meant to be plucked and played, and felt herself moisten, growing hotter and more liquid. Through the silk she felt the warmth of his gloved hand gently pressuring her pubic hair. She could feel the juice seeping out of her, knew that she was now not moist, not wet, but sopping, soaking the flimsy silk panties she wore. She was flooding in a blush-pink tide, flooding and flowing.

'Yes?' he prompted.

'Tides,' she said, the words coming from nowhere. She felt strangely disembodied, hazy, conscious now only of a slow burning sensation stealing over her body. Her breasts were full and hot, and she felt her clitoris stirring like some nipple wanting too to be fondled, plucked and sucked. Beneath the silk she was heating, perspiring, felt the drops trickling down her neck. The air was closer now, like velvet.

'Tell me,' he said, amused and felt her push against his hand. Watching her from behind hooded eyes, he saw the flushed cheeks, her lashes fanning them, breasts rising and falling. Her ready passion surprised him. He meant only to test her a little, find her resonance, watch the flames lick like a slow movement and dry her tears, but already this girl was rushing to the edge.

Deliberately he slowed the movement of his hand and extending a finger felt for her clitoris through the silk, brushing gently, feather soft, searching between the folds of fabric to find the erect little core.

'Red. Red and silky and bitter, like roses and salt,' she murmured and felt his finger stiffen, press hard against her.

She'd used the very words he had used long ago to his women when his face was buried between their thighs, licking, sucking, tasting and teasing. Salt and roses. Caught off guard, he felt himself stiffening.

'Enough,' he said abruptly, releasing her and turning away.

'But why . . . what?' Confused, disorientated, she opened her eyes.

'Enough. You're losing the flow. Handel isn't roses, not the *Water Music* at any rate. Spring flowers, perhaps, but never roses.' He stood with his back to her, apparently intent on examining the painting on the wall in front of him.

Dumbly she stared at him, feeling the unfulfilled pulse between her legs like a second heartbeat, hearing his words as though from far away.

'So, have you learned anything? One can learn even from an audition. Especially from an audition, in fact,' he said casually.

Frantically she cast her mind back, struggling to find something that made sense, words he'd said only moments before, struggling to subdue the aching void left by the imprint of his fingers. 'My body is the violin,' she said slowly.

'And your hands?'

She knew the answer he wanted, knew also it wasn't the right one. It had been his hands touching her, plucking her that became the bow; his hands that made her the violin.

'Hands are the bow,' she said, dissembling a little. He nodded, apparently satisfied.

'And Handel?'

She thought furiously. Handel's *Water Music*. Published 1740, probably composed for a royal trip on the Thames. What did it have to do with the receding tides of her body, that wet, hot flood denied release?

'Handel isn't roses,' she replied.

'Yes. I'll make my decision tonight. You should go to bed, get some sleep. You're in the Green Room at the top of the stairs. Ring for Maddie if you need anything.'

'But I—' she managed, but too late. He'd already gone. Unsteadily she rose to her feet, clutching the table for support. Her body felt disordered, confused. The waves of sensation that had washed through her

79

so violently only moments before were slackening now, leaving her weary but elated.

Carefully she walked across the room into the hall, felt for the balustrade on the staircase, grateful for its support. Her room seemed terribly far away. Finally she reached it, closed the door with trembling fingers and collapsed on the bed.

'Well?'

Surprisingly, Mika started at the sound of her voice. A few drops of Calvados marred the mahogany sideboard. He mopped them up, then finished pouring his drink. With a sigh, he selected another goblet.

'Drink, Serena?' he asked.

'I'd love one, darling. So?' Her voice rose invitingly.

Deliberately he kept his back to her, pouring out the Calvados with the concentration of a scientist mixing a particularly difficult formula.

From the buttery depths of the leather sofa, she smiled to herself. 'So?' she repeated.

'Serena.' Her name was enough to calm him. He repeated it softly under his breath. The disquiet that had flooded through him at his body's unexpected response was receding. 'Serena . . . perhaps you were right.'

'Of course I was, my love. Why are you surprised?' Some basic instinct cautioned her against pressing for the details she was dying to learn. She would find out in her own time, in her own way.

'She's locked much of it away,' he mused. 'You can sense it suppressed in the A major. But she can respond. You must listen to the CD.'

'I will,' Serena answered, a smile hovering on her lips. 'But do you have any plan, any theme?'

'*Water Music*,' he said, finally turning to her and crossing the room with her drink. 'She needs to be receptive, uninhibited. Perhaps some sleep therapy . . . would you send Maddie up with something?'

'Of course,' she said softly. Their fingers met as she took the glass from him. 'Shall I conduct?'

'No, I'll do it.'

'But Mika, you've never—'

'Allow me, Serena. I'm . . . I'm experimenting tonight. It's what you wanted, isn't it? Isn't it?'

Was it? Sipping her Calvados, she scrutinised him closely as she considered her reply.

She was asleep. No, not exactly asleep . . . dreaming perhaps? She had woken, she thought, saw him looming over her, this fair-haired god dressed in black, but then everything swam out of focus again. And now she was naked, nude. She'd felt the whisper of her night-dress leaving her skin, the cool air caressing her body, felt exposed somehow as the silk drifted down her arms, her breasts, soft swathes pooling along her belly, settling momentarily in the juncture of her thighs, then whisked along her legs.

And now there was music. She recognised it at once as Handel's *Water Music*, that stately, joyous, sensuously flowing passage. It seemed very close, almost as though she were in the front row of an audience. And then she was moving, being carried as though in a barque along the Thames, in strong arms, to the flowing source of the river. There was water running. Carefully, reverently, as though she was one of the royal princesses in that stately procession, she felt herself lowered to the cool marble of her seat. But she was naked, she knew, could feel the veins of the marble against her own skin. And then her arms, again ever so delicately, ever so reverently, were lifted from her sides, entwined with silken cords. If she were to be bound, it must be in silk, she thought, a little confused. And then those same hands were spreading her legs, opening her thighs, encircling her ankles with thick silken cords. Instinctively she knew they were white. She should, perhaps, be embarrassed, naked as she was in front of her courtiers, but she knew her skin

81

was as white as the cords, knew herself to be as sensuous and voluptuous and open and flowing as the very water they sailed on.

He stood back, breathing a little heavily. She was so slender, it was hard to believe she was so heavy to carry. Her eyes were closed, and her breathing regular. He was sure she had woken when he lifted her, but she seemed completely under now. How fortunate that Maddie had put her in the Green Room, which had its own *en suite* jacuzzi. Against the black marble of the cavernously deep tub, her skin glowed like a pearl. Spreadeagled on its surface, her long white legs spread wide, her flaming hair in disarray, she resembled the sacrifice he'd likened her to earlier. Something to devour . . . Recalling himself, he concentrated on the music and turned on the taps, testing the water to make sure it was neither too cold nor too hot, then took the showerhead in his hand. The more powerful jets from the jacuzzi would come later.

Oh God, yes, that was it, bliss, those warm summer showers moistening her skin, flowing around her, warming her. The touch of the cool marble contrasting with the warm, pulsing jets of the spray. But what a strange shower it was. It moved leisurely, slowly, starting from the soles of her foot, pulsing intimately between her toes, then tracing the curves of her calf, her thigh, then pressing against her apex, pulsing, swirling, dancing with her lips, her labia, flirting with her clitoris. Again and again the path was repeated, sometimes slowly, sometimes in sharp little thrilling, trilling, bursts . . . it followed the strings. *Water Music*, she realised, and arching toward the shower tried to capture it, summon it to the centre of her pleasure, but found her wrists bound, her legs immobile. Only her torso could move, wave towards the waves. Like some sea creature caught in the tide, a flowing anemone, she was at the mercy of the water, its creature, sucked into its dark roiling depths, then spat out and cast forth in an unrelenting rhythm.

Leaning over the tub, he was entranced with the picture she made. The water level was rising, and her red-gold hair was fanning out as though it were alive. And she was ready, he could sense it from her skin, knew it from the rocking of her hips, questing toward the jets spurting from the showerhead he held in his black-gloved hand. Swaying a little to the music, he realised that he was now the conductor and she was the orchestra. This crude instrument in his hand was the baton, with which he would call forth the entire symphony. Her body now was almost submerged, only the tips of her breasts peaking above the water. He felt the tension in his wrist returning, almost as though he were playing again. Delicately, deftly, with a mathematician's precision, he positioned the showerhead between her thighs and waved it gently, fanning it across her pubic hair.

It was humming, she could feel it, hear it, sense it humming, like a bee coming to drink the honey of her juices. Warm wet waves, pulsing towards her, stirring her hair, ruffling through it to the tender skin beneath. Her groin felt heavy, as though all her blood was rushing and coursing to settle between her legs. Under the hypnotic rhythm of that fanning warm tide, her lips were growing, engorging, plump and red and slick. Her clitoris was stirring, hard and greedy, desperate to reach that humming, pulsing jet. It had caught the rhythm, was humming and pulsing too, pushing through the swollen folds of her labia. The tides were ebbing and flowing, washing now against the inside of her thighs, now swirling through her hair. She could feel the pulsing jet coming closer, tantalising her clitoris with the faintest watery caress before swirling to lick the plump leaves enfolding it. Lightheaded, disembodied, she was at the mercy of the tide, desperate for that pounding, crashing wave to slam into her, slam through her. It was coming closer and closer, she could feel it coursing through her.

Mika saw her body tense, could almost feel the first tremor of her response.

And so he stopped.

Carefully, with long, slow strokes, he moved the showerhead under the water, tracing the long line of her legs, moving from her thighs to her knees, finding the sensitive flesh of the inner curve of her knee, then down to her feet, positioning the pulsing head between her toes.

With his free hand, he reached behind him and turned up the volume of the CD.

Just poised on the crest she felt the wave recede. Moaning, she tried to rock towards it, follow it, but it ebbed away, settled between her toes, found the little hollow between her baby toe and its mate and throbbed against the sensitive skin. Warm and pulsing, thrumming, it was the symphony of sensation she needed between her legs. Her clitoris was quivering, trembling with need, suffused with aching. And the tide understood, because it was flowing towards her again, leaving that tiny hollow between her toes, washing up along her calves, her thigh, coming closer, fluttering against the swollen lips encircling her clitoris, then receding along the path of her other leg, tracing the curve of her thigh, the swell of her calves, then settling between her toes again.

Again and again, with infinite patience, he waved the showerhead under the water, following the contours of her legs, his leather gloves sodden with water. Her torso was rocking frantically, with water sloshing against the sides of the black marble tub. This was the moment to prolong to infinity, to turn greed to need to imperious desire, so that the final explosion was a shuddering flourish.

Throbbing, aching, pulsing, all of her, every part. Drowning, submerging in the warm wet want, her toes were her clitoris, her clitoris her toes, ten, no eleven, erect little mounds of flesh dancing and palpitating for release. Her breath was coming faster and faster, she could feel the salty sweat of the sea on her brow. The waves were pounding now, dashing her against the hard black shore.

He could hear the music coming to its end now, the stately barge preparing to dock, throwing out the lines to the shore. It really wasn't long enough for his purposes, he decided, probably wasn't even the right music for this one. She deserved something from *Tristan and Isolde*, perhaps, something from the post-Classical period. Still, for the sake of symmetry . . . He smiled a little tensely, and moved the showerhead between her legs.

Crashing closer and closer and now, the warm jets were pulsing towards her, dashing against her clitoris in a surging tide, and as it throbbed in response she could feel her inner walls throbbing too. The water was beating against her faster and faster, sucking away then flashing back, sucking and flashing, sucking and crashing.

The final notes were sounding. Firmly he placed the black plastic head, still spewing the pulsing jets of warm water, against her lower lips, then turned the taps on full force.

Tense, straining for release so long denied, with the streaming pressure of the jets thrashing her clitoris she came in a rushing, screaming frenzy, a torrent of suppressed sensation, a fury of ecstasy unlike anything she had ever experienced.

He knew she could come again and again, was almost tempted to make her, but the tape had finished. Leaning over the tub to replace the showerhead he was aware of a sudden tingling in tips of his fingers. Accustomed to the phantoms of sensation that still sometimes haunted his sleep, he ignored it and reached for a large, fluffy white towel. Bending down he flicked the mechanism that drained the tub and waited while the water flowed away. Her skin was flushed from the warmth of the water and the force of her orgasm, and she was still breathing rapidly. For a moment, watching the fronds of her water-darkened hair wave in the draining water, her taut, milky breasts still heaving, the muscles in her perfectly formed calves still trembling, he was almost tempted.

Briskly he shoved the thought aside, unbound her wrists and ankles, and wrapping her in the towel carried her back to her bed. She roused a little then, he was sure, because her eyes opened for a moment. It didn't matter. Because of the draught she would not know what was dream and what was reality, would retain, only, he hoped, the physical memory of sensations. Already she was snuggling beneath the blankets, drifting into sleep.

A cool gust of air stirred the draperies, and walking to the window he peered out. Storm clouds, thick and gravid with rain, were gathering over one of the mountain peaks faintly visible in the distance. How very appropriate, he decided.

He returned to the bathroom, hastily wiping down the wet surface of the tub, and pocketed the four silken coils with which he'd bound her. Finally he unplugged the CD player and, returning to the bedroom, hesitated. She had clasped a pillow close to her breast, cuddling it close like a lover, looking for the security and warmth of another body. Her fingers, long and graceful, were clasping it close to her, drawing it into the warm, dark embrace of her body. Unthinkingly, he bent down, kissed her cheek and left the room.

The heavy carpet muffled his steps as he walked down the hall. He hesitated outside the door to Serena's suite, then moved on. He wasn't quite ready to tell her.

Tell her what?

She could respond, this girl, this violinist, had a reservoir of sensuality that could be unleashed on the music, if she learned how to draw on it, sustain it. Did it matter?

He felt edgy, unsettled. The unusual energy, the almost clinical sense of purpose that had driven him to

86

her room had deserted him, leaving him tired but restless, irritable and weary.

In the old days he would have had a woman, taken one almost automatically, to relieve the tension, the music shivers shuddering his fingers. Unconsciously he flexed his fingers, extending them and then balling them into fists. It was a simple reflex now. He knew, despite early hopes, early promises, that his hands would never recover.

Morning dawned fresh and fragrant, the world washed clean by the night's storms. Serena woke early, slicing quickly through the haze of sleep to full consciousness. She'd returned to her rooms at dawn, leaving Max sated and sleeping. She had left him only twice yesterday, once to observe the arrival of Francesca Tonelli, and once to share a brandy with Mika. Now her curiosity was at a fever pitch. She slipped into a robe and went to find Mika.

Mika was, of course, on the terrace, drinking coffee, Midas sprawled along the length of the table in front of him.

'Morning, my darling,' she said, slipping into the seat across from him and waving a dismissive hand at the cat. 'Shoo, Midas, you know you're not allowed on the table.' In reply, the big yellow cat opened one eye so malevolently that even Serena was taken aback.

'Leave him, Serena,' said Mika. Moodily he splashed more coffee into his cup, ignoring her own.

So they were both in a bad mood, cat and master. Instinct told her to stay silent, give him time, but she couldn't wait. Wouldn't wait. 'Mika? What is it, darling? What happened?'

At that he looked at her. 'I'm not sure. I tried to play the *Water Music* with her last night. It was clumsy, I suppose, not up to your standards. The music wasn't right, the motivation wasn't right, but still, I felt her resonate.'

Her heart curled in triumph. Leave him now, let him

87

come to it in his own way, in his own time. But she knew. 'I heard it last night. It was very late, though. The storm woke me,' she said artlessly, filling in the silence. 'I've never really liked Handel.'

'No, I know. But it was a good storm,' he said, remembering the lightning streaking the sky.

'It was, my love,' Serena said.

She drank more coffee, let the silence grow. Tempted Midas with a strip of bacon and let the cat delicately, fastidiously snatch it from her fingers. At last she broke the silence. 'And how did she play?'

Mika drummed his black leather fingers on the table uneasily. 'Quite well, I think. Perhaps. I'm not sure, Serena, I can't decide. Will you try?'

'Of course. *Water Music*, you think? Why don't I—'

'No, it's not the right one,' he interrupted.

'Still, we can pursue the motif,' she pointed out. 'Why don't I fetch her, take her for a swim? I'd like to meet her.'

Their eyes met, amber and blue. And in those golden depths he read their past and saw the music. If she was aware of some half-concealed, disturbing current behind his electric blue eyes, she gave no sign.

'Yes. Yes, I suppose you must,' he agreed. 'Where's Max?'

'Probably still asleep. Worn out, I expect,' she explained sweetly. 'Why? Will you see him now? It would be so good, Mika, if you would.'

'Yes,' he said, suddenly decisive. 'I will. I've hesitated, thinking how difficult it would be . . . A friend, you know, an old friend from the past. But with the girl, last night—'

'Franca,' prompted Serena.

'Yes,' he nodded. 'It wasn't as hard as I imagined.'

'I'm glad,' she replied. 'Very glad.'

'What about Max's plans for her, Serena? What do you think?'

'We haven't really discussed business,' returned Serena, fingering the gold chain links at her neck.

'I see,' said Mika drily. 'Max was always very fond of you, See,' he added slowly. 'It would be a shame, if—'

'It would, wouldn't it?' she said coolly. Without waiting for a reply, she rose from the table and walked inside. As she made her way up the stairs, her momentary, uncharacteristic irritation with Mika vanished. He was, she realised, a bit off balance. So, the girl could resonate. That enlarged their opportunities considerably, she thought, and knocked on the door of the Green Room.

It opened immediately. 'Oh,' said Franca, startled, clutching her towel to her. This voluptuous brunette in a silk robe was a far cry from the grim-looking housekeeper she'd been expecting. 'I'm—'

'I'm Serena,' said Serena, slipping through the doorway. Any other explanation seemed otiose, unwarranted. 'I wanted to welcome you to the villa. You slept well, I hope?'

Had she slept? She'd woken feeling utterly drained, with a curious sense of dislocation. But clearly Serena didn't expect a reply.

'Mika's on the terrace. I thought you might want to come down and join us, and perhaps have a swim.' Expertly Serena ran her eyes over the girl. The studio photographs hadn't done her justice. She really was quite stunning. No wonder Mika was intrigued. She smiled, a warm, inviting, intimate smile that instantly put Franca at ease.

'A swim sounds divine. But I didn't bring a swimming costume, I'm afraid,' Franca replied. So this was Serena. She seemed so friendly, so unaffected, that some of her earlier misgivings dissolved a little.

'You can borrow one of mine. We're about the same size, I think. Why don't you come with me, and you can change in my room?' Even as she spoke, Serena was drawing the girl out of her room, down the hallway. 'I'm just along here, not far away at all. And I know I have something that will suit you.'

The room they entered was more lavish than

anything Franca had ever seen, with the huge bed, the mirrored wall, huge pots filled with fresh flowers. Irresistibly her eyes were drawn to the painting occupying one niche, a man and a woman frozen in an ecstatic embrace, the colours pale and muted.

'Try this,' said Serena, handing her a small package still encased in its cellophane wrapping. 'I haven't worn it yet.'

She took the package, intending to thank Serena and return to her room to change, but was caught by the sight of Serena slipping out of her robe. She was nude underneath, and her golden skin glowed in the early morning light. Her breasts were larger, more rounded than Franca's high points, her waist slimmer, her hips more generous, the juncture of her thighs smooth and hairless.

'Try it on and see if it fits,' suggested Serena matter-of-factly, willing her to drop the towel.

Their eyes met. Serena's amber eyes were deep, fathomless, exerting a magnetic pull. She had an aura, not just of sensuality, but of command. To submit to her will seemed the most natural thing in the world. Hardly thinking, Franca let the towel fall.

Oh, yes, she was luscious, thought Serena. Slender and crisp with tight breasts, the flaming curly thatch of pubic hair barely concealing pouting red lips. Delicious.

'Your hips are smaller than mine,' she said to Franca, 'but with this style, it shouldn't matter. Just put on the bottom and we'll see.'

It was scarcely more than a G-string, a tiny sliver of black fabric just covering her pubis, ending in a long thong that disappeared in the crease of her buttocks to reappear at the waist, where it joined a narrow strip of fabric circling her waist. Surprisingly, it felt a little tight, but not exactly uncomfortable. The dense bush of her pubic hair curled around the little black triangle covering her mound.

'It fits, I'm so glad,' purred Serena, eyeing the flaming curls. The perfect opportunity to test the physi-

90

cal resonance of this vessel for the violin had presented itself. 'But of course you weren't expecting to go swimming. I have some marvellous stuff that I got in Rome, absolutely perfect for sensitive skin. You just cream it in and then scrape it off. Let me get some for you,' she promised, disappearing into another room.

'Well, I'm not—'

'No?' said Serena, reappearing with a small jar in her hand. 'Just stretch out on the bed, and spread your legs very wide. It's so much easier when someone else does it for you,' she continued conversationally, drawing the girl to the bed.

'There, now if you keep your feet on the floor, and spread your thighs as wide as possible, you can lie back while I spread the cream. Depilation. Such an ugly word, isn't it? But widely practised. In the East, you know, they believe that it enhances sensation to shave your pubis. It's quite an ancient belief, really. Even shown on ancient Greek vases of the fifth century BC.' Artlessly Serena kept up a flow of chatter, soothing and distracting the girl with the sound of her voice.

Franca's long legs were pale, the only colour the flaming swathe of pubic hair and the pink folds bisected by the slinky black grip of the bathing suit. Kneeling at the side of the bed, gently Serena massaged the cream onto the insides of her thighs, just skirting the tender inner flesh, following the line of the suit, working the cream in with circular, insidious strokes.

The cool, oily cream, the feel of fingers rasping against her crinkly pubic hair, the soft, smoky sound of Serena's voice all combined to lull her into a delicious haze. She felt relaxed, open. Against the tight black fold of fabric, she could feel her lips swelling, her clitoris wakening, her inner walls begin to pulse. She was growing wet, liquid juices creaming the fabric, lush wet folds wanting to escape the chafing restriction. Serena mustn't notice. She moved just slightly, felt the thong tighten along the crease of her buttocks. Serena's hands were moving higher now, feathering through her hair, gently tugging it from the confines of the tiny black triangle, pouring more cream onto the soft, sensitive skin.

'You know, your skin is so smooth here, so sensitive, I'm reluctant to use the scraper,' said Serena, bending close to inspect the sheaf of curls. Her breath was warm and moist, a humid caress. With her thumb and forefinger, she pulled gently at one of the hairs. Loosened by the cream, it sprang free, with only the tiniest pin prick of sensation.

'That didn't hurt, did it?' she asked softly, casting a knowing glance at Franca. The girl's eyes were closed, her cheeks flushed, although Serena had barely touched her.

Delicately Serena searched out another hair, and another, and another, placing her thumb and forefinger right at the root, then drawing it through her fingers, long and slow until she reached the tip, then tugging gently.

The sensation was indescribably arousing, tiny pin pricks thrilling through her. Her clitoris was stirring, becoming greedy, hungry to be one of those hairs, wanting Serena's fingers to close around the root, tug at it, pull at it. Franca waited, hardly daring to breathe, as slowly Serena searched out another hair, tugged gently, almost lifting the skin, then pulled it free. Again and again she repeated the action, sometimes pausing to pour more cream on the hairs, sometimes making some minute adjustment to the tiny triangle covering Franca's sex. The slow, conscientious rhythm was almost agonising. Franca was swelling, spreading, longing to burst open in a humid torrent, stop this measured dance and grind herself to orgasm. Serena couldn't possibly know the effect she was having on her, it was impossible, she had to stop this coursing, burning friction somehow before . . .

'Franca, this next bit's just a little tricky. Lie still, I'll have to get a bit closer,' Serena said smoothly. Firmly she cupped the girl's mound with one hand and pressed the fleshy folds caught in the black triangle to one side, concentrating now on the hairs feathering the very inside of one thigh.

The firm pressure of her palm, the flesh warm through the thin fabric of the bikini was delicious, relieving for a moment the hunger rippling between her thighs. But only for a moment. The pressure of Serena's hand, combined with the thrilling little jolts as she carefully plucked the flaming hairs nestled so close to her labia, were creating new tides of sensation. The tiny electric pulse of each hair as it sprang free was creating ripples, spreading along her thighs, through her belly, up to her breasts, pooling in her nipples. Warm already, she was growing hot, hotter still, burning. Her control slipping, wildly she thought of grabbing Serena, forcing her between her thighs, begging her to slide her tongue along her lips, into her entrance, dart into her again and again, to stop this desperate, aching pleasure.

Kneeling between her thighs, Serena could sense the girl's arousal, smell the musky perfume of her juices. Despite herself, she could feel the beginnings of her own arousal, a certain pulsing heaviness in her groin, a tingling awareness in her breasts. It surprised her.

Her fingers, clever and knowing, slowed in their measured dance over Franca's mound, still pulling gently, easing away the last few flame-coloured strands of curly hair.

'Perfect,' she murmured, then shifted her palm and pressed the mound of the girl's sex towards her. 'Now the other side.' Expertly she repeated her ministrations, creaming and plucking, carefully following the black line of the tiny bikini. She could take her now, she knew, release the pink folds from the tight clasp of the black thong, tongue them and taste their sweetness, bury her face between those white thighs and suck greedily, drawing out all her juices, suck each plump pink fold until the girl screamed in release.

But that, she reminded herself, wasn't the point.

Mika was waiting on the terrace, Max would no doubt be stirring in search of coffee, and besides she had learned quite enough by now. The girl definitely had potential.

Franca felt Serena's hands slowing, trailing gently along the inside of her thighs, pausing here and there to pluck at an errant hair, then rubbing a scented oil into her newly plucked skin in firm, sure strokes.

'Just to take away any of the sting,' said Serena softly. The eucalyptus oil would soothe her skin, should help soothe her arousal into a more diffuse, sensual well-being. Her fingers firm and impersonal, no longer deliberately tantalising, Serena massaged in the rest of the oil.

Franca's breathing was slowing, no longer coming in the harsh little gasps that betrayed her. She was warm and loose, still excited but not with that gnawing, aching need that had almost caused her to clutch at Serena, and grind against her mouth, her tongue.

'There, all finished,' said Serena, rising from her knees and stepping back to admire her work. 'It really is so much easier when someone does it for you, isn't it?'

'Much,' agreed Franca, opening her eyes and making an effort to speak evenly. 'I'd be happy to return the favour sometime.'

'We should go down,' said Serena, surprised into a smile. 'The pool is just beyond the terrace. And you must be dying for coffee.' Rummaging in one of the drawers, she discovered a tiny white bikini, the twin of the one she had lent to Franca, and slipped on the bottom half. Reaching behind her to fasten the clasp of the brassiere, she found Franca's hands already there, cool and smooth along the column of her spine.

'Here Serena, let me, these things can be so fiddly and awkward. There, I've got it.' But she made no move to step away, standing close behind her, the tips of her breasts just brushing Serena's back. She moved her hands forward, rested them beneath the lush swell

94

of Serena's breasts, making a minute and utterly unnecessary adjustment of the tiny white cups barely covering the nipples.

Daring, thought Serena, aware that her nipples were puckering in response. Very daring. And a quick learner. Perhaps Francesca would prove to be the challenge Mika needed.

Chapter Five

Water Games

Stepping out into the sun-drenched warmth of the terrace, Serena paused, adjusting her eyes to the dazzling sunshine. Behind her, Franca stumbled a little and reached out to steady herself. Alerted by the slight noise, Midas opened his eyes and hissed. Following the direction of his baleful yellow eyes, Max and Mika glanced towards the arched doorway.

It was an arresting tableau. Serena stood motionless, resting most of her weight on one leg, one hip thrusting forward provocatively. Her dark hair was loose, just skimming her shoulders, her eyes half-closed against the bright sunshine. The tiny scrap of material lovingly moulded to her mound shone white against the pale gold of her skin and the lush swell of her naked hips curved towards her tiny waist. Only the thin white string of the bikini circling her waist interrupted the flow of pale gold flesh. Her breasts swelled against the tiny white cups clasping her nipples, the outline of her aureoles almost visible beneath the pale fabric. To her side, slightly behind, Franca was in profile, one arm extended, resting lightly on Serena's shoulder where she had reached out to steady herself. Her red gold hair fell in a flaming tide down her back, catching the sun and reflecting its fire.

Clothed, they could have been sisters; almost nude, the physical differences between them were apparent. Where Serena was lush, Franca was spare and slender, her hips faintly angular, her belly flat, breasts high and pointed. Against the dazzling white background of the concrete terrace wall they seemed, for an instant, almost unreal, images of some erotic daydream, simulacra of sensual fantasies.

Max simply stared, his mouth dry, his body hardening in response. Then Mika coughed, and the spell was broken.

'You'll join us?' he invited the women, gesturing vaguely with one black-gloved hand. Behind dark glasses, his expression was unreadable.

Serena glided forward with the unconscious, sensuous grace of a woman who knew herself infinitely desirable to everyone present. 'Of course, darling, I'm sure Franca would love a coffee. Max, how are you? How did you sleep?'

'Well, Serena,' he replied, striving to sound casual. How strange to see the maenad of yesterday, the wild wanton who had driven him to climax after furious climax, acting the perfect hostess.

'Have you two been catching up on old times?' she continued, casting a quick glance at the table. 'Franca, why don't you sit there and I'll ring for more coffee. Or would you prefer iced coffee? It's so hot, almost too hot . . . champagne, and some orange juice as well, I think.'

She kept up a steady stream of small talk, bathing them in the honey of her voice, lulling them with the potent force of her charm, while expertly assessing the situation. There was some tension between Max and Mika, impossible to tell whether it was the natural awkwardness of a first meeting after a long time apart or something deeper.

She could feel the intensity of Max's eyes sweeping along her body, dwelling on her breasts, flicking furtively to the pale triangle at the juncture of her thighs.

She noticed too the flickering glance he darted at Franca, and was pleased.

'Such a lovely morning, I persuaded Franca to join me for a swim. Max, why don't you come too? We've barely used the pool all year, it seems such a shame.' Her voice drifted on, enfolding them. Franca was nervous, she sensed, firmly tuned to Mika's every move, drinking in his presence. And Mika? He was lounging back in his chair, a faintly ironic twist to his lips indicating he was well aware of the sensual spell Serena was trying to cast.

'Ah, Maddie, thank you. Coffee everyone? Champagne? Orange juice? Mixed or separate?' The heady aroma of freshly ground Blue Mountain, the crusty warm scent of newly baked bread, the astringent tang of oranges, rose invitingly from the tray. 'You must have a croissant, Maddie bakes them every morning and they're utterly divine.'

Ignoring her words, Mika gave her a slight frown. Serena cut her eyes at him and then looked away, casually fingering the heavy gold chain around her neck.

Fascinated by the silent interplay between the two, Franca sipped her coffee, studying Mika covertly beneath her lashes. The enigmatic man of the night before whose hands had rested with hers on her breasts, made her body the violin and plucked a response from her as surely as he used to pluck the strings was no figment of her imagination, no fevered dream. She felt his presence like a magnet.

Sensing the direction of her gaze, Serena smiled. Rising, she circled the table, deliberately brushing Max's shoulder with her naked hip, then stopped behind Mika's chair, rested her hands lightly on his shoulders.

'Swim, Franca?' she asked. Franca leaned back, tilted her chin to look directly into Serena's eyes. Whatever she saw there seemed to reassure her.

'Yes, yes, I'd love to.' She reached up and caught the

flaming mass of her hair between her fingers and began
to tame it into a thick braid.

'You'll join us, Max?' invited Serena, still resting her
hands on Mika's shoulders. There was something
going on between the two of them, thought Max, as he
watched Serena's long, slender fingers resting on
Mika's powerful shoulders, some fundamental com-
plicity that he could perceive only dimly. He'd never
truly understood the relationship between them, knew
only that sexual jealousy played no part in it. He'd
often wondered, after that wild night in Paris,
whether . . .

'Max? Swim?'

'I'll join you later, Serena,' he managed. 'There's a
few things I want to discuss with Mika first.'

Franca stood, and in unspoken accord the two
walked arm in arm towards the shallow steps leading
to the pool from the terrace. The fat braid of Franca's
plait snaked down her back like a python, swaying
provocatively with each step she took. The thin black
thong bisecting her buttocks only seemed to emphasise
her near nudity. He could see the finely tuned muscles
of her thighs and buttocks rippling as she walked, her
skin gleaming white in contrast to the pale golden tint
of Serena's flesh. The voluptuous swell of Serena's
hips, the rounded globes of her buttocks swaying from
side to side as she walked down the steps . . .

'Well, Max?' Mika's tone was dry.

Reluctantly he tore his eyes away. 'Mika. Yes. Well.
I wanted to explain about Franca, about everything,
really. But first, I want to say I'm sorry. I shouldn't
have asked about your—'

'My hands. I admit, I am perhaps too sensitive,' said
Mika smoothly, examining them, encased in the black
leather gloves despite the heat of the morning. 'And
other explanations are unnecessary. Serena and I have
discussed your proposition. I haven't yet reached a
decision.'

'But she has the potential, don't you think?' probed

Max, his voice eager. 'When I first met her, for some reason she reminded me a little of Serena.'

'Serena?' asked Mika thoughtfully.

'Strange, isn't it? To see them like this, they're not at all alike, really.' Both turned their eyes to the pool. Franca and Serena were standing at the edge, preparing to dive in, their semi-nude bodies poised and graceful, ready for the cool embrace of the still blue water.

'It's curious you should say that,' said Mika at long last. 'When I first saw her picture she reminded me of someone. We'll see,' he added abruptly. 'I need a little more time.'

'Time?' asked Max, puzzled. 'I would have thought—'

'While I make up my mind. And while I do so, perhaps you would care to join them?'

The dismissal was unmistakable.

The outdoor pool was a shining blue oval, bordered with a profusion of brilliantly coloured flowers massed in clay tubs. Carefully manicured grass formed another border and a profusion of thick, glossy green shrubs guarded against prying eyes. Deck chairs were scattered along the tiled edge.

Serena dived in expertly, slicing through the water like a shark. Franca hesitated a moment, assessing the depth, then followed. As they surfaced close together, Franca could hear the faint strains of Handel's *Water Music* issuing from the terrace.

A shiver of sheer sensual pleasure stirred her, running hot and liquid through her veins. Unconsciously she swayed, rocking to some half-remembered rhythm. She let her fingers flutter through the water, dancing to the music, creating little wavelets that pulsed against her breasts. She let her head fall back, cradled by the water, relishing the cool embrace.

She was suddenly, madly liquid, as wet as the water surrounding her. She could feel the muscles in her thighs trembling, feel her nipples tighten and pucker,

100

feel the hot flush of arousal warm her skin. She let her hands drift slowly through the water, inches away from the familiar curves of her breasts, remembering the incandescent sensations that had flowered through her body when Mika's hand had drifted down her belly to the centre of her pleasure.

The music was louder now, the joyous strains of the violins flirting with the air. The demands of her body, too, were becoming louder, a lively allegro of anticipation shivering through her veins.

One elbow draped on the side of the pool, Serena watched her intently. She could see the response to the music, a physical memory surfacing in her arousal. Mika must have used water to play her last night. How clever of him! And how right he was about the Handel. It didn't suit her at all.

The music was drawing to a close. Franca could feel her body tightening, the heavy, insistent pulse of desire drumming between her legs. The waves were stronger now, luring her to fulfilment.

Serena glanced up to the terrace. Mika was alone, standing at the shallow steps leading from the terrace, eyes fixed on Franca. Serena lifted an eyebrow at him, knowing the gesture was sufficient to recall him to her. He looked back and shrugged.

'Mika? Not like this.' Serena's voice was low, barely audible. He understood her instantly.

The music stopped, halted just before the final crescendo. Caught in the electric sensations fountaining through her body, Franca was startled, opened her eyes. The sudden silence was heavy, almost oppressive. Serena was watching her with sympathetic eyes.

Lounging in a deck chair at the side of the pool, Max was frankly bemused. For a moment he could have sworn that Franca was about to climax to the music, touched only by the watery embrace of the pool itself.

'Franca, come with me to the shallow end, we'll rest on the steps there.' Serena's voice was gentle, as persuasive in its own husky tones as Mika's was, and

101

Franca followed her automatically. She felt Serena's hands brushing through her hair, loosening the fat braid that had confined it, spreading it across her shoulders, down her back. Her heated skin welcomed the cool, moist veil. Serena was speaking, her voice soft and lulling, and she could feel the turbulence of her body slowly calming.

'Always difficult at first,' she was saying. 'And, of course, particularly difficult for you, without the proper theme. It was, oh, a bit tactless of Mika, shall we say? But you've done very well, even without being properly instructed. Are you feeling better?'

The edge of Franca's frustration was softening under the influence of Serena's warm tones, just as Serena's hands, lightly trailing down her arms, were soothing her skin. 'Yes, yes, I am,' Franca replied slowly, remembering Mika's words. The body is the violin. 'And I think . . . I think I understand.'

'I thought you might,' replied Serena, a spark of approval dancing in her eyes. 'Let me have a word with Mika.' With one lithe, graceful movement she drew herself out of the water and walked towards the terrace.

Max caught at her hand as she passed. 'Serena? Serena . . . what's going on?'

She paused for a moment, let her fingers rest in his. Unbidden, the memory surfaced of how even in sleep he had drawn her close to him and kissed her hair, a soft, blind kiss. She pushed it aside, but returned the pressure of his fingers. 'Trust me, Max,' she said lightly. 'I have to speak to Mika. Believe me, this is truly in your own best interests.'

'Serena, you must know—'

'Later, Max. Why don't you strip and have a swim?' She disengaged her fingers and walked up to the terrace.

Slipping into her chair, she said abruptly, 'Mika, she's perfect. Her body remembers the music. But we can't play with it. We'll have to channel it properly.'

'I told you the Handel was wrong,' he pointed out. 'You said we should follow the motif.'

'I know,' she said thoughtfully. 'But how do you see her?'

'I don't know. I've been running through all the possibilities in my mind, and I can't even find a composer I like for her. Bach is mine . . . shouldn't be played by a woman anyway. And that's a problem. You know I've never believed a woman had the potential to really become first class with the violin. The violin *is* a woman, needs to be played by a man.'

'Chauvinist,' she retorted automatically, knowing it was a common belief among male violinists. 'Never mind, darling, we'll think of something. But we should tell them—'

'The truth?' he interrupted, sensing the direction of her thoughts.

'Not the whole truth, of course,' she replied, faintly shocked. 'Perhaps not even half of it. But Franca suspects, thinks she understands a little of what is necessary. We'll have to tell them both enough to begin work properly . . . that is, if you've decided.'

'You're willing to trust them, then?' he asked.

'Trust them? What an absurd idea, darling.'

He relaxed. 'We'll need the right music,' he began slowly.

'Write it,' Serena replied unthinkingly, her mind moving ahead. Determining the sensual range and expanding it was the first step. The music could come later. She raised her voice. 'Max? Franca? Come and join us.'

'Write it?' Mika repeated under his breath. 'Write it? Serena, you're mad, I've never composed, can't even begin to imagine how.'

But he could, she knew it. She could sense his mind working furiously, turning the idea around, examining it for flaws. He'd lost all awareness of her presence, wasn't even aware of Max and Franca walking across the terrace, settling themselves in their chairs.

Serena poured herself some chilled orange juice, waiting for Mika to rouse himself from his thoughts.

At length he shook his head. Taking off his dark glasses, he looked at Franca, a long and appraising glance, then moved his eyes to Serena. Steepling his fingers, he began to speak.

'The first instrument of the violinist is his own body. It must be as poised, as balanced, as fluid as the sounds he coaxes from the violin. It requires a delicate subtlety, a sensual, tactile awareness. It must be finely tuned, honed to perfection, if you like, to withstand not only the rigours of playing for hours at a time, but to sustain physical concentration. Your mind and your body must be open and receptive. Some people meditate. Some even use drugs. Serena and I have developed . . . another method. Methods. Which also aid in the very subjective, very intricate art of interpretation.'

He's going to do it, thought Max exultantly! The secret behind the gates! He's going to reveal it to her, teach her!

Franca was silent, drinking in his words, watching him intently.

'So. I will find something for her to play. Something different. The structure will become clearer as we go along. In the meantime, I advise you to be led by Serena. Any tiresome business details, Max, you can discuss with her.' He rose from his chair and disappeared into the villa.

Serena smiled to herself, fingering the heavy links of her gold chain. Max was looking puzzled. Although Mika had hinted quite broadly, he had not given them enough information to allow Franca to begin. Without a theme, there was nothing yet to interpret. A void, an empty space, waiting to be shaped, mastered.

Serena smiled again. She'd always enjoyed improvising. In her own way, she was as much a musician as Mika. Music, after all, began with improvisation: precise notation demanding slavish observance to certain notes at certain places was a tyranny to which she could never submit. Spiritually she was more akin to the gypsy violinist; a rogue player prone to incredible, impulsive ornamentations, she preferred her progressions fresh and unpredictable.

She would, of course, try anything once. If she liked it, she'd try it again, improving, modulating it until the original act was so transmuted, so unfamiliar, that it acquired a spurious originality. She and Mika differed in only one dimension of expertise, she thought, watching Max and Franca.

Music and sex.

Sex and music.

Obverse and reverse of the same coin. Both relied on a natural, inescapable rhythm, a thematic, rhythmic progression to an inevitable climax. How fortunate that they had found each other, she thought. And how lucky she had been with him.

She stretched. 'I am so glad that Mika decided to explain everything. I must admit, I was a little surprised.' Her voice was husky, compelling. Max found himself nodding in agreement.

Wait a minute, said a small voice in the back of his mind. Explain everything? Mika had explained precisely nothing. Violins, bodies . . . a performer was a performer. The good ones made money, the bad ones didn't, and then there were the amateurs. Once in a lifetime you found a star . . . then kept on hoping to find another.

Serena could see the scepticism in his eyes. It didn't trouble her. Turning her glance to Franca, she lifted her eyebrows. Cool grey eyes met hers with unblinking, unthinking acceptance.

'Why don't we go back to the pool?' Serena said casually. Leaning forward slightly, she reached behind her and undid the tiny clasp that fastened the bra of her suit. Her breasts swung free, ripe and golden with large, rosy brown nipples.

Both their eyes were riveted on her. 'We can sunbathe for a while, I do so hate getting tan lines, don't

you Franca? Or swim. Maddie will tidy up here.' She
was natural, unaffected, apparently unaware that she
had changed the atmosphere, charged it with a sensual
heat.

Lazily she got up, enjoying the faint tingle in the air,
the look of frank hunger in Max's eyes. 'Max? Why
don't you bring the champagne and orange juice?'

Walking down to the pool, idly she pondered her
next move. On the purely professional level, she
needed to explore Franca's range, test the limits that
she and Mika would carefully extend, discover the
barriers that might inhibit her performance. Franca was
rousable to a woman's touch. So much was obvious,
given her response to the intimate but ambiguous scene
Serena had contrived earlier this morning. Unaccustomed to a woman? Probably. Easily shocked? Serena
doubted it, remembering the glancing touch beneath
her breasts.

And Max, what role should she assign him, she
wondered, settling herself in a lounger. He was, on the
other hand, if not easily shocked, possibly too conven-
tional for the intricate scenarios she would have to
construct. But his hunger for her might well override
any qualms. And he seemed attracted to Franca on
some subliminal level. She let her thoughts drift.
Leisurely she slipped out of the bikini bottom and lay
back, exposing her perfectly nude and golden body to
the eyes she could feel fixed on her. The important
thing, she reminded herself, was the sustained physical
concentration Mika had mentioned. It took time to
master it.

And as far as anything else was concerned . . . she
closed her mind to the thought, feeling herself warming, getting back in tune.

She turned over on her stomach and closed her eyes.
'There's some suntan oil here, somewhere. Would you
do my back?'

She wondered who would be the one to respond to
her request. Not that it mattered, not at this stage.

Then she felt oily fingertips on her shoulders, trailing gently down her spine, tracing each vertebra, pausing uncertainly at the globes of her buttocks. Impossible to tell whether it was Max or Franca. She shifted slightly, inviting the anonymous hands, the anonymous fingertips to drift lower, slip between the cleft of her buttocks, but they shifted away uncertainly, returned to her spine, her shoulders.

'All over, please,' she murmured. 'I don't want to burn. Ah, that's better.' More confident now, freshly moistened with more oil, the hands were moving down her body, palms flat in a long, fluid motion from shoulder to buttock. Max's hands, large and heavy. Franca would be watching.

She spread her legs wider apart, felt the hands moving lingeringly across her buttocks, then to the tops of her thighs, one stealthy finger darting furtively to probe the cleft, retreating as it met the taut aperture of her rectum. 'The physical concentration Mika mentioned, it's well . . . crucial, really, isn't it?' she said slowly, as if thinking aloud. 'The violinist has to be in tune with his body, has to sustain the intensity.' Languidly she rolled over and looked into Max's eyes. 'More, please.'

He swallowed hard. The luscious body that had tormented him so skilfully, so sensuously, was fully exposed, gleaming and perfect in the hot August sun, the smooth juncture of her thighs revealing the pouting pink folds of her sex. He felt his erection straining against the fabric of his jeans, felt too the presence of Franca standing nearby.

'Max, darling, you're still dressed,' exclaimed Serena softly. 'Do take off your jeans, you're wearing far too many clothes.'

He smiled a little uncertainly at the echo of his own words to her. 'Serena, I—'

'And Franca, why don't you take off your suit? You have that pale skin that tans so quickly.' Serena's voice was husky.

'Physical concentration,' Franca murmured, eyes fixed on Serena. 'I think, perhaps—'

'No, don't think, not yet,' cautioned Serena. 'That comes later. For now just . . . concentrate.' She slipped off the lounger. Standing in front of her Serena reached behind to unfasten the clasp of Franca's bikini bra. Close together, their nipples almost touching, Serena let her hands coast along Franca's hips, found the taut line of fabric encasing her mound, and drew it down to her ankles.

Franca moved to step out of the black triangle, but Serena placed a hand on her shoulder, warning her to wait. 'Max, hand me the oil,' she said without turning around.

'Serena, I'm—'

'The oil, Max,' she repeated, holding out her hand. Wordlessly he placed it in her outstretched palm.

Serena massaged it in gently, in long, rhythmic strokes, over Franca's shoulders, pausing to caress the slightly reddened patch of skin at the edge of her jaw where the chin-rest of her violin had abraded the skin, moving down her arms, carefully anointing each finger, massaging the sensitive web of skin in between, tracing the delicate blue veins of her inner wrist where a small, betraying pulse fluttered.

Her hands retraced the path, resting lightly at the top of Franca's breasts, drifted down to her belly, just barely touching the rosy brown nipples that were firming and puckering in anticipation. No, thought Serena, not yet, not for hours yet, perhaps.

With infinite patience she set about to explore every contour of Franca's body, oil every inch of exposed skin apart from the jutting nipples, apart from the pink leaves of her sex barely visible below the flaming swathe of hair.

Franca's body was drinking in the touch of Serena's hands, responding to the fluid, graceful sensation, the slinky ease of the oil, and she could feel herself moisten, knew that the folds of her labia were swelling, blushing pink and glistening with the natural oil of her own lubricious juices. Her nipples too were blushing and warming, unbearably, unbelievably sensitised not by touch but by its absence, by the implicit promise of Serena's fingers.

'Structure and proportion,' murmured Serena, feeling the muscles of Franca's inner thigh begin to tremble.

Franca swallowed. 'Structure and proportion,' she repeated, feeling the oiled hands gliding again over her body, radiating a heat that pulsed inexorably to her groin.

'Climaxes, you see, have to be graded,' said Serena softly. 'Think of the *Chaconne*.'

'The *Chaconne*,' repeated Franca mindlessly, desperately trying to concentrate, trying to ignore the pleas of her nipples, hard and distended now, begging for the warm, pulling pressure of a mouth, the tantalising, biting ache of teeth, trying to ignore the yearnings of the heavy, swollen lips at her centre, engorged with blood, greedy for the lapping friction, the moist embrace of mouth and tongue. Her body was swelling and stretching now, in tune to the oiled caress of Serena's fingers, now playing sinuously along the curve of her thigh.

'Max? Why don't you do her back?'

'Serena! Serena, I—'

'Max. I want you to help me.' Her voice was soft, inviting, almost implacable.

Aroused but uncertain, he walked toward them, his brain frantically trying to interpret Serena's cryptic reference to Bach's *Chaconne*, trying to assimilate the tantalisingly erotic sight of Franca and Serena naked together, wondering what part he played in this voluptuous venture. His body, knowing no such inhibitions, was hard and roused and ready.

He stood behind Franca, looking over her shoulder directly into Serena's eyes. Something hot and wild was glowing in those amber depths. Taking his hands,

Serena poured oil onto his palms, then lifted them to Franca's shoulders and positioned her own body exactly opposite. Dimly, he began to perceive what she wanted, their hands to dance in rhythmic unison separated by Franca's warm body. He could smell the musky perfume of her arousal, and it fuelled his own.

Losing himself in Serena's hypnotic yellow stare, he moved his hands down to Franca's shoulder-blades, smoothing in the oil, almost feeling Serena's hands move to the girl's breasts, almost feeling Serena's hands through the slim length of flesh and blood that separated them.

She was enclosed, a crossroad of desire, her trembling, enchanted back belonging to the firm male hands that sculpted her shoulder-blades, her breasts bewitched by the slim, sensitive length of the woman's fingers. Involuntarily she arched her buttocks, thrusting for the hard male member, but she swayed forward from the waist, breasts and belly avid for the soft mouth of the woman. It was an erotic envelope, deliciously voluptuous in contrasting sensations, an intoxicating symphony.

The pulsing in her groin was increasing in tempo, the leaves of her labia thrumming, the pulsing beat of her heart throbbing in time with the throbbing pulse of her clitoris. She was dazed and dizzy, dilating in desire.

'Max, darling, you're still dressed.' The silky purr of Serena's voice was another caress, close behind her ear.

Serena leaned forward slightly, lifting her chin across the slim barrier of Franca's shoulder and ran her tongue along her lips. Unthinkingly Max responded, moving his head to hers, taking her mouth, his hands tightening on Franca's waist.

His tongue tasted the swell of Serena's lower lip, danced across the contours of her teeth, while his hands followed the slim curve of Franca's hips, pausing to finger the clean swell of her pelvis. He lifted a hand to cup the back of Serena's neck, increase the pressure of his mouth, and she leaned forward willingly, breasts brushing against Franca's own. Aroused beyond all measure by the naked buttocks pressing against his erection, the oiled back warm against his chest, the warm and knowing mouth that opened under his, Max deepened the kiss, forcing Serena's lips apart even further with his tongue and teeth. He penetrated the plush cavern of her mouth, darting his tongue against her teeth again and again in the pounding rhythm of sex, using his tongue like a second shaft.

When he lifted his mouth from hers, the blood was filling his ears with a dense roar. He was too hard now, too roused and stimulated to be conscious of anything but the rearing demands of his body, his cock still painfully trapped in the tight vice of his jeans.

Franca felt their bodies enclosing hers as a tangle of oily limbs and harsh denim, heated skin and cool linen, the bruising strength of muscular thighs, the soft curves of breasts and belly. She was caught in the heated clash between two bodies, caught in a shivering struggle that was burning her body, searing it, soaking it.

'Max? Your clothes,' Serena smiled. Gently urging Franca out of the narrow black triangle still encasing her ankles, Serena took her hand and led her forward to the grass verge surrounding the pool. Together they lay on the newly-mown grass, Franca willing and submissive to the carnal choreography Serena so effortlessly, so elegantly directed. She felt Serena's touch fleetingly on her knee, and instinctively understanding, spread her legs wide. Beside her, leaning on one elbow, Serena let her hand settle at the top of Franca's breast.

Max hesitated for a moment, then recklessly tore off his clothes to stand naked before them. He knew himself harder than he had ever been, felt his shaft like an iron rod, a voracious living creature seeking its mate. Serena beckoned him with a smile, and groaning he settled himself against Franca, knowing that she

111

meant to keep the girl between them, understanding without conscious realisation that the kiss they had shared with the fragrant warm body between them was a prelude to a different dance.

The grass was warmed by the sun, slightly spiky, redolent with the rich, warm spices of the earth. Closing her eyes Franca concentrated on the oily fragrance of Serena lying beside her, the salty, heady scent of aroused male surrounding her. She was spreadeagled, open wide to the sun and the air, soon, she knew, to be enclosed in a more intimate caress.

'A sensual, tactile awareness,' breathed Serena, holding Max's gaze with amber eyes that were hot and glowing. With one slim index finger she stirred the air over Franca's right nipple, almost touching the quivering peak.

Franca moaned, then felt the aching abrasion of a softly padded thumb flick over her nipple. An electric jolt shuddered through her at the caress, so long denied, and then she gasped as her left nipple was roused by a heavier touch. The warm caress of flesh against flesh, two hands joined in a rhythmic dance at her nipples, two bodies pressed against hers glowed against her skin, and she felt her desire crystallise and harden.

Molten and delirious, she craved the heat of teeth and tongue, wanted the ferocious frenzy of a driving cock plunging into the furnace of her body, thrashing her to climax, pounding her into the earth.

'*Adagissimo*, Franca,' soothed Serena. '*Adagissimo.*'

Very slow. Impossibly slow. She waited, hardly daring to breathe as she felt the twin fingers leave her breasts, creep leisurely down her belly, linger at her navel then twine together in her pubic hair, while the humid caress of twin mouths hovered at her nipples.

Unable to bear it any longer, she gritted out, '*Affrettando*, Serena,' pleading for haste, a hurrying, pressing onwards, and heard her husky chuckle.

'*Adagio*,' Serena conceded.

The moist caress of tongues gradually descended, flicking lazily at the heated points of her breasts, bathing them, infusing and suffusing her nipples with a rosy heat. She arched towards them blindly, begging for the hot, relentless suction, the pulling pressure that would draw the heat from her, and felt her left nipple suddenly clutched between hard lips, while her right was still tormented by the soft silk of a tiny tongue.

Point and counterpoint. Where he was hard, she was soft. The man's mouth, greedy and avid now, ravaging her nipple with the hard, demanding, powerful strokes of tongue and teeth, the woman's tongue lazy and languid, a faint whisper of sensation. The contrast was arcing through her, whipping her with delicious, tingling thrills. She was lost now, poised and hovering at the edge of an orgasm too powerful to be denied, too strong to be checked.

Surrendering utterly to the tactile torment of the contrasting sensations, hard and soft, weak and strong, Franca retained only enough sense to know that she must signal her understanding, only enough breath to murmur, '*Ad libitum.*'

Serena laughed then, a low sound of surprised joy. Ad lib. At pleasure, when the speed and manner of performance are left to the performer. They had not been mistaken in this girl.

She tilted her head back. Franca was writhing now, whipping her head back and forth as she trembled on the verge of orgasm, her entrance slick and welcoming. They were beautiful to watch, Serena thought, admiring the play of muscles along Max's lean back, the shapely strength of his legs. His eyes were screwed shut in blind concentration as he suckled at Franca's nipple, the massive rod of his erection pressed tight against her thigh. His grasp on her own fingers tightened. She found herself curiously moved by his gesture, felt it echo deep in the pit of her belly.

Gripped by a sudden impulse, she returned the pressure of his hand while letting her slim index finger escape his grasp and feel for Franca's swollen centre, his hand following hers, slipping down to clasp her wrist as she pressed inwards and upwards to unlick its secretive heart.

Franca's head flicked back again as she felt the smooth, moist tip of Serena's finger push between her lips, and slide with confident ease inside.

This she had been waiting for. The man – Max – was a blur. As surely as she had ached for the male hardness, the driving possession of the man's penis claiming her, stretching her, she knew it was not the right man. It was Mika she wanted, only Mika, driving himself into her in a blind, mindless fury. But the woman was different. She was part of him, almost soothing, sweet to the touch, and her finger seemed to Franca as familiar as her own, as skilled and knowing as Mika's, exploring her very depths, testing and pressing the silken walls.

Surrendering to these thoughts she felt herself surge towards climax as Serena's finger lured ripple after ripple of vibrant energy from her vagina. Vibrant, vibrating . . . vibrating like the lowest string of her Gagliano, pulsating to its fullest amplitude under the gentle, coaxing pressure of her bow, of this finger, the fullest, loudest tones coming not from weight, not from force, but from confident, relaxed stroking, making the violin sing.

And Serena's finger, as deft, as supple, as intransigently clever as her Francois Tourte bow had found the burning, responsive string, G-spot, G string, nothing mattered except the inescapable, inexplicable molten delight coursing through her.

Her body was pliant, passive, captive, willing to surrender to this pressure, willing to yield, to allow the music to play her. Eyes closed, mind and body incandescent with the excitement of impending release, Franca arched her hips upwards, not once, but again and again, clinging to the promise of Serena's finger which filled her body, rocking against the friction in the comfortable cocoon of her two lovers.

Allowing her body to sway to the pulsing of the bow, to rise up, like the violin, to meet the caresses of the bow, she balanced herself on an equipoise of sensation, pressure and resistance.

But the grand climax of this movement of bodies that she felt so close, drifted, maddeningly, impossibly, away, softening in a gentle wash of perfect diminuendo. She felt Serena ease her finger out, until the merest tip of its pad retained contact with the begging bud of Franca's clitoris. And she was taut, engorged, ready but not yet released, under the remorseless but almost imperceptible touch of that clever finger.

Clawing for climax, angered by the deliberate, taunting, haunting withdrawal of the source of orgasm, she suddenly recognised the touch. She had been young, very young, when she learned to play harmonics, when she had been shown how to touch the strings of the violin, not pressing it against the fingerboard, but letting it vibrate freely, her finger sensing out the node, that perfectly still point. And from either side, with geometrical precision, the string would swell and pulsate.

In that instant she captured the perfect disassociation of mind and body, both perfectly aware of each other, each absorbed in different aspects of the same sensation, the intellectual and physical appreciation of the same stimulus. Her body was flying free, vibrating, as if that mysterious, unmarked node of her, that tiny hidden point of flesh, had for the first time been found with precisely the accuracy, gentleness and skill needed to allow the rest of her body to sing.

And she remembered the music, began unthinkingly to murmur to herself the great theme of the slow movement of the Sibelius concerto. Her hands moved down to find flesh . . . the one hard and masculine, her loving bow . . . the other soft and welcoming, feminine and female. Her fingers arched, poised, she pressed the strings, vibrating gently.

She was in the spotlight, heating under its glow, heating under the eyes that followed her every movement, adoring her, wanting her. She moved her fingers, dexterously moulding and shaping the bow and the violin surrounding her.

Sensing this new moment, this new movement, Serena flexed her wrist up from the warmth of Franca's mound, still keeping her fingertip on her clitoris, took Max's fingers and slid them into the wide-open sex that beckoned both of them.

It was the heart of the orchestra, the soft pad of Serena's finger controlling the very node of her, the strong firm strokes of Max, bowing deep into the centre of her. Sound and touch, mind and light, sound and touch . . . She was playing them, fingers and bow in perfect harmony, and they were playing her too . . . the bowing arm, proud, imperious, yet yielding and lovingly male, far inside her, joined in tracing the outline of that ravishing melody by the delicate finger of the female.

Franca opened her eyes to a blue and endless infinity.

Knowingly, caressingly, slowly, Serena drew Max's fingers out of Franca and brushed the lightest of kisses against Franca's lips, knowing it would go unheeded in the musical, sensual trance she had attained. Critically she admired Franca's voice as she listened to her hum the Sibelius . . . so few players, in her experience, were worth listening to except on their chosen instrument.

Easing herself away from Franca she turned Max onto his back, and, pressing her open mouth against his, laughed in a full-throated ecstasy, a blend of passion and accomplishment.

And because she was pleased, she reached down with her hand, lightly brushing the hairs on his chest, and on down to the dark mass which bordered the base of his shaft. And then, sliding her cupped hand down its full, massive length, with calm and practised assurance she eased herself around him until she was filled, brimming over with the elation of the morning's *divertimento*.

He thrust at her furiously, desperately, need driven by greed, and heard her laugh, a soft bubbling laughter like Horace's *Bandusian Spring*, a laugh that belonged to the nymphs.

Concealed in the thick shrubbery bordering the pool, Sergei watched with angry, avid eyes, wanting her with a sick desperation mixed with fury. She had no right, no right at all. He'd felt her attention shift the afternoon Max had called, remembered with sullen wrath how she had ruffled his hair, smiled at him, told him to wait. Remembered with aching greed the silken furnace of her sex, clasped tight around him, the insanely intoxicating warmth of her eyes as she dared him, taunted and tormented him to please her further, please her at all.

He imagined her again in the black dress that bared her back, barely covered her breasts as she greeted Max, remembered how she had waved him away with a casual, dismissive gesture. He had burned at the time, even knowing that she would return to him, knowing that while she might enjoy herself with the stranger, she could never, *would* never share the perverse, provocative pleasures she had taught him so skilfully.

But they had never shared a woman together, never. And as he watched them, heard the lilting ripple of Serena's laughter, he was seized with a raging desire, a desirous rage, a potent thickening of his cock and his anger.

Swiftly he unzipped himself, eyes fixed on Serena, the amber-eyed witch now spreading her legs and opening her arms to *him*. Blindly he stroked himself, hands hard and furious, knowing he wouldn't come, couldn't come, would remain hard and aching for the velvet embrace of her body, the delirious dance of her inner muscles.

She laughed again, an irrepressible husky bubble of sensual joy, and Sergei found himself coming in a powerful, exploding surge.

Chapter Six

Variations on a Theme

*A*lone in the music room, Mika prowled restlessly, absorbing the disjointed images his musical mind and relentless memory had recorded. The familiar warmth of Serena mingling with the unfamiliar, stirring strangeness of a new vessel for the violin, the burning, poignant path of Max's eyes as they followed Serena's every move, the hungry need in Franca's eyes as they watched his own hands . . . He was unbearably conscious of all of them, aware of a new, surging, tingling irritation at the base of his spine.

Was it the girl? Franca. He forced himself to use her name, remembering how Serena had forced him to use it, acknowledge her. Max had seen the similarity between them.

She was beautiful, with that fiery hair and those unusual, dark, slanting eyebrows. A competent violinist, he acknowledged; indeed, she was almost as technically flawless as she claimed. But she had yet to master the sensual sorcery of the strings, the potent, passionate, perverse demands of the violin. The violin was all things to its player: friend, lover, mistress, partner, child. But you could never rely on a single instrument, never confine yourself to only one.

Mentally, he paused. Opening one of the cabinets,

he withdrew one of his favourites, a Stradivarius made in the last years of the craftsman's life. How old had he been when he shaped this youthful creature, he wondered, opening the case and carefully drawing the silk aside. Ninety? Older? She was a dream of youth, warm and supple, ample enough to accommodate a youthful passion, accept the heavy, pressing thrusts of the tutored innocent.

Write, Serena had said. Her voice reverberated in his head as he gently stroked the satiny finish of the Stradivarius before returning her to her rest. Moving on, he paused to finger the leather case of a Januarius, offer a mindless caress to the Storioni.

Despite what he had said, that he couldn't imagine how to begin, he had known it for a lie. And he never lied to Serena. No violinist could master Bach, the six sonatas and partitas for violin alone, without being inspired to compose, stirred to create and compete, master the empty, aching void that was silence without music, silence without the violin, woman on the edge of orgasm without the thick, pounding male counterpoint of the player. It was the ultimate mastery of space.

His steps stilled before the case holding the Guarnerius, remembering the Bach he had played in Rome. She was a wanton, this one, passionate with a sheer animal vitality and incredible powers of penetration. Somehow more sophisticated than the Stradivarius, more voluptuous, richer in tone. She demanded carelessly, arrogantly, an equal sophistication, a hand that could caress silk or wield iron with equal confidence.

And beside it lay the Stradivarius from his so-called 'Golden Period', when the craftsman was in his early seventies. She was a haughty creature, perfection that demanded perfection in turn, proud and unbending, arrogant in her clarity, responding only to the lightest, most flexible touch. She might love you for a night, if you loved her without reservation, desired her passionately enough to endure the endless provocation, offer the endless patience that was her perquisite to possession.

They were all Serena. And, like Serena, they were restless in this seclusion, were meant to glow in the spotlights, bask in the dazzled admiration that their sheer perfection always commanded.

Write it. Serena's Song. Could he put her to music, capture that wayward, lawless, warm and passionate spirit with his notes? It would be the ultimate form of possession, the only fitting consummation for their relationship. And it would be played by the girl with flame-coloured hair and cold grey eyes, the first woman to have stirred his interest, however faintly, since the accident. There was a symmetry in the arrangement, he felt, a pleasingly unnatural triangle.

He could begin with his first memory of Serena, her warm husky laughter, a sound that teased the ears, teased the senses. What fingering to evoke the curve of her eyebrows, her smile, the million shades of midnight in her hair, the ambiguous amber of her eyes?

Six, he decided suddenly. Six climaxes, twice as many as Bach had given the *Chaconne*. He felt a new stirring. Something totally, outrageously different, something wild and daring and unconventional, like Serena. Six climaxes, six movements, each exploring a different Serena, each building to a peak of equal intensity. And each played on a different violin.

The change of instrument, unthinkable in concert unless for some technical flaw like a broken string, would be a master stroke of the avant-garde. Each violin has her own character, leaves an imprint on her player like a lover, ineffably shapes the music with her character. He would take six of his favourites, six of these sleeping sirens surrounding him, and let them evoke the sensual sphinx that was Serena.

Six sides of Serena. Six violins. Six climaxes.

He had never heard her moan in passion, cry out in release, knew instinctively that in this, as in all else, she must be different from other women. Did she seek oblivion in a furious, clawing frenzy, slashing and biting, fighting for release? Or was she quiet at the end, meeting the little death softly, welcoming it to the dark silence of her inner body?

It was a stirring, forbidden thought. They had decided long ago that they would never endanger their closeness with the ultimate act of intimacy, and he had never regretted it, knowing that he possessed her more completely by its absence than its fulfilment.

But to give her six climaxes, create six musical, orgasmic peaks, touch her by proxy of the strings, possess her so utterly by this act that she would be forever, indissolubly his . . . the thought was irresistible. It would be the ultimate penetration, impaling her with the notes, exploring her with the chords.

Could Franca learn to harness the sexual energy, transmute and transmit the voluptuous vitality, the searing lust, the orgiastic, orgasmic excitement that such a score would demand? A woman playing a woman evoking a woman – Franca, the violin and Serena – what intricate scenarios could they construct to create the physical reality that would translate to the music?

He pushed aside the thought as a distraction and seated himself at his desk.

She climaxed, finally, in a seething, surging torrent, her body writhing in ecstatic fulfilment, her eyes locked to the endlesss blue of his own, and cried aloud in pleasure.

But as the heady afterglow of orgasm suffused her body, filling her with a pleasant, hazy lassitude, she swam back slowly to full consciousness and recognised the empty expanse of cloudless sky.

The sky. Not Mika's eyes after all.

But that was the blue she had seen, hoped to see, needed to see . . . the electric blue of his eyes fixed on hers. As he thrust inside her, claimed her, mastered her, played Sibelius. Her master, her maestro, the enigmatic, black-gloved man who had roused the passion of the violin to unparalleled heights . . . and was rousing her, even in his absence.

A little dazed, she swallowed hard and blinked her eyes. Beside her, close enough to touch, lay Max and Serena. Serena was riding him in a graceful, pounding rhythm. Body replete but mind faintly disordered, Franca slipped away from the erotic tangle of limbs and walked towards the villa, absentmindedly scooping up the tangled black bikini at the side of the pool. The tactile awareness, the physical concentration that Serena had insisted upon as she led her through that voluptuary's voyage had resolved, at the very last moment, to the blue of Mika's eyes.

She had, she guessed, some vague understanding of what Mika had meant by becoming the violin, should, perhaps have realised sooner. But suddenly all her ambition was dissolving in one focused, driving, need. To see his eyes, warm with passion, blazing with desire, meet hers as he drove himself into her.

She accepted the thought calmly. It was as inevitable as the seasons, as the sun, predestined. Others, more jaded, less sophisticated, might have found a hundred or a thousand rationalisations. None of them would be true. She wanted him.

The terrace was deserted, the table bare, the remnants of the morning's feast cleared away by unseen hands. Only the yellow cat remained, basking in the sunshine. She bent down to stroke him, drawn to him as a familiar of Mika's, but drew her hand away at his warning hiss. Absurdly, she was rather hurt by the rejection.

Wondering whether to cover herself with the bikini, she peered through the door a little tentatively, but the hall was empty. Her feet grateful for the cool marble, she walked across to the ornate staircase, pausing at the carved doors of the music room.

He would be inside, she guessed, perhaps leafing through scores. He had promised to find her something to play, something different. He must have felt, must feel something for her to do so much. How strange to think of him alone, separated from her only by the barrier of those double doors, while she stood nude, hesitant . . . wanting him.

The palms of her hands had gone damp. Could she dare to go to him, open the doors and slip inside? 'Let yourself be led by Serena,' he had said. He must have known what would follow, the tormentingly slow arousal, the *adagissimo* anticipation building to a climactic *presto furioso*, must have expected her to submit to Serena's carnal choreography as willingly as she had submitted to his hands last night.

Instinct made her turn away to the stairs. Alone in her room, she examined herself thoughtfully in the mirror. Her skin was slick and shiny from the oil, her hair a flaming disarray, her body still flushed with the rosy aftermath of sex. Curiously, she touched her breasts, watched the nipples spring to hard points, immediately responsive. This is what he would see, the pink blush of her aureoles darkening to red, peaks tightening, demanding his mouth. He had never seen her fully nude, had touched her only through the barrier of silk and leather . . . this is what he would feel, the tender white warmth of her skin, the lush red satin of her nipple.

Her fingers were the bow, lightly tracing the strings of her nipples, just brushing the eager tips with a pointed nail that sent a thrilling vibration down her spine to her groin. Her hands slowed, remembering his words, remembering Serena's instructions.

'*Adagissimo.*'

With a slow, drugging rhythm she languorously fingered her nipples, watched the darkening hue of arousal flood the aureoles, and almost as if her body recognised a command physically imprinted on it, felt her hips rock ever so slightly to some unheard, half-remembered rhythm. This is what he would see, this is where his hands would linger.

124

The music was welling up, filling her breasts, swelling between her legs. She let her hands drift slowly down her belly, hands astonished at this new languor, and tentatively explored the flaming curls of her mound. She pictured his hands, those long, elegant fingers encased in black leather feathering through the hair, imagined the contrast of cool black leather meeting the fiery thatch, probing at her secret mouth, and found the thought unbearably exciting.

Inside she was wet, vibrating for a harder touch, his touch, but her hands were slow and lazy, laggard explorers, masters of rhythm and movement at the slowest tempo.

Idly, she circled her clitoris, freeing it from the swollen leaves of flesh, felt it swell and grow, resonate to the strange frequencies of her fingers, suddenly plucking *pizzicato*, then slowing to a measured beat. Hard and quivering, it pulsed with its own mad rhythm, hot and sure.

Her fingers were slick, glistening with the humid liquid of arousal. She was, suddenly, not violin, not harp, but an orchestra, strings and brass and percussion all at once, the throb of her clitoris an insistent drum beat increasing in tempo. Closing her eyes, she imagined Mika watching her, observing the graceful play of her hands, the enchantingly sensual symphony of her body. She wanted him to conduct this orchestra she had conjured, needed the hard baton filling her, ached for the heat of his mouth directing her, tasting her, sucking her to climax. The blue eyes watching her.

And with the image of his eyes fixed on hers, his mouth fixed on hers, she plucked her clitoris again and again, increasing the tempo until she felt herself begin to shake, throb with the first compelling convulsion, and gave herself over to the radiant explosion of orgasm.

Spent, he raised himself on one elbow to look at her. The pale gold of her skin was warmed by sex, the dark cloud of her hair mingling with the grass. Her breathing was regular and steady, her eyes closed. Asleep, or merely daydreaming, it was impossible to tell. He let his eyes wander over her, marvelling at the perfect contours of her breasts, the rosy nipples that had felt his mouth, the gently curved hips that had rocked beneath him in a sinuous, sensual rhythm. But the essential core of her had drawn away as if, at the physical separation of their bodies, she had retreated to some private refuge known only to herself.

He moved his eyes lower, lingering at the tender swell of her hips, the poetry of perfect legs sprawled in casual abandon. It was somehow incongruous that this woman, who belonged in silk sheets and candlelight, should look so natural, so right, so naked on the summer grass.

He had wanted her from the moment he had first set eyes on her, burned for her since he felt the wild and wanton force of her so long ago in Paris. Now he had finally recaptured the luscious, lascivious, exquisitely passionate creature who had tormented his dreams for so long.

No, not captured or recaptured, he acknowledged, grimly determined to face the truth. She had captivated him, recreated every wild moment they had shared, shown him new and unbearably exciting peaks, while still remaining aloof. Tenderly he smoothed away a stray tendril of ebony hair from her forehead, mesmerised by the delicate blue veins at her temples.

He wanted to bind her with chains, shower her with diamonds, keep her hidden and secluded in some private haven, away from the prying, desirous eyes of other men, wanted to flaunt her kaleidoscopic beauty to the world . . . wanted her.

He had hardly acknowledged to himself the faint hope that once he had her again, sated himself in her body, he might screw himself free of this gut wrenching, hollow persistent ache for her. Instead it had grown, expanded, found a limitless horizon of wanting. Wanting to hear her laugh, see her smile, listen to the sound of her voice. Wanting more than sex, wanting the surety of the next morning, wanting to kiss toast crumbs from her mouth, have her read aloud from the morning papers as he shaved – all the mundane, banal hopes that lovers are prey to, and Serena would despise. Obsession had become love?

He let his mind wander, recalling each heated encounter, each frenzied coupling they had shared since he arrived, finally reaching this last, most exotic, most erotic scene. In some strange way, Franca had heightened his awareness of Serena. She had become not surrogate, not substitute, but simulacrum.

With a start he realised her eyes were wide open, watching him. Careful not to betray himself, he said nothing, merely smiled and kissed her lightly on the lips, feeling her mouth soften into a smile beneath his own.

'Mmm, that was lovely, Max,' Serena purred. Sinuous as a cat, she flexed her body, then relaxed. 'Mika will be pleased.'

Male pride, male jealousy rebelled at her words. 'What does Mika have to do with this?' he asked, his voice level, unconcerned.

'Max, my dear, weren't you listening? You acted so perfectly, so well in tune that I thought . . . Are you serious?'

'What does Mika have to do with the two of us?' he persisted.

'With the two of us?' she repeated in surprise. 'Nothing. With the three of us . . . everything.' She stretched again. 'It's vital that Franca learns her sensual range, expands it, so that she can learn to channel and interpret. And tame as this beginning was, I think she did very well. Don't you?'

His brain stuttered, searching for a reply. He could, he realised, do nothing but agree unless he wished to betray himself, but he felt a nagging irritation at the base of his skull, a half-formed thought or feeling itching to be born. 'Yes, yes, of course Serena. Very well. Indeed.'

She stirred, lifted herself to sit cross-legged on the grass, and plucked absentmindedly at the grass. She could feel the tension in him, had seen his eyes widen at the word 'tame', could sense the hidden swirl of emotion he was trying to conceal.

Remembering the gentle touch of his hand as he smoothed away her hair while she feigned sleep, the unaccountably welcome touch of his lips as he kissed her, she was overcome with a swift resentment, a swift desire to shock him, rock him, shatter his persistent tenderness, his unfailing gentleness.

'As I said, lovely . . . but a bit tame. I feel in the mood for something a little more sophisticated. Join me?' Her eyes were taunting, daring.

Like some changeling she had transformed the warm mouth that had smiled under his kiss to a wicked red invitation, narrowed her amber eyes to sensual slits. Her words had been a challenge, a gauntlet thrown onto the soft green grass between them.

She was goading him, he realised, goading him for some obscure purpose of her own. As obsessed as he was, as infatuated, on the brink of love, he was nevertheless not completely stupid. It had to be a battle of more than bodies, he realised. He had to learn her, outwit her, delude her into wanting him for more, forever . . . How to accomplish it? He needed time.

'Later,' he said, reaching for her.

'Later?' Her voice was a mocking temptation, her eyes glinting dangerously.

'Later,' he repeated firmly. 'I'm hot—' he said, kissing the tip of her nose. 'Sweaty,' brushing back a stray strand of midnight hair, 'and I want a shower. And then lunch. And then I want you to show me around the villa. And then . . .' eyes close to hers, just brushing her mouth with his, 'I'm going to screw you blind, my darling.'

There was a moment of tension. He could see her

128

eyes, teetering on the verge of temper. 'I hadn't realised the house was so large,' he added casually. 'How old is it? And where does that lead to?' he added, gesturing to a flagstoned path leading away from the pool. One of her unlikely enthusiasms was architecture, or used to be. If only he could divert her long enough to puzzle things out. 'Sixteenth century?' he hazarded, releasing her and searching for his clothes.

'You must be joking,' she retorted.

For a brief moment his blood chilled, wondering if he had chosen the wrong tack.

'Have you even looked at the brickwork, the arches? The original core is late seventeenth, possibly, though I'm a bit dubious, and it was done over in the 1920s so lavishly that it's a nightmare. The entire hall was transported from a palace in Venice.'

With a certain amount of relief he stopped listening to the sense of her words, concentrating only on the tone of her voice as he slipped into his jeans.

'And the gardens are surprisingly lovely, very Victorian, a herb garden for the kitchen, a rose bower, then more formal arrangements leading to the stream that divides the property. We could have lunch in the rose garden, if you like,' she offered. The angry, feral heat that had coursed through her was muting to a dull warmth. It wasn't very smart of her to tease Max after he had performed so beautifully, she acknowledged, and unfair to challenge him in an arena where she excelled. Besides, they might need him.

She rose and slipped a companionable arm through his as they walked towards the villa.

An hour later, freshly showered and dressed in a casual, white Armani suit, Max was confident that he had pieced together the most important fragments of information and come up with a plausible interpretation. Mika's strictures on the physical properties of the violinist, Serena's offhand reference to the *Chaconne*, the murmured exchange between Franca and Serena as they had lain side by side, together all made a bizarre sort of sense. Expanding the sensual range, channelling the energy . . . they were trying to teach Franca to screw the violin. For a moment he paused, uncertain, momentarily dissatisfied with his conclusion. Creative screwing didn't create the unparalleled, ecstatic, electric effect that Mika had produced at his height, or half the musicians he had under contract would be doing as well, or better.

There had to be something more. Whatever that was, he reminded himself, was irrelevant. Mika was sufficiently interested in Franca to find her something to play, would help her, perhaps, to claim a piece for her own, as he had done with Bach. Now all Max needed was Franca's signature on an iron-clad contract and he could turn to the more provocative problem of Serena. He had made a mental note to call Sally and get her to fax a draft contract to the villa.

LONDON

Sally leaned back in the large black leather chair and negligently crossed her ankles, resting them on the edge of the desk. Across the smoky lake of glass that served as Max's desk, Eve was watching her patiently, a hint of mischief in her eyes. The huge video screen that dominated one wall showed a man playing the piano. He was young, no more than twenty, with high, Slavic cheekbones and a shock of brown hair artistically falling over his forehead. His hands were moving gracefully over the keyboard, caressing the keys with a light, deft, touch. The sound was turned off.

'He's lovely, isn't he?' purred Eve. 'Quite the most promising of the lot so far, I think. There's his biog,' she added, tapping a sheaf of papers with a long, curved nail.

'Mmm,' said Sally noncommittally, reaching for a cigarette. Since Max had left, she'd taken up smoking again, and hated herself for it.

'I think you should go and see him, Sally,' persisted Eve. 'He's young, he's eager, and like so many of these kids, stony broke. He's playing in one of the clubs up in Camden at the moment. Or—' she drew out the syllable far too long, 'I could have him brought here.'

'Eve, are you joking? And have everybody see him? Even if he is a nobody, it'll be obvious—' the indignant tones of her voice subsided at Eve's ripple of laughter.

'Just teasing, just teasing,' soothed Eve, a wicked smile curving her lips.

Nikolai was the third pianist she'd discovered whose playing created a sensual frisson down her spine, made the hair at the back of her neck tingle. Whether it was from the thrill of the hunt, the sure certainty that she was about to pull off the biggest coup of her career, or the power of his playing, she wasn't entirely sure. That's why she needed Sally who was, she acknowledged, more level-headed, more experienced.

It hadn't been all that difficult to coax Sally into this search for another musician, using the pretext that Max would be so grateful to have someone waiting in the wings if his plans with Franca fell through.

But she needed time. Time to exploit Disc-O's connections, time to work out all the finicky details, time to seduce Sally away from her absurd loyalty to Max . . . and time to find the star who would make her fortune. Not a violinist, however. She had no desire to enter into overt competition with Disc-O, wanted to break new ground.

'You know Eve, I'm not really sure about this,' said Sally, her voice breaking into Eve's thoughts. 'We still haven't assembled the short list for Max, which he'll need if Mika won't take Franca on, and that's certainly a possibility. And I'm not convinced that we should be looking for another soloist on another instrument so soon. I know you think that Max will be thrilled, but I'm not so sure.'

Eve smothered a smile. Sally still hadn't guessed her real motives. A testament either to Eve's subtlety or to the sensual web she'd woven around her. 'You're in charge,' Eve rejoined smoothly, sliding from her chair and moving around the desk. 'But look at his hands, the way they touch the keys,' she suggested persuasively. 'You can almost feel the Beethoven without hearing it.'

Idly she let her hand trail down the curve of Sally's arm, felt her shiver in response. She had led Sally so skilfully, so artfully, that her body was now immediately responsive to Eve's own, instinctively recognised the source of remembered pleasure. Even a casual, friendly, glancing touch had her skin heating, labia engorging, nipples puckering in anticipation.

'Watch his hands, Sally,' said Eve smoothly, gently removing Sally's legs from the desk and spreading her thighs apart with knowing fingers. Kneeling, she was pleased to see the brown swathe of hair, the pouting pink lips free of any concealing garment. She'd asked Sally only yesterday to come to the office naked under her clothes – 'So I can imagine you like that, all day, waiting for me' – and Sally had complied.

What to tease her with now, thought Eve idly, extending the tip of her tongue to the tiny bud of Sally's clitoris. The day before Eve had tantalised her with a screaming climax brought on only by the repeated, relentless, rapacious sucking of her nipples, denying them both any other stimulation for hours until seething frustration turned to orgasm. Nothing so protracted, nothing so prolonged, at least not in office hours, she cautioned herself.

'You see,' she said, leisurely lapping aside the protecting swathe of hair, 'I think it would be a fabulous idea if you and I were to meet Nikolai, and perhaps the other two as well. We can compare them for technique, stage presence, all that sort of thing.'

Sally watched the screen, unbearably conscious of the platinum head between her thighs, the warm, moist pressure of Eve's tongue insinuating itself between her legs, exploring the deep valley of pleasure.

132

She was open, glistening and aroused. With diabolical slowness Eve traced the plump pink folds of her sex with her tongue, found the expectant, quivering clitoris and kissed it gently.

'I'd really like your opinion,' Eve continued, licking the tiny bud that firmed under her tongue, bathing it in monotonous, lascivious strokes while titillating the entrance to her vagina with one finger.

Tentatively, tenderly, Sally ran her fingers through Eve's hair, searching for the nape of her neck to press her closer to the centre of her pleasure, remembering how not so long ago she herself had knelt before this very chair, had taken Max's huge organ in her mouth as he watched Serena captured on the video screen. Her fingers tightened, suddenly urgent. Eve had taken her sex in her mouth, was now gently suckling the tiny bud that stretched and engorged, now abandoning it to trace the furrow, now returning to suck her with increased intensity.

Sally was rising, arcing towards the molten explosion, lava boiling through her veins, filling her groin, trembling on the verge of a massive eruption. The finger tantalising her entrance slipped inside, searching the inner walls, probing, finding the magical, mysterious point that yielded pleasure so intense it was almost pain.

The demanding ache in her limbs was growing, increasing with every moist stroke of Eve's tongue, and she found herself rising to meet it even as she pressed Eve's head more firmly against her. Trembling, she felt the first warm shudders ripple through her vagina, her inner walls suddenly clenching the slim finger with desperate strength, the humid flow of her body's juices escaping. Eve's mouth was greedy, avid, voraciously drinking her in wild, hungry draughts. And just when she thought she would go mad with the pleasure shooting through her, the furious intensity of Eve's mouth, the frenzied friction of Eve's finger driving her to mindless, helpless writhing, she exploded in rapture, her body shaking uncontrollably with the force of her climax.

Kneeling before her, Eve was caught in a frantic turmoil of shaking limbs, spasming muscles and thrashing pelvis as Sally came in her mouth, sobbing out her pleasure. And even when her limbs stilled, the trembling subsiding to a weary lassitude, Eve continued the hungry play of her mouth, plunging her tongue into the slick wet opening, teasing and fondling the quivering clitoris with her teeth until Sally came again in a sweet, shuddering flurry.

Still kneeling, she looked up to see Sally, eyes half-closed, dazed and sated. 'Soon, then?' she asked softly.

'Soon?' repeated Sally, uncomprehending.

'Nikolai,' Eve reminded her, mind moving ahead. In a burst of inspiration, she added, 'We could meet him at Max's penthouse. It is business, after all.'

She felt Sally stiffen, and bent her head again, lovingly licking the plump folds clean of her juices, as assiduously and imperturbably as a mother cat with a kitten. 'Yes?' she prompted.

'Yes, Eve,' replied Sally, helpless under the tender stroking. 'Yes.'

Satisfied, Eve got to her feet, her body humming pleasurably. Mildly aroused by the depth of Sally's response, the smoky flavour of sex in her mouth, the sensuous feel of Sally's body as it convulsed, she was still in control, not yet prepared to hazard an advantage by having Sally pleasure her in turn. That would come later. Something to look forward to, after she had achieved her own ends.

Clever of her, really, she mused, to have thought of kneeling before Sally as patiently and submissively as Sally herself had knelt before Max. It should sharpen Sally's ambition a little, give her a little more confidence. Because of all the people Eve was planning to lure away from Disc-O, Sally was the key figure. That Sally was more than half in love with Max was obvious, jealous of his obsession with Serena, but still resolutely

134

loyal to his interests. Strange, really. She could play on that a little, Eve decided, crossing the room and turning off the video.

'So, what's the news from Geneva? Have you heard from Max yet?' she enquired casually, fiddling with the tape.

'No, he hasn't called in,' Sally said, stretching and then relaxing back in the depths of his executive chair. 'Odd, really. He's been gone, what? at least three days now. It's not like him not to report in.'

'Too busy screwing Serena, no doubt,' retorted Eve, deliberately crude, waiting for the shadow to cross Sally's face.

'Mika's there too, don't forget,' retorted Sally with a frown. 'And Franca. I'm sure that . . . that Max is probably involved in some rather delicate negotiations. These things take time. And Mika's never been that easy to deal with.'

'What really did happen to his hands?' asked Eve with studied casualness.

'I don't know,' replied Sally slowly. 'I'm not even sure that Max does, to tell you the truth. It was a car accident, I think, but the details were never made public. He was scheduled to do a concert in Milan. He'd taken a few days off to drive along the Amalfi coast. We heard nothing until Serena called and told Max to cancel the concert. No reason, no explanation. Max had to fly to Milan, sort out the mess. It was awful. It was about three months before you started here, wasn't it?

'About that,' agreed Eve. 'I was still in New York then. I imagine Max must have been a tremendous help to Serena,' she added slyly. 'Mika in hospital, his career shattered . . . she must have needed someone to lean on.'

'No, that's the strange thing. He couldn't find a trace of them. They just disappeared. It was months before we heard from her.'

GENEVA

Lunch had been laid out in the rose garden. The heavy perfume of a thousand varieties of rose scented the air, not quite overpowering the more subtle fragrance of smoked salmon and dill. Serena, wearing a white sundress with a tight bodice that bared her shoulders and a flowing skirt that almost touched the ground, was plucking the heads of fading blooms as Max paused at the trellised entrance. She looked absurdly young and impossibly romantic with her flowing skirts, her hair in a casual knot from which a few loose tendrils had artfully escaped.

Without turning around, she said, 'As you requested, Max. There's cold chicken, asparagus, some smoked salmon, and a lovely bottle of local wine. I'll just fetch Franca.'

'No, don't bother, Serena,' he replied, slowly entering the garden. 'I saw her just now. She won't be joining us.' The dreamy, languorous creature who had greeted him when he knocked on her door had dismissed the notion of food with a wave of her hand, her eyes far-away. Just as she had dismissed his attempts to discuss business, contracts and percentages. Irritation had replaced any lingering tenderness left on his part from the sensual fantasy they had shared with Serena: Max was back on track, hard-headed, hard-nosed, and ready to deal.

'Is she all right?' asked Serena swiftly, turning to face him with an expression of concern on her face.

'She's fine,' he replied shortly, trying not to reveal his annoyance. 'Just not hungry.' In both senses of the word, he realised. What had happened to the hard-edged, ambitious girl with cold grey eyes whose only driving desire was to be the best in the world? She should have been avid to discuss the contract, claw concessions and barter for better terms. Instead she had merely smiled dreamily.

'I'll have Maddie send a tray up to her later,' said

Serena, seating herself at the table and gesturing to the chair opposite.

'What about Mika?' Max said, warily watching her open the wine, hoping it was better than the dreadful stuff she had served the night he arrived.

'In the music room, I expect,' she replied offhandedly. 'I seldom see him during the day anyway. He always has morning coffee on the terrace, but after that he usually goes to the music room. We sometimes have dinner together.'

'Lonely for you,' he commented, settling back in his chair, watching her pour thick yellow wine into two glasses. 'How do you pass the time?'

A small smile tugged at her lips as she framed her reply. In the beginning there was Hans, she remembered. She'd turned to him in a raw and desperate fury, needing some distraction, any distraction from the pain of Mika's injury, the collapse of his career, the silent icy shell he had become. It was with Hans, under the guise of sex, that she could scream her fury, vent all her frustration, lash the uncaring fates. And what an accommodating whipping boy he had been, loving the slashing arc of leather as it whistled through the air, loving the white-hot pleasure-pain that reverberated with each blow. She had discovered then a dark side to her nature that she had never truly suspected, a penchant for pain, a cold voluptuous appreciation that verged almost on sadism.

Slightly horrified by the discovery, she had dismissed him before she could harm either of them, replaced him with a gentle Asian boy whose name, she realised, she had completely forgotten. But his skin, warm, golden, hairless, faintly scented with sandalwood . . . how well she remembered his skin. His body, lithe and slender, supple as a girl's, had entranced her, and she had spent hours admiring it with her fingers, with her mouth, relishing the almost androgynous feel of soft silken skin free of any body hair except the dense, curling bush around his groin.

As if to atone for the furious, frenzied violence she had shared with Hans, she had been gentle with him, tender and considerate, solicitous of his desire, sensitive to his needs. It had palled, soon enough.

'Serena?'

'Pass the time? This and that,' she replied. 'A bit of gardening, listening to music . . .' remembering the intricate scenarios she had constructed with Mika which roused the heavy, delicious ache between her thighs 'and then I read a lot.' Exploring for the first time the classics of erotic literature from De Sade to D. H. Lawrence, from the *Kama Sutra* to *Cleland*, she had briefly experimented with recreating the fictional scenes she had most admired but found herself unable to comply with the regimentation of scripted eroticism. Always she had discovered some delightful variation, some intriguing deviation to enhance her pleasure. It was no use, she reflected, shaking her head. She simply couldn't follow rules, even ones she established herself.

'I never knew that,' said Max, intensely curious. It was a side of her he had never suspected. 'What have you been reading?'

'Poetry,' said Serena, a little at random. And she had immersed herself in love poetry for a while, Shakespeare, Donne, even reviving her rusty Latin to read Catullus in the original. She had found him more passionate, more perverse than she remembered, more vibrant. She had felt a certain affinity with that Roman poet, felt instinctively that they would have recognised each other. That he would have known her. '"In wind and running water", Max. Some chicken?'

Apparently not recognising the quotation, he silently helped himself from the platter she offered him.

Thoughtfully, she sipped her wine. A woman's words ought to be written in wind and running water, Catullus had written scornfully, maddened by the sly provocations of his mistress. It was as much of a warning as she would give him. Deftly, she diverted the conversation along other lines, asking Max about the London music scene, the newest jazz clubs, the latest trends.

He replied easily, watching the graceful play of her hands as they hovered over the asparagus, long elegant fingers reaching for one of the tempting green stalks, then hesitating between bowls of vinaigrette and mayonnaise. She ate with a fastidious greed that fascinated him, casually tossing a woody stalk of asparagus on the grass at her feet, gnawing on a chicken bone with pointed, little white teeth. She ignored the heavy silver cutlery and used her hands, licking mayonnaise from her fingers with a childlike enjoyment.

She ate far more than he did, even taking a second bowlful of strawberries and lemon, which he, regretfully, had to refuse. Finally replete, they shared a comfortable silence while Max smoked a small cigar simply to prolong the pleasure of watching her bask in the sunshine, surrounded by roses.

The afternoon was simply too perfect to mar with business, he decided, aware that the sensual delight of observing her was eroding his earlier determination, though he would have to broach the subject soon. Mika surely couldn't be expecting a fee for his involvement with Franca? Max thought, fleetingly returning to Mika's parting remark about 'tiresome business details', shorthand for money in his lexicon.

That Serena had been the driving force behind the incredible contract Max had eventually been forced to offer Mika he had no doubt, though she had played a shadowy role. He hadn't even met her then, he realised. Mika had little interest in money, it seemed, allied to a positive genius for spending it, never failing to unearth some antique treasure of a violin or bow that he simply had to possess, while Serena seemed largely indifferent to material things . . . or was it merely that she took them for granted?

He knew almost nothing about the raven-haired woman before him, he realised with a shock of surprise, was barely acquainted with her even though he had shared the secrets of her body so intimately and had wanted her so intensely for so long. Gardening, architecture, music, poetry . . . they seemed such solitary, isolated pursuits for someone as lusty, as uninhibited as he knew her to be.

Over lunch she had been graceful, amusing, the taunting devil that had dared him to join her in more sophisticated couplings submerged in an elegant, witty companion who spoke knowledgeably about jazz and devoured her food like some half-starved street urchin, letting the strawberry juice run down her chin while she reached for her wineglass with sticky fingers.

He had promised to screw her blind in a moment of cornered bravado, he acknowledged to himself, wondering how he could have been so rash, so confident. But there was no erotic charge to her silence now, nothing in the pose of her body to suggest that she even remembered the uneasy bargain they had struck beside the pool.

'You wanted to see the villa, Max?' she asked, stretching and then rising from her chair. 'Why don't we do the inside first, and then come back here and I'll show you the gardens. It'll be cooler inside.'

Already absorbed, she accepted his hand unthinkingly as she described the plan of the villa, differentiating between the original core and successive restorations and additions with the air of an expert. As she led him through room after room, pointing out incongruities and interesting features, he lost the thread of her words in a gradual but overpowering awareness of her every move, the sensual caress of her fingers on carved wood as she described the staircase, the lingering mockery of her laugh as she disdained some Victorian fakery.

As she walked beside him, her skirt almost trailing on the ground, he imagined her legs, smooth and golden beneath the crisp white cotton, the softly rounded curve of her belly. He knew instinctively that she was naked beneath her dress, wore no flimsy scrap of lace or silk to protect her mound. And as she paused before the great carved doors of the music room he pictured her sex, the petals of her labia as lush and velvety and perfect as any of the roses in the bower.

'We can't go in, of course, as Mika's working,' she was saying, 'but it's quite lavish, temperature-controlled for the collection, of course, and all the latest stereo and recording equipment. These doors, however, are really quite interesting. Some exotic hardwood, and originally probably part of a much larger work, a screen or something. The craftsmanship is superb, and from the motifs – you see the acanthus there? and the lotus? – I imagine it must be Chinese, perhaps eighteenth century.'

She was bending forwards from the waist, intent on tracing some leafy pattern, and beneath her dress he could almost see the smooth globes of her buttocks, ripely inviting, made for his hands. Mouth suddenly dry, he knew how he would take her, how he wanted her. He let the smooth litany of her words wash over him, savouring the sound of her voice and the sure and certain knowledge that he could, that he would surprise her into orgasm.

As they toured the vast villa, exploring the network of passages that expanded from the central core, rooms that led into rooms in a bewildering labyrinth, the wine cellars sunk deep into the ground, and as he examined the thick slabs of interlocking stone that Serena pointed out as particularly significant, he kept her close, using any pretext to touch her, any excuse that offered itself.

Peering over her shoulder to look more closely, he breathed in the scent of her hair, apparently absent-mindedly fingering the nape of her neck. Taking her arm in his as they walked up the heavy stone stairs to the kitchen he caressed the sensitive inner skin just below her elbow as he questioned some feature of design that seemed to interest her, having no interest at all in her answer, relishing only the sound of her voice as she replied. And he could feel her body responding, becoming a little more pliant, a little less aloof, a little less hers alone. Was she aware of his hand resting lightly at her waist as she pointed to the skylight, his fingers sliding gently down her arm as they walked through the kitchen into the herb garden?

'Delightfully old-fashioned, with thyme and verbena, sage and mint. Maddie was thrilled when she saw it. And if you go through here,' she said, gesturing to a sculpted opening in a thick hedge, 'you're back in the rose garden.'

That was where he had to have her, Max realised, in the rose garden, surrounded by the plush perfume of roses whose velvety petals reminded him of the rosy leaves of her sex, where the heady, intoxicating scent of roses and Serena could intermingle, sheltered from the villa and enclosed in a private, sweet smelling bower.

Giving himself no time to think, he reached out for her, pulled her half-laughing, half-protesting through the carved greenery to the rose garden, drew her down to the grass and urged her onto her side with insistent hands. She gave a low laugh as he lifted her skirt to her waist and twisted to face him, but he held her still with one hand on her belly as he fumbled with his fly. Feeling for his organ, he was relieved to find himself barely tumescent, and nudged himself between her buttocks, questing for the taut opening. He slipped in easily, feeling only a slight protest from the tight muscles of her back passage. He kept one hand curled protectively around her shoulder, the other splayed across her belly to keep her still.

Settling back against the hard length of his chest she could feel the dull thud of his heart against her back, the heat of the sun on her face. She wriggled slightly, arranging herself more comfortably, and felt him ripple inside her, growing and stiffening, pulsing against the tight walls of her anus, testing the channel that sheathed him. Conscious of his touch as she had led

142

him through the villa, she hadn't read the intent in his eyes.

He would have to withdraw soon, he knew, or risk hurting her with his full length, too massive for her to sustain this way without pain, but he was unwilling to move just yet. He concentrated, determined to remain semi-erect, wanting to relish the intimacy of this new penetration. He felt for her hand and brought it to his lips, forcing himself to admire the fine tracery of blue veins at the inside of her wrist, the slim elegance of her fingers. The skin of her inner arm was pale, almost translucent, and he imagined the blood flowing through her veins. With the tip of his tongue he traced the course of one vein, following it from her wrist to the fleshy pad below her thumb, then drew her thumb into his mouth, sucking it as gently as an infant.

She moved against him lazily, relaxing to the comfortable, moist embrace of his mouth enveloping her thumb, the warm pressure of his rod now thickening even further, the drowsy hum of bees now kissing the roses. His mouth was moving, releasing her thumb, tracing the path to her index finger, enclosing it with his lips and bathing it with the warmth of his tongue. She was barely conscious of feeling stretched, the delicate tissues surrounding him responding to his hardness, a supple, melting warmth in the pit of her belly.

So intensely attuned was he to her every breath, every movement, that he felt the quiver that ran through her, a quiver so slight she might even have been unaware of it, like an electric jolt. Releasing his finger he bit his lip sharply, drawing blood, trying to distract the growing excitement of his shaft with the pain. He was hardening now, starting to reach his full length in this delicate sheath far too small to hold him, fighting against the primitive commands of his body to find the friction, the pounding rhythm that would ignite the explosion curling at the base of his spine.

Sweat beading his brow, he sought her ring finger

with his mouth, traced the contour of her nail with his teeth, furiously trying to distract himself from the heating demands of his body. She wore no rings, ever, he thought distractedly, no jewellery apart from the heavy gold chain around her neck. He would change that, find yellow diamonds for her fingers, with icy, shimmering depths to reflect the fiery brillance of her eyes, and topazes, and amber. He felt his concentration harden as he began to master himself. Pearls for the golden lustre of her skin, a long, long strand that he would trail down her body, drape along the alabaster apex of her thighs, push with gentle insistence into the velvety valley between her legs. He could see them already, gleaming pearls warm and glistening from the perfumed musk of her body, shining white in the ruby enclave of her hidden mouth.

Despite himself, he was hardening further. Resolutely he forced his mind away from the enticing, erotic image of Serena in pearls and tried to concentrate, searching for something to deaden his increasing arousal. He had to control himself, had to tame the insistent, aching need that was thickening his shaft. Tame. The word she had used to describe the most exotic, most erotic encounter he'd ever experienced. Involuntarily he rocked his hips just slightly, driving himself further into her, cursing himself for his weakness. He had to tame her, had to keep her, had to master her. Mindlessly his mouth moved to her little finger, drawing it in deep and sucking with a blind, driving need.

Pleasure caught her unprepared, slamming through her veins, fisting through her muscles, arcing, engorging and exploding her in a cataclysmic fury. For one brief moment she clawed for detachment, the aloof, amused reserve that she cloaked herself with, but the searing, boiling maelstrom of orgasm claimed her, sucking her down, stiffening her spine, clenching her muscles. She screamed once, in heated denial, then lost herself in the electric frenzy shuddering through her body, the encompassing, unpredictable explosion, desperately thrusting against him, arching to encompass his hardness.

He forced himself to stay still as she surged around him in a silken torrent, tried to force himself to ignore the maddening torment of her buttocks grinding against him, could no longer check the clamouring demands of his rod buried deep inside her and felt himself engorge to full arousal.

Ecstasy knifed through her, an overflowing, overwhelming crescendo electrifying every cell of her body, saturating and suffusing her. She was helpless, drowning in the torrential flood of the storming climax.

Fear feathered his spine, fear that he had hurt her with the invasion of his full length, but the cry that reached his ears was not a cry of pain. It was a full, keening, moaning scream of utter pleasure. He gave a low, triumphant laugh as he eased himself out to find her other entrance, the moist cocoon pliant to his shaft, and drove himself into her. He let the frantic urgings of his body master him then, pounding himself faster and deeper into her until he too climaxed, shaking and shuddering in release.

She waited until his rasping breathing had subsided a little to a regular, rhythmic murmur and then disengaged herself, rising to her feet and letting her skirt fall around her ankles. Disinclined to speak, a little dazed by her own reaction, she extended a hand to Max, still lying on the grass. He kissed it gently, then released it as he got to his feet and arranged his clothing. They returned to the villa in silence, Serena walking a few paces ahead of him.

Later, much later, when the light had thickened and then dimmed, and the gibbous August moon had risen, bathing the rose garden with a spectral haze, he came for her as she slept. She was nude, as he had known she would be, and he paused beside her bed to look at her, feasting greedy eyes on naked curves illuminated by moonlight. She barely stirred as he leaned over her, passed the vial of sweet smelling hypnotic fluid beneath her nostrils.

Her breathing deepened almost imperceptibly. He nodded once in satisfaction, then gathered her in his arms. He was hardly aware of her weight as he ran lightly down the staircase and through to the kitchen, down the massive stone steps leading to the wine cellars. It had been a dungeon, once, he had heard her say, and the idea pleased him.

Chapter Seven

Rehearsing

Mika leaned back in his chair and felt a faint twinge of protest in his shoulder muscles. Crossing his arms behind his neck he gave a long, shuddering sigh. Dawn light, soft and pale, was just beginning to filter through the window. He had been working almost ceaselessly since yesterday. Almost twenty hours and he had completed nearly twenty pages of manuscript. Perhaps ten minutes' music, possibly a bit more.

It had come with breathtaking speed, music soaring from his imagination, searing the page, the colours, the textures, the contrasting shadows. The skeleton of the work was perfectly formed in his mind, the hard white bones of exposition and development, recapitulation and coda, the fundamental elements waiting to be transformed into living flesh. He could see the final, aching frenzy of the ultimate climax, almost feel his nerves shivering in anticipation of capturing the intense and seamless scream with his notes. Absent-mindedly he caressed the page in front of him.

The first movement was a flirtation, a teasing, provocative and evocative. He had decided to call it *The Kiss* and had abandoned, for the moment, the idea of six equal climaxes. This was the first stirring of desire, the sideways glance, the touch that lingers a suggestive second too long before slipping away, the prelude to intimacy, the moment when two mouths hover uncertainly before meeting. The climax was the kiss, he decided, a warm and tentative exploration of lips and tongue, bow and strings, with just the merest hint of teeth. He knew exactly how it needed to be played, the capricious supplication, the sweetly hypnotic stroke of tongue against tongue, bow against strings.

It was pink warming to rose shading to red, lips blushing and swelling, nipples hardening under silk, unseen, untouched, the first quivers of response.

He stretched to ease a knot in his neck and rose from his desk, still concentrating on the kiss. Technically it was well within her range, with none of the virtuosic demands, the double stoppings, harmonics and left hand pizzicato that would dominate the fourth. In some perverse way that might well make it more difficult for her, he realised. She would have to etch it with desire, allow her soul to colour the music, summon the deep reserves of passion and allow them to infuse the strings without relying on the cold brilliance of her flawless technique.

Still deep in thought he crossed the room and opened the double doors leading to the hall, idly wondering whether Serena had coaxed some response from her, encouraged the fundamental physical receptiveness.

Her. She. Francesca. Franca.

It was so different from the old days, when he and Serena would spend hours talking through the music, exploring the sensations, setting the stage, designing the complicated and intricate scenarios that he used to rehearse. He had, he realised, no real idea of how to continue, apply the lessons they had learned together. Yet still he was aware of a growing confidence, an inner conviction that was gradually soothing and suppressing his doubts.

He made his way to the terrace, suddenly eager for the freshly brewed coffee Maddie would have waiting for him, the plump and perfect croissants. It was a ritual he had established shortly after convalescing, to have his coffee on the terrace, enjoying the morning sunshine, the morning sky, in peaceful solitude. Serena would join him later, mindful of his privacy, respecting his wish to begin the day alone.

So accustomed was he to this established routine that he had already taken his seat, poured a cup of steaming black coffee into a heavy white pottery mug and reached out a hand to feel for Midas, always prowling round the terrace at this hour, before he noticed her.

She had drawn one of the chairs away from the table and was sitting motionless, long legs encased in skin-tight jeans stretched out in front of her. Her feet were bare. A loose white shirt with sleeves rolled to the elbow but buttoned demurely to her collar bone. Her hair was unbound, a coppery red stream flowing around her shoulders. She was waiting, poised, serene but wary, looking at him with changeable grey eyes that darkened at his stare.

A nameless, blind, roaring surged through him as he met her eyes, a hot writhing anger that she, that anyone, had dared to intrude and sully his private horizon, and at the same time he was aware of something else coiling softly in the pit of his belly, stirring languidly like a drowsy snake. With deliberate slowness he brought the mug to his lips and sipped his coffee, concentrating on the bitter, savoury, smoky flavour, willing his reactions to subside. She had, as yet, not uttered a word, for which he was grateful.

Instinct kept her silent and motionless, waiting for him to speak. It was enough this morning simply to be near him, feel his presence. She let the silence grow and watched the light change, the muted pale wash of dawn sharpening and thickening, acutely conscious of his every move, his every breath.

In some strange way she felt suspended, almost lightheaded, intoxicated by the mere proximity of his body. Conscious thought, rational reflection played no

149

part in her actions. Somehow he had changed her, altered her, and she was content to wait, let the transformation he had wrought unfold gradually.

Midas arrived, stalking up the steps that led to the pool like an actor making a stage entrance from the wings, paused for a moment, apparently surprised by his audience, then growled at Franca, a low strangled howl of surprised outrage.

The sound reflected his own emotions so perfectly, so graphically, that Mika was surprised into a laugh. 'He's rather jealous of my privacy,' he explained, finishing his coffee and pouring himself a second cup. After a moment's hesitation, he poured a cup for her.

A faint smile curved her lips, but she said nothing, let her glance move away to the vista beyond the terrace to the seamless blue of the pool, its surface reflecting the sky. The sound of his voice, rich and warm, was a caress in itself

'Coffee?' he offered finally, gesturing to the cup he had filled.

She shrugged slightly, made an idle gesture with one hand, perhaps indicating disinterest, perhaps merely acknowledging his words.

But his attention was caught by the sight of her hand, the long, elegant fingers, the slim wrist. It was a musician's hand, supple and sensitive.

'I've been working on something,' he said abruptly. 'Something that might suit you.' Her eyes now fixed on his face, he saw the grey eyes widen, her body tense. 'I shall be curious to see what you make of it.'

Excitement flooded through her, a tide of anticipation. 'When will you show it to me?' she asked softly, tentatively.

'Now, if you like.'

'Please.'

'Drink your coffee,' he said, rising from the table and disappearing inside the villa. Suddenly awkward, almost gawky, she rose and scraped her chair closer to the table. She was trembling, grateful for the almost

150

bitter brew that scalded her lips. She took a deep breath, and then another, trying to tame and channel the nervous thrills clawing her spine. It was the same before any concert, the tingling sensation close to panic, senses heightened, nerves scraping.

He returned almost at once, bearing a sheaf of densely annotated manuscript which he set beside her. Quickly she immersed herself in the score, experienced eyes scanning the pages, pausing now and then to reread a passage. He was amused to see her unconsciously flexing her fingers tilting her head, mentally playing the music. She frowned, the dark, slashing arcs of her eyebrows almost meeting, then shook her head. When she lifted her head, her eyes were puzzled but her voice was sincere.

'But it's lovely,' she cried. 'So simple, so clear. Not difficult at all!'

'No?' he inquired smoothly. Her eagerness was charming, if a little rash. 'Perhaps you would care to try it then?'

'Oh, yes! Very much!'

Two hours later, hot, sweating, in the throes of a frustration so acute it was almost sexual, the muscles in her arm beginning to tremble from rage as much as strain, she placed her bow with clinical anger on the music stand and wheeled round on him.

'Damn you! It's impossible! It's simply not there!'

'Again.' His voice was level, unconcerned.

'The hell I will!'

'The hell you won't,' he corrected, smiling a little. 'Again.'

'There's no point!' she exclaimed furiously. 'I don't know what you want, what you see. I've played it perfectly, and you damn well know it!'

'It's not a kiss,' he said, still patiently. 'You're not kissing the music, making the strings make the kiss.'

Angrily she wiped her forehead, brushing aside stray wisps of hair that had turned to curls in the heat of her exertion. He was sitting casually relaxed in one of the deep black leather chairs, a small smile playing around his lips.

Bastard! she fumed to herself. Sadist! Asshole! Any reverence for the power of his genius, any physical glow from the power of his presence had dissolved in the gruelling torture of playing for him, the tortuous agony of every attempt being met with a small shake of the head, a simple command. 'Again.' Her control was slipping, finally, and she was losing any vestige of concentration.

'Didn't Serena show you anything?' he asked, fishing a little. He had suspected *The Kiss* might be too deceptively simple, too achingly close to the bone. He had no way of knowing what she might have experienced at Serena's hands, knew only that it would have, should have, loosened the inhibiting coils just a little. Still, he reminded himself, Serena had been working without a theme.

'This is a kiss,' he repeated.

She didn't respond, merely looked at him with narrowed eyes.

'A kiss. The first tentative stirrings of attraction, of desire. The sly moment when you first consider the curve of another's lips, wondering how they'll respond to yours, soft or hard, practised, inexperienced, whatever. It's a haunting moment in any relationship, the first kiss.'

'It's usually the first fuck I go by, personally,' she said bitingly.

'So much is obvious from your interpretation,' he returned smoothly. 'Again.' Perhaps with repeated effort she might capture the effect he wanted. He could feel her simmering just below the surface, knew that she was capable of suffusing the music with the heady, potent, elusive romanticism he envisaged, sensed also that she was close to losing her temper.

'Show me,' she challenged, eyes almost black with suppressed fury. 'Why don't you show me?'

And that was when the drowsy snake in his belly stirred a little, loosened its coils just fractionally, raised a somnolent head. Her anger was warming him, even enticing him a little. From his chair he could sense the heat of her body, the electricity of her frustration. Her eyes were spitting rage. He remembered seeing her photograph for the first time, how she had summoned the image of Vivaldi's *Autumn* with eyebrows that belonged to Ravel, and found himself rising from his chair.

He hesitated for a moment, closing his eyes, forcing himself to concentrate. The score. Only the score mattered. The kiss. The soft searching, tender and tentative.

Even lost in anger, she was aware of the change in him, a deliberate focusing and pooling of energy. Eyes still closed, he shuddered faintly, as though gripped by some kinetic surge.

And then he was walking towards her, stopping a calculated arm's length away, eyes rapt and intent. She had the curious sensation that he was looking through her, past her.

'It begins here,' he said, just gently touching the curve of her lips with a black-gloved finger, 'and here,' a glancing, light caress at her nipple, a touch so delicate, so fragile, so graceful she wondered a second later whether she had felt it at all, 'and here,' the merest whisper against her belly.

'Franca.' His voice was low, persuasive, coaxing. 'Close your eyes and think of the kiss.' He moved nearer then, so close he was almost touching her with his body.

'The kiss,' she retorted, in a tone meant to be sarcastic and biting, but it changed to a gasp as she felt his hands cup her face, fingers gently stroking the curve of her cheeks.

'When a man wants a woman, wonders if he wants a woman, he kisses her first with his eyes, tests the texture of her skin, the contours of her mouth,' moving

153

a finger to her full lower lip, gently pressing it against her teeth, 'the feel of her hair.'

And his hands were moving through the fiery silken mane, stroking her skull with skilful fingers. She felt herself relaxing to his touch, growing smooth and pliant, relaxing to the dark honey of his voice. Hypnotic and compelling, he was changing the notes of the score to the pure poetry of desire.

'Kissing your body with my eyes, tasting you in my mind, licking you with my eyes, exploring you.' His hands were moving to her shoulders, down her arms, so impossibly lightly that it was as if he was caressing the white cotton of her shirt, a sensation somehow more intimate, more erotic than if he had touched her skin. She could feel the hair on her arms rising, her skin tingling.

'Wondering what lies beneath, conjuring your breasts in my mind, sucking them with my eyes, feeling your nipples harden to the touch of my imagination.' Leisurely he retraced the path he had taken, moving his hands up from her elbow to the shoulder, hovering at her collar-bone then descending to the points of her breasts. His touch, so deliciously delicate, so achingly faint was enchanting her body, melting it to liquid. He had barely touched the soft cotton over her breasts but her nipples were hard, aching points, avid for his mouth, greedy for his teeth. She was moist, a swelling heat growing between her legs: a prelude to the hot, rushing wetness of utter arousal.

'Teasing you just a little, daring you.' His hands were moving lower, flirting almost imperceptibly with the zipper of her jeans, moving lower to the swell of her mound. She was ripening under his touch, flesh engorging, the juices of her arousal now thick and sweet.

'Tonguing you with my eyes, finding the curves your clothes conceal, wondering how you will taste when I finally lick you.' Lightly he ran his hands along the swell of hips, the curve of her buttocks, one provocative finger trailing along the cleft defined so brazenly by the tight fabric of her jeans, then slipping gently away to trace the taut line of her thigh, the slender length of calf. He was kneeling before her now, head level with her belly, mouth so close she could almost feel his breath, voice so soft she had to strain to hear his words.

'Screwing you with my eyes before I kiss you with my mouth.'

Caught, trapped, in thrall to his words and his hands, she felt an ecstatic shiver ripple through her, centring in her groin, an abandoned luxury of sheer sensation. She felt a sudden impulse to reach out and touch him, draw his head between her thighs, knowing that the mere reverberation of the rich ice of his voice against her sex would be enough to make her come instantly. But almost as if he read her mind, he rose and captured her hands in his.

Their lips were almost touching. She could sense the heat of his body, smell the sharp, irresistible, musky smell of him that made her mouth grow dry.

'All those things in a single glance, a kiss of a look.'

Body hot, sex fervent, she felt herself poising on the edge, ready to fall, inflamed and aflame. She wanted, needed, was ready to scream for the supple black leather finger poised at her entrance, barely touching, igniting the cleansing explosion of orgasm. His mouth was so close that she knew that the first touch of his lips against hers, the first tender probing of his tongue would have exactly the same effect.

She was shivering a little with the sheer physical intensity, he noticed, cheeks flushed and breathing rapid.

'Do you understand, Franca? The kiss,' said Mika.

'Yes,' she murmured, aching for it, waiting for it.

'Excellent. Try that for the first six bars.'

'You utter, despicable bastard!' Her eyes snapped open in surprised rage.

155

He smiled a little ironically, walked across the room and sat down. 'Again.'

Seething with frustration she took the bow with trembling fingers.

'Begin.' Mika lounged back in his chair and closed his eyes wearily, absentmindedly running his fingers through his hair. Damn the girl! She was attacking the first movement like a lioness mauling a raw piece of meat! And she knew it, too. Well, he'd allow her her temper for the moment. Music, he mused, is a demanding mistress, offering a sublime ecstasy, however ephemeral, only to her slaves. And as he had slaved for her, so had this girl. Francesca. Franca. And when the music eludes you, swaying provocatively and slyly just out of reach, you know that you can only blame yourself for courting her ineptly.

Suddenly, silence. It was a relief to have the void, after her ferocious attack on *The Kiss*.

He sighed. 'Again.'

Better. Just slightly, almost infinitesimally, but better.

LONDON

The hard cock was pounding into her, the rhythm erratic, the force varying, driving into her, full length, then withdrawing to circle the slick entrance of her body. Eve lay back in sprawled abandon, enjoying the unaccustomed sensation of a thick male member filling her, a hard male body above her. She could, of course, never come this way, but it was still quite delicious, she mused.

In the huge mirror fixed to the ceiling above the bed she watched their bodies, admiring the taut globes of his buttocks as he thrust into her, the well-muscled back, the shapely legs. The length of his body obscured her own in the mirror's reflection; they seemed to form some strange animal, with a woman's head and a man's body. It was strangely, clandestinely erotic, and she shifted a little underneath him, wanting to see more of herself.

He withdrew then, moved lower, moved his mouth to her breast, sucking one hard point and then the other, swaying his head from side to side. Her breasts looked lovely in the mirror, high and pointed, nipples washed to rosy pink.

It was almost as though it was happening to someone else. She felt the warm mouth move down to her belly, a soft, moist path, the tongue thrusting into her navel, and saw the man's head move lower, watched the woman spread her legs further apart, felt him tonguing her pubic hair, now searching through the slick, secret folds. It intensified her pleasure, watching the two strangers in the mirror.

He had found her clitoris, was licking it gently with the tip of his tongue. She was surprised by his gentleness, by his intuition – his touch was as deft as a woman's, as tender, and she felt the first stirrings of voluptuous pleasure swelling her lips.

A different animal in the mirror now, the torso of a woman, legs wide apart, the man crouching between them, head fixed between her thighs. She half-closed her eyes, blurring the picture.

As she was blurring, losing the sharp edges of control, becoming indistinct, she was suffused with pleasure, luxuriating in the sensual wash of his tongue.

He probed at her opening with his finger, found her tight and wet, thrust his finger deeper, exploring her inner walls, testing the humid corridor. He felt her shiver, inserted another finger, then a third, still delicately stroking her clitoris with his tongue. His fingers, long and supple, were stroking her inside, sculpting the tunnel of her body with fluttering, fragile fingers.

He was, she acknowledged, half-opening her eyes, very good. He used the same exquisite intensity, the same controlled passion in bed as he did on stage with the piano, fingers and tongue flexible and sure. That smoky little club in Camden had been hiding a considerable talent. And now he was devoting his considerable talents to playing her, surely convinced that he was screwing his way into a contract with Disc-O. She had hinted as much, perhaps, inviting him to Max's penthouse suite for a drink . . .

Sally had given her the spare key Max always left her when he was away from London. Sally. Loyal assistant to Max Schiller. What would she say if she knew her own assistant was using her beloved boss's apartment, not for Disc-O's benefit, but to further her own, hidden agenda? Sally's need to make sure she did the best possible job for Max had played neatly into her hands. If Francesca Tonelli and Mika did not hit it off, Max's trip to Geneva would be abortive. He'd return to London angry and frustrated, still needing another artist to fill the void left by Mika's retirement.

Eve shifted a little, letting Nikolai's fingers probe her more deeply.

Her flirtation with the gifted young Russian expatriate had made *almost* perfect sense to Sally – she'd required some persuasion. But Max's luxurious penthouse was the ideal setting to spring the seductive trap on a man so long deprived of those many good things of life which money alone could buy. But what nobody knew but herself, this side of the Atlantic at any rate, mused Eve, were the long-term business implications of this meeting of minds and bodies in Max's flat.

And what a gorgeous setting it was for her little scheme . . . and who would have guessed that Max would have such a huge, glittering mirror fastened to the ceiling above his bed; a third eye, a silent witness to enhance the senses?

Diverted by the thought, Eve opened her eyes to the mirror. Her hair was tousled, her lips faintly swollen, Nikolai kneeling between her thighs like some supplicant. The two sexual sides of Eve seemed suddenly perfectly encapsulated, perfectly expressed, in the contradiction of her detached admiration for the strangers in the mirror, her increasingly intense physical pleasure as his fingers throbbed against the walls of her vagina.

Intrigued by this contradiction, she slithered away from him, then drew him close, gently persuaded him onto his back and straddled him. He was erect and throbbing, and her fingers closed around his penis, gently exploring the hard, pulsing muscle that rippled a little at her touch. It was, she decided, somehow less aesthetically pleasing than the cool length of ivory she preferred. But she was entranced with the picture they made as she straddled him, head flung back to expose the cool lines of her throat, her high and pointed breasts in perfect relief, thighs parted to receive the thick red rod into her body.

Leisurely, she parted her lips, slid the head of his organ into her, watched the strangers in the mirror as the woman's body swallowed the man's organ, drawing it deep inside her. They were both beautiful, this man and this woman, she with her platinum hair and perfect breasts, he with a thick pelt of brown hair covering his chest, blunt features coarsened a little in passion.

She moved a little, rocking him inside her, felt the thick rod press against her belly as she moved forward, the pressure against her rectum as she moved back. The stranger in the mirror was graceful, elegant, swaying above the male body in a languid, fluid rhythm.

The man's hands were reaching for her breasts now, cupping and squeezing them, pinching the rosy brown nipples into even harder points, and the mirror captured the contrast of his hands, the long fingers silky with brown hair, striping her white breasts.

She arched, found that leaning forwards she could find the friction for her clitoris, brush it against the wiry coils of his dense pubic hair even as she moved his organ inside her.

She saw the woman's hips begin to move faster, more urgently, rocking almost wildly, a turbulent frenzy. Beneath her he groaned, lifted his hands to her hips, clutching at her, forcing her to slow the feverish ride.

'Slow,' he said, voice thick. 'You'll make me come.'

The sound of his voice jolted her a little, recalled her from the strangers in the mirror. For a brief moment she flirted with the idea of making him come, rocking him to orgasm, driving him over the edge before he was quite ready, expressing her power, her will. But the lure of the woman in the mirror was stronger. She was smiling now, licking her lips, subsiding, subduing the furious rhythm, enjoying the thickness of the shaft inside her.

And then she moved, arching away from the hard male rod, swarmed up his chest to his mouth, obliterating his face. The woman in the mirror watched as his hands grasped her buttocks, pulling her closer. His tongue was thrusting through the slick folds to find her entrance, slipping inside, one finger probing at the taut aperture of her rectum.

GENEVA

Serena woke feeling hazy, slightly distorted. Clinging uncharacteristically to sleep, she tried to roll over and bury herself in the covers but found herself unable to move. Languidly, she tugged at a wrist curiously unresponsive to her will. Irritation drove her fully awake, annoyance clearing the drowsy mist she had been trying to recapture.

She was lying on something soft and silky, spread-eagled, wrists and ankles snared. She lifted her head, flexed her arms, experimented with the range of movements allowed her. Her wrists and ankles were bound. Cold steel flirted with silky mink, and she recognised the fur-lined manacles she had bought in an impulse of deliciously bad taste in New York.

Incredulously she jerked her wrists again. Nothing. So fully was she extended that even her range of vision was limited, but she could lift her chin just a trifle, and

160

knew the hard stone ceiling, could see the impressive forest of racks either side of her.

She was in the cellars, captured in the tiny aisle space between the wine bottles, limbs bound to the racks on either side. Experimentally she shifted, knowing even as she did so that it was useless. Handcrafted of the finest oak, burdened by the weight of thousands of bottles of Mika's prized Burgundy, she couldn't shift the shelves. And the cuffs that bound her, mink-lined stainless steel, would be impervious to any pressure she could bring to bear. Mentally she cursed the lapse of aesthetics that had led to the purchase of the cuffs now imprisoning her wrists and ankles . . . it was just that at the time they seemed so American, so deliciously, lecherously, lubriciously vulgar that she hadn't been able to resist them

Irritation and amusement were struggling with something a little deeper, a little more intense.

Deliberately she regulated her breathing to smooth, even breaths. Inhale. Exhale. Inhale. Exhale. She was not frightened. She had been frightened only once in her life, when she entered the hospital room in Milan after the operation and found Mika comatose, unresponsive to her presence. Having experienced that moment of utter horror, of total panic, of her world splintering apart before her eyes, there was nothing left in the world to frighten her ever again.

She ran her tongue around her teeth, testing and tasting the contours of the inside of her mouth. Valerian. He must have used Valerian, that sweet soporific, to thicken sleep. He.

Who was he?

She had shown Max the cellars, taunted him, dared him, but she felt instinctively that this wasn't his style. Perhaps, just possibly, but unlikely. He had chained her to the bed that first night under the influence of the aphrodisiac she had given him, but that was a spontaneous, lustful, impulsive urge . . . which, she

161

decided to acknowledge, had been really quite wildly wonderful.

This sort of premeditation wasn't like Max, or was it? She cast her mind back to the rough idyll in the rose garden, the pleasure that had splintered through her. Thought of the tender, loving touch of his hands, just scant hours ago, surely, that had brought her to such a sweeping, swamping orgasm that she had been almost frightened.

She had felt, at the instant of orgasm, curiously joined to him. A melting, melding sensation that had heightened her pleasure, and urged her out of his bed as soon as her breathing had slowed. She owed him no explanation, none at all, but something deep inside had prompted her to give him one. She had told him she wanted to be alone.

Impossible to imagine that he could have taken offence.

Perhaps, she thought, casting her mind further back, he had been mulling over the taunt she had flung at him beside the pool that afternoon, to taste more sophisticated delights than their heady coupling with Franca. She had done it, she acknowledged, merely to shock him, rattle the middle-class morality she was sure he possessed, as he kept rattling her own composure with his kindness, his gentleness.

So. Whatever she knew of Max, the facts didn't fit. He was, ultimately, too tender, too romantic, too inexperienced to respond to the dark side she had been flirting with. She was almost sure of it.

Sergei. She thought back to the last time with him, remembered how he had tried to rebel, and how she had enjoyed taming him. She had seen practically nothing of him since Max and then Franca had arrived at the villa, hadn't needed him for the car, hadn't used him for pleasure. That he might try to extend the clear boundaries of his duties – a stud to be summoned at her whim – seemed almost impossible.

She hissed in frustration. Franca? Could this be some

erotic scenario that Mika had constructed to allow her to fulfil her interpretive range? But the stage was set more for something from the murkiest depths of punk rock or the most extravagant excesses of Victorian pornography, not the classically romantic range which Mika had been moving towards at the time of the accident.

And besides, Mika would never do anything like this without consulting her. It would destroy every covenant of their relationship.

Irritation was becoming anger. Gritting her teeth she closed her eyes and inhaled deeply. But it was not the cool air of the wine cellars that assailed her. Instead the potent, faintly spicy fumes of one of her most powerful potions, a herbal distillation flavoured with amyl nitrate, immediately sent the blood rushing through her in a pounding roar. Her eyes flew open, and for a brief moment she caught the sight of a black-gloved hand drawing away the cut-glass vial.

For a split second her brain foundered. Mika? *Mika?* And then she was drowning, helpless, swamped by waves of sheer pleasure.

He stood above her, watching her eyes close, sensing her body warm with the rush of physical sensation. Quickly he drew a length of black velvet from his pocket and covered her eyes. She must see nothing, know nothing, think nothing. She must be only a creature of sensations, prey to the captive delights of torment and ecstasy. And fear. Just enough to provide the cutting edge, the searing wildness of the unexpected. She would be a difficult woman to frighten. But he was sure he had learned enough at her hands, knew her well enough to create the moment. And prolong it.

He began with mink gloves, the soft, seductive, sensuous flow of wild mink against naked flesh, first rubbing it gently on the soles of her feet, finding the achingly sensitive arch, letting her body become accustomed to the rich texture. He let it purr along the curve of her calves, describe the tender mesh of tendon and muscle at the inside of her knees, flirt with the silken contours of her thighs.

And she was purring, arching towards the enticing stimulation of fur against skin, the rippling, silky, decadent wash of sensation that was tightening her nipples, flooding her loins, stirring her clitoris.

Her head stirred a little, and he knew her eyes would be opening, finding the dense black velvet, eyelashes fluttering against it, still in thrall to the first heady rush of the amyl, too strong not to begin to fight it.

Swiftly, he held one hand to her centre, fighting the urge to press hard against the ripe, rosy folds of her sex, revealed so nakedly to his eyes. Instead, with a delicate lechery new to him, he moved the mink against her slowly, taunting her with long, sure strokes that moved from the tip of her clitoris to the base of her spine. Again and again he dragged the mink against her, pleased when he saw the glistening evidence of her arousal dewing the fur, the first quivers of the muscles at the inside of her thighs.

The regular, delicate torment of the silky pelt kissing her furrow, fluttering against her clitoris, flirting with the ripe folds of her labia, insinuating into the deeper crevice of her rectum then stealthily withdrawing, was engorging her, enlivening her skin, shortening her breathing. Distantly she knew her arousal was artificial, drug-enhanced and therefore dangerous in the hands of this unseen presence. She tried for a brief moment to distance herself, concentrate on any clues to his identity, but the hands that stroked her were mink, and the delicious, hot, hormonal flush of increasing desire was submerging her.

Naked, chained, the black strip of velvet concealing her amber eyes, the pale gold of her skin flushed slightly, her hips arching to his hand, she was the image of every febrile fantasy he had ever had, the slave in the harem, the captive houri. And he was master.

Her breasts tempted him. The taut peaks of rosy nipples strained for suckling, the full curves that cried out for palming and stroking and kneading, but he was stronger than before.

Without interrupting the rhythmic caress of the mink against her mound, he moved his other hand to her breasts, moved back and forth between the engorged nipples, deftly stimulating them with the tanatalising brush of fur, watching them pucker and harden under the silky caress. Soon, it would time for steel, the cool kiss of the knife blade to chill the languorous warmth of fur, to stretch the nerves under the skin.

She was becoming soft, hazy, melted by the rich wash of silken fur teasing her breasts, warming her sex. Desire, thick and heady, was pooling in her groin, moistening her, ripening her. Her clitoris, teased to almost unbearable sensitivity by the rhythmic caress of mink was hot, aching now for a firmer touch, ready to explode in pleasure. She could feel it growing, feel her body suffusing with the glowing heat of impending orgasm.

He felt her stiffen and arch under his hand, knew from the almost inaudible moan that she was ready. He was surprised to find her so quickly responsive. Frowning, he drew the fur away.

LONDON

'Nikolai, sweetheart, be a darling and fetch me a robe. Max is bound to have spares somewhere. We really must talk.'

Reluctantly the young Russian pianist sighed, licked each of Eve's nipples tenderly, lingeringly, before pulling his right arm from under her waist and rolling onto his back. She could not resist bending down to take the head of his cock in her mouth, and kissed it before nudging him gently towards the edge of the bed.

'I haven't enjoyed making love to a man so much ever before,' she whispered, with more truth than

Nikolai could possibly imagine. He raised himself to his feet and walked unsteadily to the door which connected the bedroom to Max's dressing-room.

'And you, my dear Eve, for a woman, have pleased me more than I have ever known,' he replied.

The implication was not lost on her. She made a mental note to check whether Nikolai's history could be rather racier than she had so far discovered.

He returned with two luxuriantly thick towelling robes, a black one which he took for himself, and a white one which he tossed onto the bed for her.

'Let's have some sparkling mineral water,' she suggested, stretching out a hand for the robe. 'There's bound to be a few bottles in his fridge. Perhaps some fruit and chocolate too, if you can find any. And then we'll talk.'

Nikolai went off obediently.

He certainly seems biddable enough, thought Eve. But would he take the bait she was about to dangle before him? She thought back over the last few months.

New York. City of opportunity for people who could see it and, like her, knew how to exploit it. New York, where she had worked in financial services before joining Disc-O. New York, where she had recently gone on an errand for Max and Sally, to size up the potential for Disc-O in the North American market. Toronto should have been able to hack it, what with their government's naïvely ambitious agreements with the Americans over free trade. But the Canadian branch had its problems, and Max had wanted an independent pair of eyes on the spot.

So Eve had gone. And she had taken her chances. Taken Jeff Brooks, too, as it happened. Jeff, music lover, *bon viveur*, billionaire's son and venture capital investment adviser who was retained by one of the world's leading banks. Jeff was convinced that the recording industry was wide open.

No one had exploited the upsurge in the popularity of classical music in the States as effectively as it had been done in Europe. Disc-O certainly could do it, with the right marketing strategy. But Disc-O's image was tarnished, largely through a plodding pedantry stemming from Toronto's senior management.

A new label, however, could do the trick. Under the aegis of Disc-O. Or maybe not? And so the idea of a new independent entering the scene had arisen. And naturally Eve would head it up, with Jeff fixing finance and handling the legal set-up in the background.

But she needed other expertise, too. Wider knowledge of the recording industry than was possible for a comparative newcomer, such as herself. Sally, with her knowledge of Disc-O, its artistic management, its marketing, its distributors . . . Sally, with her knowledge of Max Schiller, based on ten years' experience as his personal assistant, her access to the most intimate details.

'You are sure that you only want mineral water?' asked Nikolai, interrupting her train of thought. He was holding a tray with two crystal glasses, a bottle of mineral water and a bowl of fruit.

'Yes, darling, I need a clear head for the next few hours,' she replied. 'But you can put a couple of bottles of Brut in the fridge. I think that later we'll be having a visitor.'

'Not Max Schiller, I hope.' His voice betrayed his nervousness. 'I thought you said he would stay in Geneva for another day or two.'

'So he will, I'm sure of that, darling. No, I wasn't thinking of Max. I'm hoping Sally will come round.'

'Your boss, Sally? Why?' he asked, setting the tray on the bed and handing her the glass of mineral water she had requested.

'Because,' Eve purred, 'with her knowledge of what's happening in Geneva we can steal a march on Max's plans for Francesca Tonelli. We'll plan your début for the same week as hers.' She smiled, sipped some water and continued in a rather dreamy voice. 'Think of it! The public will flock to hear the new genius of the keyboard. The violinists have been over-exposed recently, I'm sure of it. A fresh image, a fresh repertoire, that's what we need.'

'But Schiller would never agree!' he objected. 'If he takes me I'll be part of a sales pitch including Tonelli, not competing with her!'

Her voice was watered silk. 'Nikolai, we do not need Max Schiller.'

'We do not need Max Schiller?' he repeated, frowning. 'But my contract with Disc-O that you are promising me, what of this?'

'Nikolai,' she soothed. 'Tell me . . . have you ever heard of the Brooks family?'

'Of course,' he replied, his eyes puzzled. 'Even in our pig-ignorant Soviet days we Russians learned English, read smuggled Western magazines. Family fortune based on old Texas oil money. More better invested since the fifties than most. But what is this doing with me?'

In his agitation his text-book English was slipping a bit, Eve noted, suppressing a smile and setting down her glass. 'Jeff Brooks,' she began, then hesitated a little. How much of her hand should she divulge to him? He was anxious now, and no possible threat. And she wanted to gloat a little, bask in the surprised admiration her plans would excite.

'Jeff Brooks is backing me to start a new independent record company,' she said. Her eyes glittered . 'If you're prepared to go along with it, your début will coincide with the launch of the new company. All the media attention will be on you, on us. Just think of it!'

She rose from the bed, pulling the robe around her, and began pacing the floor. 'RUSSIAN PIANIST TAKES NEW YORK BY STORM! FROM NIGHTCLUB TO CARNEGIE HALL!' Excitedly she sketched the headlines with her hands. 'It can't fail. I can't fail. You'll be made!'

His eyes widened at her words. 'But this Sally,' he said, 'why involve her?'

168

'Because she knows everything that makes Max Schiller and Disc-O tick. And right now she's the only one who can tell me what is going on in Geneva.'

He still looked puzzled.

'Trust me, darling,' she said, moving beside him to place a reassuring kiss on his cheek. 'I know what I'm doing. Sally's just about ready, now. I think I'll give her a call.'

'This is the way you do business here?' he asked a little uncertainly.

'Baby, as they say in New York, you ain't seen nothing yet,' said Eve, patting his shoulder before leaving the room.

Alone, Nikolai bit into a nectarine, savouring the sweetness of the juice flowing over his tongue, savouring too the almost sensual delight of surrendering control to the woman called Eve.

GENEVA

The last, aching chord spiralled away, rippling, haunting, leaving in its wake a warm, melting quality to the silence. It lay between them like a living presence, warm and pulsing. *The Kiss*.

Finally, reluctant to break the spell, taint the magic, Mika exhaled, a long, deep sigh. He hadn't even known he was holding his breath.

'Yes.' The single word betrayed his relief, his astonishment, delight and awe at the musical poetry he had created and she had brought to life.

Face flushed, eyes glittering with triumph, Franca looked over at him challengingly. 'Yes?' There was just a hint of scorn in her voice, which surprised him.

All morning she had played with the piece, played at it and around it, striving to discover the colours and textures he envisaged until, after four gruelling hours, he had got up and left without a word. Astounded, puzzled, then angry, she had waited for ten furious minutes for him to return. Rage bubbling through her like lava, she knew she couldn't contain the molten flow of her emotions much longer. The old childish impulse to smash something, hear the crash of something fragile – and preferably very, very expensive – splintering to tiny shards was surfacing.

And this room, with the antique glass-fronted cabinets protecting his much publicised collection of violins, the ultra-modern monster of a sound system along one wall, the various *objets d'art* scattered decoratively on tiny tables, was too, too tempting. As her eyes lit on a Lalique bird, wings poised to fly and escape the shimmering glass, she realised the impulse was becoming overwhelming.

Damn him! How dare he walk out and leave her here alone without so much as a word! Angrily she had flung herself out of the room, stalked up the stairs, and changed into the black bathing suit Serena had lent her, hurling her jeans and shirt and tiny lace panties to the three corners of the room.

A frenetic half-hour doing laps in the pool had soothed her frustration somewhat, but increased the trembling tension in her arm muscles. At last exhausted, mentally, physically and emotionally, she floated on her back and looked up at the sky.

Was it only yesterday that she had lain on the grass, opened her eyes to a seething orgasm, seen his eyes in the blue of the sky? Her moods had been so changeable since coming to the villa, awed by Mika, wanting Mika, enraged by Mika, that she barely recognised herself. Fury at his cold insensitivity had cleansed her of sentiment: coldly, dispassionately, she decided to find some perspective – any perspective! – and adopt a plan.

She wanted to be the best in the world. He could help her achieve that, not least through the lustre of their association – if it became known and if she could capitalise on it. She had been foolish yesterday to turn Max away when he appeared at her room eager to discuss business, but contracts and percentages and royalties seemed so trivial, so boring, so ultimately meaningless compared to the sensual heat of being close to Mika, wanting Mika.

And she wanted him. Wanted to see him plunging into her, wanted to feel the heat of his mouth moving over her body, wanted to see the hard blue eyes softened with passion, wanted to pierce the cold veil of his self-composure, shatter his aloofness. To do that she had to find in herself the resources for *The Kiss* and then, and then . . . go beyond it.

'Yes!' His voice was forceful, cutting through her thoughts. 'It's almost exactly how I heard it in my mind! You've captured the warmth, the gentleness, the subtle exploration of eyes and tongue and mouth.' His blue eyes were impossibly bright, sparkling.

Hers were cold, grey shading to onyx. 'I'm not completely convinced,' she said clearly, laying down her bow and moving to look out of the large picture window. Blind to the idyllic vista of terraced gardens, she concentrated on mastering her reactions.

'And the final down bow, long and lingering, the moment before the lips part, reluctantly,' he carried on, unheeding. 'It's just as I wanted. Poignant. Expressive.' He moved his black-gloved hands eloquently, sketching the movements.

'I'm not convinced,' she said again, interrupting him, turning to face him, voice now etched with acid. Unwillingly she admired the graceful play of his hands, felt herself responding to his excitement even as she steeled herself to resist it.

'Just the hint of teeth, it was clever of you to finally catch that with the extra emphasis . . . What did you say?'

'I said,' she repeated, acid mingling with sugar, 'I am not convinced.'

He looked at her in some surprise. Standing against the window, the afternoon sun firing her hair to a blazing nimbus, she stood spare and elegant. He became aware for the first time that she had changed from her unisex attire of the morning, jeans and loose shirt, and was wearing a brightly coloured sarong that barely covered a tiny black bikini. She must have gone for a swim after he left, he realised. He hadn't noticed, had been concentrating on her hands, the movement of her arm as she plied the bow.

Arrogance flavoured her stance, one hip thrust aggressively foward, chin tilted, eyes dark. It was on the tip of his tongue to reassure her, congratulate her on finally achieving the delicate balance between technique and interpretation that allowed *The Kiss* to flower, but the tilt of her chin warned him.

Let her speak, he decided. She was, after all, a gifted musician. She might, conceivably, offer some minor criticism that could enhance the work. Unlikely, of course, but conceivable.

'Why not?' he asked. 'You played well. I think you're starting to uncover the pervading sensuality it requires.' It was a compliment, the first he had given her. She deserved it, he decided magnanimously, still flushed with the triumphant enthusiasm of hearing *The Kiss* played as he had imagined.

'It's not a real kiss,' she replied coolly, moving away from the window towards him. She paused beside a small antique hardwood table that held the Lalique bird she had been so tempted to shatter earlier.

'Not a real kiss? What do you mean?' Obviously she was still piqued by her failure of this morning, by his patient tolerance.

'When a woman wants a man,' she began, consciously turning his earlier words against him. 'Wonders if she wants a man, wonders if a man wants her, she plays with different textures, different tones.' With her index finger she traced the smooth arc of the wing of the Lalique bird, apparently absentmindedly.

He said nothing, watched her with narrowed eyes.

She could feel the shift of his concentration like the hot glare of stage lights. 'You assess, if not caress, with your eyes,' she continued lightly, letting her own eyes travel appraisingly over his body. 'Wondering if your body will like his, if he can make you want him.'

The implicit challenge hovered in the air, faint and tantalising. Let him wonder if there was some sub-text. She would make him acutely aware of her body, of all the earthy wild wonders she could bestow upon him, if she chose, cloaking it all in the mystery of music.

She abandoned the Lalique bird, moved closer to him, sinuously, aimlessly, stopping to admire a small but perfect enamelled snuff box, apparently oblivious that the clinging folds of her sarong were slipping.

'Woman,' she said softly, almost as if to herself, 'like the violin, is the essence. She has the empty hollow that evokes the sound, the reverberations. Mouth and womb, the deep dark, secret space where music and orgasm fuse.'

Thoughtfully, she drew the folds of her sarong up to her shoulder, outlining the taut peak of her breasts, the nipples already hard. 'In the moment before his mouth touches hers, before his hands move along her body, she wonders if he will be too hard, too gentle, too yielding, too rough.' She let her hands drop to her breasts. 'Can he rouse the deep heat she has found only in dreams or in fleeting moments? Will he press too urgently, or will he wait to make friends with her lips?'

He was watching her intently, blue eyes darkening. Without premeditation, almost unconsciously, she felt her fingers moving to the knot of the sarong, undoing it, letting it fall to the floor. Brazen now, almost naked but for the tiny scraps of black bikini moulded to her body, she stood before him.

'We are the womb.' Her fingers drifted to the black triangle encasing her mound and splayed across it.

'The tomb for the little death, warm and welcoming.' She let her index finger slip inside the black triangle, watched his eyes following her finger.

Long, elegant, impossibly white against the black triangle, he saw the three fingers splayed across her

173

mound, saw the concealed movement of her fourth finger searching through the folds of flesh and fabric.

'While we can see you, hard, hot, red and thick, that shaft between your legs rearing and pulsing, sometimes intensely desirable, sometimes infinitely ridiculous, you can never see the hidden heart of us.'

He watched her hand, the hidden finger burrowing deeper, slipping through the pink folds to find the bud of her pleasure, could sense her body flowering around it.

'It has to be more mysterious, hotter, darker.' Her cheeks were flushing with arousal, her eyes bright.

'The caverns of the mouth, the hollow of the violin, the cave of the womb.' Her voice seemed to be coming from some great distance. There was a roaring in her ears as, trance-like, hypnotised again by the blue in his eyes, she brushed one hand against her nipples, feeling them strain against the fabric.

'Saliva and semen mingling, because we are all of us mother and lover, you find both of us when you suckle our breasts, when you thrust into the canal that gave you birth.' Languidly she withdrew the hand that had caressed her nipples, extended it towards him, inviting him to rise.

He got to his feet, eyes never leaving the intricate dance her finger was weaving through the tight black fabric.

'Deeper.'

He knew she had found the entrance to her body, was questing against the taut, plushy walls of her vagina with her finger, could feel the humid heat of her.

'Darker.'

He was suspended in the grey mist of her eyes, in the perfumed incense of her body wafting towards him. He watched, disbelieving, as she withdrew her finger, slick and glistening with her body's pleasure. She took a step towards him. They were almost touching now. Without volition he felt his hand move towards her, reach to grasp her wrist, but before he could move she had touched her finger to his lips.

With unfocused eyes she traced the contours of his mouth, anointing his lips with the heady musk of herself, moving slowly across the sensual swell of his lower lip.

It was a gesture so shockingly profound, so incredibly primitive, so intense, that he found himself unbearably moved.

'And that, Mika, is the kiss.'

Chapter Eight

Heavy Metal

She turned away from him, rescued the gaudy sarong from the floor. 'So I think the bowing at the end should be deeper, slower.' Unhurriedly she wrapped the bright folds around her, knotted them over one shoulder. 'And the vibrato should be slow and wide, not fast and wide as you've indicated. It should be more velvety.'

Still he said nothing.

She moved further away, paused again by the Lalique bird that she had been so tempted to shatter earlier. With the index finger that had probed her sex, touched his lips, she traced the arcing curve of the glass wing. There was still enough of her liquid left on her finger to etch her presence on the shimmering surface. For a moment she admired the dusky smudge she had created.

'Of course, it all depends on how you see the harmonic texture developing, as well as the melodic texture,' she continued. 'You'll forgive me if I point out that at this moment it's a little too clear, a little too circumscribed for what appears to be your theme. A little too Hindemith, in fact.'

She turned to face him. He was standing rock still, black-gloved hands clenched at his side.

'With Hindemith, you're always aware of the clarity of his vision underlining even the most complicated and intricate passages.' She couldn't read him, wasn't sure she had reached him. His eyes were expressionless. Anger flared again.

'Of course, he once composed a double canon on a train,' she concluded bitingly. She had no idea why she said it, knew only that it would hurt him. And was pleased to see a tell-tale muscle in his cheek jump.

'And I'm hungry.' She swept out of the room without a backward glance.

Lunch was waiting on the terrace, a festive array of cold meats and salads, cheeses and fruit, bottles of sparkling mineral water and the local white wine. There were no place settings, but glasses, plates and cutlery for four were banked at the edge of the table, near the earthenware coolers protecting the wine.

Shading her eyes, Franca looked up at the sun. It must be past two o'clock, closer to three. She touched the edge of one platter, a heavy yellow earthenware dish displaying paper thin slices of prosciutto and bresaola on a bed of endive. The plate was cool, the endive crisp and fresh.

'How does she know?' she asked curiously, seeking the safe refuge of small talk. She was starting to reel from the self she had found confronting Mika, still felt poised and confident but was becoming aware of a peripheral anxiety tugging at her nerves.

'Who? What?' Mika had already seated himself at the table, was pouring thick yellow wine into two glasses.

'Your housekeeper . . . Maddie, isn't that her name?'

'Yes.' Despite herself she was entranced with the spare economy of movement as he poured the wine, then reached for a bottle of mineral water. He was elegant, precise. Not a single wasted gesture. Not a single wasted syllable. He poured the sparkling water with the deft precision he might bring to a particularly difficult passage of Bach.

'How does she know when you'll be ready, when

you'll want . . .' her voice trailed off at his blank stare of incomprehension. 'I didn't know that you had left orders for a meal,' she tried again.

'Oh. This.' He glanced around the table indifferently. 'Maddie is used to our ways.'

It was a feast for the senses, an array of delicacies arranged so temptingly, so artistically that even the most jaded gourmet would have rejoiced.

Plump slices of red, juicy tomatoes bursting with green seeds basked voluptuously on a blue plate, kissed with olive oil and lightly dusted with pepper. Fat wedges of mozzarella were interspersed, decorated with the glowing green of fresh basil. A careless eye might merely accept the random scatter of black, wrinkled olives; a second glance showed how cunningly they had been placed against the delicate curve of a fresh green leaf, nestled close to the gleaming, milky sheen of the cheese.

A cluster of purple grapes, gravid with juice, so lush and perfect that they might have been grasped by the infant Dionysus, lay wantonly exposed on a white plate. A faceted crystal bowl held peaches and apricots, furry skins still dewed with drops of water, a spray of mint interrupting the tonal palette of yellow, orange and rose.

At the centre of the table there was a glazed, low-lipped dish, vibrant with fantastic flowers in purple, green and red, their contours edged with gilt. Perfect oysters on the half-shell flaunted themselves, plump and delectable as the choicest specimens from a sultan's harem. Lemon wedges challenged the flowers.

'Will Serena and Max be joining us?' she asked, glancing at the unused plates and glasses, still curious, seeking to fill the silence and avoid the unasked and unanswered questions that lay between them.

'Serena and I have never kept to any schedule, any established routine.' He lingered automatically, lovingly, caressingly over the syllables of Serena's name.

Jealousy flared, hot and thick as she heard him lick

the name with his voice. And then she remembered Serena kneeling between her legs, plucking delicately at the hairs between her thighs, Serena smoothing her hair as they rested together at the edge of the pool, Serena oiling her body, amber eyes hot and compelling.

'She's extraordinarily beautiful,' Franca heard herself say.

'Yes.' Meditatively he took an oyster, supped it from its shell, avoiding the gulping slurp that is the time-honoured homage to that creature.

Again, unwillingly, she admired his grace, his elegance.

'Extraordinary, and beautiful,' he added, reaching for his wine.

He was unbending, at last. 'You've . . .' she hesitated, searching for the right word, foundered, forged ahead, 'been together for a long time.' She let her voice rise at the end of the sentence, a half-tone, a half-question.

'Yes.'

Another monosyllable. Frustrated, she reached for an oyster, heard the involuntary slurp as she sucked at the salty sea-juice. And decided she didn't give a damn.

'Forever, really,' he added, looking beyond her, beyond the pool, into the past.

She could have pushed him then, artlessly, manipulatively, but she knew that the questions she asked would be the wrong ones, the answers, if there were any, would not be the ones she wanted to hear. Back in the music room she had rocked him, reached him, if only for an instant. She was sure of it. Let that be enough for the moment.

Mika poured more wine, lounged back, carefully studying the amber liquid in his glass. Not quite the colour of Serena's eyes, he decided. Hers were darker, lighter, flecked with a thousand shades of yellow and gold.

Forever.

An aeon of a word.

179

It was with Serena that time, real time, had begun. Before was a nameless, meaningless void. The drudgery, the hopeless despair. Moving automatically in a hostile world that despised, cheapened or patronised his deepest hunger.

Together they had buried the past so quickly, so completely, so irrevocably, that to even think back to those days was to exhume a corpse still fresh. Strange, it hadn't bothered him to recall and use his first memory of Serena, her husky warm laughter, in *The Kiss*. Yet now that he allowed himself to remember, he could see her, thin, scrawny, eyes like saucers, crouched behind the organ in the ice-cold chapel of the orphanage. Laughing.

Laughing, a warm, surprised bubble of joy at the music he had coaxed from that poor, tawdry excuse for an organ, laughing because the sound pleased her. Laughing, perhaps, because, they had discovered each other, escaped for some tiny fraction of time from the intolerable, intolerant, regimented goodness of the nuns.

He had been Michael then, she was Sally. No last names. No family. No identity. No mother.

Was that why Franca's words had moved him, her reference to mothers and lovers? The womb, the tomb, the birth canal. Primal, primitive images.

Together they had reinvented themselves, fled to London, little more than children. Created, together, the new identities of Mika and Serena. Dedicated themselves to his art – his mistress, his music, – as their only hope of escape. Had finally discovered together the key to unlocking the essence of himself, freeing it into the music.

Vivaldi's *Four Seasons*.

The dazzling energy that had first captured the attention of the critics had deserted him. And, curiosity aroused, he had known they would be circling like sharks at his next performance, wondering if he could recreate the magic, fully prepared to devour him in print if he couldn't.

Rehearsal had gone well by almost anyone's standards. But the violin in his hand had remained a violin, never changed from wood to flesh, refused to become the spring-like, ardent body of a young girl open to rapture. He had been rooted onstage, unable to break free into the sunny fields strewn with flowers, pound her body into the moist earth with his, spill his seed in ecstatic communion with nature and music.

Serena had known.

And when he had returned home, slightly drunk, unbearably frustrated, he had found the flat they shared transformed into a floral fantasy of chintz and ruffles, drifts of spring flowers, daffodils, violets, narcissus, Vivaldi playing in the background. Two girls, young and slender with flowing blonde hair dressed in blue and green had greeted him. 'Spring' and 'Summer'.

Wordlessly he had let them lead him into the fantasy, closed his eyes, let the music wash through him, over him, around him. Felt their hands, as gentle as petals, sift through his hair, glide over his shoulders, loosening his shirt, then drifting lower to his torso.

Fresh and innocently beautiful, delicately perfumed, they had been as sensually inviting as the first fruits of the season. The music was a palpable second presence as they swayed slowly together, loosely clasping each other, kissing softly, like sisters, to the music.

It was Summer who had led Spring, kissing her cheek, her eyebrows, feathering kisses along her neck and throat.

And watching them he felt a surge of wonder at the languid grace of their entwined bodies, the leisured, knowing, slow exploration of hands and tongues. No thrusting of separate parts striving to join, but a subtle celebration of the female body, woman pleasing woman with the innate sense of how a nipple felt to be sucked, a clitoris licked, a labia to swell. Entranced, he had moved closer, sensing the violins rippling and

181

shivering like the bodies of the two girls. Spring knelt to Summer, paid homage to the flower bud nestling in the warm labia leaves, drank the flowing, sap-like juices in delicate sips.

When they had uncoiled from each other, smiled and opened their arms to him, he had been profoundly moved. He had felt at once too hard, too rough, too male, to join that graceful duet. But they drew him down, enfolded him, embraced him, lost him in a tangle of breasts and mouths and tongues, licking him as gently as they had licked each other. Enveloped in their warmth, his maleness, his hardness was a fundamental element in the celebration of the seasons. They had needed his hardness, flowed around it, shared it generously between them, Spring riding him on top in long, cresting waves, Summer crouched between his legs, licking his balls, fingering his anus.

He had never heard Vivaldi so clearly. And when he came, emptying himself into Spring in a final, joyous thrust, he had known exactly how he needed to play it.

Serena hadn't come back that night. The next morning he found the flat restored to its pristine minimalism, not a trace of the floral fantasy left behind.

The night of the concert he played brilliantly, fantastically, left the critics open-mouthed and searching for superlatives.

And the next day he had gone out and spent much, much more than they could afford on a gold chain for Serena.

Across the table Franca watched him, saw the small smile playing at the corners of his mouth, one black finger meditatively tracing a complicated pattern on the snowy tablecloth. The sun was highlighting his hair, discovering every shade from yellow to gold and gilt.

How to recall him from this silence, bring him back to her?

'Have you decided on the overall scheme of the

work?' she ventured, helping herself to salad. One of the tomatoes slipped from the tongs and fell beside her wineglass. 'There's obviously more . . . is it a concerto, a tone poem, what?'

He answered her easily. 'Six movements. Six climaxes of equal intensity.'

'All the same length as *The Kiss*?' she asked in surprise.

'Yes.'

'That would be almost an hour,' she calculated rapidly. 'It's almost too long, don't you think?'

'No.'

Her hand tightened on the wineglass just as Max emerged from the arched doorway of the villa.

'Mika, Franca, there you are. I've been on the phone to London all morning it seems,' he explained, dropping into a chair. 'Anyway, I'm starving, this looks delicious. But where's Serena?'

Mika seemed engrossed, pouring a glass of wine for Max, handing him a plate. It was Franca who broke the silence. 'I – we – I haven't seen her,' she said with a sidelong glance at Mika. 'We've been working almost straight through.'

'Working?' repeated Max, accepting the wine. The excited relief in his voice was obvious. 'You've found something for her then, Mika?'

'Yes.'

'Not Bach, I hope,' said Max, mind already moving ahead to marketing and promotions. 'We'd like to retain your niche there . . . Or Paganini, there's that Japanese fellow contracted to EMI and they've scheduled a release for September. Nothing too obscure either, like what's his name? Warshawski?'

'Wieniawski?' offered Franca doubtfully. Hardly obscure. Perlman had played Wieniawski's *Concerto in F sharp minor* at his first appearance at Carnegie Hall, and subsequently recorded his Violin Concertos 1 and 2 . . . Surely Max wasn't as crass as he sounded?

'Yes, that's right . . . and Bruch's been done to death

recently. We need something different, something to capture the market. The male market,' he added, remembering his conversation with Sally back in London.

'Max.' Mika's voice was cold.

'Something sexy,' continued Max, unheeding, 'something erotic. Ravel might have worked, if they hadn't used it in that movie—'

'Max.' There was enough ice in Mika's voice to freeze the headlong rush of Max's words. 'We are progressing. I have found the theme and . . .' he paused briefly, 'and Franca has demonstrated a certain artistry in evoking it. Leave the music to me. You may be confident,' he added, a hint of mischief in his eyes, 'that it will meet the demands of your marketplace.'

'Excellent!' enthused Max, savouring his wine. 'But you'll have to give me lead time, Mika, I'll have to let the office know so that we can book the studio, start working on publicity and promotions. I know Carnegie Hall is booked solid—.'

'*Festina lente*, Max,' warned Mika, a crooked smile on his lips.

'What?'

'Make haste slowly. A favourite saying of the Roman emperor Augustus.'

'Yeah, well, he didn't have to deal with the recording industry.'

She was waiting to fall, wanting to fall, hovering precariously on the edge of orgasm, hot and almost incandescent when she felt his fingers searching through the pink folds of her sex. No longer masked in mink, his fingers were thick and cool, leaving a burning, ambiguous sensation like hot ice.

A sharp smell, not unpleasant, assailed her and she dimly recognised the fumes of the ointment. Amyl nitrate, vaseline, a bit of this and that, it stimulated the tissues, enhanced sensation. But it had to be used sparingly and he was spreading it thickly, layer after

184

layer, forcing it into the tiniest fold, rubbing it into the insides of her outer lips, outlining the entrance to her vagina.

Burning, icy shivers engorged her labia, melted her with a delicious heat. She was swelling, swollen, the delicate tissues thickening and pulsing voluptuously.

The world contracted to the movement of his finger, the infernal heat consuming her sex. Stimulated to the threshold just below pain, she was pulsating, radiant, mindlessly numb and swamped in sensation. She felt his fingers probe her clitoris, felt the glacial heat suffuse it, making it grow thick and hot. She was throbbing now, clitoris and labia as stiff and engorged as any prick, the impossible hollow between her legs wet and avid, wanting to screw and be screwed.

She arched her hips, moved to capture his fingers, draw them into her so she could appease the gnawing hollow, find the pressure that would allow her to convulse the pleasure, tighten it into a knot of orgasm, but it slipped away, seeking the intimate density of her other entrance.

He was opening her, exploring her, heating the sensitive tissues, probing deeper, penetrating, then withdrawing, leaving a trail of fire. She writhed furiously, torn between pleasure and frustration so intense they were almost pain, desperate to recapture the pressure.

The gnawing ache between her legs was growing, heating, needing the hard, plunging length, the fast, fervent, feverish rhythms.

She felt his tongue move lightly against her slippery folds, a ghost of a sensation, fiendishly delicate, hardly touching. She moaned then, aching for something hard and rough and wild to maul her pleasure, rip it to shreds in orgasm, but his touch was tentative, gentle.

With a final, lingering kiss on the inside of her thigh, he rose to his feet.

LONDON

Sally cursed to herself as the private line rang. She had let the temp go for an hour's lunch-break five minutes ago, and had just settled herself on the couch with a glass of sparkling apple juice from the refrigerator and a black cherry yoghurt. Max had spent hours on the phone to her this morning discussing the Canadian situation and then, typically, as an afterthought, asked her to fax draft contracts over to Geneva for Francesca Tonelli. This she had done half an hour ago, almost as soon as he had rung off. Surely there was nothing wrong? They had used that dummy contract so many times.

She stretched out a reluctant arm to the phone perched on the table by her side.

'Disc-O. Sally Jenkins.'

'Sally. Eve. How goes the lonely vigil at the top?'

'Piss off, Eve,' retorted Sally, uncharacteristically stung by the tone of Eve's voice. 'How goes Nikolai, or should I say how is he coming along?'

'Everything has come up to my expectations here,' Eve replied, with the merest hint of lechery in her voice. 'But why don't you come round and join us? There are things we should talk about. Outside the office,' she added coaxingly.

Sally sighed. 'Eve, there's just too much going on here. Max took up my whole morning with a string of calls about the Canadian office. Things are reaching a crisis point there, or at least he thinks they are. He wanted to have details of the quarter's figures, which arrived by fax overnight. Then he wanted to discuss your report from the States, and get your impression of Ashby in Toronto. You did a good job there, by the way.'

Better than you know, thought Eve, remembering her meetings with Jeff Brooks in New York. 'Thanks, Sally, I did my best.'

'Thank God I had all of your reports here,' Sally

continued, 'He seems obsessed with the American market at the moment.'

'I thought he'd be more obsessed with the Geneva situation,' Eve cut in tartly. 'Given what we know about Serena.'

'Yes, that's what I thought, too,' Sally replied slowly. Eve's jibes about Serena never failed to hit their mark. 'Odd. He mentioned nothing until right at the end when he rapped out an order to send faxes of draft contracts over for Franca.'

'Ah, so she's buying in then? And Mika, does this mean he's coming out of seclusion?'

'Apparently,' Sally hedged. She'd asked about Mika, of course, and in a brief flood of enthusiasm before hanging up Max had mentioned Carnegie Hall, a large piece for solo violin and his plans for a première before the year was out. 'Mika is composing,' she said aloud. 'A piece for Franca. Solo violin.'

'So . . . things are moving fast,' exclaimed Eve, more to herself than Sally. 'But Serena must have had a hand in all this, surely? What did Mr Schiller say about his favourite lady?'

'Max said nothing, really. Strange, I suppose.'

'Not strange at all,' said Eve quickly. 'Think a moment. He's probably totally enmeshed by her now. She would have seen Franca's potential, guessed at the effect on Mika of having such a talented young beauty around the villa. No doubt they've all been in bed together to celebrate their new partnership. I bet Max wouldn't have turned that offer down,' she giggled, 'even if he did have to pull Serena off Franca to get at her.'

Sally winced at the thought. Eve was so crudely direct, so blatant . . . so right. It really was ludicrous how much she had let herself become Max's creature. Because she wanted him, had imagined fondly for years that she might get him to want her in some way that was not just sexual. What a dreamer she had been. And Eve had seen it so clearly.

'Are you still there, Sally?' Eve enquired artlessly.

'Yes, yes, I am,' replied Sally, forcing her mind back to the conversation.

'Well, as I said, Nikolai is really quite good. A more diverse talent than I imagined. And I really think you should see him, come and join us. I promise you'll enjoy yourself. We always do together, don't we?' Eve's voice lowered to a soft purr.

'Yes, yes, we do,' Sally replied softly, her body already warming to the implicit promise in Eve's voice.

'Delightfully diverse, in fact,' Eve coaxed. 'You will come, Sally?'

The images flashed across her mind, of Max's apartment, of lying on that great bed with its expanse of mirrored ceiling, and watching Eve, seeing Eve, seeing herself, seeing Nikolai. 'Yes, look,' she said impulsively into the phone, 'I could do with a break. I'll organise the rest of the day's work with the temp, get her to keep the world off my back, and leave for Max's place at five. I'd love to hear Nikolai playing Max's baby grand.'

'Don't worry, Sally love, he'll be here,' said Eve, carefully concealing the triumph in her voice. 'And he'll play anything you like.'

GENEVA

'Has he always been like this?' asked Franca.

Mika had left them abruptly, offering no explanation, no apology. One moment he was smiling rather cynically at Max's story about the flautist who was having an affair with both her conductor and the first violinist, and the next moment he had risen from his chair and disappeared into the villa without so much as a word.

She and Max had exchanged glances, idly exchanged gossip and opened another bottle of wine, tacitly agreeing to ignore Mika's mood. But one part of her mind stayed with him, wondering if he had returned to the music room to compose or merely to think, wondering if he sought Serena's company in preference to hers, wondering why he acted as if the normal rules of polite interaction applied to everyone but himself.

'Like what?' asked Max.

'So, so brusque. No, that's not the right word,' she replied, shaking her head. 'It's not even that he withdraws, retreats, switches off. It's more like he switches *you* off, that you simply cease to exist. Was he always like this? Or is it since the accident?'

Max sipped his wine, wary of the question, remembering the fierce blast of Mika's temper when he had ventured to ask about his hands. 'He's never been a particularly easy person to deal with,' he responded slowly. 'But yes, yes he's changed. He's colder now than he used to be, more reserved.'

'You've known him for a long time, Max,' she probed, stretching out her legs, pushing aside the folds of her sarong to expose them to the sun. She felt relaxed with Max, at ease. A curious intimacy that had nothing to do with sex or business was developing between them, a bond of some sort.

'Ten years, more or less,' he agreed. 'I was just starting out then, Disc-O was only a couple of years old. It was in Paris. EMI had thrown out a few lures to him, RCA was getting interested.' He smiled briefly at the memory.

'But he signed with you.' She couldn't keep the surprise from her voice.

'Yes, he signed with me.' Looking back, Max still couldn't believe the incredible risks he had taken, the loans, the creative accounting that allowed him, on paper at least, to offer Mika £250,000 for an exclusive lifetime contract. He remembered Mika's thoughtful nod, and later, the regretful phone call. More creative accounting, driven by the sure certainty that he couldn't afford to lose this talent, needed it to fuel Disc-O's rise to the top. The final agreement, at double the sum. Reeling with relief and horror, he had thrown a party at Maxim's. And seen Serena for the first time.

'What was he like, then?' she asked.

'The greatest,' Max replied simply.

'I mean—'

'You know what Previn said about Perlman?' he continued, ignoring her interruption. 'He said that there's a lot of good violinists. Quite a few very good ones. Several excellent ones. But only a meagre handful of great violinists. That,' he smiled, drank more wine, 'was before he met Mika.'

'But you were asking me what he was like.' He searched through his memories, found them clouded with Serena. He sensed that his answer was important to Franca, that she needed to know more about the man, not the violinist. But was there any difference?

'There's a story Serena told me once,' he said finally. 'Mika was very young when he first heard the violin, three perhaps, or four. Demanded one for himself. His parents misunderstood, bought him a toy. Classic, isn't it? Same thing happened to Perlman, to Menuhin. Perlman threw his under the bed, Menuhin stamped his to bits.' He paused, sipped some wine.

'Mika, well, Mika apparently threw his on the fire,' he said at last.

It was as if he was talking to his wineglass, she thought. He swirled the last amber depths of it reflectively, as if there were some answer to be found there.

And when he finally spoke again, she was surprised to hear him say, 'Strange. I've never really believed a word of it.'

Were six movements really too many? Mika wondered irritably, glaring at the page in front of him. Was it too long, too self-indulgent? He had decided to rival the *Chaconne* on an impulse, a whim . . . Perhaps she was right, and it should be shorter, tauter. But that would require a major reworking of the underlying concept . . . which she had disparaged unthinkingly, without even knowing the full structure, as too Hindemith.

Damn the girl!

He tried to focus on Serena, repeated the soothing

mantra of her name under his breath. For once it failed to calm him.

He shut his eyes, tried to recapture the smooth flow of notes, the cadence of fugitive dreams pooling to delirium, the melody arching to exaltation.

Nothing.

Four, he decided angrily. He could compress it to four movements without losing the soul of the work. *The Kiss* was perfect; he would leave it as it was, ignore her comments about the vibrato.

And then . . . questing hands finding naked flesh beneath the silk, testing, exploring the contours and textures. He would combine the nucleus of the unwritten third movement with the kernel of the second, make it deeper and darker, more thrilling. Silk slipping to the floor with a sinuous rustle. Black lace against golden skin. The capricious drift of knowing fingers. *The Embrace.*

His concentration was returning.

Unconsciously he flexed his hands to relieve the creeping, tingling sensation pulsing through his fingers. He wasn't even aware of it. The gesture had become automatic, unthinking.

He could hear the opening of the movement, a slow sensuous glide against the skin and strings, heating and growing deeper as they pressed closer, thigh to thigh, belly to belly. An electric sweep of pizzicato for the first tingling flush of excitement teasing the spine. The ending, too, was clearly etched in his mind, the crisp rustle of white linen sheets slowly eased to the foot of the bed, the warmth of naked flesh meeting, breath just beginning to quicken.

The middle was still annoyingly obscure. The erotic transition from clothed embrace to the naked fall on white linen – the long, hot, deep kisses, the caressing exploration of heated skin, the shaft thickening and stirring – refused to transmute into notes and chords.

With a groan of frustration he threw aside his pencil and wandered over to the window. The sun was setting, a glowing red orb descending into a thick bank of puffy grey clouds. It was an unusually dramatic sunset, flamboyant, almost tropical, not the well-mannered sun he associated with Geneva. It hung suspended for a long moment, so long he could almost imagine it was glaring at him, before sliding behind the clouds.

Light softened, thickened as day became dusk. If he were rehearsing the piece, he thought, it would be in this light, with banks of ivory candles unlit, waiting patiently for the flame that darkness would urge. And in this room, where his violins rested, wrapped in silk. And she would be wrapped in silk, ivory silk, long and flowing from throat to floor like a waterfall.

There would be tiny pearl buttons, hundreds of them, tracing the line of her spine, the pizzicato pulse as each was loosened, the tempo quickening as his fingers became impatient, threaded through with the warm line of naked flesh, a rougher urgency as he reached the hollow of her spine, the rending tear as the fabric split asunder under his hands, the rippling cacophony of pearls cascading and dancing across the marble floor.

A long note, lightly bowed, almost hesitant, as he turned her to face him, drew the dress from her shoulders, let it slither to the floor.

Yes, he thought, rubbing his hands together, it felt right. But then . . . something a little more wanton, titillating, naughty even. The faintest suggestion of the slut, the merest whiff of the whore, the vibrato deep and slow.

A black corselet clasping the milky flesh of her breasts, pink nipples visible beneath the tracery of lace. An intricate, delicate web of black cradling the lush white swell of her breasts, emphasising the tiny waist, flowing to the soft lines of her hips. Black lace stockings to reveal the creamy expanse of thigh, the merest sliver of black lace to cover her mound. Black and white. The fiery tendrils of her thatch curling softly, protectively around the inky mesh of lace.

Engrossed, he returned to his desk, hardly aware that the image of Franca was gradually altering the contours of *Serena's Song*.

Alone in the rose garden Max smoked a cigar, watched the sky. He and Franca had lingered over lunch, enjoying the sun, enjoying the wine, enjoying each other. She had seemed relaxed, at ease, yet he could feel a simmering undercurrent in her as she spoke about *The Kiss*.

He drew thoughtfully on his cigar. Using the draft contract Sally had faxed through to the villa, he had lured Franca inexorably into Disc-O's orbit. The contract was the usual take it or leave it offer made to first-time recording artists, tying them into low percentages of net proceeds. And Franca, unlike many in her position, was good enough to have felt free to negotiate a better deal.

But she'd looked at the document only briefly while listening to him make his offer, an exclusive five-year contract, only ten per cent of net proceeds on the royalties. Max was surprised she had agreed so readily, without seeking independent legal or financial advice.

Was her ambition to be accepted as Mika's pupil or protégé so great she would accept any terms to be with the same company? Max found this unlikely. Perhaps there was something more. He had felt an urgency in her voice as she quizzed him about Mika, more than simple worship of an artistic hero.

Perhaps Serena played a part here . . .

No. Unwillingly he dragged his mind away from Serena.

But his business instincts told him that he must tie Franca into a final contract soon, tonight, before she could have second thoughts. He would ring Sally now, before the office closed, and get her to fax two copies of a final contract with complete details of percentages. That was essential.

And Mika. What were his expectations? The phrase he had used, 'tiresome business details', lingered uncomfortably in Max's mind. Idly he tried to recall the exact wording of Mika's contract. Presumably he would have been astute enough to specify that Disc-O owned every aspect of Mika's creative output, which would include composition. At £500,000 a year – all for nothing in the past eighteen months! he reminded himself irritably – Mika couldn't reasonably expect any more.

His mind drifted on, snagged on the complicated North American market, zeroed in on the Toronto office. Eve's report, as dictated by Sally over the phone, had been quite precise, but he wasn't reassured by her conclusions. The last quarter's figures hadn't met his expectations and he was beginning to suspect that something was wrong. Or at least not right.

The cigar was almost burning his fingers. He got to his feet, ground it out in the warm earth nurturing the roses. Their scent was almost overpowering, thick and sweet. He reached out to fondle a garnet leaf, feel the velvet texture of a perfect petal, remembering the lush folds of Serena.

She had left his bed last night after they had made love, slowly, gently, a tender contrast to the rough, heated mating in the rose garden. In the slow climb to the peak of pleasure he had moved her just as intensely as he had among the roses, he was sure of it.

'I want to be by myself, Max,' she had said coolly, drawing the white folds of her robe around her, slipping from his room like a wraith. Propped on one elbow he had watched her leave, hurt, almost disbelieving, his prick still hard and wet with their mingled juices.

He had slept badly, tossing and turning, searching for the warmth of her naked body, waking to find himself alone. He couldn't confront her with his need, blurt out the aching longing he felt for her without risking her disdain, her pity. She owed him nothing, he thought resentfully. What Serena wanted, she took. It had pleased her to take him, and she had. And now it pleased her to be alone.

He lit another cigar as the sun disappeared behind fluffy grey clouds. From the villa he could hear the thin wail of a violin colouring the air.

He ignored it. He was not, as he would be the first to acknowledge, 'musical'. It was an advantage, really, in this business.

At some point she must have slept, for when she next opened her eyes the velvet blindfold had been removed. She let her lashes fall, feigned sleep, careful to keep her breathing deep and regular. She could sense his presence nearby, feel the dark smell of oiled leather.

Tilting her head, Serena looked for him through the screen of her lashes. He was standing at the end of the aisle, his back to her. Dressed all in black. Mika's colour. Black leather pants that clung tightly to muscular thighs, to the taut bulge of his buttocks. A black leather shirt that outlined powerful shoulders. His sleek, dark head was bent.

He looked unfamiliar. And when he turned to face her, she realised why. He was wearing a mask, a black leather hood with only the tiniest slits for eyes and nostrils, the mouth a thin gash.

And he held, in hands encased in black leather, a knife.

She recognised the hood. She had bought it herself in New York, the same shop that had supplied the mink-lined manacles now braceleting her wrists and ankles, binding her. She had worn it when she was exploring bondage, flirting with the cruel delights of pain inflicted under the guise of pleasure; the heady, potent, powerful blend.

It had been an experience. One she had enjoyed. Revelled in. Until she had frightened even herself. The mask. The manacles. The power.

And as she well remembered, the hood had power. It masked her features, somehow masked herself from herself, from her victim-lover. She had felt powerful. Almost euphoric. Anonymous.

It went beyond sex, found darker realms. Mystery. Pain. Pleasure. Power.

Fear was the key. It triggered the natural adrenalin rush, made the nerve ends scream, magnified sensation. The skilful manipulation of erogenous zones blended titillation with terror, created the cutting edge of carnality.

Mentally she winced at the words as the knife blade glittered in the dim light.

These were dangerous games, blood sports to be played only by lovers who agreed on the rules in advance. Otherwise it could spiral out of control, become truly dangerous. As she had felt herself spiralling out of control, becoming truly dangerous. Wearing the mask.

He was walking towards her now, and quickly she let her lashes fall. But before she closed her eyes she glimpsed the thick-set, almost bullish column of his neck, and knew, with a flood of ecstatic relief that the black leather figure was not Mika, not Max.

Sergei. Or whoever Sergei became when he wore the mask.

She would have to be careful. She had no real doubt that she could control him, manipulate him to her will, but she had to take into account the fact that he had some of her most powerful stimulants, potions that dissolved the will in the maelstrom of arousal . . . and he was wearing the mask. Her confidence wavered slightly. But only slightly.

He was kneeling beside her now and she could feel his eyes intent on her face. She made her decision instantly.

She wriggled slowly, languorously, as though half-awakening, and made a low sound in her throat. His hand touched her cheek, and she opened her eyes.

Close up, the hood was more chilling than she remembered, scarcely human, the blank, black face of a sexual executioner. She let her eyes drift over it slowly, then smiled, a warm, red curl of lip.

'Good morning, darling,' she purred, stretched as far as the manacles would allow. 'Or is it morning?'

As she had expected, her opening gambit surprised him. 'No,' he replied, voice muffled behind the hood.

She smiled again, allowed a little of the warmth to reach her eyes. She had to create the illusion of collusion, become a carnal conspirator. 'I must have slept,' she said slowly.

He nodded.

She gave a low laugh. 'No wonder. It was . . .' she paused meditatively, 'it was quite truly . . . spectacular.'

'Will be,' he corrected. He lifted his hand to reveal the knife. It was a long, thin blade, curving in a cruel arc.

She laughed again, a wicked little laugh. Mentally she approved of the sound, decided it sounded natural, unforced. A faint chill was icing her spine, the instinctive response of naked flesh to the blade. It gleamed silver in the murky light.

He laid it flat on her belly.

'Sensation is all,' she commented, making her voice and eyes hot. Her mind was clear. There were two Serenas now, the actress Serena and the observer Serena. The observer would guide the actress. She had to reverse the roles, master him by her passivity. And it was going to be difficult.

She knew nothing of the convoluted paths of his sensuality, his mind, his emotions, had only ever concentrated on the length of his cock, the skill of his hands and mouth. With her body she had dominated him effortlessly, bent him to her desire, used him at her whim, secure in her position as mistress, his as servant.

'Yes,' he was saying. He moved the blade of the

197

knife between her breasts, laid it flat, the curved point just pricking her right nipple, the shaft cold down her cleavage, haft resting on her belly.

She shivered, only half simulating fear, smiled a feral smile.

'It's cold,' she murmured, eyes challenging.

'Too cold?' he asked, pressing the haft gently into the swell of her belly.

Be victim, be passive and pliant, counselled observer Serena. But an interesting victim. Learn more.

'Too cold,' she agreed, arching her back so that the chilly steel pressed more firmly against her.

He was silent. Beneath the tight black leather she could see him stirring, the bulk of his erection growing. Be careful, Serena, said the observer. The idea of hurting you excites him.

'Pleasure and pain,' she mused aloud. 'There are centres for pain and centres for pleasure in the body. Sometimes the signals become confused. That is why some people can only find pleasure in pain, and some can only find pain.' Serena, warned the observer, be careful. 'It takes consummate skill to blend the two, to create the ultimate fusion.'

'Fusion,' he repeated, fingering the haft of the knife.

He liked to come inside her, she remembered, not a form of sex that gave her the greatest pleasure, but she had allowed him to, once or twice.

It pleased you with Max, reminded observer Serena impartially.

'Fusion,' agreed actress Serena, letting the pointed pink tip of her tongue touch the swell of her upper lip suggestively. If you can make him remove the hood, advised the other Serena, you may have won. Or at least tipped the odds overwhelmingly in your favour. 'Belly to belly, tongue to tongue, Sergei.'

'Tongue to tongue,' he repeated, lifting the knife. 'And this is my tongue.'

Eyes unreadable behind the narrow slits of the mask, he lifted the knife to her mouth, placed the pointed tip of the blade against the full swell of her lower lip. It was a pin-prick of sensation, not hard enough to draw blood. The knife was cold as it traced the contours of her lips, the tip of the blade outlining the ripe swell of her lower lip, exploring the sensual curve of her upper lip. It was a delicate touch, too light even to leave a trace, but the threat of the glittering steel made her nerves pulse even as her mouth welcomed the thrill, the chill.

The dark side of her was responding, the self not governed by actress or observer.

He was toying with her now, toying with the knife, drawing it in sharp, tiny little flicking motions across the red bow of her lips, with a sharp, stinging metal kiss.

Be careful, cautioned Serena the observer.

I'm enjoying it, said Serena the actress.

More, urged the dark side.

She opened her mouth, caught the cold steel with her tongue. His hand stilled instantly. She opened her eyes wide, let the amber heat blaze out of them, licked the knife once, a lascivious caress, then closed her lips on the blade, yellow eyes never leaving the tiny eye-slits of the black leather mask.

She pressed her lips together, caught the steel with her teeth. He was fixed by her eyes, intent on her mouth. She smiled again, let him see the tip of the knife caught between her perfect, white, pointed little teeth.

Don't challenge him too soon, warned observer Serena.

It's an interesting role, shrugged the actress.

It's . . . rather intriguing, observed the third voice.

She let her lashes fall, breathed deeply, softened the pressure of her teeth, let the pressure of the blade open her lower lip to him. Let her tongue snake out to play with the blade, dance with it, caress it, enfolding the razor-sharp edge so delicately that it was a mere whisper of sensation, licking the flat of the blade blatantly, wantonly.

She could sense his control loosening, becoming lost in her knife-play. With the pressure of her mouth she drew the blade towards her, sucked it into the warm cavern of her mouth, then released it.

'Lick me, then,' she said softly, invitingly. 'Lick me.'

To use his tongue, he would have to remove the mask. As the cool side of the flat of the blade travelled down her throat, she wondered, fleetingly, which she would prefer, knife or tongue.

He used the knife cleverly, teasing the points of her nipples with the tip of the blade, tracing the aureoles in a metallic kiss that made the flesh shiver. Even as her nipples hardened she felt the muscles in her belly clench in icy anticipation, felt the liquid heat between her thighs. The vague, background fear that the honed blade of the knife might slip sharpened her sexual tension, carved every nerve into screaming awareness.

He drew the flat of the blade down her body slowly, saw the muscles of her belly and thighs quiver with the strain. Spreadeagled before him, flesh pearly white in the dim light, the iridescent gleam of arousal moistening the soft pink folds of her labia, she had never seemed so desirable. The mocking amber eyes were half-closed, the raven hair tumbled around her shoulders, her wrists and ankles bound. She was, now, his creature. As he had been hers.

Through her lashes, she watched him intently. He was rapt, absorbed, apparently fascinated by the contrast of the whiteness of her skin and the silver blade, now tracing the blue vein of her inner thigh, skirting the tender flesh of her apex. A frisson of fear, of pure sensual excitement shuddered her spine, swelled the lips enfolding her clitoris.

Her senses sharpened; she felt him probe delicately, lightly unsheathe the tiny bud with the tip of the blade. It sent the heat flooding through her, the dark, feral hunger.

'Sergei,' she whispered softly, infusing her voice with the humid promise of a thousand carnal delights.

Yes, approved observer Serena. Stop him. You're letting it go too far. Recall him. And make him remove the mask.

Not just yet, objected the dark side.

'Serena.' It was a measure of his newfound power that he dared to use her name.

It annoyed her.

She smiled, drew the tip of her tongue along her lips, outlining the plush, red contours of her mouth. 'Kiss me.'

'With my tongue, Serena?' he asked, lifting the knife. Slickened by her juices, it glowed softly in the shadowy light.

She opened her eyes wider. 'With your mouth on my mouth,' she said huskily. 'I want to feel your lips on mine, your tongue on mine, before that tongue licks me.'

Caught by her eyes, by the play of her pointed little tongue dancing across the swell of her lower lip, he moved forward, settling himself along her body, one hand still clasping the knife, the other reaching blindly for her hair. He had licked every part of her body, probed almost every orifice with his fingers and tongue and prick, entered her from every angle, taken her in every conceivable position. She had never before allowed him to touch her lips.

It was, as she had mockingly, even dismissively explained, a simple matter of taste.

Through the narrow gash of the hood, the tip of his tongue darted forward to touch hers. She met it cunningly, flicking the tip of her tongue against his in quick, darting rhythm.

He growled, deep in the back of his throat, thrust his tongue harder against the black leather hood, strained with his teeth against the mask. She retreated gently, circled the narrow slit of the mask with her tongue, tasting the leather. She could feel the bulk of his

201

erection hardening further against her thigh, smell the musky heat of him, sweat and salt and leather.

'Kiss me, Sergei,' she murmured. 'Kiss me.'

With a muttered curse he dropped the knife, fumbled with the fastenings of the mask, and tore it off. His yellow hair was rumpled, his eyes hot and unfocused as he drove at her mouth. He used his tongue like a knife, stabbing at the soft caverns of her mouth, slicing through the barrier of her teeth.

'Darling . . . darling,' breathed actress Serena, moving voluptuously beneath him, nudging his erection with her thigh.

A bit over the top, reproved observer Serena. Now get him to free your hands. Even one hand.

I really think I preferred the knife, the dark side commented.

Max lifted the receiver in his room, dialled for an outside line and waited for the villa's private exchange system to clear him to reach the London office. He had programmed the number into his handset's digital memory system for one-button dialling. He pressed the button, heard the ringing tone and waited. Surely Sally would still be there? In his absence he couldn't imagine her skimping on her exacting attention to business. She hardly ever left the office before seven, sometimes worked as late as eight or nine, and it was barely five o'clock in England.

The ringing tone was clear and undistorted. He fingered the calf-skin cover of his personal organiser. The ringing continued, then broke off with a barely perceptible click, followed by the echoing silence which always preceded a recorded message.

Damn it! Sally must have left early, and not instructed the computer to route calls through to her flat.

He put the phone down and repeated the procedure, this time dialling Sally's home number. From across the valley he heard the mournful resonance of cow bells. A farmer bringing in his animals for the evening's milking, perhaps. The sound mingled with the tone of the international trunk call.

How long should he give it? Two, three minutes? Surely that was long enough to fetch her, even from the shower?

He threw his filofax onto the bed and replaced the receiver. Obviously she wasn't in. And he had been looking forward to getting Franca's signature on the final contract tonight, before she could change her mind.

Damn!

Franca studied herself in the mirror and impulsively reached up and began pulling the pins from her hair, quickly destroying the immaculate coils of the chignon she had just spent twenty minutes creating. The effect had been subtle, sophisticated, elegant, and didn't suit her mood at all.

She dragged her fingers through the once elegant coiffure, disarranging it, rearranging it, tousling it until it was wild and crackling with electricity. A hoyden's hair, streaming in tumbling waves down her back, flowing over her shoulders like molten lava. Better, she decided. The simple white cocktail dress she had selected was perfect foil, elegant, almost demure.

Dinner at eight. The message, conveyed by the impassive housekeeper, appropriately enough on a silver salver, had arrived just as she was waking and carried all the enigmatic mystique of the man himself. The writing cramped, the capitals angular, the signature a bold, dramatic flourish.

Incredibly, it had sent her pulse racing, a heady flurry of expectation overwhelming the unexpected ennui that had led her to her room for a nap after lunch with Max. She had felt unaccountably tired after agreeing to sign with Disc-O, selling herself to an agent who didn't know the difference between Warshawski and Wieniawski. The first, if she remembered correctly, was the name of some fictional female detective recently portrayed in a movie by Kathleen Turner . . . Wieniawski was one of the most internationally famous violinists of the nineteenth century, had toured America with Rubinstein, succeeded Vieuxtemps as professor of violin at the Brussels Conservatory, composed concertos and fantasias . . . Could Max Schiller possibly be as cretinously ignorant about music as he appeared? It was a chilling thought.

He probably got the Rubinsteins confused as well, Anton and Artur, might even call Artur 'Arthur' . . . God knows what sense he made of the Strauss family – all of which was irrelevant.

She had agreed to sign with Max because Mika was with Max, she reminded herself, because she was now with Mika. The future had telescoped itself into their next meeting.

She surveyed herself in the mirror. Good, but not quite perfect. The dress was too severe, designed to please, not tease. On impulse she kicked off the matching stiletto heels.

Perfect.

Barefoot, hair wild, the elegant white dress was now faintly jarring, an intriguing contrast to make the male eye linger on the curves and angles it concealed.

Mixed messages. And tonight she would be cool, unapproachable except as the flawless professional. Not an original strategy, she acknowledged to the mirror, but at least it was a strategy.

One last look in the mirror and she left the room, running lightly down the staircase. As she began to open the doors to the music room, she heard the sound of voices and then a shout of laughter. With sure instinct she recognised Mika's voice, and paused for a moment, relishing the sound. She had never heard him laugh before. She frowned slightly, a puzzled expression on her face, then entered the room.

Max was sitting on the black leather couch, casually

dressed in jeans and a white shirt, glass in hand, smoking a small cigar.

'Franca, come and join us,' he said, voice curiously taut, motioning her further into the room with his glass, rattling the ice-cubes. 'We were just having a drink before dinner.'

Mika was standing by the window looking at Max, eyes bright, a strange expression on his face.

She missed a beat before replying, waiting for Mika's eyes to reach her. When she saw him raise one eyebrow fractionally, taking in her wild hair, naked feet and elegant dress, she moved towards them.

'So I see,' she replied, favouring Max with a smile, giving Mika a rather cool nod of the head.

'What will you have?' asked Max, apparently assuming the role of host. 'I can recommend the Scotch. Fifty years old, tastes like liquid gold mixed with fire. But of course, Mika only has the best.' There was a faintly bitter undertaste to his tone.

'The same, then,' she replied. 'No ice.'

She let her eyes drift to the massive desk, almost obscured by a drift of papers, some crumpled, others fanned out in some bizarre order, and a neat pile meticulously stacked at one corner pinned in place by the Lalique bird.

Surprised, she darted a look at Mika. He'd been following the direction of her gaze, met her lifted brows with a quirk of his lips that might have been a smile.

'Wise of you,' he said smoothly, moving towards the bottles. 'One should never dilute one's pleasures.'

'I agree with you entirely,' she said coolly, but Max saw her eyes widen at his remark.

Their remarks had all the force of innuendo, he thought irritably, and why were they both staring at that silly paper weight? Lalique, if he wasn't mistaken . . . how typical of Mika to use something priceless to anchor his papers. And how annoying.

He watched Franca move towards the desk, caress the glass wing of the bird. The gesture was idle, apparently meaningless, but he could sense the intensity in her. Across the room Mika turned his head to give her a swift, penetrating stare, before turning his back to pour the Scotch.

Max caught his breath. For a moment there had been such a palpable charge between them that the air seemed to crackle, become alive and electric.

She abandoned the bird and came to sit beside Max on the couch, drawing her legs up under her. She was speaking naturally, unaffectedly, her manner so casual and relaxed that he might almost have imagined the heat that flared between them.

A moment later he was sure of it. As Mika handed her the crystal tumbler, her fingers brushed his gently, a gesture so fleeting it might almost have been accidental, but somehow so intimate it could only be contrived.

His resolution to treat her carefully tonight in the absence of a final contract had been completely unnecessary. She was totally absorbed in Mika.

'Your work went well?' she was asking Mika, inclining her head to the papers strewn about his desk.

Mika was silent for a moment, didn't reply, but stood looking at the desk, the scattered papers. The glass bird, its wing still smudged. He frowned a little, flexed his hands. 'Yes,' he replied finally. 'Yes, I think so.'

'But you still haven't told me the scheme of the entire work,' Franca reminded him in a faintly provocative voice, sipping her Scotch. 'Oh, that's divine, you're right, it is liquid gold.'

'And probably costs more,' remarked Max, gulping the last of his drink. 'I'll have another, Mika.'

The faintest twitch of his lips betrayed Mika's reaction. Wordlessly he moved to the cabinet.

'But what is the scheme?' persisted Franca. 'An étude, a tone poem, what?'

'Well,' replied Mika thoughtfully, 'I suppose you could describe it as a form of tone poem.' He poured Max's Scotch, then added more to his own glass. 'It certainly owes something to the *Four Seasons*.' There was the faintest trace of amusement in his voice.

'A tone poem?' Franca's voice was frankly puzzled. 'But *The Kiss* isn't anything like—'

'Conceptually, at any rate,' interjected Mika, cutting her off. 'And I think you may be right. Six movements may make it a trifle long. I've decided to compress it to four.'

'Oh,' she exclaimed, clearly surprised.

'Yes,' he went on. 'I'll lose nothing of the core of the work, and I think structurally that two halves may be even better. Your comments,' he added slowly, eyes shifting to the Lalique bird, 'were . . . not without merit.'

Seated beside her, Max could almost feel the heat that flashed from her, but she covered it quickly, concealed it in a barrage of questions centred on harmonic progression and melodic textures. He listened with half an ear and drank more Scotch, losing interest altogether when Mika and Franca became involved in an impassioned discussion over rhythmic impulse.

Musicians! he snorted to himself. Artistic temperament. Sensitivity, creativity . . . Sensitivity, my arse! he thought. Polysyllabic children with too much money. And Serena still hadn't appeared.

Unlike her to miss a meal, he thought bitterly, wondering where she had been at lunch. And where was she now? She could be having a tray in her room, a meal in the village. Hell, for all he knew she could have flown to bloody Paris for dinner at Maxim's!

Oh, God. What had made him think of Maxim's, of Paris. The first sight of her. The first night of her.

He swirled the Scotch in his glass reflectively. The ice had diluted the smoky gold liquid to amber, the colour of her eyes. He loved watching her eyes as he thrust into her, to see the amber shift to topaz as he moved inside her body, tiny points of gold flickering as he drove himself deeper, losing himself in the velvet

207

of her inner body, the shining gilt of her eyes until he could feel himself coming in her eyes as he exploded into her body.

He was hardening now, even at the memory. Resentfully he drained the last of his Scotch and poured another.

He tried to divert himself by listening to Mika and Franca, now intently discussing quavers, triplets, and semi-quavers. The intensity, the electricity between them should have captured his attention, even if the words meant nothing, but all he could feel was the image of Serena, floating behind his eyes, Serena the siren, Serena the wanton, Serena the cool sophisticate, Serena the greedy urchin licking mayonnaise from her fingers. The woman, warm and vibrant, absorbed in her rose garden.

The Serena who, coolly, dismissively, had said, 'I want to be alone.'

'Garbo did it better,' he said aloud, and drank more Scotch.

'Sergei, darling,' breathed the actress against his mouth, 'I want to touch you . . . feel you . . . finger you. Free my hands, darling, so I can feel your skin.'

Her voice, her words were compelling, inviting. But it was the silent message in her eyes, the tilt of her head, that held more heated sensuality, more erotic promise, more fire than any words could convey.

Garbo couldn't have done it better, approved Serena the observer.

Chapter Nine

Moonlight Sonatas

'Max wasn't himself at dinner,' remarked Franca, accepting a glass of Strega.

'Do you know him so well, then?' asked Mika, his voice amused. He was eyeing the selection of liqueurs Maddie had left with the coffee. Strega was too sweet, Calvados didn't strike the right note. He wanted something to complement the thick, pungent espresso, break the rich aftertaste of the profiteroles smothered in chocolate and whipped cream . . . Grappa, he decided.

'Not that well, no,' she replied. 'But he seemed, oh I don't know. Preoccupied? Worried? And he barely ate a thing.'

And that, she reflected, was almost sacrilege. The mouth-watering salmon mousse, so light, so delicate it seemed to mist on the tongue like sea-foam, a tantalising introduction to the robust seafood symphony that followed. Clams, mussels, scallops, lobsters and crabs in a buttery wine sauce perfumed with garlic and parsley. Freshly baked bread, still warm to the touch, still exuding the irresistible, yeasty fragrance of childhood memories. A summer salad of dandelion leaves, crisp and fragrant, lightly dressed with walnut oil that enhanced, rather than replaced, flavour. All served with a local white wine so fresh it was almost sparkling. Then a selection of cheeses ranging from stilton to mascarpone. The decadent finale of profiteroles smothered in bitter-sweet chocolate which melted like dark magic on the tongue.

No, the food would have seduced the most uncompromising gourmet, shattered the resolution of the most stringent dieter.

But the empty place-setting across from Mika, smoothly removed after the first-course, had seemed to haunt Max, almost as though the shining wineglass waiting to be filled and the pristine white plates were a taunt, a dare.

She had seen Max's eyes shift to Mika as the impassive housekeeper removed the setting, seen the swift, slightly rueful smile that crossed Mika's face, seen Max's jaw harden.

'Perhaps he wasn't hungry,' said Mika lightly, his tone of voice edging towards boredom. He finished his coffee and leaned back in his chair, sipping the grappa, savouring the heated explosion at the back of his throat. Not the liquid gold of his favourite Scotch, this was a thin, snaking flame of taste that danced across the palate like the flickering lights of the candles on the table. They were burning low now, casting her face into shadow while still striking sparks from the red-gold mass of her hair.

'No, it was more than that,' she persisted, looking Mika in the eye. 'There was some tension, some awkwardness between you two . . . I felt it as soon as I walked in.' The slight darkening of his blue eyes warned her not to persist, but the words came out before she could bite them off. 'And I heard you laugh, just before I went into the room.'

He lifted his brows, poured another grappa. 'Is that so unusual? Another Strega? And then I think I shall walk through the gardens.'

Not a warning this time, but a command. No trespassing. Well, she thought, watching the black-gloved

210

hand pour more Strega into her glass, at least it was more politely phrased than usual. He seemed to be mellowing. No indication that he expected her, or even wanted her to join him strolling through the gardens.

Nor would she ask. She would simply, she decided, take it for granted that she would go too.

It was a warm night, almost sultry, the sky midnight blue, stars impossibly bright. She walked beside him, the grass thick and cool beneath her naked feet. The heavy perfume of roses mingled with subtler scents she couldn't identify, something elusive and faintly spicy. She stumbled a little as they turned onto a gravelled path, the sharp pebbles biting into the soles of her feet, and was surprised to feel his arm reach out to steady her.

It was the first time they had been so close since this afternoon when she had taunted him over 'The Kiss', etched the essence of her body onto his lips. She slipped her arm through his as naturally as if he had intended to offer it, rather than merely steady her as she stumbled, and continued walking.

'Foolish girl, not to wear shoes,' he said, a slight tremor in his voice that might have been amusement.

'One should never dilute one's pleasures,' she retorted softly.

He didn't reply, but turned so that they were walking once again on the grass. She felt his body as a warm and comfortable presence, reassuring somehow in the shadowy landscape of the terraced gardens. For a moment the manicured hedgerows had seemed to loom almost threateningly, but she dismissed it as a trick of the light.

Mika turned again, and just ahead of them was a small fountain, the moonlight glinting off the white marble in a playful chiaroscuro. It was a fanciful confection of tritons and mermaids, streams of water jetting from the mouths of four impudent looking dolphins. The underwater lights illuminated the slippery coils of a mermaid sinuously escaping a lustful triton, and highlighted an irate turtle snapping at his staff.

She exclaimed involuntarily in surprised pleasure. 'How beautiful!'

'Borromini, or so Serena would have it,' came his reply. 'I doubt it myself, but it pleases her. "School of", most likely,' he added, 'but then Serena is a bit of a romantic.'

'Can we stay, just for a moment?' she asked, still holding his arm.

'Of course,' he replied courteously, moving towards the fountain.

She slipped away from him then, feeling drawn to the water, walked ahead to perch on the rounded edge of the basin and dipped her fingers in the fountain, knowing how well the play of light and shadow would become her.

Serena, a romantic? What a strange thing for Mika to say! Serena seemed too cool, too sophisticated, too subtle ever to be described as romantic. Determinedly she moved her mind away from Serena, knowing her impulsive tongue would lead her to blurt out the question that had lurked in the background throughout dinner, the cause, no doubt of Max's abstracted behaviour. Where was she? Somehow she was just as much a vibrant presence even when absent, colouring the atmosphere . . . and she didn't want Serena between them now.

As players, as musicians, as violinists she and Mika shared the music in the way Serena never could. They had, surely, a more intense communion than any lovers could hope to achieve, however intimate, however long-standing the relationship.

'Did you mean it, this afternoon?' she asked impulsively, not daring to look at him as he replied, watching the water dance away fom her fingers.

'I imagine so, whatever it is you may be referring to,' he said coolly. 'I generally mean what I say. I find it more efficient.'

'When you said to Max that I played artistically?' she said, almost holding her breath.

'I said that you showed a certain artistry in evoking the theme,' he corrected. 'And yes, I meant it.'

'And then, later, you said that you'd decided to compress the work into four movements,' she persisted, 'but you never really explained the underlying structure . . .' she let her voice trail away, thinking of the Lalique bird now resting atop the pile of manuscripts that surely represented the second movement.

He was standing in front of her, face unreadable in the shadows. She felt the same, hypnotic heat begin to flow through her body, the same centred intensity as she had that afternoon when she had kissed him with her finger, traced the contours of his lips with the balm of her body. She trailed her fingers deeper in the water, losing herself in some half-remembered, half-forgotten rhythm of response.

'After *The Kiss* comes the second movement,' she said softly. 'What happens after the kiss, Mika?'

The question, multi-layered, hovered in the air between them. She might have been referring to the kiss she had given him, or to *The Kiss* she had played for him. Perhaps she didn't really know herself. Perhaps there was no difference, she thought.

'The second movement is, naturally, more complex,' he replied levelly, clenching his hands in his pockets to relieve the annoying tingling sensation coursing through his fingers. His nerve ends seemed to be becoming more irritable, more prone to this phantom torment of unreal sensation. 'As you say, what happens after the kiss? You withdraw lingeringly, regretfully, look into her eyes to see if they are warmed with the first stirrings of desire, taste and test your own response, the lull before hands become bold enough . . .' he paused reflectively, then roused himself. 'Never fear, the second movement will stretch you.'

Seated on the cool stone basin, trailing her fingers in the cool water of the fountain, she found herself moistening at his words, the thick, hypnotic heat pooling between her legs. Stretch her. Stretch her. She imagined him inside her, stretching the tight inner walls of her body with the thick, plunging length of his cock, stretching her arms above her head to feast on her breasts, stretching her legs even further apart as he drove himself into her.

'The chords will be complicated, the minims of chromatic descent to be played at a semi-quaver, long enough for resolution and dissonance to emerge,' he continued. 'Your "flawless technique" should carry you through the most demanding sections,' he said, the extra emphasis in his voice highlighting his words.

The thwarted child in her longed to scream at him, the woman sitting on the edge of the fountain, desire beating hot and heavy in her groin, longed to grind against him. They coalesced in the provocative colleague, who replied, 'An embrace then, I take it.'

'My working title,' he admitted, surprise etching his voice. 'Yes.' He fell silent, watching her finger the water, remembering the first night she arrived, the sight of her naked body straining to the sounds of Handel, the water-darkened fronds of her hair waving like some sea creature fished from the depths of the ocean. It seemed so long ago, especially when he remembered the mesmerising heat of her as she described the kiss and touched her finger to his lips.

His voice altered, he went on, 'Given the initial difficulties you experienced with *The Kiss*, you may find it useful to concentrate on some external symbol, some physical embodiment in which you can find the inner heart of the music.'

At that she flicked her fingers through the water impatiently, almost contemptuously. He must have misread her, he decided.

He waited until it became apparent that she would not reply. 'Serena, I know, will help you,' he said gently.

'I don't need Serena for *The Kiss*, Mika,' replied

Franca, a faint smile hovering at the corners of her mouth. 'Nor for *The Embrace*. Not even for the third movement, or the fourth. Will you conclude with climax or afterglow?'

'With the climax,' he answered, taken aback by her perception, intrigued by the possibilities her comment had raised.

He had heard, had seen, no further than the orgasmic rapture of the climax, the primeval, thrashing frenzy of two bodies striving to unite, the ultimate co-mingling, separated by the merest barrier of flimsy tissue . . . but the aftermath, the afterglow, the soft untwining when sweat-slickened skin parts, when heated breath cools . . . that, surely, was the domain of the violin, the aching tenderness, the sadness after the little death.

After sex, all men are sad, wasn't that what Aristotle had written? *Post coitum, omnes tristes.* It was all he could recall of Serena's flirtation with Latin when they were living in London. It hadn't occurred to him to use the third movement for the climax, the fourth for the heady afterglow, the lazy lassitude as the tingling thrills subside gradually in the bliss of relief . . . what a good idea.

LONDON

Sally paused at the door of Max's penthouse. She had left the office just a fraction before five o'clock, lingered just long enough to select a long, cool caftan from the fitted cupboard beside the fridge, darted into the executive washrooms to change, and then went down in the lift to the waiting taxi. All without giving Eve and Nikolai much thought at all.

Her head full of reports, analyses, market assessments and marketing strategies, she had lost herself fully in the intricate and complex machinery that was Disc-O after speaking to Eve. The teams of secretaries, accountants, lawyers and consultants who inhabited the nether regions of the building all funnelled their various reports through superior after superior until a very condensed, very concise version reached her, and then, after due consideration, Max.

It was easy to lose yourself in work, in details, in contracts. Shut out all the nagging doubts and worries that surfaced when she wasn't concentrating on Disc-O. But now, staring at the massive but familiar, somehow reassuring, entrance to Max's private domain, she hesitated. Why was she here? Why had she allowed Eve to interview Nikolai in the very private place that belonged to Max alone?

Eve had been so convincing, so compelling, so persuasive. She couldn't remember the reasons now, the carefully worded whys and wherefores that had resulted in her handing over Max's second set of keys to Eve.

Franca was going to be booked, as soon as Max had time to discuss the contract with her. Nikolai was not needed now, unnecessary, at least in the role Eve had designed.

On the other hand, Eve had said there were things to discuss. Max was away in Geneva enjoying himself while she was slaving away in London. What harm was there? How could he complain, even if he knew about it? Which he never would. The image of Max and Serena in bed together swam before her eyes, strengthened her determination.

The door swung open easily as she pushed. She had cleared the security check at the entrance to the block using her Disc-O identity card, and all that had been needed was a call from the hall porter to alert Eve.

Sally walked in. Eve was lying back on the ottoman, glass in hand, wearing a white towelling robe tied almost negligently at the waist. Sally caught a glimpse of smoothly curving leg, the shadow of the deep cleft between her breasts as Eve altered her position, stood and came towards her.

'Sally,' she greeted her, voice warm and sincere. 'I am so glad you came.' Eve let her eyes wander over

Sally, pausing at the swell of her breasts almost concealed by the loose caftan. 'We really must talk. But first, some champagne?'

'I'd love one,' Sally replied, moving towards the ottoman. 'Nikolai? Is he still here?'

'Of course, I promised, remember? He's so sweet, I've just sent him off to the music room to tinker with the piano for a while. He went into raptures when he saw it, a Steinway is it?'

'Yes, I think so. Funny, I'm sure Max can't play it,' Sally said.

'Oh, it's probably just there to impress people,' Eve retorted. 'It's the sort of philistine thing a record tycoon like him would do. I mean, look around here!'

Her expansive gesture took in the room, a masterpiece of restrained luxury that served as a setting for Max's collection of modern art. Abstracts for the most part, they were harshly vibrant, angular, discordant and disturbing. It was the collection of a man who either had an unerring instinct for the newest trend or abysmal taste in art. It was impossible to tell.

But it was certainly impressive.

'Yes, he's like that,' said Sally obscurely. The faintly bitter tone in her voice encouraged Eve.

'Of course he is,' she agreed. 'And Max probably wouldn't have the faintest idea what you meant.' Nor did Eve, but that hardly mattered. 'He takes it all for granted. Money, success . . . people.'

'Success,' repeated Sally slowly, seating herself on the ottoman. 'It's what shaped him, shaped his whole life. It came too quickly for him, I think. He's never really had to understand what it's like for the rest of us.'

'Of course he doesn't,' said Eve, 'and when you consider the salaries he pays!' she added suggestively, handing Sally a glass of champagne.

It was a mistake, and she realised it as soon as she said it. Eve was making good money at Disc-O, very good money if the truth be told, and Sally was drawing at least double her salary.

'Oh, I don't know. I live pretty well,' Sally said.

'But not like this,' Eve interjected quickly.

'No, not like this,' agreed Sally, looking around the room. 'Not like this.'

'And you could be doing better,' suggested Eve. Her nerves were singing with tension. She had never been one to rush her fences, but she had a feeling that the time was ripe, that to hesitate now would be to lose the advantage. Max was away, Sally was feeling resentful, a resentment Eve had done everything she could to encourage, and Nikolai was in the next room.

'Mmm,' Sally replied noncommittally.

'Relax, have some more champagne, and let's put our cards on the table,' Eve said gently.

Sally lay back on the ottoman as Eve sank to the floor beside her on a large cushion, her right arm trailing carelessly beside Sally's feet.

'I think,' Eve began, shifting slightly so that her side rubbed against the edge of the ottoman and her blonde hair lightly grazed Sally's legs, 'I think that Max needs to wake up a bit. And perhaps we can help him.'

The sounds of the piano drifted into the room. Sally lifted her head from the cushion and listened. It was Chopin's *Revolutionary Polonaise*. A call to arms, she thought vaguely.

'I'm not sure I really feel like helping him at all,' she said suddenly, surprising herself a little. Perhaps the paintings were annoying her. She knew exactly how much each one had cost, and how much each had appreciated over the past year. The obnoxious red and green splash on the wall opposite would have paid her rent for a year. 'Waking him up, perhaps. But I guess I'm not feeling very charitable at the moment. Mmm. Nikolai is very good, isn't he?'

'Darling, he's a world-beater. And also very, very cooperative,' Eve added, pouring more champagne into Sally's empty glass.

As she replaced the bottle on the table she moved her right hand up Sally's bare leg, and began to caress it gently. Sally felt herself growing a little lightheaded, a little flushed from the champagne and the heady sensation of Eve's fingers stroking her calf, her thigh.

'Maybe Max is just too monomaniac about the violin,' she mused, admiring the Chopin. 'Maybe he can't see beyond his early success with Mika, has lost touch with what the audiences are wanting and waiting for.'

Eve's hand moved higher, to the top of her thigh. 'You're so right, Sally. But then, you've always been the one with your fingers on the pulse of the public. Max barely pays any attention to the marketing summaries any more.' Her fingers crept toward Sally's mound tentatively, almost surreptitiously.

'True,' Sally said, remembering the brief discussion she had with Max that had resulted in the search for Franca. 'Very true. I wonder sometimes . . .' her voice trailed off, and she drank more champagne.

'Yes?' coaxed Eve, her hand suddenly still.

Unconsciously Sally arched towards it, moving just slightly, just fractionally, just enough so that Eve's fingers grazed her sex.

'I wonder if his infatuation with Serena—' she halted, began again. 'I wonder if Franca is only Max's way back into the charmed circle of Mika and Serena. I wonder if he'll ever see that?' The words were out, irreclaimable.

'Sally, I've seen that from the first,' Eve agreed sadly, secretly exulting. Sally's words might be a little unclear, but her dissatisfaction was obvious. 'That's why Nikolai can be so helpful, so important. For both of us.' She let her index finger slip between the leaves of Sally's labia. She was already moistening, perhaps hardly aware of it.

'No, I don't see it, Eve. Max won't be interested,' Sally replied, wriggling a little. 'He'll be signing up Franca soon, she's agreed in principle to the draft contract.' Eve's eyes widened, but Sally hardly noticed.

'What possible use would Max see for some pub pianist? No recordings, no major concerts or awards to his name.'

'So the problem, as you see it?' prompted Eve, her finger still.

'Basic PR,' said Sally automatically, arching her hips instinctively even as she assessed the situation as Max would see it. 'He'd have to have had a distinguished career at the Moscow Conservatoire, perhaps a tragic tale of blocked opportunities at the end of the Soviet era. Maybe be a son persecuted because his father fell foul of the KGB over human rights, something like that. Otherwise Max would never go for it.'

Eve's eyes brightened. What a clever ploy. Sally never disappointed her. Or hadn't yet.

'But just think, Sally,' she coaxed. 'Think. If you had a free hand, a free rein, how would you use him, market him, make him? And wouldn't you love the chance to try? Wait until you meet him. Nikolai! Join us.'

GENEVA

He looked into yellow eyes now slumbrous with desire, golden glints of fire dancing in the topaz depths, and was lost. No man could resist the mute invitation of those amber eyes.

With a muffled groan he reached for her wrists, fumbling with the manacles, even as his mouth searched for hers again. He had never experienced anything so intimately erotic, so enticing, as the touch of her tongue meeting his, the ivory hardness of her tiny pointed teeth nipping at him, the humid warmth of the contours of her mouth.

As the manacles fell away, he heard her sigh against his mouth, felt the delicious play of her hands as they travelled down his shoulders to his waist, his buttocks. His mouth never left hers as he tore at his shirt, tore at his trousers, eager, passionate, demented, to remove the last barrier between them, the barrier that had already been weakened by possession of her mouth.

Impersonally she admired the feel of taut muscles bunching beneath his skin at her touch, the involuntary shudder of his body as she rasped one long nail against the base of his spine. His erection lay between them like a thick iron rod, trembling against her inner thigh, now questing for her entrance even as he plunged his tongue deeper into her mouth. She let her hands drift idly along his torso, enjoying the tensile warmth of his skin, slickened with the sweat of arousal. As her fingers moved lower along his rib cage she felt, bunched at his side, the supple smoothness of leather. Carefully she drew it away from their entwined bodies, explored it with her fingers and recognised, with a slow flush of excitement, the contours of the mask.

He was avid, engorged, blindly driving into her mouth, his cock searching through the soft pink folds to find her hidden lips. She arched her neck, forcing his mouth to her throat, shifted beneath him until her neck and shoulders were free.

He groaned hoarsely in protest, moved to recapture her lips, but she guided him to her breasts, fingers urgent at the back of his neck, and moaned deep in her throat.

Primitive excitement arced through him at the sound, a soft mewling moan of surrender. She had never been so eager for him, so submissive, so subdued to the will of his body.

And as his teeth closed on her nipple, she drew the mask over her head.

She waited for the black heat to envelop her, the dark sensual thrum to pulse through her, then suddenly thrashed beneath him, coiling and uncoiling, thrusting with her pelvis, grappling with her arms in a sudden frenzy that might almost have been passion. And in the tangled welter of furious, flailing limbs that was his response, she somehow managed to free her ankles.

Breathing harshly, finally he managed to subdue her, pinning her still by her shoulders. And found himself looking into the expressionless black visage of the hood.

Her hand curled around him, nails poised at the tender flesh of the head of his cock.

'Sergei,' she whispered, eyes yellow points of flame behind the slits of the mask, 'give me your hand.'

The heat in her eyes became the heat in his cock as, utterly mesmerised, he lifted his arm from her shoulder, reached out to take the one outstretched hand she offered, unbearably conscious of the warm, predatory pressure of her fingers around his shaft. The sharp click as she snapped the manacle into place was almost explosive.

There were no multiple Serenas now, no actress, no observer. The dark side smiled a little as she straddled him, felt the pulsing length of his rod along her furrow, saw the first stirrings of fear in his eyes as slowly, thoughtfully, almost meditatively she reached for the knife that had fallen beside them.

'Serena,' he said, voice cracking a little. 'Serena.'

She let the other hand drift to the side of his neck, slim fingers gently exploring, a touch so tender it might have been a caress. Found the pressure point that would induce unconsciousness in seconds, death in a few minutes. Kept her fingers there as she gently eased the hot, long length of him into her body.

He was gone again, as surely as if he had turned on his heel and walked away, instead of moving to the edge of the fountain to sit beside her. His eyes were rapt, unfocused, a look she had seen before.

In the soft moonlight and flickering underwater lights of the fountain his face wore the absorbed expression of a medieval monk in contemplation, a Byzantine saint at prayer. There was something paradoxically ascetic about the sensual planes of his face, the high cheek bones, the full, lower lip, the deep-set eyes now the midnight blue of the sky.

She looked up at the sky, trying to subdue her frustration. What had Menuhin said? 'To play great music, you must keep your eyes on a distant star.'

A distant star. Scattered across the heavens like winking diamonds they seemed as impossibly bright, as impossibly far away as Mika himself, even though she could feel the heat of his body beside her.

'That I should love a bright, particular star.' The words came unbidden to her mind, their origin obscure. But she knew the despairing desire, the same wrenching, aching for the impossible, and promised herself that she would have it. Regardless of the cost.

She would have him, seduce him with his music, with her body, with every potent promise they both embodied. He was lost in the music now, as completely and utterly as he would lose himself in her.

'An embrace,' she said softly, trying not to shatter the spell of his concentration, 'can be so many things. Gentle. Enfolding. Tender. Rough. Wild. Passionate.'

'Yes,' he replied, eyes glowing, 'all those things. Before the pizzicato, before the pearls fall to the floor.'

It wasn't necessary to understand his words. She caught the meaning in his voice, the timbre of suppressed excitement.

'Contrasts. Cock and nipples hard, hands soft,' she ventured, eyes intent on his face, aware her own nipples were hardening.

'Yes,' he said again, 'tongues thrashing, hard, pointed, bodies still, bowing deep and long.'

Her vision was flowing with his now, the heat between her legs firing the heat of creative excitement. 'And laughter,' she exclaimed excitedly, 'there must be laughter. The kind of laughter only shared between soon to be lovers, warm, intimate, excited.'

'Plucked, not bowed,' he agreed, turning to look at her. Her eyes were shining, her hair tumbled around her shoulders.

The heat flowed between them, a sudden crackling, electric rush that fired every cell in her body. She remained still, waiting for him, knowing that he would move closer, touch her, embrace her as she had kissed him.

'It's late, and I have work to do,' said Mika coolly. 'We'll go back now.'

Max dialled Sally's flat for the third time. For the third time he listened to it ring. And ring. And ring.

Dinner had been a disaster. Without a final contract he couldn't follow his instincts and snag Franca – so receptive this afternoon, so engrossed in Mika tonight that she barely seemed aware of anything else. And where the hell was Serena?

Irritably, he replaced the receiver, and almost as a reflex, to ease the frustrations of the day, dialled his home number to pick up any messages on his answerphone.

A few minutes later he hung up the phone and rubbed his eyes as if he could erase the confusion clouding his mind. Doubtfully he eyed the Scotch bottle on the table beside him. Still half full, he hadn't had that much to drink. Maybe it packed a hidden punch, he thought, and poured himself another to find out.

He had been astounded to hear Sally's voice on the other end of the line. In his initial relief at getting hold of her he had merely instructed her to fax two copies of a final contract to the villa and hung up. But she had sounded . . . different. And what was she doing there anyway?

She had, of course, a spare set of keys to the flat, for any emergencies that might arise, but he didn't remember asking her to check the mail and water the plants.

Reflectively, he drank more Scotch. Water the plants? He cast his mind back to the London flat. He wasn't sure, couldn't quite remember, but he had a faint, sneaking suspicion, a nagging doubt . . .

Another gulp of Scotch.

No, dammit, he was certain. He didn't have any plants.

LONDON

Sally replaced the receiver with trembling fingers and reached for a cigarette.

'Well?' Eve's voice was as smooth as honey.

'Well?' echoed Nikolai, his gravelly voice a rough contrast to Eve's sensuous purr.

She fumbled with the gold-plated lighter, lit the cigarette on her third attempt. 'That was Max,' said Sally in a tense little voice.

'Darling, I guessed as much when you called him by name,' rippled Eve. 'What on earth made you pick up the phone . . . especially at a time like this?'

'I don't know,' she replied a little numbly. 'Just . . . reflex, I guess.' And it was true. She had never been able to bear the sound of a ringing telephone, would leap from the bath, drop groceries in the hall and fumble with the locks of her door, unthinkingly reach for the receiver even in the middle of sex.

She looked over at them, sprawled across the rumpled white sheets of Max's huge bed. Eve's platinum blonde hair was tousled, her eyes bright, her scarlet lips pouting. Nikolai's erection was still thick and hard, a few glistening drops still pearling the head of his shaft. His semen? she wondered a little wildly, or her saliva? He had been in Sally's mouth as she knelt between his legs, Eve pressed close behind her, her clever fingers teasing her rectum, her knowing tongue dancing along the slick folds of her sex, Nikolai's hands squeezing her nipples.

She took a deep drag of smoke and exhaled, trying to push away the sound of Max's voice. His familiar deep baritone had sounded puzzled, furred a little with Scotch, she guessed.

'Clever of you to say that you were just checking the flat,' approved Eve, privately thinking that she had never heard a more lame excuse. Fortunately, it didn't matter now. But twist the knife a little, just to make sure. 'He'd naturally assume that sweet, subservient Sally would worry about his plants, about his mail, even check his laundry, while he's in Geneva shagging Serena. It's amusing, isn't it, darling?'

Sally crushed out her cigarette, lit another.

'Clever Sally,' agreed Nikolai, dropping a kiss on Eve's shoulder. 'Put out that cigarette and come here.'

She edged closer to the side of the bed. 'No,' she began, 'Eve, I, I don't think we should – I can't. I don't feel right about this. Max trusts me.'

She looked down at her hands, missing the glance that passed between Nikolai and Eve. And then Eve was beside her, deftly plucking the cigarette from her fingers, easing her onto her back, soothing her with a soft litany of reassuring words, and Nikolai was between her legs, bathing the tender folds of her labia with long, rhythmic strokes of his tongue.

'Clever Sally, beautiful Sally, so soft and sweet here,' murmured Nikolai, nipping at her clitoris.

'Clever Sally, lovely Sally, so hard here,' breathed Eve, her mouth closing on her nipple.

Fingers, tongues, teeth becoming more insistent, more urgent, moving to her belly, hands gliding across her buttocks, a squirming tongue insinuating itself deeper in the pink folds, finding the entrance to her body, sucking at her, drinking her.

The drowsy warmth heating and curling, becoming hotter, undulating through her, hollowing her to a hot, wet void waiting to be filled.

'Clever, clever Sally,' rumbled Nikolai, positioning himself, rubbing the head of his penis against her anus. She was so slick, so wet he could drive himself into her now.

'Clever, clever, Sally,' whispered Eve beneath them, thrusting her tongue into her vagina.

GENEVA

The life pulse was beating under her fingers, between her legs. She rocked gently, moving the hard shaft inside her, pressing forward, feeling it thrum against the muscles of her belly, leaning back until it urged against the hollow of her rectum. She tightened her inner muscles, imagining them as steel sheathed in silk that could snap the rod buried inside her . . . or caress it.

She let her index finger press gently against the side of his neck, feeling the artery there, let her inner muscles clench him as she pressed down more firmly.

'Serena. Serena.' A hoarse voice from far away kept repeating it. 'Serena. Serena.'

She smiled a little, even as she deepened the pressure. Serena.

What a pretty name.

And the faint whisper of fear edging the voice pleased her, made the name more compelling, the slithering sibilants writhing like snakes. Sssserena.

The male body beneath hers was shuddering, thrusting into her, striving for release, for domination, a body in thrall to the movements of hers, with enough instinct left to shiver at the knife in her hand.

She could sense the muscles in his belly tightening, his hips thrusting harder, knew from his laboured breathing that he was soon to explode within her.

And he must not be allowed to please himself, find the ecstatic flood of release inside her. Dreamily, waveringly she wondered why, but her mind refused to focus . . . it had something to do with the name he kept repeating in a mindless litany.

'Serena.'

'Sssserena.'

'Sssereeeenna.'

As he thrust again, desperately, wildly, the penultimate push for orgasm, his eyes were screwed shut in

227

blind concentration. He didn't see the yellow flash of fire behind the hood.

'Serena.' It was almost a shout.

Eyes glittering in sudden recognition she looked at the body beneath hers, the curling, matted golden hair on his chest, the bullish neck, thick arms upraised, held by the manacles.

Sergei.

Her chauffeur.

He really shouldn't have dared to use her name. It was just a little too familiar, she decided, a little too intimate.

The dark side behind the hood, the actress, the observer all coalesced as she moved swiftly in retaliation, riding him hard, chafing the hard rod inside her, denying him the rhythm he needed, no longer stroking him with her inner muscles, but striking him, thrashing him, keeping him hard, hovering on the edge, denying him.

He groaned hoarsely, once, twice, again, a disbelieving aching sound that enfolded her in a warm flush of pleasure, made her acutely aware of the engorged folds of her sex, her body's mindless response. She let the hot flood run through her then, gloried in the tides of sensation centring in her groin, the heavy ache of arousal.

Furious, riotous, rampant, she plunged on until she felt the first burning presage of his orgasm flickering through her. And as her muscles contracted in response, she willed herself to increase the pressure. He had no right.

There is a moment on the verge of orgasm when a change of rhythm, a change of pressure, even a change of mood can halt the impending flood. As much physical as psychological, it can provide the most intense frustration, the most intense and abrupt pain. Serena knew very well how to provoke it.

Sensing him poised but struggling on the very brink, she fleetingly looked back over the years. The orphanage. The deprivation. The early days of self-denial with Mika. The moulding of his talent. The rewards and the riches . . . the accident. All culminating in this greedy homunculus beneath her, Serena D'Angelo.

As if in celebration of her name, the hallmark of the successful identity she had created for herself, her inner muscles contracted again tightly, so tight that they held Sergei's manhood in a vice-like grip. And, triumphant, she felt him waver, slacken unwillingly, subside disbelieving.

She had won. He had lost the will to orgasm, without knowing why.

In one swift, slick movement she hauled herself away, let herself slide to his side as the electric shocks flared through her, wrapped her arms around herself and laughed as the glorious flames ignited and exploded.

He watched with stunned eyes as she held herself, convulsed with laughter and orgasm, the milky white skin flushed to an almost luminous pink, the black leather hood an almost sinister foil.

The primitive, primeval urge for release triggered in his brain, but unattainable in his body, was almost unbearable. It flared hotter as he saw her remove the hood and shake her head, releasing the perfumed cloud of her raven hair.

'Sergei,' she purred, her smile a warm, red curl of lip that he recognised with a sense of foreboding.

'Serena, for God's sake,' he mouthed hoarsely, thrusting his pelvis, aching for her mouth, her limbs, the final friction that would surely recreate his arousal and release the demon desire from his body.

'Sergei, my dear.' She looked at him tenderly, he thought, almost lovingly. She leaned forward, kissed his cheek with smiling lips. The soft touch of her breast against his shoulder almost released the explosion.

'Sergei . . . you're fired.'

She got to her feet and stretched, ignoring him, looked around for something to fight the chill of the cellars. Humming softly to herself she found the black leather shirt he had worn, sniffed it appreciatively, and wrapped it around herself. It came to mid-thigh. The trousers would be much too large, she knew, so she contented herself with removing the black leather belt and twisting it around her waist.

A pity there was no mirror, she reflected, fluffing her hair and smoothing the shirt over her thighs, but then life was like that.

You had to learn to take the rough with the smooth.

Mika was alone in the music room, bent over his desk, a stack of neatly folded papers to one side, the Lalique bird perched on top as an impromptu paperweight. In the harsh light of the desk lamp, the only illumination for the vast room, his hair looked like molten gold. She slid inside, softly replacing the huge carved doors so that they shut without a trace of a sound.

He looked up immediately.

'Serena.' Something in the undertone caught her attention, some faint edge that she had never heard before. Irritation? Relief? Annoyance? Perhaps it was merely surprise.

'Sorry, darling, I didn't dress for dinner,' she said, deflecting whatever he might have meant to convey by his tone, and sprawled herself on the black leather couch.

'Serena.' A wealth of meaning in his voice, the indulgent parent confronting a childish misdemeanour, the rueful lover forgiving yet another indiscretion.

'Yes, Mika?' she said, eyes challenging, the merest suspicion of a whiplash to her voice as she crossed her legs.

'You've missed dinner, my love,' he replied, rising from his desk. He reached out for his glass, drained the last of the grappa as he looked at her, took in the glittering yellow eyes, the flowing black shirt rolled back at the cuffs to expose her slender wrists, the heightened red of her mouth.

'A bit camp, I agree,' she acknowledged, smoothing the shirt over her thighs. 'But I simply couldn't find a thing to wear.'

He smiled a little wryly, she thought. She sensed he was hovering on the edge of some statement, some remark, something she didn't want to hear. She warned him with her eyes, lowering her lashes just slightly, and shrugged.

'You must be hungry,' he said casually.

'Ravenous, darling,' she admitted. 'And thirsty.'

'Wait here, I'll fix you a tray.' He hadn't moved, was still standing by his desk, looking at her as though he would never look away.

'Mmm, lovely,' she purred, flexing her body. 'Caviare, perhaps, asparagus, smoked salmon . . . greedy things, Mika.' She smiled at him, relaxed.

He moved then, paused to drop a light kiss on her hair, smelled the sex scent rising from the shirt, from her body.

'Greedy child,' he reproved, hand lingering on her shoulder. 'You'll have leftovers if you have anything at all. You should be sent to bed without any dinner the way you've behaved.'

Her laughter, warm and surprised, followed him out of the room.

It was an old joke, from the early days, one they hadn't made in years. It belonged to the orphanage, to those days in London when they could barely afford to eat, when baked beans on toast sometimes seemed an unparalleled luxury. How strange that the old days had risen so clearly in her mind tonight, and in Mika's. But there had been an edge to his voice, something she didn't recognise. Didn't like. Something she wouldn't concern herself with, at least tonight.

She was hungry.

When Mika returned from the kitchen with a tray, clutching several bottles of white wine, Serena inspected it with the impersonal air of a connoisseur even as her mouth watered. Fresh bread. Smoked oysters. Cold asparagus. Half a lobster. To one side, profiteroles smothered in chocolate, drowning in cream. Not a single knife, fork or spoon. He knew her preferences in private.

'No caviare?' she exclaimed in a tone that would have the most experienced maitre d'hotel shivering in trepidation.

'I hate it when you eat caviare with your fingers,' Mika returned, opening the wine. 'It gets all over the place, and then Maddie complains. Eat up like a good child.'

With a sigh of contentment she reached for an oyster, loving the oily, slippery feel of it on her fingers. 'You've been working,' she said, gesturing to the desk, the sheaf of papers spilling from its polished surface.

'Yes,' he said, pouring the yellow wine into two glasses and handing her one.

'Lovely,' she purred, taking a long swallow and then setting the glass beside her. Her fingers left a sticky mark on the crystal surface, and involuntarily his eyes flickered over to the Lalique bird poised on the completed pages of his manuscript.

'Tell me,' she invited, tearing at the bread. 'Tell me.'

And so he told her, speaking as she ate. Told her about the changing, shifting patterns of the work, how it had moved from six movements to four, how the passion of the violin was expressing itself in the passion of the body, how perfectly the first movement had flowed from him onto the page, the difficulties Franca had experienced in capturing his vision. For the moment he shied away from the strangely moving experience when she had . . . kissed him. He would, he knew, tell Serena everything in time. Except the title. She would never know whose song it truly was until it was perfectly formed, perfectly executed, his most perfect gift to her.

'Darling, it's brilliant!' Serena exclaimed, waving a lobster claw for emphasis before moving it to her lips and sucking out the tender white flesh. 'It's everything we've ever learned about the violin, about music, even about sex! It's a rehearsal in the form of a score!'

'You're right,' he said slowly, moving to sit beside her. 'I hadn't thought of it that way,' he admitted, reaching unthinkingly for one of her oysters. His hand was poised just above the plate when his mind registered the sight of his fingers enclosed in black leather, and he drew his hand away.

'Silly,' she murmured softly, taking his hand and squeezing his fingers briefly before lifting an oyster to his lips.

'Silly child, to hate knives and forks,' he returned, acknowledging the touch of her fingers with his own.

'But difficult,' she said, mind hardly diverted from the music. 'How do you rehearse a rehearsal? We played on the underlying passion . . . when passion is the theme, how does one rehearse?'

Her fingers hovered undecidedly between the lobster and the asparagus, and watching them Mika was conscious of a sudden, overwhelming feeling of tenderness. Long, slender, elegant fingers, bare of rings, nails unpolished, the hands that had held his in fear, in delight, in plots and counterplots, held fast to his throughout the nightmare of Milan and later, soothed him, petted him, never clenched his in passion.

He could tell her anything. Everything.

Except, perhaps, the problem that had been worrying at him since he began to compose, since Max and Franca had come to the villa.

She pounced in favour of the asparagus. 'Well, my love? What have you been doing?'

'Well, nothing really,' he said, grateful for the respite, sipping some wine, savouring her presence. 'Nothing, except . . .'

'Mmm?'

He watched her prise more meat from the lobster, heard her hum in appreciation. She could lose herself so easily in the pleasures of the flesh, something he

233

had never been able to master so abandonedly, so joyfully.

He spoke with difficulty at first, then with increasing confidence, describing how he had tried to ease Franca towards *The Kiss*, move her without touching her, how she had . . . kissed him. The words she had used. The womb. The tomb. And how he had felt the work coalesce tonight at the fountain.

'At my Borromini,' she corrected, a sidelong glance at him as she drained her glass.

'At your Borromini, love,' he acknowledged, hiding the smile he knew she could sense on his lips. 'And I realised then that the fourth movement had to be the afterglow, the aftermath. I hadn't seen it before.'

'You have, at times, a selective blindness, Mika,' she replied. 'You only have to look at the curves, how cunningly the angles are placed, how sinuously the whole piece moves together. Of course it's Borromini.' She held her glass out for more wine, which he obligingly poured. And he knew she wasn't talking about the fountain. At least, not entirely.

'And she said she doesn't want my help?' asked Serena dipping into the profiteroles and licking the chocolate from her fingers.

'Yes, that's what she said.'

'I wonder if that's true,' she mused, 'I wonder if she really knows what this level of playing requires, whether she can sustain it. Of course, she may be right. She may already have identified the physical stimulus she needs to interpret.' Her voice was soft, coaxing.

He looked away, his gaze lighting on the bird.

'How long before it's finished, Mika?' she continued, unwilling to press him.

'A month, six weeks at least,' he replied. 'It's gone so quickly, it feels so right, but I know I'll want to play around with it, explore it, expand it. It's remarkable, See, hearing the music in my mind in a different way. It seems to be with me all the time, even though I'm not always conscious of it, and then suddenly I know what I need to do with it. Does that make sense?'

'Stravinsky said something similar, darling,' said Serena through a mouthful of whipped cream. She giggled suddenly. 'What a pity you're not American!'

He laughed with her. It was an old joke they shared. 'Of course, the way to write American music is simple,' he began.

'All you have to do,' she joined in, 'is be an American and then write any kind of music you wish! What impossible names they have, too. Virgil Thomson!'

'And what improbable names we have,' he remarked, suddenly serious. 'Serena. Mika. And what improbable lives we have led.'

'Serena suits me,' she replied levelly, reaching for her glass.

'A curious thing happened this evening,' he said abruptly. 'Max and I were having a drink before dinner and he was talking about Disc-O, plans for expansion, business. I wasn't really paying attention, my mind was on *The Embrace* but then he mentioned Sally.'

She went utterly still, hand poised to take her glass.

'I must have shown something, or perhaps not. He changed the subject then, asked where you were, if there was any sort of problem.'

'And?' Her voice betrayed nothing but slight curiosity.

'And I laughed. God help me, it suddenly seemed so ludicrous, so bizarre, such a strange coincidence. I think I offended him.'

'Coincidence?' she inquired.

'Sally, as it turns out, is his assistant at Disc-O.'

Some of the colour returned to her face. Her hand was, she was pleased to see, absolutely steady as it grasped the glass, lifted it to her lips.

'What a curious coincidence indeed,' she said lightly. It might have been thirst, might have been agitation that drove her to drain her glass at a gulp and extend it for more. It was impossible to tell.

'Yes,' Mika replied, refilling her glass. 'Later I wondered . . . but Max isn't subtle enough, devious enough to play mind games like that. Or is he? Serena?'

'Devious? Max? Subtle? Max?' Amusement bubbled through her voice.

'Mmm.'

'Mika, my love, that's as absurd as, absurd as—' Comparisons failed her. 'It's absurd,' she said decisively, outwardly calm, remembering with lightning clarity how convinced she had been at the outset that Max had some hidden agenda.

Convinced enough to add the aphrodisiac to his wine. Driven by suspicion, or some subconscious desire to know what he would be like under its influence? She filed the thought away and concentrated on Max.

Whatever suspicions she had initially had been soothed away by his frank, open manner when he discovered her going through his papers that first night, allayed by his willingness to surrender to erotic play with Franca, disarmed by the unfailing tenderness he had shown.

'There are things that don't ring true.'

Mika's voice broke into her thoughts, recalling her.

'He can't be as cretinously ignorant about music as he pretends and have made Disc-O what it is today,' observed Mika.

'I wouldn't have thought he was particularly ignorant about music, darling,' she replied absentmindedly.

'You weren't at lunch,' he reminded her, recalling the expression of horror on Franca's face when Max had mistaken Warshawski – whoever that might be – for Wieniawski.

'No,' she agreed, suddenly yawning, exposing her perfect, pointed little white teeth. 'Perhaps he was merely, merely, umm, sending you up, isn't that the English expression?' Having no real nationality of her own that she chose to claim, Serena had adopted an attitude of utter ignorance about the most commonplace, colloquial expressions. It was her way of patronising most countries. Usually it amused him.

'It is,' corroborated Mika patiently. 'But Max isn't English.'

She dismissed that for the irrelevancy that it was.

'He did act strangely during dinner,' Mika persisted, again remembering Franca, how she had commented on Max's lack of appetite, how his eyes had kept returning to Serena's empty place.

'Max wouldn't harm either of us,' she said with utter conviction. An expression of complete trust she swiftly undercut by pointing out, 'It could do nothing but harm him. And Disc-O.'

'No,' he agreed, a bit reluctantly. Serena had a shark's instinct not only for blood but for self-preservation that had saved them many times. But was it possible that she had the selective blind spot she accused him of?

'I've been wondering, See, wondering if perhaps something hasn't happened that might make him dangerous. Very dangerous indeed,' he said finally.

'What on earth do you mean?' she asked in surprise, opening her eyes wide.

'I think he loves you, See,' he said bluntly, fixing his blue eyes on hers.

Amber eyes winked back. 'Of course he does, darling,' she said, laughing a little. 'How could he not?'

'Serena.' Mika's voice was suddenly harsh, compelling. 'I think he's in love with you.'

She shrugged, dipped her index finger in the decadently rich chocolate sauce smothering the profiteroles. Another irrelevance. Max English, not English, loving, in love, what difference did it make?

He replied to the language of her body by clasping her shoulder, his fingers urgent. 'Listen to me, Serena. "Loving", "in love", they're both dangerous, but "in love" – it's passion, it's heartache, it's hatred, every primal, visceral emotion rolled into one. It's clawing for the stars when it's tearing at your guts, it heightens

237

every sense, turns the world upside down, shifts angles, perspectives. Do you understand?'

'Ah,' she purred, a sweet malice decorating her voice, 'the voice of experience?'

His grip on her shoulder loosened, but his eyes never wavered. 'Yes. You can't play the violin without being in love.'

'But I interpret the violin, Mika. You're making a distinction without a difference. A rather trite and boring little distinction, too, if you'll forgive me.' Her eyes were hot and angry and he could feel her body tensing under his hand.

Deliberately he loosened his grip on her shoulder. He felt the tears gather at the back of his throat, feeling her recoil from his touch, his words.

Impatiently he rose from the couch, paced before the large picture windows, which were blank with the darkness of night.

'Serena,' he said aloud, 'Serena.' His mantra.

She watched him with iron in her eyes, and sipped her wine.

His back to her, looking out the window, he spoke again. 'Serena, it's perhaps dangerous for us, but it's not a terrible thing. I've expressed myself badly.' He halted, fumbling for the words that refused to come.

Another sip of wine. Not by the flicker of an eyelid, by the faintest gesture would she betray how he had wounded her.

'I like Max,' he said to the window, apparently at random. 'And I've been thinking about you, about . . . things.' Without turning around, he gestured to the antique cabinet holding his Stradivarius. 'Like her, you belong in the spotlights, See, you've been restless, I know it, and I've been thinking about the future—'

She interrupted him, her voice silky. 'Ah. The future. Such a portentous word. Or do I mean pretentious? This *is* the future, Mika. The one we dreamed of, planned for, worked for.'

'Not exactly,' he said, looking down at his hands.

'No, not exactly,' she returned, her voice surprisingly cold. 'But we have money. Independence. Freedom. And you've found another way to work,' she added more gently.

'But you haven't.' He spoke to the window. They were terrible words, best left unsaid. And he had said them. He had known from the first instant she appeared in the room, wearing the smell of sex and the black leather shirt that something had drawn her back to the dark side, the side that made her something other than Serena. Not more, not less, just other. He couldn't express it better, even to himself.

'Darling, I've never truly espoused the Protestant work ethic in my life. And I have no intention of starting now.' The silk in her voice became taffeta. It scratched, just a little.

She was avoiding the meaning, responding to the words alone, as flippantly as if he were some meaningless acquaintance at a cocktail party. He had to break down the barriers, find some way to express the whirling confusion, the growing conviction that both he and she could find something new to guide them.

As usual, she guessed his intent, even supplied the words.

'So, Mika. The future. I should have one perhaps? You think so? One different than the one I lead? An object in life, even?'

'Perhaps,' he ventured, turning to face her.

She smiled, a slow, slumbrous smile. 'Mmm. Something to give my life meaning, you think? A goal?'

He nodded encouragingly, a smile beginning to light his face.

'Well,' she said meditatively, 'I see where you're leading. Max. A man who loves me. Involved in an industry of which I have some knowledge and expertise. A rewarding, challenging career . . . or at least an opportunity to flee these walls and – no, I can't say "find myself", now, can I? Outdated jargon, and for

239

various other reasons, completely impossible. But this is what you're suggesting?'

'Yes.' His voice held the slightest tremor.

'At one stroke relieving your rather nebulous concerns about Max as a threat, and creating for me . . . some . . . work?'

He was silent.

'And, then, in the future, who knows?' she mused. 'Respectability? I have, certainly, a cachet which could translate with the proper outside arrangements into "respectability". Marriage? I suppose marriage is not inconceivable, is it Mika?'

Softened blue eyes met her yellow stare.

'And then . . . children? I wonder.' She looked down at her perfect body, scantily clad in the black leather shirt, ripe, luscious, still faintly exuding the scent of sex.

She laughed, the warm husky bubble he knew so well. 'Why not a rose covered cottage while we're at it, my love?'

'Serena—' His voice was tentative.

'Darling, you're a romantic, it's something I've always loved in you, it's what made you Mika.' Her voice was caressing.

Which made the whiplash that followed so shocking.

'But a bourgeoisie romantic at heart, I'm afraid, my love. You'd be well advised to save your clichés for your score.'

She rose in one lithe, controlled movement and walked to the door, disdainfully licking the last of the chocolate from her fingers. And because he knew her flashes of temper so well, he called to her at the door, ventured the question that had hovered at the edges of his mind all day, even though he was sure he knew the answer.

'Where were you today, Serena?'

Half through the door, she inclined her head towards him. Should she, could she, resort to another cliché?

Why not?

It had turned out to be an unexpectedly cliché-ridden evening.

'Well, darling, I was tied up.'

Alone in her suite, sitting at her black lacquered dressing-table, the anger, the outrage, the outrageous events of the past hours clashed and collided in a sudden, horrible wave, thudding against her with such force that Serena actually gasped for breath. She reached out a hand to steady herself and found herself grasping one of the carved ivory dildoes scattered in erotic disarray along the polished black surface.

She dropped it as though it had scorched her fingers.

With a sudden, instinctive, unthinking sweep of her hand, she dashed the entire collection to the floor, the dildoes, the love beads, the whips, the unguents and potions. One of the bottles broke, releasing a pungent, aromatic scent.

She ignored it, looking deep into the mirror, rubbing her hands along the lacquered surface of the dressing-table, as if its rich, black patina could warm the darkness within her.

Chapter Ten

Rhapsody in F Minor

M ax was awake. His mind was a rat's nest, a labyrinth, a maze of stray thoughts jostling and scrabbling, fretting the fabric of sleep with needle-sharp claws.

He shifted irritably. It was something of a triumph of mind over mattress not to have succumbed to the crisp linen sheets, the feathery pillows that cradled like a lover, the faint caress of cashmere blankets. The bed could have been designed by Morpheus to waft mortals to the world of dreams, to blissful sleep, to some erotic paradise of slumbrous, sexual luxury . . . damn it!

He shifted again.

The ceiling was another matter. Intricately moulded in a complex, asymmetrical pattern of scroll work, flowers, leaves and entwined lovers, it was florid, flamboyant and could only have been inspired by Eros himself. Baroque? Rococo?

Serena would know.

His mind closed on the thought like a steel trap, crushing the syllables of her name in a metallic grip, sibilants wavering softly, like perfect white legs under water.

Sleep was impossible. He moved to the side of the bed, reached for his silk dressing-gown, and turned on the bedside light. His gaze fell on the Scotch bottle, but he discarded the notion almost immediately. He needed childhood remedies, a warm, milky drink, an impenetrably dull book . . . perhaps a tot of brandy in the milk. An array of the latest magazines and current bestsellers had been thoughtfully placed by the bed, but none of them appealed to him.

Dickens, perhaps, or Trollope. Surely in the vastness that was the villa there was a library. He didn't remember one from Serena's tour of the place, but then he hadn't paid much attention to anything that afternoon except the movement of her body beneath the flowing white dress, the thought of taking her in the rose garden, her body as lush and fragrant as any flower.

He gritted his teeth. Dickens and some warm milk. Knotting the tie of his robe, he left his room and made his way down the vast corridor.

He had almost passed her room when his mind registered the thin spill of light from beneath her door. His heart twisted. He felt himself slowing, stopping, turning to stare at the blank, closed face of the door. She was inside. He knew it with every bone in his body, every fibre of his being. And the door was closed.

A tiny, detached, ironic portion of his brain approved his position. His Latin was every bit as good as Serena's, his memory of Catullus undimmed. *Exclusus amator.* The locked-out lover. He had been too surprised by her quotation to respond, too aware of what she might have meant by wind and running water to challenge her by his understanding. Too afraid. And now, pathetically, miserably, he was hovering outside her door, longing for her.

Why not some other poem, some other coda? *Vivamus atque amemus*, perhaps, let us live and let us love?

The door stood between them. It might have been a wall, a fortress. He could never, would never breach it . . . she wanted to be alone.

He reached out his hand to touch the door, caress

the wood, just like some besotted elegiac lover, he thought bitterly, when he heard a thin, tiny laugh from behind the door. A strange sound, almost inhuman, it shivered his spine, froze his hand on the door handle.

Without conscious thought, without volition, his hand moved, twisted the handle, and he felt himself moving into the room.

She was sitting at her dressing-table, staring into the mirror. Her reflection in the mirror swam towards him, pale but for the red warmth of her mouth. She was wearing black, and the black lacquered surface of the table, the black leather moulded to her back, the shining raven sweep of her hair all melded into an inky cloud. She was oblivious to his presence, utterly absorbed.

'Serena,' he said softly, trying to recall her, afraid of startling her. 'Serena.'

He moved closer, gently stretched his hands towards her, still speaking softly. She was crying, a pale wash of tears falling along the sculpted planes of her face. It seemed to fascinate her, because her eyes never left her reflection in the mirror. Her hands were moving over the black lacquered table in reflective strokes, as if her fingers would learn something from its silky surface.

He put his hands on her shoulders, leaned forward tentatively. His face joined hers in the mirror. Her gaze shifted. She eyed him dispassionately, calmly. As though she had expected him. As though she had never seen him before.

'Serena.' The rhythmic, meditative wash of her fingers along the table was beginning to disturb him. He reached out to take her hand, and found her fingers icy cold.

'Serena, my love, you're freezing.' He knelt beside her, took both her hands in his and began to rub them gently, trying to infuse her with his warmth. Something warned him not to turn her towards him, clasp her in his arms, turn her away from the image in the mirror.

The room was pleasantly cool, not cold, he thought distractedly, and the heavy leather shirt she was wearing should have warmed her. She smelled of leather and salt and something musky . . . he moved sharply, trying to evade the memory of the smell, and his knee shuddered against something hard and jagged. Looking down he saw, scattered on the floor, vials and bottles, whips and carved images, curious looking instruments shining softly in the dim pool of light.

Her hands were still cold. But she was looking down at him now with impersonal amber eyes, tears still falling.

He rose then, took her by the hand, led her docile as a child to the huge, *en suite* bathroom. She stood passive as he stripped the shirt from her body, turned the taps on the marble tub full force until they were surrounded by a boiling mist of steam, tested the water and lifted her in his arms.

He eased her into the tub. Limp, almost boneless, she lay quietly. Guided by some instinct, he said nothing, but simply took the soap and washed her tenderly, every part of her body, fingers, arms, shoulders and neck, breasts, belly, thighs and legs. For once her naked body failed to stir him sexually; she might have been his sister, his child.

His sleeves trailing sodden in the water, he moved her onto her side, supporting her head like the child his mind had likened her to, soaped her back, her buttocks. Her skin was warming, a faint flush of pink beneath the ivory. Passive and quiescent she submitted to his hands, made no move either to aid or obstruct him as he turned her yet again, coaxed her head back into the water.

Her eyes were on his, yellow, blank, incurious but watchful. She had stopped crying. But he wasn't reassured. The thought came to him that she would watch him with that same yellow stare even if he forced her head beneath the water, would watch him with drowning eyes, make no move to save herself.

He raised her head, searched blindly on the marble shelf behind her for some shampoo, found it and squeezed some of the liquid onto her hair. His hands were clumsy as he lathered, too big for the small circumference of her scalp, but he persisted until he was satisfied, then lowered her head back into the water.

The frothy confection of white foam dissipated under his fingers, and he raised her head, now sleek and shining, hair plastered to her skull. He was sweating in the steamy heat, becoming aware of his sodden silk robe clinging uncomfortably like a second skin.

He lifted her from the water and set her on her feet. So tractable, so unresisting had she been that it would not have surprised him if she crumpled to the floor at the loss of his hands as he searched for a towel.

But she stood, patiently, pliantly as he wrapped a towel around her, found another for her hair, and dried it gently, then let the damp black snakes of her hair fall to her shoulders.

She was amenable, lifting her arms as his hands directed and suggested, watching him now with faintly curious eyes as he dried her body.

She might have been a statue. An effigy. A priestess accepting her rites. A virgin waiting to be sacrificed. A tired child.

She was all of them and none of them.

The strange thought occurred to him that she held within her some secret, deep, dark and pulsing slowly; some cleansing madness waiting to be born. And so, frightened and awed, tender and gentle, tired and unhappy, Max rubbed her skin gently with the white towel, knew the impulse to wind it around her neck and force the secret and then the life from her when he saw the imprint of teeth on her breast, the abraded aureoles of her nipples.

His touch was even more gentle than before.

And when he lifted his eyes to hers, saw the almost imperceptible twitch of the muscles at the side of her mouth, he knew exactly what she would do if the madness moved his hands to her throat. Tightened their grasp. Pressed his love and anger and fear into the white column of her throat.

She would laugh.

If he left no breath in her body she would laugh with her eyes, strangle him with the yellow fire, suffocate him with the deathless, breathless gold of her gaze.

But the eyes he had seen in the mirror were a child's eyes, wide and wondering as she had watched her own tears fall.

Carefully, cautiously, almost reverently he dried her, found a silk robe hanging on the back of the door and wrapped her in it, carried her to her bed. He knew a moment's hesitation as he settled her head against the soft pillows, but some tiny shift of her expression reassured him, prompted him to strip off his robe and move beside her, hold her close.

She fell asleep almost immediately, her breathing deep and regular, the soft rise and fall of her breasts as compelling, as hypnotic, as the waves of the sea.

He felt his eyelids drooping, then dropping, lulled by the now familiar warmth of her body, even beneath the silk robe he had wrapped her in, the reassuring rhythm of her breathing, the seductive warmth of Serena next to him, silken limbs beneath a silken robe.

And so he slept.

Curiously, it was Max who dreamed. Of beautiful, silken coils that wrapped themselves around him, enveloped him in a humid, vegetal warmth, the loamy smell of damp earth rising to his nostrils, then clogging them, suffocating him.

He moaned, held Serena closer as the white, etiolated strands clung more closely, as the flickering, darting petals became tongues and then fangs, as they twined around him, binding him.

Of fangs that turned to steel, of hands that moved to his throat and became a shining steel blade . . .

'Max.'

Moving over him, caressing him, carving him with the slick kiss of steel.

'Max.'

Slow motion, now, seeking and finding the life blood with vampiric instinct, loving it, wanting it . . .

'Max!'

He swam up darkly, slowly, saw her eyes, not yellow, not gold, but amber, searching his.

'Max. It was a dream. A nightmare.'

The sheets were twisted and coiled around his waist like the snakes he'd been dreaming of, drenched with sweat and his fists were clenched, his body tensed.

'A dream, Max. Wake now, then sleep again.'

Her hands on his body, smoothing the sheets, cooling them, unwrapping them, drawing him close.

'Sleep, Max.'

'It was the knife,' he muttered almost indistinctly, as sleep took him. 'The knife.'

Serena watched him sink back against the pillows, his dark lashes falling, his hands groping blindly for her body, clasping her with desperate, drowsy strength.

The knife.

Fleetingly she wondered why that image had come to haunt Max in his dreams. Wondered, again fleetingly, what it might mean. Then slept.

Mika paced the length of the music room irritably, restlessly. He couldn't go to Serena now, apologise, explain, make her understand the disordered thoughts scrambling through his mind. He barely understood them himself.

He should have known better. He knew when she had the devil in her, driving her. She would accept neither love nor logic, reason or affection.

248

And he had not been particularly logical or reasonable.

Why, tonight of all nights, had he tried to express his vague unformed fears and hopes, his clumsy fumblings toward the future? Ruefully he looked down at his hands, the black leather gloves. His fingers were tingling again, itching, almost burning.

Perhaps it was because he had felt himself changing, being changed, had assumed that she, as always, was with him, changing, being changed, responding as he was.

The sight of her in the doorway, clad in a black leather shirt many sizes too large, the heavy black belt wound around her waist, the disorder of her hair, the feral heat of her eyes . . . They belonged to time past. To a time and place he had hoped she had no need to revisit.

He had been aware of the games she had played ever since they came to Geneva, the endless string of chauffeurs and gardeners, accepted her needs as she had accepted his. But the black leather shirt, the look in her eyes had disturbed him. Reminded him of the first few months at the villa.

Suddenly he felt caged, trapped, almost claustrophobic. He threw open the huge windows, breathed in the soft scents of the night.

They were growing apart. The knowledge pierced his heart like an icicle. The cold truth he had feared to acknowledge even to himself.

In this strange metamorphosis from performer to composer, from invalid recluse to creator, they had grown apart. She was no longer vital for the work that was his life's blood. He forced himself to drag the words from the depth of his subconscious. Examined them dispassionately, coldly.

The act of composition, the needs of a composer were fundamentally different. As a performer he had grown with Serena, thrived on the sensual counterpoint she provided in their lives. She had been able to take him to new heights of interpretation, forced him to go beyond the purely intellectual, the purely technical and succumb to the sensuality. Without shame, without guilt.

She had laid the foundation for his new role as composer. And, ironically, it was a role that excluded her. Because he was not seeking to describe, to interpret sound and sensuality, but create it. It was a new landscape, foreign yet somehow familiar, a new journey that he had to make alone.

Abruptly, he turned away from the window, suddenly unsure. Perhaps he was wrong. Perhaps he was simply tired, disturbed by their quarrel, flinching at shadows.

With a slightly bitter smile, he remembered what Brahms had said about the art of composition. 'It is not hard to compose, but it is wonderfully hard to let the superfluous notes fall under the table.'

Superfluous notes. Why had he dragged Max into the conversation, voiced his nagging doubts, his growing certainty that Max was in love with her? That he might provide some path to a future. And Serena, as always, was two steps ahead, quick to grasp the unsaid, pursue the merely imagined.

'Keep your clichés for your score,' she had said.

Superfluous notes. He moved around the room slowly, switching off the lights, pausing to lift the tray of food Serena had abandoned on the floor. Her plate looked like a second-rate still-life by some neurotic Renaissance painter, the rosy lobster claws broken into jagged pieces where she had prised them apart with her fingers, the asparagus stalks now limp and tired looking.

He placed the tray on his desk and hesitated, looking at the sheaf of papers. Notes and ideas spilling to the floor. The completed manuscript. The Lalique bird.

There was another difference between playing and composing.

Practising, rehearsing, playing, he had had scores of women. Needed them to pour out the restless energy, the adrenalin high after a concert that left him tightly, explosively hot and hard. Wanted them, quickly aroused by the sight of lovely legs spread around a cello, graceful fingers pulsing against a flute. Used them to fuel his interpretations in a variety of intricate and elaborate sexual scenarios.

Music was sex and sex was music.

He hadn't had a woman in almost two years.

Franca slept deeply and dreamed. The image of the fountain, gleaming white marble and dark, mysterious shadows, the play of light and running water, the sinuous coils of the mermaid, the triton, hugely erect, grinning lustfully, all tangled and merged, coalesced. She was sitting on the edge of the fountain, long legs dangling in the cool water, behind her the solid warm frame of a man, holding her shoulders, easing her forward, urging her to the marble phallus.

She glanced down, saw her legs parted, the white dress swimming around her waist, the flaming strip of her hair, the plump, moist leaves of her sex shining in the uncertain light. Her body was running wet and liquid like the fountain, pulsing on the cool surface, heating in the chilled embrace. The hands on her shoulders were coaxing her forward, lifting her, moulding her, gently positioning her on the veined white marble rod.

She knew a moment's fear, tried to struggle, arch away from the spear of penetration. She was too small, too tight, too mortal to take him in her body, envelop the marble hardness.

In sleep, her hands clenched the pillow.

And even as she parted her lips to moan, to protest, her body flowered, expanded, fountained around the hard sex plunging within her. Her inner contours were heating, accepting, moulding the white marble to pink

251

flesh, softening the marble to muscle, glorifying and exulting in the metamorphosis.

The hands on her shoulders twisted suddenly, clenched her with bruising strength, could not recall her from the primal, primitive, mindless rhythms. In a frenzy she drove herself harder, drove him deeper, felt him reach the mouth of her womb and tremble there. Her body began to shake, driven by the first, faint tremors, riven by the electric shudders now coursing through her.

Expanding and contracting, clenching and releasing, the hidden heart opening, hot and pulsing. Her head fell back and she saw that the hands gripping her shoulders were black leather. And then she exploded, soaring, falling, consumed and convulsed, felt the hot wash of him pour into her as she writhed around him.

She moaned once, as the throbbing heat enveloped her, infused her. Stretched slowly as the heat diffused, leaving a blissful warmth, a torpid languor. A deeper sleep.

LONDON

'Don't wake her,' cautioned Eve in a soft whisper, slipping from the bed. 'She'll sleep now, for a little while.' She looked for her robe, saw it tangled in the sheets at the foot of the bed, and decided to ignore it. Nude, she walked to the bedroom door and gestured to Nikolai to follow her.

Nikolai, also nude, had paused beside the bed and was looking down at the sleeping Sally, his expression slightly bemused.

'Come on, Nik,' whispered Eve impatiently, surprised to find herself annoyed by the look in his eyes. 'Move. I don't want her to wake up just yet.'

He stood a moment longer, obviously reluctant to move his eyes from the sleeping form on the bed. Sally was sprawled in the abandoned pose in which she'd climaxed, legs spread wide, arms flung out, face half-buried in one of the pillows. He shook his head, then turned to look at Eve standing by the door.

Two women. So different, both in bed and out of it. Eve was lush, voluptuous with a powerful, driving sexuality that had enveloped them all, banished any constraint. Sally, nervous and reluctant, then brash and uninhibited, finally losing herself in the sex-play with total abandon. He wasn't sure how much of Eve's plan she had truly taken in, he thought, looking down at Sally again. Eve had skilfully interlarded her proposition with kisses and caresses, artful touches, and encouraged him to do the same.

When Sally had screamed yes for the first time, a long, drawn out scream of intense surrender, he had wondered whether she was accepting Eve's plan or his tongue, buried deep inside her. And she had moved so beautifully beneath him, following his rhythms, matching his strokes, allowing him to set the pace.

'Nikolai!' Eve hissed urgently 'Now!'

Sighing, he reached for the black towelling robe he had dropped by the side of the bed. Eve was another matter, he reflected, following her out of the room.

It was Eve who established the rhythm, set the pace, rode his cock like it was some iron shaft, not a living, pulsing organ. And it was Eve who knew Jeff Brooks, had the support of that Texas billionaire, Eve who was about to launch a new recording company. Eve, who could propel him to the forefront, make his name a household word.

Still, he'd sooner place his career in her hands than his cock.

'Some champagne,' Eve was saying imperiously, running her hands through her platinum blonde hair. Her eyes were glittering with excitement. 'I've done it! Or rather, we've done it!' she added, glancing at Nikolai. 'We've got her, you clever, clever boy. She's mine now.'

He unpeeled the gold foil from the neck of the bottle slowly, watching her as she paced the length of the room. 'I'm not sure—' he began doubtfully.

'She's betrayed Max now on a basic, personal level,' Eve carried on heedlessly, 'letting us use his flat, his bed, the three of us together. For Sally, that's very significant. And you heard her, she said yes! Just at the end, I asked her again, just to make sure, absolutely certain. And she said yes!'

The champagne foamed out of the bottle. He cursed under his breath as he slopped it into two flutes. 'She might have meant something else,' he ventured, handing her a glass.

'Oh no, Nikolai,' replied Eve, eyes turning hard. 'A deal's a deal. Remember that.' The threat in her voice was unmistakable. She raised her glass to his.

'To me,' she said, clicking the rime of her glass against his.

'To you,' he echoed. And drank deeply.

GENEVA

Max woke before Serena, lazily swimming to full consciousness to find her nestled against him, buttocks against his groin, the smooth curve of her back against his chest. His right arm was flung across her, cradling her breasts. Slowly, reluctantly he drew it away, careful not to disturb her.

As he did every morning, he quickly reviewed the events of the previous day, dividing them, compartmentalising them, then mentally tagging them. Business. Personal. Important. Insignificant. Action. Delay.

The most pressing thing today was to get Franca's signature on the final contract. No foreseeable problems there. Sally would have faxed over the two copies by now, Mika and Serena could act as witnesses. He doubted that Franca would draw back now, insist on extra concessions or outside advice. She simply wasn't that interested.

But something was wrong at Disc-O. He could smell it, as surely as he could smell the faint perfume of Serena's hair on the pillow beside him. He had nothing to go on, no obvious cause for concern, no actual doubts or suspicions, but he knew something was wrong. And it involved the North American market.

Max operated largely by instinct and intuition and right now his thumbs were prickling. Speculation was pointless. He would have to return to London, sight things out, perhaps go on to New York and then Toronto himself. Or send Sally.

But before he left, he'd have to speak to Serena, clear up any 'tiresome business details', make it quite clear, in fact, that there was nothing to discuss. If Mika wanted to renegotiate his contract based on his new interest in composing, he'd send over the legal team to explain just why that was impossible. All twenty of them.

So much for business.

Next item on the agenda, please, he mocked himself. Personal. Serena. He looked over at her, the black cloud of her hair on the white linen pillow, the regular rise and fall of her breathing. Even the thought of leaving her, being without her, was painful.

But it was a pain he would learn to live with. Had lived with so long.

Who was she, he asked himself for the thousandth time? She slipped through his fingers like water, the wild and beautiful wanton, the greedy child licking mayonnaise from her fingers, the woman, sleek and elegant . . . the pale creature of the night before, fascinated by her own tears. Who had twisted him to such untold heights of fury that he could only express it with tenderness.

His heart clenched. If only she could bore him, disgust him, annoy him . . . even her flaws intrigued him, her arrogance, her perverse waywardness.

He should leave before she woke, he thought, leave her to wake alone, spare them both the awkwardness, the embarrassment of acknowledging last night in the cold light of day. He had seen her weak . . . No, not weak perhaps, he realised, struggling to define her mood. Vulnerable? Mentally he shook himself. It didn't matter now. He couldn't allow it to matter.

He leaned over to kiss her hair and found himself looking into her eyes.

'Good morning, Max.' She stretched a little, blinked, then surprised him by touching his lips with her fingers. 'You look very serious.'

'Serena—' he hesitated a moment, then began again. 'Serena, I'm sorry, I was just going to leave, I thought you were still asleep.' He smiled a little awkwardly and moved over to the other side of the bed.

'As you like, of course,' she replied easily. 'But you're welcome to stay. I'll send down for some coffee and rolls. I feel a bit lazy this morning.'

His robe was a sodden puddle bunched miserably beside the bed. Absurdly, he suddenly felt shy, reluctant to rise naked from the bed.

'You had a nightmare last night,' she was saying, rising from the bed and smoothing her silk robe around her. 'Do you remember?'

He lay back against the pillows. 'Yes, yes, I do,' he said slowly. 'I remember the knife.'

'Curious symbolism,' she said, sitting on the side of the bed. She spoke fluently, knowledgeably about Freud and the interpretation of dreams, but it was clear her mind was elsewhere. 'Coffee?' she asked, interrupting herself.

'Yes, thanks,' Max replied, a little at sea.

She spoke softly and rapidly into the intercom fixed to the carved headboard, then rose to her feet. She moved across the room, paused at her dressing-table, looked down at the scattered array of erotica on the floor and smiled.

'So did I, I think,' she said cryptically, gently nudging aside a small whip with her foot. 'An interesting word, really, nightmare. When I was a little girl I always imagined them as horses, huge black horses with steel hooves and huge, flaring nostrils. But it's actually from Old English, *maere*, an incubus or evil

256

spirit that came to suffocate the sleeper.' She knelt on the floor, sifting through the various objects.

Max fumbled for a reply. First Freud, then a brief foray into etymology . . . what next? And what was that strange looking thing in her hands? 'A nightmare?' he asked uncertainly.

'I think so. Or perhaps merely a day-dream, meeting the incubus while I was still awake. Ah, there's Maddie,' she said, rising in response to a soft knock at the door.

Max frowned, puzzled. He had rather expected Serena to be cold, distant, dismissive. Instead she seemed utterly at ease with him, but strangely obscure, open and withdrawn at the same time, offering mysterious remarks with the bland assurance of someone discussing the weather.

She was smiling as she placed the tray on the bed, uncovered silver chafing dishes to reveal crisp bacon and frothy scrambled eggs, poured coffee into two white mugs.

'What incubus?' he ventured, accepting the mug she handed him and sipping the coffee.

'The incubus I created, of course,' she replied lightly, sitting cross-legged on the bed and taking a piece of bacon in her fingers. 'Or perhaps merely summoned. The distinction between the subconscious and the unconscious, between fantasy and reality frequently blurs, don't you find?'

'No,' he said honestly, adding, after a moment's thought, 'Serena I haven't the faintest idea what you're talking about.'

'It doesn't matter, Max, just a stray thought,' she said, heaping scrambled eggs onto a plate and reaching reluctantly for a fork. 'Mika and I quarreled yesterday.'

'Oh,' said Max, relieved and disturbed at the same time. So that's why she had disappeared, then acted so strangely last night. He hoped to God it had nothing to do with Franca. 'I'm sure it's not serious, Serena,' he began awkwardly. 'After all, you two have been—'

Been what? he wondered a little wildly, remembering the imprint of teeth on her breast that he had seen last night when he bathed her. 'Been together so long,' he finished.

'Serious?' she repeated. 'I'm not sure. It might be. He said some truly unforgivable things. But then, so did I. He's working well, though, isn't he?'

'He seems to be,' agreed Max tentatively.

'Franca's been good for him,' Serena observed, rapidly disposing of her eggs and reaching for a roll. 'I'm very pleased. Max, you're not eating a thing. More coffee?'

Thoroughly disconcerted, Max held out his mug. She was changing topics so rapidly it was hard to get a grasp on the conversation. Nightmares, an incubus, a serious quarrel with Mika, unforgivable things said . . . and yet she seemed curiously light-hearted, looked rather pleased with herself if anything.

'Bacon?' she asked, taking another strip between her fingers. 'Or would you prefer ham? The strawberries are delicious, you must try some.'

Alone on the terrace Mika watched the sun rise, drank coffee and brooded, grateful for the rumbling warmth of Midas on his knees. The cat had disappeared yesterday, out hunting, he guessed, perhaps merely annoyed by the presence of strangers in the villa. He was, like his master, a creature of routine.

Mika had slept badly the night before, a thin, disturbed sleep that left him weary but restless. He had returned to the music room, determined to finish *The Embrace* and sketch out *The Climax* but the notes refused to flow and instead he had found himself staring blankly into space, thinking of nothing.

They would return, he knew, could almost feel the notes dancing at the periphery of his consciousness, but whenever his mind reached out to grasp them, they floated away, replaced by other sounds magnified a thousandfold. Mundane, everyday sounds seemed preternaturally loud, Midas's rumbling purr a dull roar, the early morning birdsong a violent cacophony.

So when he heard the fall of her footsteps as she walked across the terrace, the whining scrape of metal as she drew back a chair, he almost flinched.

'Good morning,' she said softly, pouring herself some coffee.

She was wearing only a tiny black bikini imperfectly concealed by a large, white shirt, her hair a flaming mass tumbling over her shoulders. In his heightened state of awareness he could almost hear it crackling with life and energy as she smoothed it behind her ears.

'Perhaps,' he replied.

She puzzled over that, decided to ignore it. Decided also to ignore the cat arching under his hands and staring malevolently at her. 'I thought I'd swim before we begin work,' she said, sipping coffee.

It was a carefully planned remark, one that assumed an almost equal status, a collaboration, an emerging routine, while still allowing them both a measure of independence. He could, of course, rebuff her, slash her overt assumption to ribbons with a simple, cutting remark. She wondered if he would.

'You respond to the water,' Mika said after a time, thinking of the play of her fingers in the fountain, the way her body had trembled to Handel the first night she had come to the villa.

An equivocation? she wondered. 'I've never done much swimming,' she responded simply. 'But since I've been here, I've felt very drawn to it. Perhaps it's just the ease, the luxury of a private pool. And your own fountain too,' she added with a slight laugh.

'To say nothing of the stream at the bottom of the gardens,' he said wryly.

'Oh, is there one?' she exclaimed. 'Will you show me?' She could have blushed to hear the naïve pleasure in her voice. Damn! She was behaving like a child instead of some cool sophisticate.

259

'Later, perhaps,' he said, hardly hearing her words, concentrating instead on the sound of her voice, the surprised delight. It belonged in *The Embrace*, the moment when two bodies recognise each other, know instinctively that they were meant to join, would join.

She finished her coffee, setting the cup on the table with a sharp click that recalled him somewhat. As it was meant to.

'I'll take my swim now,' she said, standing up, willing him to look at her as she slipped off the white shirt, willing him to admire the high breasts, the long legs, the swell of her hips.

'Yes, yes, of course,' he replied distractedly, mind clearly elsewhere even as he surveyed her body.

She left with a haughty swing of her hips, ran lightly down to the pool. He heard the spray of water as she dived in, the rhythmic pulse of her body slicing through the water, and felt himself relaxing, felt the notes gathering form and definition. Wary now of chasing them away, disturbing them with his impatience, he waited, heard the swell of sound soften and recede, the weighty roar of Midas's purr muting to a dull rumble, the shrill waves of birdsong subsiding to a faint trill.

He let his mind drift, avoiding the dark shadows cast by Serena, the uncertain clouds of the future, thought instead of the girl in the water. Franca. There was no real reason for her to stay while he finished *Serena's Song*, no foundation for her easy assumption that they would work together. Still, for some reason, he was reluctant to have her leave just yet. She had provided some interesting insights, some valuable suggestions that had helped to shape the work.

And he was becoming more aware of her as a presence, a woman, something other than a conduit for his music. The heat that had flashed between them the night before in the music room had startled him, surprised him. He had dismissed it as easily as he dismissed the burning tingling in his hands.

But both were becoming more insistent. Almost annoying.

Finally replete, Serena stretched and rose from the bed. She was feeling restless and lazy, impatient and languorous. Time to escape from the villa, for just a little while, take one of the cars and drive, dawdling sedately through the twisting, leafy lanes or speeding recklessly, it really didn't matter which.

'We'll take one of the cars and go out today, Max, and I'll show you the countryside. Have a picnic, perhaps. I'll get Maddie to make something up for us. It's a beautiful sunny day,' she said, moving to the window, parting the heavy draperies. From the window she could see Franca, swimming lengths in the pool, Mika alone on the terrace. Best, perhaps, to leave him alone today, after last night. Perhaps not.

'Serena, I'm sorry, I can't, I'm afraid.' The words were wrenched out of him before he could recall them. Thankfully.

'You can't? Why ever not?' she said, curious, turning to face him.

It wasn't that she expected him to leap at her every whim, follow her every desire. It was just that it had never occurred to her that he wouldn't.

'I need Franca to sign the contract, Sally will have faxed it over by now,' he began awkwardly. 'And thanks, by the way, for having a fax machine put in my room. It was very thoughtful of you.'

Serena nodded absentmindedly. It hadn't occurred to her to do anything of the sort. Maddie really was a jewel.

'Well, that will hardly take all day,' she pointed out. 'There's a marvellous little restaurant by the lake, we might have dinner there. I feel like driving a long, long way.'

'Serena, I have to get back to London.' His voice was stronger now, more determined.

'Really, Max, Disc-O can survive without you for a

few more days, surely,' Serena retorted, rather piqued. 'I'd like you to come with me.'

Words he would have embraced, hugged to himself, leapt at, only a few short days ago. But last night he had plumbed the depths of love and obsession. To stay longer would jeopardise more than his heart, more than his soul. He remembered the impulse to crush the breath out of her when he had seen the marks of another mouth on her breast.

He blanked out his thoughts, reverted to business.

'Not a question of that, Serena,' he began to reply briskly, then stopped. She was taking off her robe, letting the white silk slither to the floor. He swallowed. 'But I have to get back. Something's brewing, something's wrong. Or at least not right. And I have to find out what it is.'

'What's brewing, then?' she asked, moving towards the mirror and examining her reflection. There was a faint, bluish mark beneath her right nipple. She winced a little as she applied some salve. 'And how do you know?'

Half his mind was focused on her body, the movement of her fingers as she massaged her breast, while the other half struggled to define the problem. Strangely, it seemed to enhance his concentration.

'It's instinct, Serena, a feeling. Nothing I can put my finger on, exactly. But I'm suspicious, and I always follow my instincts.'

Serena smiled slightly. So did she. 'So?' she prompted, coming over to perch on the side of the bed, fingers darting for the last strip of bacon lying on his plate.

She barely listened as he began to describe percentages and market forces, marketing strategies, the increased interest in classical music in Europe, the solid tradition that the modern market had seized on, but her attention was caught by one phrase.

'What did you say, Max?' she asked, licking her fingers.

'I said it's basically a public seduction, or seducing the public, if you prefer,' he answered, still engrossed in his train of thought.

She smiled again. There wasn't much she didn't know about seduction.

'And that's what's missing from Eve's report, I hadn't seen it before now. No strategy, no tactics!' he exclaimed, striking his fist on the bed. 'And why didn't Sally pick up on it? We can't merely assume that we can't equal or better our European sales in America! She cites their lack of tradition, but hell, we can capitalise on it!'

Mildly interested, she scanned the tray. There was a stray strawberry under the edge of his plate.

He continued, green eyes bright. 'We have to stimulate the market, massage it into awareness, tantalise it into wanting more.'

'Of course,' she shrugged, reaching for the strawberry. Obviously big business wasn't much different from sex. 'To create need, find greed.'

'You understand, then,' commented Max, not quite asking a question.

'Need and greed? Very well,' she responded, biting into the strawberry. 'But there's obviously something else on your mind.'

He hesitated, unwilling to confide his nagging, unfounded, unreasonable doubts. Just because your PA of ten years leaves the office unprecedentedly early, forgets to reroute urgent calls on the private line and then inexplicably answers the telephone in your penthouse apartment in a strange voice, attending to non-existent greenery . . .

'Max?'

'Maybe,' he conceded. 'But I hope not. And there's something else we've got to nail down, Serena, while we're talking.'

'Mmm.' She rose from the bed and started padding towards the bathroom.

'You've got to understand, or Mika does, and I have

to make it clear. These "tiresome business details",
Serena, it's—'

'Of course, darling. I'm going to shower. Franca's
down taking a swim, I saw her from the window. Why
don't we meet down there in half an hour or so? You
did say you needed her signature before you left?'

He couldn't read her voice, her emotions, her
responses.

It hardly mattered.

She'd already left the room. He could hear the sound
of the shower. In wind and running water, he
reminded himself, looking at his empty plate. He'd
been saving that last strip of bacon.

'Nothing to worry about at all,' said Max, handing over
his gold Cross pen to Franca. 'A standard contract that
protects both of our interests and no hidden clauses, I
promise you. The dotted line, as they say, on page
seven, and that's that. And you're Disc-O's new star.'

Franca leafed through the pages quickly, scanning
the dense print and denser legalese, and had just
touched the pen to the paper when Serena appeared
on the terrace. She was wearing a saffron yellow silk
dress that left her arms and shoulders bare and
enhanced the glossy black of her hair.

'You were quick, Max,' she said, walking over to the
table. 'Franca, good morning. Mika.'

Mika turned abruptly in his chair to face her, upsetting the wrought-iron table just slightly, and the beginning of Franca's signature dissolved into jagged line.
Serena touched him lightly on the shoulder before
moving to stand behind Franca.

'Ah, so this is the contract,' Serena observed. 'May I
see?'

'Serena, hello, yes, of course—' Franca began, but
Serena had already plucked it from the table and
slipped into the chair beside her.

'I really don't think there's anything—' Max began
to say.

'Serena, I'm glad you've come down to—' Mika said at exactly the same moment.

They both broke off.

'Sorry, Max.'

'No, no, I was just going to say—'

'How interesting,' observed Serena, ignoring both of them. 'Have you read all this, Franca? An exclusive five-year contract? You're tying yourself down, rather, don't you think? And only ten per cent of the royalties? It's not a great deal, really.'

'I haven't read it that closely,' Franca confessed, a little bemused. 'But—'

'Serena, you're not an agent, and you have no idea how these things are done,' interrupted Max. 'This is a standard contract I've used countless times for new artists—'

'Ah, but she's not a new artist, is she?' interrupted Serena sweetly, eyes fixed on the contract. 'A recording for Deutsche Grammophon, the prize last year at the Lucerne International Music Festival. You're bidding low, Max.'

'Listen, Serena, that's hardly a stellar background—'

'But she's hardly an unknown,' countered Serena, lifting guileless eyes to his.

'Ten per cent?' Mika commented, beginning to look mildly interested.

'Ten per cent is standard, for your information,' Max ground out, 'and in any case—'

'No, my dear,' Serena said, turning to Franca, 'I really think this requires a little more thought than you've given it. Perhaps you should consult an agent, a lawyer. Of course, I really don't know how these things are done,' she added, an expression of shining innocence on her face.

The urge to strangle her was returning. 'Serena, for your information,' Max began, gritting his teeth. 'Our legal department—'

'Ten per cent of the royalties?' Mika repeated, as

though Max hadn't spoken. 'How much do I get, Serena?'

'You don't get any royalties!' Max exploded. 'You have an inflation-proof base salary that only an utter lunatic would have—'

'Now, now, Max,' soothed Serena. 'Don't get testy. Isn't that what they say in England, Mika? Testy?'

'Perhaps I should read it over more carefully,' offered Franca, looking at them all with fascinated eyes.

'Actually, I think the word you're looking for is "tetchy",' said Mika seriously.

'Let me make something quite clear,' said Max, in a voice of barely controlled rage. 'The legal department in London—'

'Ah, yes, London,' interrupted Serena, mischief gleaming in her eyes. 'Unfortunately Max has to return to London soon, isn't that a shame?' she said to Mika and Franca. 'And I was thinking that we would go off together today, leave the two of you alone to work, explore the countryside, have a picnic perhaps, but no, business before pleasure, I'm afraid. Isn't that right, Max?'

Max ground his teeth. Was she capable of sabotaging this deal merely because he had refused to join her today for a drive and a picnic? Impossible. Inconceivable. Strangling was too good for her, too quick.

'But since I'm feeling a bit restless, I thought I might go with him, perhaps visit the shops, have a mild fling on Bond Street. While I'm there, Franca, I can look into this contract a little more closely for you, if you like.'

'But Serena, you hate London!' exclaimed Max and Mika in unison, distress colouring both their voices.

'Perhaps I'm just feeling a trifle masochistic,' she said airily, favouring them all with a delightful smile.

Chapter Eleven

Double Fugue

*S*erena hummed softly to herself as she leafed through the racks of the huge built-in wardrobe. London in August. It was a daunting thought. Dismal, chilly, grey and rainy, or hot and steamy, it was impossible to tell. The Thai silk jacket in rich and vibrant yellows and reds, of course, the white silk trouser suit, the slim, black leather dress . . . On second thoughts, perhaps not. She'd been wearing black leather a little too often recently, she decided with a chuckle.

'Serena?' Franca's voice was tentative. 'I'm sorry, I knocked, you didn't hear.'

'Franca, I'm glad to see you,' said Serena, turning to face her with a smile. 'You can give me some advice. What do you think I should take? The weather's always so unpredictable in England.'

'Well, it was hot when I left,' Franca offered, gazing with some awe at the serried ranks of blouses, skirts, dresses, trousers and evening gowns, the rows and rows of shoes, sandals and boots in every conceivable colour, fabric and style. 'How long are you planning on being away?' she asked diffidently.

'I really haven't decided,' replied Serena, thoughtfully fingering a suede skirt. 'Packing is such a bore, don't you find? Perhaps I should get Maddie to do it, she always manages everything so perfectly. Or just pick up a few things over there, and not bother with luggage at all.' She pulled out a Gucci overnight case and set it on the bed. 'Make yourself comfortable,' she said to Franca, gesturing to a settee.

'What made you decide to go to London?' asked Franca, perching on the edge of the settee and watching Serena toss lingerie into the case.

'Oh, just a whim, really,' said Serena airily. 'I thought I'd surprise Max.'

'Well, he certainly seemed surprised,' remarked Franca dryly.

'Surprised? Darling, he was utterly aghast!' Serena said with a laugh.

'And so was Mika,' Franca replied, watching her closely.

'Mika?' Serena seemed to consider the matter carefully, then shrugged her shoulders. 'Mika should keep his mind on his work. He told me about it last night, and what an inspiration you had been,' she said, abandoning the delicate pile of white silk and coming to sit beside her.

'He said that?' exclaimed Franca in surprise.

'Well, perhaps not exactly. But I could sense that you have been,' said Serena, placing a reassuring hand on her thigh.

Franca shivered a little at the touch, remembering the sensual heat of Serena, but this touch was light, friendly, almost casual. 'You'll need a great deal of controlled passion for the piece as he seems to envision it,' remarked Serena, looking into her eyes.

'Yes, yes, I know,' Franca admitted. There was something compelling, almost hypnotic in those amber eyes.

'And will you be able to find it?' asked Serena softly.

'I think so. I hope so. Yes.'

'You want him, don't you?' said Serena. Eyes widening slightly, she continued, 'You're using him, aren't you? Clever. Quite clever indeed.'

She made no effort to pretend to misunderstand her. 'Yes.'

'But are you strong enough to ride the desire, keep it for the score? The music,' she added gently, 'the music has to come first.'

Franca was silent. The suppressed sexual tension she felt with Mika, the yearning, the liquid ache between her thighs, were all colouring her playing, enriching it, allowing her to interpret more freely. But he was haunting her dreams.

'You'll have to be careful,' warned Serena, 'very careful. You'll have to play him as delicately, as precisely, as passionately as you would play Bach. But you must keep the essence for yourself, for your music. After you've mastered that, of course, completed the recording, the première, you can do as you please.'

'You don't mind?' asked Franca simply.

Serena's laughter rippled to her ears. 'Darling, Mika and I go far, far beyond sex.' She smiled a little at Franca's look of puzzled incomprehension. She didn't understand. Perhaps no one would. 'No, no, I don't mind.'

Franca felt suddenly relieved, the nagging doubts and tensions she had hardly been aware of dissolving and leaving her at peace. Serena was more than an ally, more than a friend, she was, simply . . . Serena. She touched the hand resting on her thigh, brought it to her lips and kissed it lightly. 'Serena, thank you.'

'Just play well, my dear,' replied Serena. 'Nothing else matters.'

Franca leaned back more comfortably on the settee as Serena wandered back over to the bed and began sifting through the silken white pile of lingerie. 'It was good of you to look over the contract Max is offering me, Serena. Do you really think the terms are unreasonable?'

'How would I know?' said Serena carelessly, frowning down at her case.

'But you seemed so confident, so sure that he should be offering a better deal, that's why I didn't sign!' Franca said, drawing her eyebrows together.

'Bluff and double-bluff, darling, I really haven't the faintest idea,' said Serena vaguely.

There was something decidedly unconvincing in her attitude, Franca thought. Or was it just unnerving?

'I must see Mika before we leave,' Serena said, 'and have a word with Maddie. I wonder if she's managed to book this afternoon's flight. And I suppose I'll have to leave the car at the airport, what a bore.'

'Won't you be using the chauffeur?' enquired Franca.

'Not today,' Serena replied, a slow smile curving her lips. No doubt Maddie had already managed to dispose of Sergei, sent him off with a fat bonus and made arrangements for a replacement. 'No, not today.'

LONDON

Sally sat at her desk, massaged her aching temples and puffed irritably at her tenth cigarette. Her desk was awash with computer print-outs, phone messages scrawled in the temp's barely legible handwriting, several densely typed reports from the marketing division, and a single sheet of paper that surely spelled doom or salvation. If only she could decide which.

She'd slipped away from Max's apartment in the cold grey dawn, leaving Eve and Nikolai entwined and sleeping. Like some hunted animal, she had made straight for her office, her lair, and locked the door behind her. She looked down at the sheet of paper.

On it she had jotted down everything Eve had said last night, every detail she remembered of her schemes and dreams. Some of it was still a bit blurry, tangled in her mind with the memory of naked limbs, mouths and hands moving over her, but she was sure she had the gist of it. A bold little venture, Sally acknowledged, with a fair chance of success. At the very least it would deaden the impact of Mika's comeback, deflect a certain amount of attention. In the long-run, it couldn't topple Disc-O, but it would certainly rattle it a little.

She was hesitating, on the brink of a crucial decision. It wasn't too late to draw back, tell Max everything, have Eve unceremoniously sacked, and galvanise the Toronto office into immediate action.

Or she could join Eve.

She stubbed out her cigarette and sighed.

GENEVA

'Serena, why are you doing this?'

She turned at the sound of his voice. She was prowling through the garage, trying to decide which of the immaculately kept cars to drive to the airport. The Rolls was far too stuffy, the Lamborghini far too red – whatever made her order that colour? she wondered, momentarily irked – perhaps the black Maserati?

'Doing what?' she replied absently. The silver-grey Jaguar was quite fun to drive, but she rather preferred the feel of the Maserati.

'Rushing off to London like this,' Mika said, coming towards her.

'A whim, an impulse,' she returned lightly.

'Serena, you've never acted on impulse in your entire life. It's not because of what I said last night? And if it is—'

'Don't be ridiculous, darling,' she said, 'and don't distract me when I'm trying to make an important decision. Do you think I should take the Jag or the Maserati?'

'Serena, listen to me,' he said seriously, taking her by the shoulder and forcing her to look at him. 'What are you up to? Max was furious this morning, we had words after you left, and I've been worried, concerned about you, about last night—'

'Mika, my love, don't worry,' she smiled up at him,

enfolding him in the warmth of her eyes. He relaxed a little at her smile. 'Everything's fine, and I think I've finally come to a decision.'

'Yes?'

'I'll take the Maserati.'

And that was Serena, he reflected a few hours later, watching the Maserati disappear beyond the gates and the dust settle on the drive. She had in her own delightful, annoying, impossible fashion parried every question, eluded and avoided any direct confrontation, reduced Max's rage to a bemused acceptance, charmed them all like some sorceress and then disappeared in a cloud of smoke.

He would miss her, he thought, flexing his hands.

As always, work was the anodyne. *The Embrace* had begun to bore him a little. He could hear it now so clearly in his mind that it hardly seemed worth the effort to transcribe the notation. *The Climax* was calling to him, beckoning with increasing intensity. Ripe, and hot, and melting, he thought, moving towards the music room.

Franca barely looked up as he entered the room. She was sitting cross-legged on the black leather couch, making notes on a score with a soft pencil. She nodded a greeting as he moved to his desk, then bent her head to the pages. He knew a moment's irritation at her invasion, but thrust it aside, impatient to capture the chords fluttering through his mind. He would ask her to leave, politely, shortly, just as soon as he had captured the essence of *The Climax*.

He was becoming easier and easier to read, thought Franca, suppressing a smile as she gazed down at the pages in her hand. She had almost felt him stiffen when he saw her. Idly she wondered if the best way to pierce him would be through anger, drive him to a fury so intense it would break down all his reserves, rouse him to express the heat that flashed between them with his hands, hard and bruising.

She found herself mildly excited by the thought,

moistening as she pictured his eyes flaring blue and brilliant, his hands rough on her body, tearing away her clothes, driving into her wildly in long, shuddering thrusts, losing his anger in her body. And that, she decided suddenly, was how it would be the first time between them.

She knew now when it would be. At the première of this work, the night the world was introduced to Mika's first composition. In her dressing-room, in the euphoric high after playing, swiftly, urgently, in a feverish, white-hot frenzy.

But first, the seduction. It would be a long time, a very long time before the première, six months at least, perhaps longer.

She could wait, she decided, husband and harness the melting heat in her belly, the dense yearning between her thighs, master it for the music, let it enhance her interpretation. In the meantime, there were sure to be many delightful variations, improvisations. She was content to wait.

They worked in silence for several hours, Franca memorising and making notes on 'The Kiss', Mika engrossed in 'The Climax'. She was startled by the sound of his voice, the brief curse he uttered as he rose and thrust a sheet of paper at her.

'No, I need to hear it,' he said impatiently. 'It's not quite right.'

'I'll get my violin,' she said, rising unhurriedly to her feet.

'Don't bother,' he said curtly. 'What is it you're using, a Cappichioni? I don't favour the contemporary violin makers, myself, and besides, it's too robust for what I want. Good God!' he exclaimed, shoving a distracted hand through his hair, 'that might even account for some of your problems with *The Kiss*. I just wasn't thinking. I want the Golden Strad for *The Climax*, my other Strad for *The Kiss*, the Guarnerius for *The Embrace* and then . . . I haven't decided about

273

Aftermath. I'm tempted by the Amati, but it's not really meant for a great hall. Nor is the Grancino.'

Even as he spoke he was moving towards one of the cabinets, withdrawing a case and lifting a violin from its silk wrappings. She caught her breath as he unveiled it.

Like some precious and priceless wooden jewel it gleamed and glowed with a life of its own. Moving closer she saw with awed eyes the deep and velvety perfection of the varnish, the sinuous, perfect curves and was tempted, for one incredible moment, to actually reach out and touch it.

Impulsively, she clasped her hands behind her back. A violin can only be held at the neck and the chin-rest, not so much as a finger should touch the body anywhere else. And her fingers itched to caress it.

Releasing the Strad from its silk bag, Mika turned to her, holding it almost casually at the neck, and saw her hands fastened behind her back. His face softened.

She had, of course, tested a Stradivarius or two in some of the more elite music dealers' rooms in London, was quite familiar with the craftsman's work, but she had never seen, never imagined anything quite like the unique and beautiful instrument currently dangling from Mika's gloved hand.

'She's beautiful, isn't she?' he asked, a smile playing around the edges of his mouth.

'Exquisite,' she breathed. 'Utterly exquisite.'

'Made in 1741,' he commented unnecessarily, handing it to her. 'Almost impossible to believe that he was seventy-one when he fashioned her. She has enormous power, fabulous clarity. It's what *The Climax* requires, the power, the purity. We'll use the other one for *The Kiss* as she's supple rather than powerful.'

It slipped as easily into her hands as if it had been made for her. 'Do you mean you want each movement played on a different violin?' asked Franca incredulously.

'Of course,' he replied matter-of-factly, adjusting a

music stand and retrieving the paper she had let fall to the floor. 'Now, read this and play. Your Tourte bow will do, though I prefer Peccate. You'd find it a bit heavier than the Tourte, and you'd need to get used to it.'

Her mind reeling, she cast her eyes over the score. If *The Kiss* had been deceptively simple, this looked incredibly complex. The rhythmic structure was quite unconventional, almost incongruous, a long note at the start, long notes that became shorter, and short notes which became more numerous. Dear God, he couldn't really expect her at a moment's notice to master this?

'Don't worry about the actual notes at the moment,' he instructed her curtly. 'It's the sensation we're cultivating, I need to hear it. Play.'

Settling the chin-rest against her neck, she had the curious sensation of a tingling warmth spreading through her body, enveloping her, as though the violin itself was alive, transmitting a glowing heat.

'Play.'

Drawing a deep breath, she began. It was a searing progression, quick and plunging, that grew like wildfire, a conflagration, phrases overlapping with impossible speed.

'Harder,' he said. 'Harder.'

She ignored him, focused on the music.

Eyes closed, hands clenched into fists, Mika stood behind her, gripped by a burning irritation as much mental as physical. Yes, she almost had it there, but it had to be harder, bowed harder with the desperate intensity of the male rod thrusting and lunging into the slick, hot void of woman, the explosion gathering at the base of the spine.

'Harder!' he exclaimed, voice rough. The tingling sensation in his fingers was becoming more intense.

It was drawing to a climax, an elaborate variation of the first phrase. Her attention fiercely concentrated on the score, modulating again to the dominant, she was shocked to feel his hand on her shoulder, the violin plucked from her hand, the bow snatched rudely from her fingers.

'Harder!'

She watched, dazed, as in one fluid motion he settled the Strad against his neck and began to play. Astonishingly, his black-gloved fingers moved swiftly and precisely, left hand dextrous and delicate on the violin, right hand gripping the bow easily.

It was far from perfect. There was none of the lightning speed that characterised his style, his finger fall was rather rigid and his bowing faintly jagged. For all that, he managed to evoke a power, an intensity, a soaring ardour that almost eclipsed the technical flaws.

And he was playing, she thought, amazed.

He was playing!

LONDON

In the swarming hell that was mid-afternoon Heathrow, Serena looked around a trifle disdainfully. Fashions had certainly changed since the last time she visited London, she thought with a sniff. She caught sight of a young man in black leather with a Mohawk haircut, a gold ring through his nose, long feathers dangling from one ear, and hastily looked away.

'Edward, my chauffeur, should be here to meet us,' Max was saying. 'Yes, there he is now, this way, Serena.' One hand solicitously placed on the small of her back, he urged her forward. Cutting a path through the shifting crowds he felt suddenly protective, anxious to shield her from stray elbows and shoulders. Felt, too, unreasonably glad to have her by his side. She was a perfect companion when she put her mind to it, amusing and informative on the drive to the airport, gracious to the awed officials there who recognised her, content to sip champagne and read a magazine as he looked through his papers during the flight. Her charm, her warmth, dispelled any unease, soothed any suspicions, almost made him forget how angry he had been with her.

Almost.

'*Why* in God's name did you interfere, Serena?' he had asked her.

'Darling,' she had said, resting the tips of her fingers on his arm, 'I didn't mean to cause any trouble. But Franca's so innocent, so naïve, so unsophisticated. No match for an astute businessman like you. I was simply concerned that she was out of her league.'

Angry, vaguely flattered, vaguely puzzled, Max had let the matter rest. And before he left he had got Franca's promise that she would do nothing without offering Disc-O first right of refusal. He had explained to Mika, simply and patiently, in terms that a child might understand, that his contract continued unchanged, and Mika *had* seemed to understand, had, by the end of his lengthy explanation, seemed rather bored if anything.

So, Disc-O owned this new work, whatever it was. Mika had obstinately refused to disclose the title, annoying in terms of pre-publicity, but they could work around that, even exploit it. Catchphrases floated through his mind. Mysterious. Enigmatic. Passionate.

'That little man who looks like a dissipated monkey?' asked Serena, eyeing the unprepossessing figure darting towards them.

'Not quite as beautiful as your chauffeur, I agree,' replied Max, hastily recalling himself. She stiffened slightly, but he carried on unheedingly. 'But a very good driver. Edward, hello. Here, you can take these. Where's the car?' He handed Edward their cases and continued chatting as they made their way to the waiting limousine, Serena trailing along behind them.

Just as she had suspected, Serena thought, settling back in the plush interior, the weather was cold, grey and dismal. She was pleased she had decided to change into a three-piece suit of light cashmere in dull gold. She was always cold in London, for some reason.

'Disc-O, boss? The penthouse pad? And what about the little lady here?'

Serena's eyebrows rose in astonishment. How decidedly impertinent! Yet Max was hardly offended, replying easily, 'The office, I'd like to get there as soon as possible. What's the traffic like?'

'Bloody horrible, boss, bloody horrible. But never mind, never mind.'

'Serena,' Max began, pressing a button that moved the partition smoothly into place, 'where would you like to go?' He fumbled awkwardly with his briefcase. He hadn't thought ahead to this moment, had let Serena's supremely efficient housekeeper arrange the flight, only calling ahead to alert Edward. It occurred to him now that Serena might have made plans of her own. 'Do you have a reservation anywhere? The Dorchester? The Connaught? You know you'd be welcome to stay with me, if you wanted to,' he added, mind whirling.

'Max, darling, of course I'll be staying with you,' Serena said absentmindedly, crossing her beautiful legs. 'What a decidedly original driver you have! Little lady, indeed! And penthouse pad?'

'Oh, that's just Edward,' Max replied, admiring the soft swell of her calves, the slender ankles. 'He works for me, not Disc-O. Driver, general factotum, bodyguard even. None of this martial arts stuff, he's a street fighter, as quick and dirty as they come,' he added, surprising her. 'You'll like him when you get to know him.'

'Mmm,' replied Serena noncommittally. 'So, you're going to Disc-O first? I'll come with you, I'm looking forward to it. Have you meetings arranged or anything like that?'

'No, in fact they don't even know I'm back. I thought I'd surprise them.'

She looked over at him curiously, alerted by something in his voice. It had been some time since she had actually looked at him rather than through him. His dark hair, an indeterminate shade between brown and black, shone thick and healthy, the faintest tint of grey showing at the temples. His features were pleasant, unremarkable even, except for the piercing green eyes and strongly defined mouth. He was, she realised with a start of surprise, really quite attractive. Almost handsome.

A stranger would recognise the strength of that mouth, the determined set of that jaw and no doubt conclude that he was not a man to be trifled with.

'You are concerned, then?' she said aloud, not really interested, thinking other thoughts.

'No, not really,' he answered, shaking his head. 'But it's often useful to catch people unprepared, off guard. I'm reasonably sure it's nothing more than a bit of carelessness, over-work perhaps. But I like to keep people on their toes.'

Eve's tongue flicked slowly along the arch of her foot, and Sally's toes clenched spasmodically. In the huge chair behind the glassy lake of Max's desk, she twisted, tried to draw her foot away, but Eve's hands were suddenly strong, imprisoning.

'Eve, please, I won't reconsider, I've made my decision, Max will never have to know. Oh, God, Eve, please!' The tongue was insistent now, darting between her toes like a plump, moist little snake, twisting and sinuous.

She had chosen to confront Eve in Max's office, imagining that the imposing chair and the huge, smoky glass desk would give her an air of extra authority, introduce a note of formality, keep Eve at a distance while she explained, coolly and dispassionately, why she had decided to stay with Max.

But instead Eve had wound her way around the desk, slipped to her knees, begging her to reconsider, coaxing her to think again as she coaxed the shoe from her foot, began the warm and rhythmic massage that had soothed and excited her so often in the past.

Even as she wriggled back into the chair, she could feel the thick heat beginning between her legs, feel herself moistening.

'Eve, stop, you must, I promise I won't tell Max a thing, you can leave Disc-O with no one the wiser, carry on with your plans. Oh Eve . . . you can't. You mustn't. Eve. Eve. Eve.'

GENEVA

Mika was looking down at his hands with absorbed fascination, almost as though he had never seen them before.

'You can play!' Franca exclaimed. 'I don't understand, what's happened? Your hands, they all said you would never play again after the accident! Mika? You can play!'

Without replying he slowly began to draw the leather glove from his left hand. It was soft, supple, thin as a second skin, and he tugged at it gently, slowly, first the thumb, then the index finger, with a measured deliberation that sent her nerves screaming. She wanted to rip the gloves away, free his hands in a rush, hold them to the light, hold them in her own.

'For God's sake, speak to me! Could you do this all along? Why the gloves? What's happened?'

He was plucking leisurely at his ring finger now, hand still concealed by the length of the glove.

She watched him in an agony of impatience. 'Say something!' she cried, her voice perilously close to a shriek. 'Tell me!'

'It's quite curious,' he said at last. 'They held out some faint hope at the time, one of the clinics Serena took me to. Was it Boston? Baltimore? Possibly even Bonn. I don't remember now.' Unhurriedly he grasped the leather tip of his little finger.

'*Hope of what??*' She held her breath as he tugged at the glove.

'That the nerve might regenerate. It wasn't badly

damaged, you see, not irreparably, but sufficiently for me to lose sensation.' He paused, the body of the glove still concealing his hand. 'We were driving along the Amalfi coast, a beautiful sunny day. It's a spectacular road, with sheer drops down to the sea, winding tunnels bursting into blinding daylight. Have you ever been along it?'

She shook her head, eyes fixed on his hand.

'I was driving, of course, I loved to drive in the old days, speeding a bit, perhaps. It's a wonderful way to ease the tension, and I had a concert scheduled in Milan the next week. I'd been working hard. We were coming out of one of the tunnels, and I'd just glanced down to switch off the lights when I felt it. I've often wondered if I'd been driving one of my own cars, whether it would have made any difference.'

She waited for him to continue, hardly daring to breathe.

'The road,' he continued at last, 'is quite narrow in places. Quite narrow. There was a thud, a sickening sort of dull thud. It's a cliché, isn't it? "A dull thud". That's the trouble with clichés, they generalise the specific. But it's true. He must have been travelling at ninety, perhaps a hundred. It crushed his motorcycle, sent him flying across the hood, and then the glass shattered.'

'The glass shattered?' she echoed. 'It was flying glass, then?'

'He came through the passenger side. It was like an explosion of diamonds, I remember seeing them fly towards Serena in a splendid, beautiful, deadly shower. In that moment she looked more exquisite, more *Serena* than I had ever seen her. I remember thinking that diamonds suited her very well.'

'But your hand?' she prompted, confused.

'I never bought her diamonds, you know,' he continued, then fell silent for a moment. 'I must have braked, swerved into the other lane, before I reached for her, tried to pull her free. A shard of glass buried in

281

the seat, perhaps, I'm not sure. And suddenly there was blood everywhere.'

He pulled off the glove, examined his hand. She stepped closer, staring. It was a shapely member, long elegant fingers pale from lack of sun but without the trace of a scar. He examined the palm closely, pointed to an invisible mark on the fleshy pad below his thumb. 'There. She was furious with me, utterly furious. Screamed at me even as I reached for her. "Your hands, your hands!"'

Franca nodded, understanding. It must have been something utterly and completely overwhelming for a violinist to risk his hands. Serena.

His eyes were in the past. 'And she was so wildly angry when, by some fluke, she escaped without a scratch. And so did the boy.'

She looked at the hand he was gazing at so intently. 'So it's healed, then? You can feel your fingers?'

He drew off the other glove swiftly, let both of them fall to the floor. 'So it would seem,' he replied softly. 'So it would seem.'

He flexed the fingers of both hands once, then smiled at her. 'I must tell Serena, tell Maddie. And perhaps then we should have some champagne.'

Several hours and several bottles of Cristal later, she asked the question that kept nagging at her. 'Why the gloves, Mika?'

'I simply couldn't bear to look at my hands,' he replied slowly. 'And now they look strange to me.' He poured the last of the champagne into their flutes and reached for another bottle. 'A symbolic gesture, perhaps. An abbreviation for mourning.'

'But now that you can feel them,' she began, sobering slightly as the full implications of his astounding recovery began to sink in, 'now that you can feel them, you can return to playing.'

'Perhaps,' he agreed. 'It's too soon to decide.' He prised the gold foil away from the neck of the bottle, relishing the cool, metallic whisper beneath his fingers.

282

It had been so long since he had truly felt anything except the burning, tingling phantom pains. His fingers itched to discover anew the tactile pleasures of old wood, smooth glass . . . the warmth of a woman's skin.

If only Serena were here, he thought, easing the cork from the bottle. He had decided not to call her in London, unwilling to share the news with Max just yet. He wanted to tell her in person, see the joy and relief flooding her amber eyes. And he was still shaken by Maddie's tears, by her rough, abrupt, almost absurd attempt to behave as though she had expected it all along.

They had shared a glass of Cristal together as she had spoken distractedly about the menu for this evening, wildly debating the merits of pheasant or beef, clutching his hand while the tears coursed down her cheeks.

Franca remained quiet, silenced less by his reply than the whirlwind of her thoughts. And the strange, awed conviction that she had witnessed something close to a miracle.

Mika poured more champagne, watched the curve of her arm as she lifted her glass. Yes, the warmth of a woman's skin, supple and warming under his hands, the fiery silk of her hair as he ran it through his fingers, the lush velvet of her inner lips, the taut, responsive bud of a nipple rolled between his fingers . . . So much, now, to discover again.

He felt strangely disordered, euphoric, exultant, unfamiliar to himself.

Celibacy, like the black gloves, had been a form of mourning. There had been no need for sex without music. But now that he could feel, but wasn't rehearsing, could play but was composing . . . The thoughts, the rationalisations whirled disjointedly even as his body hardened.

Her breasts, under the loose white shirt she was wearing, were sharply defined, her long legs beautifully sculpted in the tight jeans she was wearing. He could almost feel the crisp rustle of the cotton, the harsh folds of the denim as he stripped them from her, freeing the warm ivory of her flesh.

Cool, warm, hard, soft, she would be all of them under his hands, under his fingers. He flexed them again, glorying in the pliant yet fleshy resistance, the susceptible skin over hard muscle and bone. Not a phantom, burning, tingling irritation, now, but an itch to touch her.

Yes, it would be soon, he decided.

Tonight.

Perhaps now.

On impulse he moved towards the shelves containing his vast collection of records, tapes and CDs, thinking of Ravel and the first time he had seen her photograph, how the slashing dark brows and flaming hair had stirred him to Ravel. How he would take her, rehearsing, quickly, swiftly, from behind, in silk and candlelight.

But even as he reached out, the sight of his naked hand changed his mind. There was no need of the black leather gloves between them now. And there would be no music between them, no second skin like the glove.

Only a woman's music, the sighs, the cries, the scream of pleasure, the soft moan. Her music.

She sat silently, drinking her wine, watching his back as he hesitated before the imposing collection of spines, and felt the quality of his silence change, become thicker. More intense. More potent.

And when he turned to her, blue eyes brilliant, a small smile playing at the edges of his mouth, she felt the electrical, sensual current flowing from him, flowing around her.

'Yes?' It was hardly a question, but he was suddenly, inexplicably, almost a stranger. Her mouth grew dry even as her nipples hardened before his eyes.

LONDON

Max reached the door to his office, leaving Serena a few paces behind as he forged ahead. The fluttering temp had been left in their wake, sputtering and apologising even as Max had shut the door in her face. An ostensible, gracious concern for his privacy had caused Serena to efface herself, effectively masking her curiosity.

The building was ugly, stark, modern, and not to her taste at all. The Eskimo prints in the hall had struck her as slightly bizarre, but she was willing to look again. This ante-room to Max's office, however, was slightly shabby. She slung her jacket over her shoulder and gave a dismissive glance at the desk littered with papers. Modern trash, she decided disdainfully, glancing at the desk, even as her eye was caught by a name on one of the papers. Intrigued, she bent over to take a closer look.

Max entered his office.

Eve straightened up as the door opened, her voice light and easy as she greeted him. She was standing beside Sally, who was seated in the executive chair behind his desk.

'Boss, hello! We weren't expecting you back today, were we, Sally?'

He had no real objection to Sally using his office while he was away, had been meaning, in fact, to have her office re-done, replace that slightly shabby couch with something better, fitted cabinets perhaps, instead of that clumsy little fridge. Irrationally, his mind fixed on decorating details while he struggled to assimilate his first impression. That if he had opened the door scant seconds earlier, he would have seen them together. Close. Intimate. Embracing like lovers.

'A surprise, indeed,' Eve was saying, moving away from Sally, away from the desk. 'I do hope this doesn't mean anything's gone wrong in Geneva?'

Sally was looking as though she had been suddenly,

brutally slapped. Her eyes followed Eve like those of a hunted animal, and slid away from his as he watched her.

He found himself replying naturally, enquiring about day to day details, watched some of the colour return to Sally's face as he responded to Eve, knowing that his instincts hadn't played him false.

He could smell it, as surely as he could smell the stale cigarette smoke.

The air of conspiracy.

'A huge success,' he said smoothly, 'and an exciting opportunity for us all. For Disc-O.' There was a brittle quality to Eve's laugh, or was he simply imagining it? 'Sally,' he said, 'you're smoking again. I was sure that you had quit for good. The pressure hasn't been getting to you while I was away?' He moved smoothly behind his chair, scanning his desk. Not a clue as to what they might have been discussing.

'No, no, not at all,' Sally replied with an unconvincing little laugh. Thank God he was standing behind her. She didn't think she could meet his eyes just yet. Eve was brilliantly under control, voice and movements natural and unselfconscious, just as if they hadn't moments before, been touching. Just as if they hadn't, moments before, been arguing. For a brief flash she hated Eve for her self-possession.

'Well, you know the old saying, where there's smoke, there's fire,' Max was saying genially, green eyes bright at he looked at Eve. His hand closed over the pack of Marlboro 100s. 'A health hazard, Sally, a definite health hazard. If the stress is getting to you, just say so. Maybe we can arrange some time off, a brief holiday.'

'That's just what I've been telling her, boss,' said Eve, eyes glinting. 'That she really does need to get away. Right, Sally?'

No mistaking Eve's meaning, thought Sally a little wildly, reaching instinctively for a cigarette. Max, who had been turning the red and white pack over and over in his hands, hesitated for a moment before handing it back to her.

The banalities of the conversation barely disguised the growing tension in the room. Light and prickly, it seemed to her that it was etching every word Max and Eve spoke.

'Well, no one's indispensable, isn't that what they say?' Max responded, eyes still fixed on Eve, dropping a friendly hand on Sally's shoulder. It had the uncomfortable effect of reminding Sally that she was sitting on his chair, but when she begun awkwardly to rise, he increased the pressure. The gesture wasn't lost on Eve. 'Ah, Serena, there you are.'

All three turned to look at her. She stood for a moment, framed by the doorway, negligently clasping a piece of paper in one hand, before moving into the room.

'Sally, Eve, this is Serena D'Angelo, Mika's sister.'

Sally mumbled a polite greeting as an icy hand gripped her heart. She had never met Serena, come face to face with the woman who was her rival. And her striking beauty, the physical warmth of her presence was a shock. And the paper she held in her hands, folding and twisting into some strange shape . . . as Serena moved towards her, she recognised, with a sickening jolt, her own handwriting.

'Such a pleasure,' Serena was saying in her warm, husky tones, extending a hand to Sally, who took it numbly. 'How strange that we've never met before. Then again, perhaps not.' She smiled, looked down at the piece of paper in her free hand, then turned to Eve.

The blood was rushing to Sally's head, pounding through her ears in a dense roar. She couldn't move, couldn't think, could barely breathe. Her eyes were fixed on the paper in Serena's hand. The list she had drawn up, recording every detail of Eve's proposal. And, improbably, as Serena gracefully dropped to a black leather chair, she was folding it, origami-style, into a complicated shape that gradually resolved into a boat.

'Don't let me interrupt, Max,' she was saying, 'I'm sure you have many, many things to discuss. Max treated me to quite a dissertation on the music business, foreign markets and so on. It's all quite fascinating. I take it that's your speciality, Eve?' she smiled.

The boat was disappearing now, new angles and complicated folds rising to form a flower.

'Not speciality, precisely,' Eve replied, eyes wary. If she had been a cat, her tail would have thickened. Instinctively she recognised her own species, recognised a more powerful predator.

It was a beautiful creation, the stiff angularity of the paper folds somehow capturing the lush and flowing curves of a rose, suggesting the essence of the flower.

'Eve, you don't do yourself justice,' Max said easily. 'That report on your trip to America was really quite good.'

And now the rose was losing definition, petals dissolving. Sally felt Serena's eyes on her and looked up unwillingly. The amber eyes were warm, somehow reassuring, almost friendly.

The flower became a sunburst, rays exploding from the core so vibrantly that it almost seemed to glow. And Serena was smiling at her.

The waves of panic receded a little, and Sally felt her mind clearing. Eve and Max were talking about the Toronto office, old business, nothing too threatening. If there was a sub-text to their words, she couldn't grasp it. And Serena was dismantling her sunburst.

Had she left the paper on her desk? She couldn't have been so careless . . . she might have been. Why had Serena said nothing? She obviously recognised its significance. Was there some obscure message, some symbolism in the shapes she kept creating? A boat, a flower, a sunburst . . . senseless imagery. Perhaps it wasn't her notes at all. Perhaps she had merely imagined her handwriting covering the page. Surely she had locked it in her desk drawer before hastily ushering Eve into Max's office. She almost remembered doing it.

Her confidence was returning. 'That's clever work,' Sally said aloud, looking at Serena's hands. The sunburst had become elongated, a long thin point, the end obscured by Serena's fingers.

'Do you like it?' asked Serena casually, folding the paper again and again. 'Then it's yours.'

And opened her palms to reveal a knife.

GENEVA

His eyes were the deep Mediterranean blue that had coloured her orgasms, haunted her dreams. And her body was responding to it like water, becoming liquid. Her heart was pounding and she could feel the deep, fluttering pulse between her legs. And he hadn't even touched her.

'A kiss,' she said softly, feeling her belly clench. 'Only a kiss.'

'Only a kiss?' he repeated, apparently amused. He was beside her now, his thigh against hers, one arm draped along the edge of the couch, just lightly dusting her shoulders.

It would take nothing, the smallest movement, a twist of position to pin her against the black leather, pin her beneath him. He was stronger, taller, could easily take her. And she wanted him to. With a thudding intensity, she realised just how badly she wanted him to.

There were tears in her eyes when she said again, 'Only a kiss.'

She closed her eyes as she felt his hands sift through her hair, turning her face to his, shuddered at the warm breath of sensation grazing her temples, her eyebrows. He was barely touching her skin, playing with air above it as he traced the slashing arcs of her brows with his mouth, touched the tip of his tongue to her lashes, delicately licked the tear from the corner of her eyes.

She parted her lips unconsciously, waiting, willing the firm heat of his mouth, the pressure of his tongue, his teeth. Her jeans were becoming tight, too tight. She was swelling with arousal, flowering to ripeness as his mouth strayed to her ear, her breasts now chafing against her shirt, her nipples hard. And when she felt the tip of his tongue on her lobe, she almost screamed.

His mouth moved over her gently, lightly, so lightly, too lightly, tracing the contours of her face, her cheek bones, the curve of her jaw, avoiding her mouth. Her nerves were screaming, stroked into unbearable sensitivity by the fragile tracery of his lips. The fluttering pulse of her inner lips was thickening, becoming a dull ache, swelling to a greedy hunger.

She moaned, licked lips that were suddenly dry, and felt his mouth whisper against hers, his tongue tracing the swell of her lips, moistening them, tantalising them, teasing them with the faintest brush of his teeth. Her tongue flicked out to meet his, to draw it into the waiting warmth, but he moved away.

She kept her eyes closed, knowing that if she opened them to his she would ignite the explosion simmering in the pit of her belly, forced herself to remain still, knowing that the slightest movement would trip the wires that her nerves had become and unleash a screaming, frenzied orgasm. And she mustn't come, not yet.

It seemed hours later when, with a small sigh, he moved his lips to hers, strangling her scream of pleasure with his mouth.

LONDON

'I knew something was wrong,' Max was saying, 'but of course, I couldn't put my finger on it while I was away.'

'Mmm,' murmured Serena absently, gazing up at

290

her reflection. She had left Max's office, casually dropping the paper knife into Sally's hands, and been driven by Edward to Max's apartment. She'd amused herself for an hour or two with Max's impossible collection of abstracts, then bathed and slipped into bed. The mirror on the ceiling had been a surprise.

'Sally's had her suspicions for a while, apparently, but wanted to give Eve time.' Propped on the pillows beside her, Max reached out and touched Serena's hair. 'Frankly, I'm not sure Sally's entirely right, but it's her assistant. And if she feels that she can't work with Eve, then so be it. It's Sally I really depend on.'

'Mmm,' Serena said again, not entirely feigning disinterest. It had been an urgent, wild coupling under the glass-eye of the mirror, and she was feeling pleasantly relaxed. She smiled at herself and fingered her hair, wondering if it was time for a change of style. A cut, perhaps.

'And when we talked to Eve about it, she took it surprisingly well, has even been thinking of returning to the finance industry.'

'Really?' said Serena, turning on her side to look at him. So Sally had used the knife, not to slit her own wrists, nor to drive it into Max's back. Either she had sheathed it, or left it pricking between his shoulder-blades. That was interesting.

Idly she wondered about Eve, how much of a threat she might pose to Max, to Disc-O. Perhaps she should have handed the knife to Max. It had been a whim, an impulse, nothing more, that had led her to give it to Sally.

She forgot about it as Max reached for her again.

Chapter Twelve

Interlude

VIRGIN ISLANDS

*T*he yacht was moored off the tiny island of Virgin Gorda. It was a clear, calm day, the sun glinting off the water in a rapid, dazzling shiver.

'The weather's perfect,' said the man beside her. He sounded as though he was congratulating himself on the fact. Perhaps he was.

Serena, lying on the chaise beside him, made no reply, merely reached for her sunglasses. The movement of her arm caught the light, reflecting and refracting the dazzling diamond bracelet circling her wrist. Max's diamonds. They shimmered at her throat, shone from her ears with a brilliant, icy fire. As her hand moved for the sunglasses, the ring on her hand struck the light, cold, hard, bright and flawless.

Ridiculous that some people still thought it was vulgar to wear diamonds during the day, she mused. It wasn't, of course. Especially not if you weren't wearing anything else.

'And the sea's like glass,' he continued, still in a self-congratulatory tone.

She cut her eyes over at him. He had a slight, self-satisfied smile playing at the corners of his mouth, the smile of a man who owned the world, or at least everything in it he wanted. That smile was beginning to get on her nerves.

He did have every right to look smug, she reminded herself. After all, she was here beside him.

Idly she cast her mind over the past six months, her vague irritation disappearing as she thought of Mika. She smiled at the memory of her return to Geneva, how disappointed she had been that he hadn't come to the airport to meet her, wasn't even waiting at the steps. Entering the villa, she had heard the strains of Bach from the music room. Expecting to find him sunk in one of his black depressions, she had hesitated at the door, finally entering reluctantly.

To find him playing.

The tears, the joy, the overwhelming relief, the champagne and the laughter.

Her euphoria dimming a little at his decision to continue composing, to play only for his own pleasure.

He should be with her now, she thought. He had decided to remain in Geneva, refused to be coaxed into joining her, claiming the pressure of work. She wondered if Franca was still with him, or whether she had accepted the three-month stint in Rome that Max had dangled before her.

Max. Sometimes she wondered about what he was thinking, whether he realised, truly appreciated what she had done for him. Probably not.

Alerted by her sigh, the man beside her set down his book. 'Serena, is something wrong?'

'Nothing at all, Jeff, nothing at all. But perhaps we should order lunch. I'm starving.'

ROME

The eternal city, Franca thought derisively, city of lovers. What a horrible place to be alone in November.

It was raining again, the soft, relentless, warm dull rain drumming against the window.

Max had arranged rooms in the American Academy, and for the first few weeks she had rather enjoyed the change, the conversation of the students and scholars studying painting, sculpture, architecture and music. She had rooms across from the young female pianist who had won the Rome Prize, and they had become friendly, sharing meals together, visiting the open-air market in Trastevere, sipping beer in front of the Pantheon. The sheer novelty of it all distracted her a little from the ache of leaving Mika.

And the Italian string quartet that Max had arranged for her to play with were good, very good.

She couldn't have stayed in Geneva any longer without yielding to him.

The sheer, sensual torture of being near him, moving from kiss to embrace while refusing climax had gone on too long. Her body warmed as she thought back, remembering his hands, his lips on hers, the skill of his mouth and fingers as they stroked her.

Not long, now, she reminded herself, looking down at the letter in her hands. The première was on the books for January, Max had written, the Royal Albert Hall. Everything moving forward as planned.

Not long, now.

GENEVA

Mika sat on the terrace, drinking coffee. It was becoming too chilly in the mornings to really enjoy it, but he did it all the same. He was grateful for the warmth of Midas on his lap, rumbling contentedly.

He looked at the postcard propped against his mug. It showed a statue of Aphrodite at her bath. She had sent it from the Vatican. For a moment he admired the flowing marble curves of the goddess bending forward, then turned the card over to read the message again.

It was simple, consisting only of a single word.

'Soon.'

Well, *Serena's Song* was ready for her, worked and reworked, honed now to a brilliant perfection.

He'd begun work on another piece, loosely based on Midas, his purrs and yawns, growls and yowls, but it wasn't holding his attention as completely as it should. And he missed Serena.

What on earth had possessed her to fly from Geneva to New York, New York to Houston, and then disappear to the tropics with Jeff Brooks?

And he had thought, when she left for London in August, a city she detested, that perhaps she was trying to make some sort of relationship with Max, steel herself to some sort of commitment.

Instead, she'd simply been following a pattern established long ago, moving from place to place, man to man. He hoped she'd return soon for one of her flying visits.

Soon.

And the première was approaching, only six weeks away now, or was it seven?

Soon.

HOUSTON

From the third floor of the luxury condo she had rented, Eve looked out at the shabby, dilapidated eatery next door and could have screamed in vexation. Was Houston the only city in the world without any concept of zoning laws? Like her well laid plans, the city was chaotic, disordered, expensive condos and houses nestled in apparently placid luxury beside derelict laundries, garages and BBQ joints.

She gritted her teeth in frustration and turned to the phone. She had been waiting for Jeff to return her calls for almost a month now and time was running out. Her severance pay from Disc-O had been astoundingly generous, more than enough to keep her for the next couple of months while she got the new company off the ground. But she couldn't do it without Jeff Brooks.

She was pleased she had decided to leave Nikolai in London, content with the club in Camden until she had established herself in America, New York, Chicago, wherever she and Jeff decided to make their headquarters. But Jeff didn't seem to understand how crucial the time element was, how necessary it was to move quickly.

He'd been agreeable enough at first, eagerly entering into her plans, entertaining her at some of Houston's finest restaurants, taking her out to his ranch. And she hadn't pushed him hard then, relishing the high life, the freedom, the sun.

'He'll be in touch with you soon, Ms Drake,' his secretary kept saying in her impossible drawl, making every vowel last an eternity.

Soon.

It had damn well better be soon!

LONDON

'I don't know, Sally, he doesn't really do anything for me, know what I mean? No tingles, no thrills.'

'Well, he does for me,' she responded sweetly. Tingles and thrills weren't the half of it, actually, she thought to herself, smiling a little at Nikolai's photograph.

'It's a generous starting contract for some unknown Soviet keyboard artist playing in Camden,' Max objected, looking over at her. She'd had her hair cut. It was short now, almost like a helmet, with a straight fringe across her forehead. It made her look older, more self-assured.

'Always a mistake to underestimate the novices, Max,' she replied, a none too gentle reminder of his blunder with Franca Tonelli.

Max winced a little at the jibe. Damn Serena! He had eventually been forced to double his offer to Franca and include a solid yearly salary as well. While it would barely dent the spectacular profits he expected in the next year from *The Song* – the only title Mika was prepared to divulge, and a damn silly one it was, too! – Max still smarted at the memory.

She would be calling about now, he thought, looking down at his watch, pretending to think. She called every week, sometimes twice or three times. He realised how important it was, now, for her and Mika to be alone, coping with the stresses and strains of his recovery, and she had gently but firmly discouraged him from calling her. But he missed her.

'So, Max, what do you say?'

He stalled a bit longer, to preserve the illusion of reluctance, then agreed. As she had expected him to.

Sally returned to her desk, which was now a shining sleek monster of black wood and chrome. As she reached for the phone to call Nikolai with the good news, she unlocked and opened the upper right-hand desk drawer.

It had become a habit to smile at her talisman, just touch it gently, whenever she got her own way with Max. Which was quite often, these days.

The drawer was empty, except for the talisman.

More of a good luck charm, really, she thought, gently tracing one of the angular folds of Serena's paper knife.

Finale

ROYAL ALBERT HALL, LONDON

*T*he stage lights were hot. On the raised dais the
four violins were arranged in a semi-circle, the
protective silk drawn aside to reveal the polished gleam
of old wood. From the wings she could hear the
muttering of curious voices, almost sense necks craned
to catch a glimpse of Mika's prized beauties.

With the sixth sense ingrained in every performer
she probed the atmosphere, felt for the audience,
found anticipation mixed with curiosity. There was
none of the rapt expectancy that would have greeted
Mika or any other of the virtuosi: she was a relatively
unknown quantity. That the hall was filled, overflowing, was a tribute to Mika. They were here to pay
homage to him, to welcome his return to the stage in
the guise of composer, catch a glimpse of the man who
had abandoned them so suddenly amidst so much
mystery.

In her imagination she saw them all as a collection of
animals, some wild and exotic, some tame, mundane.
The critics, sleek and predatory as panthers, waiting
with feral eyes, prepared to pounce. Friends and col-
leagues of her own from the world of music, as mutable

as chameleons, poised to praise or condemn, following the critics. The flock of music lovers and culture vultures, as brightly coloured in their silks and jewels as tropical birds.

Like Orpheus, she would have to tame them, transfix them, beguile them . . . and him.

She could sense his presence, almost hear the sound of his voice.

They had not met, not even spoken, before tonight. At her expressed wish. Serena had been there, friendly, supportive, helping her through the torture of relearning the piece, lightening her mood after the first day of rehearsal.

Serena, who had casually torn apart the first note from Mika she had shown her, which had read 'I wouldn't consider even spitting at a woman who could treat *The Climax* with such consummate inartistry,' and had produced, like magic, a bottle of Calvados and a box of tissues.

Serena, who, during the second rehearsal, had laughed when she intercepted a frantic telegram pronouncing that 'Your pizzicato would shame a cat in heat!'

Serena, who had glanced at an envelope delivered after the third and final rehearsal, and merely said, 'Perhaps you should read it alone.'

There was only one word written on the thick cream paper.

'Soon.'

The hall lights were dimming now. She took a deep breath, closed her eyes, began focusing and pooling her energy. Excitement began to ripple through her as she heard the cultured voice describe the programme. Stray phrases floated past her, meaning nothing, white noise that only enhanced her concentration.

'Ladies and gentlemen, it is my great privilege tonight to introduce to you an extraordinary composition by an extraordinary musician.'

Anticipation dancing through her body, she felt her

fingers begin to tremble, itching for the smooth, satin contours of the Stradivarius, the hard rod of the bow, the warm silk of his skin.

'A work of breathtaking originality, it springs from the heart of the classical period, yet is decisively neo-romantic in conception.'

She ran the tip of her tongue over lips which were suddenly dry, moistening them, imagining his lips, tempting them with the caress of her tongue, a delicate, questing touch. His mouth opening to hers, the gleam of his teeth, white and hard under the slick wash of her tongue, his breath sweet against her lips.

'The art of writing for the unaccompanied violin has a long and fascinating history; it can be traced beyond Bach to the sixteenth century to Striggio's feat of playing four parts simultaneously on a *lira da braccio*.'

His body rippling under her touch, muscles clenching, spasming in desire as she lightly plucked at his nipples, plucked at the strings for laughter in the second movement, his cock as hard as the bow, her fingers as skilled, as dextrous, as fluent as his own.

'Even Striggio might have found himself stretched by the incredibly demanding score that we have the privilege to hear tonight, performed for the first time by a fellow Italian. Please join me in welcoming Francesca Tonelli, who will perform *Serena's Song*, described by the author as an odyssey in four movements.'

In the audience, Serena caught her breath at the title. Beside her, Mika clasped her hand, his eyes fixed on the stage. Max shifted a little uncomfortably in his seat. Well, it was a damn sight better than just *The Song*, he decided, holding her other hand tightly. A damn sight better.

Franca opened her eyes, hearing the applause, enthusiastic but guarded, waited for the pleasure-panic to subside, willed it to pool between her thighs, then walked out to the middle of the stage.

Under the hot stage lights her hair caught fire, a

blazing, sizzling nimbus of red-gold that cascaded down her back. The simple black sheath-dress bared her arms and shoulders, left her back naked to the waist and was slit to mid-thigh. Her only adornment was a thick gold chain that Serena had slipped around her neck before leaving her dressing-room. 'For luck, darling,' Serena had said, unfastening it from her own throat where it had been hidden by the white fire of Max's diamonds.

She fingered the heavy gold links once, then bent to lift the Strad from its case. As she turned she heard a small sigh escape the audience, a purely male sound, an instinctive response to the perfect, elegant curve of her leg, the milky perfection of naked skin against black velvet. For a moment, at least, in their eyes, the perfection of her body had eclipsed the Stradivarius.

Mika was there, somewhere. She could feel his eyes on her, feel the force of his mind searching for hers. Was he backstage, front row, in a box? She couldn't tell. It didn't matter.

She faced the audience feeling, suddenly, brazen. Wanton. Wet. A bit daring. Not at all the dreamy, tender, tentative creature that *The Kiss* demanded. She was hot and sultry, steamy jazz arcing to her finger tips, the heavy pulse of rock & roll beating between her legs.

She caught them with the flickering intensity of the first note of *The Kiss*, suggestive, cool and challenging. Held it, drew it out, beckoning with her mouth, soft and warm, tantalising with her eyes, cold and impervious. She imagined him, fingers curling into fists, disbelief turning to fury as she held the note a fraction too long, then capriciously she relented, slid into the next, softly, meltingly.

She was watered silk, ready to flow around him, envelop him in her warmth, intoxicate him with the elusive scent of her perfume, torment him gently with her tongue and teeth.

Mika cursed once, softly, under his breath.

The audience was still, intent on the unfolding melody, intrigued by the implicit promise of strings that whispered seductively then retreated.

Rising and falling, with deft grace she stroked the violin with her bow, stroked his body with her eyes, lingering on the firm, muscular thighs, flirted with his zipper, felt him harden at the artless, stray touch of her fingers. She was all heat and wetness now, a seamless radiance bathing her groin, hardening her nipples. For a brief moment she wanted to shock him, release the zip in one swift movement, draw the stiff engorged length of him into her mouth, feel his hands tighten on the back of her neck, but caught herself before she bowed too firmly.

And then, with a poignant, aching tenderness almost too painful to bear, she let the note fall. Into silence. Drew away from him, as she had left for Rome. In the quiet, black stillness of the night.

The silence was thick and potent. There were no dry coughs, no rustling of programmes, no whispered exchanges as she replaced the Strad in its case and turned to the Guarnerius.

As poised, as confident, as sure as if she were guiding him between her legs, she settled the chin-rest against her chin, relishing the hard patina of the wood, the hard length of him.

The Embrace flowed like water, flirted with the air like a stray breeze, rustled seductively, sensuously like falling silk, crackled suddenly like a restless flame. She was lost now in the exploration of his body, the voyage of discovering naked skin beneath silk and linen. With practised deliberation she let her fingers stray to the buttons of his shirt, eyes never leaving his face, lingered lovingly at the column of his throat, exposed the finely muscled chest, flicked the hard nub of his nipple with her tongue as she began the pizzicato.

It was hot and heavy, thick and thickening, aroused and arousing.

Eyes glowing like blue coals, Mika cursed again.

'What is it, darling?' whispered Serena, lightly touching his arm.

'Too intense, too soon,' he replied angrily, forgetting to lower his voice. 'She can't sustain this . . . there'll be nothing left for *The Climax* . . . damn her! This is intimacy, not intimation!'

An enraged whisper from behind them commanded him to hush.

'She may yet surprise you, darling,' said Serena against his ear, dropping a light, placatory kiss on his cheek, careful to keep the smile from her voice. Franca was playing brilliantly, had enveloped the audience in a steamy haze so compelling that she could feel even herself succumbing to it. Beside her, Max was absorbed, his hand tightening on her thigh.

The last, insinuating chord rustled through the air, crisp as white linen falling to the floor. Melted. Died away.

On stage, she reached for the Strad like a lover.

Hot and urgent, the frenzied fall, hands rough and impatient, greedy and ravenous, any barrier between them intolerable. She was bowing hard now, almost too hard, already reaching the plunging, lunging rhythm of penetration.

In the audience, people shifted in their seats, feeling caught, confined, overpowered. Heated.

And the heat grew, notes thickening the air, foreshadowing the screaming, rapturous, blissful frenzy of release, the ecstatic, electric dissolve.

She felt him inside her then, knew that he would thrust hard and deep, then withdraw, circle the mouth of her entrance merely to torment her, plunge again, thrust again, withdraw just when she was ready to come and move his mouth to her centre, kiss her there gently, smooth the heated tissues with his tongue until they longed for nothing more than that soft and gentle lapping.

And then he would thrust again.

Fill the wet, aching void that longed for him, fill her

body with pounding rapture as he drove into her, carry them both to the explosive heart of orgasm. She could feel her own climax approaching, the muscles in her thighs trembling as she reached the end, bowing long and hard. She refused it, even as she let the last notes scream their frenzy.

There was a palpable difference in the silence as she replaced the Strad and reached for the Amati.

Mika was right. The Amati didn't carry in a great hall. But the choice had been deliberate. The lingering, aching loving loss wasn't meant to master space, but to enhance it.

It was the little death, the fulfilment, tender, poignant. Bodies cooling, breathing slowing.

And she captured it perfectly, the subsiding physical shocks melting into the eccentrically placed pizzicato, the warm, enveloping peace of perfectly muted and muting notes.

And when she went backstage after the third encore, sweating, high, hot, delirious from the thunderous applause, he was waiting for her in her dressing-room.

NO LADY
Saskia Hope

30 year-old Kate dumps her boyfriend, walks out of her job and sets off in search of sexual adventure. Set against the rugged terrain of the Pyrenees, the love-making is as rough as the landscape. Only a sense of danger can satisfy her longing for erotic encounters beyond the boundaries of ordinary experience.

ISBN 0 352 32857 6

WEB OF DESIRE
Sophie Danson

High-flying executive Marcie is gradually drawn away from the normality of her married life. Strange messages begin to appear on her computer, summoning her to sinister and fetishistic sexual liaisons with strangers whose identity remains secret. She's given glimpses of the world of The Omega Network, where her every desire is known and fulfilled.

ISBN 0 352 32856 8

BLUE HOTEL
Cherri Pickford

Hotelier Ramon can't understand why best-selling author Floy Pennington has come to stay at his quiet hotel in the rural idyll of the English countryside. Her exhibitionist tendencies are driving him crazy, as are her increasingly wanton encounters with the hotel's other guests.

ISBN 0 352 32858 4

CASSANDRA'S CONFLICT
Fredrica Alleyn

Behind the respectable facade of a house in present-day Hampstead lies a world of decadent indulgence and darkly bizarre eroticism. The sternly attractive Baron and his beautiful but cruel wife are playing games with the young Cassandra, employed as a nanny in their sumptuous household. Games where only the Baron knows the rules, and where there can only be one winner.

ISBN 0 352 32859 2

THE CAPTIVE FLESH
Cleo Cordell

Marietta and Claudine, French aristocrats saved from pirates, learn their invitation to stay at the opulent Algerian mansion of their rescuer, Kasim, requires something in return; their complete surrender to the ecstasy of pleasure in pain. Kasim's decadent orgies also require the services of the handsome blonde slave, Gabriel – perfect in his male beauty. Together in their slavery, they savour delights at the depths of shame.

ISBN 0 352 32872 X

PLEASURE HUNT
Sophie Danson

Sexual adventurer Olympia Deschamps is determined to become a member of the Legion D'Amour – the most exclusive society of French libertines who pride themselves on their capacity for limitless erotic pleasure. Set in Paris – Europe's most romantic city – Olympia's sense of unbridled hedonism finds release in an extraordinary variety of libidinous challenges.

ISBN 0 352 32880 0

ODALISQUE
Fleur Reynolds

A tale of family intrigue and depravity set against the glittering backdrop of the designer set. Auralie and Jeanine are cousins, both young, glamorous and wealthy. Catering to the business classes with their design consultancy and exclusive hotel, this facade of respectability conceals a reality of bitter rivalry and unnatural love.

ISBN 0 352 32887 8

OUTLAW LOVER
Saskia Hope

Fee Cambridge lives in an upper level deluxe pleasuredome of technologically advanced comfort. The pirates live in the harsh outer reaches of the decaying 21st century city where lawlessness abounds in a sexual underworld. Bored with her predictable husband and pampered lifestyle, Fee ventures into the wild side of town, finding an urban outlaw who becomes her lover. Leading a double life of piracy and privilege, will her taste for adventure get her too deep into danger?

ISBN 0 352 32909 2

AVALON NIGHTS
Sophie Danson

On a stormy night in Camelot, a shape-shifting sorceress weaves a potent spell. Enthralled by her magical powers, each knight of the Round Table – King Arthur included – must tell the tale of his most lustful conquest. Virtuous knights, brave and true, recount before the gathering ribald deeds more befitting licentious knaves. Before the evening is done, the sorceress must complete a mystic quest for the grail of ultimate pleasure.

ISBN 0 352 32910 6

THE SENSES BEJEWELLED
Cleo Cordell

Willing captives Marietta and Claudine are settling into an opulent life at Kasim's harem. But 18th century Alergia can be a hostile place. When the women are kidnapped by Kasim's sworn enemy, they face indignities that will test the boundaries of erotic experience. Marietta is reunited with her slave lover Gabriel, whose heart she previously broke. Will Kasim win back his cherished concubines? This is the sequel to *The Captive Flesh*.

ISBN 0 352 32904 1

GEMINI HEAT
Portia Da Costa

As the metropolis sizzles in freak early summer temperatures, twin sisters Deana and Delia find themselves cooking up a heatwave of their own. Jackson de Guile, master of power dynamics and wealthy connoisseur of fine things, draws them both into a web of luxuriously decadent debauchery. Sooner or later, one of them has to make a life-changing decision.

ISBN 0 352 32912 2

March '94

VIRTUOSO
Katrina Vincenzi

Mika and Serena, darlings of classical music's jet-set, inhabit a world of secluded passion. The reason? Since Mika's tragic accident which put a stop to his meteoric rise to fame as a solo violinist, he cannot face the world, and together they lead a decadent, reclusive existence. But Serena is determined to change things. The potent force of her ravenous sensuality cannot be ignored, as she rekindles Mika's zest for love and life through unexpected means. But together they share a dark secret.

ISBN 0 352 32912 2

MOON OF DESIRE
Sophie Danson

When Soraya Chilton is posted to the ancient and mysterious city of Ragzburg on a mission for the Foreign Office, strange things begin to happen to her. Wild, sexual urges overwhelm her at the coming of each full moon. Will her boyfriend, Anton, be her saviour – or her victim? What price will she have to pay to lift the curse of unquenchable lust that courses through her veins?

ISBN 0 352 32911 4   *April '94*

FIONA'S FATE
Fredrica Alleyn

When Fiona Sheldon is kidnapped by the infamous Trimarchi brothers, along with her friend Bethany, she finds herself acting in ways her husband Duncan would be shocked by. For it is he who owes the brothers money and is more concerned to free his voluptuous mistress than his shy and quiet wife. Allesandro Trimarchi makes full use of this opportunity to discover the true extent of Fiona's suppressed, but powerful, sexuality.

ISBN 0 352 32913 0   *April '94*

HANDMAIDEN OF PALMYRA
Fleur Reynolds

3rd century Palmyra: a lush oasis in the Syrian desert. The beautiful and fiercely independent Samoya takes her place in the temple of Antioch as an apprentice priestess. Decadent bachelor Prince Alif has other plans for her and sends his scheming sister to bring her to his Bacchanalian wedding feast. Embarking on a journey across the desert, Samoya encounters Marcus, the battle-hardened centurion who will unearth the core of her desires and change the course of her destiny.

ISBN 0 352 32919 X   *May '94*

OUTLAW FANTASY
Saskia Hope

For Fee Cambridge, playing with fire had become a full time job. Helping her pirate lover to escape his lawless lifestyle had its rewards as well as its drawbacks. On the outer reaches of the 21st century metropolis the Amazenes are on the prowl; fierce warrior women who have some unfinished business with Fee's lover. Will she be able to stop him straying back to the wrong side of the tracks? This is the sequel to *Outlaw Lover*.

ISBN 0 352 32920 3   *May '94*

Three special, longer length Black Lace summer sizzlers to be published in June 1994.

THE SILKEN CAGE
Sophie Danson

When University lecturer, Maria Treharne, inherits her aunt's mansion in Cornwall, she finds herself the subject of strange and unexpected attention. Her new dwelling resides on much-prized land; sacred, some would say. Anthony Pendorran has waited a long time for the mistress to arrive at Brackwater Tor. Now she's here, his lust can be quenched as their longing for each other has a hunger beyond the realm of the physical. Using the craft of goddess worship and sexual magnetism, Maria finds allies and foes in this savage and beautiful landscape.

ISBN 0 352 32928 9

RIVER OF SECRETS
Saskia Hope & Georgia Angelis

When intrepid female reporter Sydney Johnson takes over someone else's assignment up the Amazon river, the planned exploration seems straightforward enough. But the crew's photographer seems to be keeping some very shady company and the handsome botanist is proving to be a distraction with a difference. Sydney soon realises this mission to find a lost Inca city has a hidden agenda. Everyone is behaving so strangely, so sexually, and the tropical humidity is reaching fever pitch as if a mysterious force is working its magic over the expedition. Echoing with primeval sounds, the jungle holds both dangers and delights for Sydney in this Indiana Jones-esque story of lust and adventure.

ISBN 0 352 32925 4

VELVET CLAWS
Cleo Cordell

It's the 19th century; a time of exploration and discovery and young, spirited Gwendoline Farnshawe is determined not to be left behind in the parlour when the handsome and celebrated anthropologist, Jonathan Kimberton, is planning his latest expedition to Africa. Rebelling against Victorian society's expectation of a young woman and lured by the mystery and exotic climate of this exciting continent, Gwendoline sets sail with her entourage bound for a land of unknown pleasures.

ISBN 0 352 32926 2

BLACK
lace

WE NEED YOUR HELP . . .
to plan the future of women's erotic fiction –

– and no stamp required!

Yours are the only opinions that matter.
Black Lace is a new and exciting venture: the first series of books devoted to erotic fiction by women for women.

We're going to do our best to provide the brightest, best-written, bonk-filled books you can buy. And we'd like your help in these early stages. Tell us what you want to read.

THE BLACK LACE QUESTIONNAIRE

SECTION ONE: ABOUT YOU

1.1 Sex (*we presume you are female, but so as not to discriminate*) are you?

Male ☐ Female ☐

1.2 Age

under 21 ☐ 21–30 ☐
31–40 ☐ 41–50 ☐
51–60 ☐ over 60 ☐

1.3 At what age did you leave full-time education?

still in education ☐ 16 or younger ☐
17–19 ☐ 20 or older ☐

1.4 Occupation _____

1.5 Annual household income

- under £10,000 ☐
- £10–£20,000 ☐
- £20–£30,000 ☐
- £30–£40,000 ☐
- over £40,000 ☐

1.6 We are perfectly happy for you to remain anonymous; but if you would like us to send you a free booklist of Nexus books for men and Black Lace books for Women, please insert your name and address

_____

_____

_____

_____

SECTION TWO: ABOUT BUYING BLACK LACE BOOKS

2.1 How did you acquire this copy of *Virtuoso*

- I bought it myself ☐
- My partner bought it ☐
- I borrowed/found it ☐

2.2 How did you find out about Black Lace books?

- I saw them in a shop ☐
- I saw them advertised in a magazine ☐
- I saw the London Underground posters ☐
- I read about them in _____
- Other _____

2.3 Please tick the following statements you agree with:

- I would be less embarrassed about buying Black Lace books if the cover pictures were less explicit ☐
- I think that in general the pictures on Black Lace books are about right ☐
- I think Black Lace cover pictures should be as explicit as possible ☐

2.4 Would you read a Black Lace book in a public place – on a train for instance?

- Yes ☐
- No ☐

SECTION THREE: ABOUT THIS BLACK LACE BOOK

3.1 Do you think the sex content in this book is:
    Too much ☐   About right ☐
    Not enough ☐

3.2 Do you think the writing style in this book is:
    Too unreal/escapist ☐   About right ☐
    Too down to earth ☐

3.3 Do you think the story in this book is:
    Too complicated ☐   About right ☐
    Too boring/simple ☐

3.4 Do you think the cover of this book is:
    Too explicit ☐   About right ☐
    Not explicit enough ☐

Here's a space for any other comments:

SECTION FOUR: ABOUT OTHER BLACK LACE BOOKS

4.1 How many Black Lace books have you read? ☐

4.2 If more than one, which one did you prefer?

4.3 Why?

SECTION FIVE: ABOUT YOUR IDEAL EROTIC NOVEL

We want to publish the books you want to read – so this is your chance to tell us exactly what your ideal erotic novel would be like.

5.1 Using a scale of 1 to 5 (1 = no interest at all, 5 = your ideal), please rate the following possible settings for an erotic novel:

Medieval/barbarian/sword 'n' sorcery ☐
Renaissance/Elizabethan/Restoration ☐
Victorian/Edwardian ☐
1920s & 1930s – the Jazz Age ☐
Present day ☐
Future/Science Fiction ☐

5.2 Using the same scale of 1 to 5, please rate the following themes you may find in an erotic novel:

Submissive male/dominant female ☐
Submissive female/dominant male ☐
Lesbianism ☐
Bondage/fetishism ☐
Romantic love ☐
Experimental sex e.g. anal/watersports/sex toys ☐
Gay male sex ☐
Group sex ☐

Using the same scale of 1 to 5, please rate the following styles in which an erotic novel could be written:

Realistic, down to earth, set in real life ☐
Escapist fantasy, but just about believable ☐
Completely unreal, impressionistic, dreamlike ☐

5.3 Would you prefer your ideal erotic novel to be written from the viewpoint of the main male characters or the main female characters?

Male ☐ Female ☐
Both ☐

5.4 What would your ideal Black Lace heroine be like? Tick
     as many as you like:

Dominant	☐	Glamorous	☐
Extroverted	☐	Contemporary	☐
Independent	☐	Bisexual	☐
Adventurous	☐	Naive	☐
Intellectual	☐	Introverted	☐
Professional	☐	Kinky	☐
Submissive	☐	Anything else?	☐
Ordinary	☐	_____	

5.5 What would your ideal male lead character be like?
     Again, tick as many as you like:

Rugged	☐		
Athletic	☐	Caring	☐
Sophisticated	☐	Cruel	☐
Retiring	☐	Debonair	☐
Outdoor-type	☐	Naive	☐
Executive-type	☐	Intellectual	☐
Ordinary	☐	Professional	☐
Kinky	☐	Romantic	☐
Hunky	☐		
Sexually dominant	☐	Anything else?	☐
Sexually submissive	☐	_____	

5.6 Is there one particular setting or subject matter that your
     ideal erotic novel would contain?

     _____

SECTION SIX: LAST WORDS

6.1 What do you like best about Black Lace books?

     _____

6.2 What do you most dislike about Black Lace books?

     _____

6.3 In what way, if any, would you like to change Black
     Lace covers?

     _____

6.4 Here's a space for any other comments!

_____

_____

_____

_____

Thank you for completing this questionnaire. Now tear it out of the book – carefully! – put it in an envelope and send it to:

Black Lace
FREEPOST
London
W10 5BR

No stamp is required!